KING OF IMMORTAL TITHE

BEN ALDERSON

KING of IMMORTAL TITHE

BEN ALDERSON

To my readers, you found me, welcomed me and breathed life back into me. Thank you.

Please be aware this novel contains scenes or themes of toxic relationships, murder, loss of family members, death, abuse, manipulation, anger, grief/grieving, depression and blood/gore/ suicide.

As much as I work hard, with multiple editors, mistakes and typos happen. Please forgive any that have slipped through the net. If you have any concerns please do contact me on b e n a l d e r s o n a u t h o r @ g m a i l . c o m

COPYRIGHT

I smiled in the face of death, welcoming it like an old friend.

My reflection was etched into the wide, moon-round eyes of the vampire pinned beneath me. Even in the lightless cavern, my smirk was visible.

But to a vampire, I was no friend. Far from it, because friends rarely plunged stakes into each other's chests and watched the insignificant life they had left drain away into nothingness.

Killing a vampire was easier than one would have imagined. It involved a good deal of stealth, for the fuckers were known for having a keener ear than an owl. There was also a healthy helping of fearlessness required. Vampires were monsters of nightmares, except no longer figments of imagination but real. As real as me and the stake I had gripped hard in my hand.

I no longer feared them. I couldn't. Being scared was not an option. But I could still recognise the danger they possessed. There were hordes of vampires. Thousands. The figure likely higher than I could ever imagine, which made them far more deadly than I. I couldn't pull the true number out of my ass to tell it even if I wished.

The corpse beneath me would have been young when he was turned. Its creaseless skin and innocent eyes revealed as much. His harsh face was crowned by sun-kissed locks of yellow and gold, long enough to fall around his skull like the petals of a picked flower.

I usually followed a rule I'd set for myself, as strict as a religion. Don't kill the young ones. The discomfort which followed once I buried wood in their heart was too much to bear at times.

However, today was an exception.

I had slipped from Tithe later than I would have liked. It was easier to clamber out of the town during the shift of the wall's guards around early dawn. The Watchers, as they were aptly named because it was all they ever seemed to do, were tired by the time they were swapped out, which meant they grew lazy—lazier than normal at least. Not that I complained. For years I had been completing this dance of leaving town before dawn and returning all before the break of the morning fast.

All day I had searched for the undead, seeking desperately through the ruins of long-forgotten buildings overgrown foliage had claimed. Usually they were easier to find, but it seemed today every single vampire had fled the world entirely.

If only.

Darkmourn, a city lost to death and time, nestled in the shadow of Castle Dread, was a major nest for the creatures. Today, the old town was utterly dry of the bounty I required.

When the sun ruled the skies, the creatures would flee to the darkest corners of the world. Light, much like my trusted stake, was deadly to the undead.

The more time slipped by, the harsher my desperation grew. Then I heard the familiar weeping of the creature, which finally led me to my prey.

The vampire was cowering in the cellar of an old bakery in Darkmourn. Years ago, this building would have been filled with the luscious smells of fresh bread and the tickling scents of sweet delights. Now it was a cavernous place, home to rats the size of cats and shadowed corners hiding other unseen horrors.

Fuck, I hate rats.

The vampire was whimpering in the dark belly of the bakery, its light voice enough to slice the skin of anyone without a stomach forged of iron. I knew it had been a child the moment I caught the dulcet tones lifting from the shadows of the cellar.

I had paused for only a moment, looking up at the rising sun and knowing my window of time to return to Tithe was short.

I could have turned my back and continued searching for one of older age. If I had the supply back home, perhaps I would have. But being picky with my prey was not a luxury I possessed, and I refused to return to Tithe without what I needed.

Blood. To be more specific, vampire blood.

I had made sure the vampire's death was as swift as I could gift it. It had hardly had a chance to scream in terror before I had pounced into the shadows of the cellar, straddled it and then drove the stake into its heart.

Even after years of the Hunt, the sound of wood through flesh turned my stomach. It was wet and loud, like the smacking of lips as a greedy Watcher chewed on meat.

I sat there for a moment, watching the pale colouring of the child's skin darken, as though years of rotting caught up to it within seconds. Guilt stabbed through me, but only for a moment. It was all I allowed.

Reaching for my leathered belt, I tore the short dagger from its sheath alongside two glass vials I kept in a pouch as easily accessible as my weapon.

"Sorry," I muttered, taking the dagger and lifting the blade toward the creature's throat. With a keen, swift slice, the flesh tore open and dark, pinkish gore splashed across the vampire's chest.

"At least you have found peace," I told the corpse as its cold, thin blood poured over my hands as I filled the vials to their rim.

There was a time I used to fill more than a couple of glass vials at a time, but then my sister grew older, and her eyes sharpened alongside her mind. She was inquisitive, which I had convinced myself was a bad thing. Sometimes those with watching stares noticed flaws as though it were their gift.

Auriol could not discover my greatest secret.

The pale colour of the blood and its almost transparent texture revealed the vampire had not fed in a while, likely because of the absence of prey. Humans who were lucky enough to survive since the curse of the vampires spread across the world, now lived within walled communities like Tithe. For years, the bloodthirsty creatures had little but vermin and wild beasts to feast from.

This child was certainly a victim to starvation. But regardless, its blood would do. It would serve its required purpose.

Once the vials were filled, the vampire's corpse melted beneath me, staining the ground in a puddle of bones and mush. Two was not as much as I had hoped to get, but it would do. It would keep me from needing to leave Tithe for a month or so. Two vials for two blissful and painless months. Only then I would have to hunt again.

I left the bakery's cellar and the melted stain of death in my wake. Vials tucked carefully into the pouch at my waist, the knife gripped in my hand. Who knew when another vampire would take their opportunity to show themselves to me.

The world beyond was quiet, almost peaceful. I walked the empty, forgotten streets of Darkmourn, cutting down the main cobbled pathways with my bounty bumping against my hip. Only the clink of the full flasks and my padding footsteps gave me company as I began my return to Tithe.

I could hardly imagine what life was like for the occupants of this town before the curse had spread. But one thing I was certain of was they had something I did not: freedom. Must have been nice. I admired the wall-less view around Darkmourn, looking towards the faint outline of rolling hills and the dense forests which filled the horizon for miles.

Even the towering, charred remains of Castle Dread did not displease me. I drank it all in every time I came, hoping the vision would sustain me until my next visit.

Tithe was not like this. It was not a place of freedom like the outside world. It was surrounded by a wall so high it blocked out the view of anything and everything beyond it. Many of Tithe's occupants hardly cared for the world beyond the walls. But I did. Even when I did not need to leave to get blood, I longed to step outside if only for a moment, just to see, to look around and let my eyes stretch for as far as they desired.

Trading freedom for safety was the price to pay for being kept alive. Most felt it was a fair trade. I was still not convinced.

The coughing began as I stood knee-deep in a shallow lake closest to Tithe's boundary, scrubbing the vampire's melted flesh from my leather breeches until the body of water turned grey. The sound was terrible. Wet gargles scratched up through my throat and made my lungs feel as though they would implode if I took a full breath in.

A sudden pain clamped across my chest and squeezed. I stumbled a step, almost falling completely, as the world seemed to shudder beneath my feet. If it was not daylight, I would have sent a message to all the vampires close enough to hear that I was ready for the taking.

I caught the droplets of blood in my cupped hands. It filled my mouth with the taste of copper, staining my teeth red and leaking out the corners of my lips. At least it happened now. The thought was not helpful. These fits were warnings my body was failing. They would start small, tickling spasms in my chest. Soon, becoming heavy rasping breaths which sounded wet and gargled in my chest, as though water filled my lungs and I drowned in it.

It was the warning I needed to know when it was time to devour a vial of my bounty. Vampire's blood was the only thing which gave me relief from the pain and the impending doom the agony revealed. I was dying, and only one form of medicine could keep death from claiming me. Medicine. I had tried to convince myself that was what the blood was. It made drinking it less... sickening.

It took a while for the coughing to finally calm before I had the energy to clean myself again. Only when I scrubbed my blood from my hands and face did I sit myself on the bank of the lake, weak and tired.

Begrudgingly, I accepted my need to drain a vial immediately. I just sat there, trying to catch my breath as I felt the familiar draining sickness dance through my body, as though it rejoiced to be overcoming me again.

A shiver passed across my arms. The weather was growing increasingly colder with the welcoming of autumn, my most hated season of all. I could only face sitting in my stupor for so long before taking one vial from the pouch, uncorking it with my teeth and draining the contents into my mouth.

As I drank the vampire's blood, I allowed myself to think of him. Small and pathetic, crumbling beneath my touch as I held the stake in his chest. I recognised the guilt as I did the sickness within me, trying to justify my murder by reminding myself why I did what I did...

A nd who I did it for.
Get up.

I repeated this mantra to myself four times before I got the strength and courage to stand again. It would take hours before the vampire's blood finally took effect. Until then, I just had to hope another fit did not return.

One vial left. Fucking pathetic, I should have found more.

Angry at my truth and failure, I discarded the empty, pink-stained vial and smashed it beneath my feet as I trod back towards Tithe's outer wall.

Today had started like shit, and I had a feeling it would not end any better.

2

I squeezed my tired body through the narrow gap beneath Tithe's boundary wall, far later than I would have liked to return. It was still morning, but I'd wasted precious minutes waiting for the Watchers atop the towering stone wall to turn their backs for me to slip inside town.

Any other day, I would scrutinise my narrow frame compared to the built, muscled bodies of the other young men within Tithe. At the fruitful age of twenty-five, I was still slight and painfully short. My body knocked years off my appearance, but without it, I would never have been able to leave and enter Tithe at my leisure. I was thankful for that.

Dirt and crumbled stone scratched across my chest and belly as I dragged myself through the hole which time had worn away. Only when I passed entirely beneath could I surrender a breath of relief.

Tithe was a cramped place. Narrow streets, and old black beamed and white painted buildings which seemed to lean on one another for support. I could see it now, through the thinning of trees I stood within.

My hand went to the pouch at my belt, fingers dusting over the swell of the glass vial within. Then I ran, as fast as my legs allowed, through the small patch of woods, across a field littered with the sheep who grazed upon the little patches of grass they could find this time of year.

With any luck, Auriol would have still been asleep when I reached home. At least I hoped so. It would have saved me the need to lie and if there was one thing I hated more than the Watchers and the immortals who commanded them; it was lying. Even if I was the self-proclaimed master of it.

۞

Auriol was awake by the time I pushed open the door to our home. Home was at least one word which could be described for the run-down apartment we dwelled within. Located in the upper floors of Tithe's most infamous apothecary, it was a place where the floor-boards screamed and every window rattled, as though the very building expressed its displeasure for us living there.

Two steps inside and she called out for me. "Are you ever going to learn that your bed is likely a better place to stay than lurking in the sweat-drenched sheets of Tom's?"

I winced, still feeling the tickle of the cough lurking at the back of my throat. It took a lot of effort to keep it at bay.

Auriol must not know.

"But his bed is far warmer... and bigger," I called out, dusting the dried mud from the sleeve of my jacket. The gilded mirror which hung drunkenly upon the wall beside me revealed the complete state I was in, as if I had been pulled through a bush over and over. Or through a wall. My straw-blond hair was a mess and heavy bags hung proudly beneath my mismatched eyes.

At least I looked the part of a dishevelled, tired patron of Tom's company. Even if he was not the reason for where I had been.

I could hear the smile in the way my sister responded, distracting me from the way I looked. "Out of all the men in Tithe and still you keep returning to him. When are you going to see Tom for what he is and leave him behind you?"

Ah, time to lie.

"I don't imagine you would appreciate me listing the reasons as to why Tom has me ensnared, sister, unless you want me to go into very long detail..."

She forced a fake gag, which conjured a deep laugh from me in response, and I said, "I shall take that as a no."

The first doorless frame to my left led into the main room of our apartment. I tore my jacket from my back and rested it on the back of the chair tucked under the worn dining table. By the time I looked back towards the slightly wonky corridor, Auriol's head had poked around her bedroom door.

"Arlo," she said, stifling a yawn. "Even Tom's long ego would entice no one else into his bedroom. At least not anyone with a lick of taste. I had believed you would be more interested in meaningful conversation."

"When I'm with Tom, there is no need for conversation... put it that way."

Auriol huffed, rolled her eyes dramatically and

grimaced without diluting any of her expression. "Men, you are all the same."

"Hungry?" I said, happy to divert the conversation before she picked up the truth that I had not, in fact, been at Tom's. Well, not the entire time, at least. I had warmed his bed before leaving Tithe at dawn, but she did not need to know that part.

"As if I am going to let you cook." Auriol wrapped her arms around her slender frame and padded barefoot down the corridor towards our kitchenette. "The last thing I need is to catch a sickness before tomorrow. If I miss out on their arrival for another year, I will be pissed. It could be my turn and I'm not missing that for the sake of your cooking. Sit. Eggs?"

My skin crawled at the brief mention of tomorrow's festivities. I hated the elves on any day, but the idea of their visits always made me feel terrifying dread. Especially with the idea that Auriol was seen by them. My sister was beautiful, stealing her looks from our mother, from the flow of her thick, chestnut hair that fell all the way down to her tailbone, to the sharp etchings of her face. High cheekbones, narrow chin and eyes so wide it seemed she held the secrets of the universe within them.

The only thing that signified us as siblings was our eyes; one a deep brown, the other a bright diamond blue. Everyone in Tithe knew us from them, just as they had known our mother before she had passed.

Looking at Auriol was both wonderful and painful, unknowingly dragging memories to the surface, ones I had spent years burying.

"About tomorrow," I started, already sensing Auriol's dramatic roll of her eyes and tongue kissing across her teeth in displeasure. "What if I told you I would prefer that you sit it out?"

I watched her crack an egg into the lip of a bowl, noticeably harder than it needed to be. "Every year you do this. And every year I obey like the good little sister I am. This time, Arlo, I am going."

Inevitably, this conversation was to happen one day. Auriol was twenty years old, younger than me by five years. But she had become an adult years ago. It forced Auriol to grow up far younger than she deserved. As scarless as her skin was, there was no denying the mark the lack of child-hood had left upon her.

Upon us both.

Last year was the first time she had pushed against my refusal for us to both sit out the immortal's visit to Tithe. So, I made her breakfast the morning of their arrival, which left us both bedbound with the shits. It was the effect of ensuring she was not placed before them like willing meat to the slaughter. Because I knew, if she was to have been seen by the elves, she would have been taken from me.

For that was what they do. Take. It was payment. At least that was what the Watchers reminded us of. A tithe for our safety. It was the reason our commune was called Tithe. Payment to be protected from the vampires beyond the wall.

But Auriol was worth more than keeping the occupants of this god-forsaken hovel safe. I could not see, nor allow her to be chosen. Selfishly, I needed her.

Likely more than she needs me.

"What if I begged?" I said, looking through my lashes as I watched her beat the eggs into a scramble. "Pretty please with a cherry—"

"I am allergic to cherries so you can shove your pleading in the same dark cavern that Tom sticks his long ego..."

"Okay, okay!" I forced a smile, trying to hide the true torment the idea of her going made me feel. "Stop whilst you're ahead before you put me off your wonderful cooking."

She lifted the egg splattered spoon at me as though it was the greatest weapon, one that won wars and defeated ancient demons and witches. Auriol looked down her nose, with narrowed eyes which screamed with threats. "No more then, understand? I am going and that is the end of that."

"Then I am coming with you."

"But you never go." Auriol almost sounded disappointed in the idea of me following.

"Nor do you." I shrugged, trying to keep my expression void of the genuine panic I felt inside. "I suppose it will be a first for us both. Don't you just love the idea of spending some time with your brother? Quality time? We could feast on sweet breads and eat cured meats until our bellies explode. Make the most of it."

Even though I had stayed clear of the immortal's visits, I still watched the festivities that Tithe put on in honour of their return. Stalls overwhelmed with food and the contagious laughter that came from unlimited tankards of ale and stronger spirits. The streets were full of Tithe's blinded occupants dressed in finery which they could hardly afford, and only came out of their closets once a year. It was as if they were peacocks exposing feathers to catch the attention of the fey-kind. For the unlucky few, it worked.

But no one was like my sister. Not a single person in Tithe could come close to comparing. And that fact had me pushing the pile of peppered eggs around the plate as I tried to keep my anxiety from overwhelming me entirely.

"You are welcome..."

I shook myself out of my head, forcing a smile that even I knew Auriol would never believe. "Are you not joining me?"

She had only given me a plate, her chair left neatly tucked beneath the table, forgotten and unwanted.

"I am a wanted woman," she said, brows furrowed as she scanned my face for a hint as to what caused my turmoil. She would never outright ask. Auriol had learned never to pry, which I respected. "I am heading into town to pick up some last-minute supplies for tomorrow. Kaye is helping me put together my outfit for the festival."

It took everything in my power not to kick up from the chair and demand that she did nothing of the sort. Instead, I focused on the plate, stabbing the fork into the pillowy clumps of egg I toyed with.

"Have fun," I lied.

"Could you at least pretend to be excited with me?" Auriol leaned in, wrapping her arms around my shoulders, her fingers interlocking over my chest where she held on.

"I just don't want you getting your hopes up," I replied coldly. It was not a complete lie.

"That I might not get picked?" Auriol's voice was equally cold. She pulled away from me, clearly over my lack of enthusiasm and vibrant displeasure at the idea of her being chosen by the elves. "Do you really think it is such a terrible thing for me to be chosen? How can you sit there and tell me you do not wish for a better life when you spent half our childhood conjuring fantasies of leaving Tithe and living in the world beyond as though those fucking bloodsucking pricks haven't poisoned it all!"

I stared at my plate, arms and legs numb. Auriol stood behind me, breathing heavily and although I knew I should turn and face her, tell her she was right, and I was wrong... I couldn't do it. That was one lie I was not prepared to say.

I kept silent, counting each of her deep breaths as I waited for her to lash out again. I deserved it.

"Sometimes you need to remember..." Auriol trailed off.

"Say it." I knew what was coming. It had been for a long time and part of me desired for her to speak the words aloud.

"It doesn't matter."

I pleaded, "Say it."

Auriol sighed, one filled with years of turmoil and dark emotion. She was always better at letting it out and making sense of how she felt. I admired her for it.

.   .   .

"You are not them, Arlo. I do not blame you for stepping into their shoes and doing what you had too as the oldest of us both. But you are not Dad. You are not Mum. I think it is time you remember that and release the burden. It would be a shame if it ruined what little we had left."

She left swiftly, feet slapping against the floor as she hurried towards her room.

Just like the coward I recognised myself to be, I swallowed what I truly wished to say and kept it buried in the darkest part of my soul, wondering how much room I had left there before those feelings I kept hidden had nowhere else to go but out.

FAENIR

Claria was not the Queen of Evelina by choice. The title should have been passed to my mother many years ago. She should have been the one to retire my grandmother from the heavy burden of the crown.

Should have.

Except I had killed my mother and prevented that from ever happening. And Claria had spent the hundred years that followed, making sure I did not forget.

Not that I ever would.

"It has been many a year since you last requested an audience, Faenir." Queen Claria's voice was rugged with age. It cracked and popped as though she needed to clear something from her throat. I hated many things in life, but her existence made everything pale in comparison. "I admit I would have preferred not to have seen your face for an even longer period of time. Looking upon you is a painful reminder of what you took from me. Tell me, child, what has dragged you before me like the unwanted mutt you are?"

Child. Even now she degraded me as though a century was nothing but a blink in time. I supposed to be someone so withered and ancient, one hundred and thirteen years of living was youthful in comparison.

I stood rigid before the curved oak throne her hunched frame sat upon. She looked small within it, like a child sitting on a chair meant for adults. The twisting, intricately woven back of the throne was polished and twisted together like the antlers of the proudest stag. It had been carved from a stump of dark wood, with its roots still rising and falling out of the earth beneath it.

The heart of Evelina.

Where the dense foliage reached above the throne, explosions of blood-red roses crowned the glade as their petals fell like snow around us. If one did not look close enough, they would have been fooled by the trick of life and beauty. I was not privy to such blindness. The glade should have been a place of colour, now it was far from it. Dull and muted, entrapped in the grasp of death. Every year, Evelina seemed to retreat into death a little more than the one before.

I recognised death, for it sang to my soul.

We were one in the same.

"Apologies if my presence disturbs you. My visit will be brief," I replied, hearing the careless tone that had entered my voice as it echoed across the enchanted forest we stood within.

Claria waved a veined hand as though she wished our meeting to end quickly. "Then get on with it so your presence does not encourage Evelina to perish any more than required."

I fought the urge to drop her hateful, judging stare. With great effort, I swallowed the stone of defiance and cleared my throat. "I request to be pardoned from the day's Choosing."

"Denied," she barked quickly.

My breathing quickened, my body growing stiffer where I stood. "It is not required for me to visit Tithe. You know what will happen if I partake in the Choosing. It would not bode well for our relationship with the humans."

As Myrinn had warned me.

Claria leaned forward in the throne, thin arms resting on each armrest as they trembled to hold her weight. "There could have been a time that your Choosing of a human mate would have been celebrated. As heir to this world, it would have secured your succession and ensured your mother, my dearest Eleaen, to step down. You could have been King."

"Could have," I echoed back. "Being the optimal words, grandmother."

"Indeed," she said through a scowl. All at once she rocked back into the throne, bones cracking with even the most subtle of movements. "You, like your dearest siblings, will visit Tithe and take your mate. If we have hopes of preventing the demise of our kind, then we must continue with the Choosing. I understand you may not see the importance and the part you have to play... you have always been such a selfish, twisted child."

I am no child. I wanted to scream it. My shadows coiled within the far corners of the forest, begging for me to call upon their comfort.

The child had died when I was old enough to recognise

what I had done, what my being alive had caused and why it had made me so hated by Claria. By my family.

"You are aware of what will happen if you force my hand to do this."

My grandmother smiled. It was the first time I had seen her smile in countless years that I believed it was not something she had the potential for. Bright and gleaming, it smoothed the many wrinkles of her bitter, old face and caused her amber eyes to glow from within. "You will kill the poor soul that you pick. For that is what you do. Your touch is as cursed as you are, Faenir. And it will further prevent you from stealing the crown I have worked tirelessly to keep from you."

"I never desired to be King, Claria," I spat, sensing the dancing shadows as though they waited for my command to devour her where she sat. "I have said it many times, yet still, you do not listen. Or simply choose not to."

"It is all well and good, but until it is proven to the realm that you are barren of possibility to find a mate to rule beside, then I will go to all measures to ensure your failure."

At that, I dropped her gaze just before her light, amused chuckle spilled out.

"Let the humans see you in the same light that we do. Let them come to know the monster that is Faenir."

3

T om was rushing, made clear mostly from his frantic thrusts and his not so careful hands. The most telling sign was his lack of focus, chestnut eyes flicking towards the window as if the impending light of dawn would reach Tithe quicker every time he would look away.

It killed the mood for me. He was so distracted by the arrival of morning that he hardly noticed when I stopped gyrating on his hard, long cock.

It took Tom a moment to look back up at me, beads of glistening sweat tracing down the prominent bones of his strong face. His brows furrowed with a mixture of confusion and annoyance.

"What's wrong?" he asked, deep voice enough to clear my frustration and lose myself in the sex again. I was certain his voice alone could remove my clothes from my body.

Among many other things, some not as nice as the

others, Tom was handsome. For me, it was his only redeeming feature that kept me returning most evenings. I had slept, tangled within his sheets, far more times than I had my own. He served his purpose, of course, acting as a distraction from my mind and the world around me.

His chestnut eyes, the same colour as wet oak after a downpour of winter rain. Tom was a labourer on a farm north of Tithe towards its outer walls. Close to where I would escape.

Working beneath his father, he would tend to their livestock, mainly sheep, but with the odd milk cow. His physical work had crafted his body in ways that should only be possible for the heroes of ancient stories. Arms as hard as boulders, every muscle defined with proud lines. Tom was strong, not that it was required when dealing with me. He often reminded me how he just loved to pick me up and throw me around. Unlike me, Tom was obsessed with my body; he worshipped it.

With the turn of the last month of summer, Tom's skin was kissed and golden. Freckles dusted across his broad shoulders, matching those that spread over the bridge of his sharp, straight nose. And now, looking up at me where I sat upon his crotch, sheets a knot around us, I could not deny his heroic beauty.

"At least have the decency to give me your full attention when you are fucking me, Tom," I said finally.

He did not laugh like I expected, instead rolling his eyes as he harshly pushed me off his lap. I was forced to lie beside him, feeling stupid for even speaking. If I had thought the mood was ruined before, it was destroyed now, shattered into too many pieces to possibly put back together.

"Sometimes you are impossible to please... do you know that?"

I gazed up at the beamed ceiling of his room, admiring the intricate spiderwebs that had lived among the shadows for as long as I could remember. No matter how many times I asked Tom to clean them, he never did. And why would he? For someone who was so engrossed in his vanity, Tom was excellent at pushing the not so pretty parts of his life into the dark corners of himself. Like the spiderwebs, they were out of sight and out of mind.

"Harsh," I said, rolling over and placing my palm across his chest. Coarse hairs tickled beneath the tips of my fingers. "Just forget that I said anything."

I could see from the proud, tall cock still raised skyward between his legs that Tom was not satisfied. It glistened in the light of dawn that filtered through his window, covered in the lubricant that he purchased from the apothecary beneath my home.

"How about we go again..." I encouraged, running my fingers from his chest, down the mountainous lumps of muscle across his stomach, following the lines that pointed down to his lower hip. I didn't get close to the manicured hairs that crowned his cock before Tom grabbed my hand and tore it from his skin.

"Perhaps we'll finish later." Tom swung his legs over the edge of his bed, which groaned with every slight move. No wonder his father and mother could never look me in the eyes. They knew what happened when I visited, ratted out by the noise his bed made when I dwelled within it. "Arlo, I think you should leave... or like just go home and get ready or something."

I popped my elbow up, resting my head in my hand as I watched him stand. Tom stretched, the glow of morning outlining his deliciously conjured body with a halo of light.

"But I would prefer to stay here with you all day. Tom, come back to bed. I promise we will have a more enjoyable day within it than out there." There was a forced pleading in my voice. It was not exactly Tom I wished to spend time with. But his body and the power of distraction he held were what I needed to get me through the day and those who came with it.

The elves.

Hanging off the wooden pillar at the end of his bed was my jacket, tunic, trousers, and most importantly, my pouched belt. Tom reached for it, fisted my clothes and threw them upon me before I had a chance to raise my hands to protect myself.

"Get up," Tom scoffed, pulling his own trousers up over the bulges of his thighs before tucking his still hard cock into the band over his waist. "May I remind you, Arlo, that you are the only person in Tithe that does not wish to see the elves. I am going, like your sister. You can either wallow at home all day or join us."

I should never have told him about the conflict between me and my sister the day prior. Tom didn't care for my emotions and turmoil, but he listened like a patient dog, knowing that his treat would come for his good behaviour. My sex. It was always the same. Even if I could practically feel Tom's discomfort when I expressed the worries of my life, I still never refrained from talking. Tom was a shit conversationalist, but it was better than speaking to a brick wall. Similar certainly, but better.

"You are like the rest of them," I said, gladly climbing out of his sticky sheets. I was damp with sweat and my arse glistened with lubricant. I needed a wash as desperately as I wanted this day to be over.

"Always thinking this will be your year to be chosen. Tell me, Tom, are you going to get yourself ready and parade yourself hoping to claim the attention of the elves that visit?" It was not a question, more of a statement fuelled by a speck of jealousy at the idea of the elves taking him from me as well.

Tom was handsome enough for the elegantly pompous creatures to choose him as their boon. The creatures were equally vain and loved pretty and lovely things. Auriol. Tom. If they were taken from me, I truly would be left alone.

"Would it be so bad?" Tom turned on me with wide eyes full of pity. "A new life where you could live like a king whilst knowing your family's lives would be changed. No more work. No more poverty. Unlike you, I actually care what happens to my family and if being picked by the fey will give them a better life, then so be it."

My blood chilled. Arguing with Tom was not how I saw this morning going, but since he was clearly so ready for one, I supposed I could give him what he wanted.

"That is not fair, Tom." My feet smacked onto the floor as I began dressing myself hurriedly.

· · ·

"Is it not?" His voice peaked, mouth drawn into a fine line. "You are so adamant to keep your poor sister trapped in your depressive life that you can't possibly imagine what it would be like for her to be given a chance."

"Fuck you."

"I already did."

I was almost lost for words. Tom grabbed at my insecurities and brandished them towards me like a weapon, sharp and thirsty for blood, slicing me open.

"Don't speak about matters you could not possibly understand."

"Understand?" He barked a laugh. "How can I not understand when you waffle on about your problems and emotions every time you visit? Arlo, for your own sake, face the day like a man and stop trying to stop others from doing what it is they wish to do."

My fingers were numb as I buttoned up my tunic. There was no doubt the wrong buttons were put into mismatching holes as I focused entirely on not letting Tom see me cry; not from sadness, but from anger and humiliation. Those were the worst tears to shed.

"You can be a real prick, Tom. Do you know that?" I was shouting now, mouth laced with copper from the blood that spilled from my bitten cheeks.

"The truth can hurt," he replied, brushing past me as he paced towards his bedroom door. "I think you should go. Take the day to think how your moods affect others, and maybe if I am still here tonight, which I really do hope I am not, you can come back, and we will finish where we left off."

I could have vomited across my bare feet. Tom truly believed that I would come running back, even after what he had said. And the truth was... I would.

Auriol was right about him—of course she was; my sister was a keen judge of character when it came to everyone but me. The price I paid for Tom and the distraction he provided was this. When things were good with him, they were amazing, but when they were bad... well, he had a way of worming into my feelings and causing more pain than the sickness that the vampire blood kept at bay.

Sometimes I wished to tell him. To see if he would have not had any lick of honest, caring emotion if I told him I was dying. Then someone would know. But he would use it against me... I had no doubt.

The door to his room screeched open, and Tom held it wide, standing beside it like a silent guard.

I was not fully dressed, my boots lost in the mess of his room. There was no time to find them. Defeated, I kept my head down as I walked away from his bed. I could have said so much to Tom as I left, but instead I bit down on my tongue to keep myself silent.

A firm hand reached out and grabbed my shoulder. His touch shattered the spell of silence. "Arlo, I hope I see you among the crowds today."

He didn't. Tom's emotionless tone told me as much. It was as though he forced himself to say it, his own way of apologising for his brash reaction this morning. Tom didn't care. He was simply saying what he thought I wished to hear to feed his own twisted conscience.

I looked up at him, standing half a foot shorter than him. "For your sake, I hope you are chosen by them."

Tom smiled; it reached his eyes, as though the idea of it brightened his very soul. Then he replied, voice alight with hope, "As do I."

4

Many years had diluted the story of how Tithe came to be. Although the story was Darkmourn's ugliest scar, those who still clung to the realm of the living chose to forget it. Mother used to tell Auriol and me the tale repeatedly, as though it was her most important lesson for us to remember. Not that I could ever have forgotten.

It started with the witches, as all things do. Selfish beings whose personal vengeance destroyed the world as it was known. Vampires may be creatures of nightmares, but witches were the masters who pulled the strings of that dreamscape.

The beginning of the story was hazy, or unimportant, as I had deemed it. But I remembered it started with heartbreak; most called it that, but I recognised it for its ugly truth. It was revenge and jealousy, or love if you wished to give it a name.

It was the end that mattered most, like all stories. The world changed when a male witch had been sent to Castle

31

Dread to kill the creature that lurked within its walls. He failed and thus doomed Darkmourn and the world around it. Jak, his name still a painful reminder to everyone, was the last Claim of the old world...

Which was why I never understood why Tithe had given a name to the elves' visits and made a festival out of it: the Choosing. It was no different to the old Claiming, reminiscent of the tales of the old world. The Choosing was simply a way of giving a terrible thing a pretty name in hopes to hide the truth of what the day came with: thievery, elves stealing what didn't belong to them, taking loved ones away as payment for keeping us safe from the vampiric curse that spread through the outside world.

I had vowed to never take part. It was my parents' last wish before they both passed. And like the witch boy who could not kill the first vampire, I had failed. Now I raced through Tithe, searching frantically for Auriol.

I pushed through the crowded streets, slipping past people squashed together like fish in a barrel. A trail of disgruntled sounds and comments were left in my wake, likely because of the sharp elbow I provided those who didn't hurry and get out of my way. I didn't care, I just had to find Auriol.

Searching for her among the crowd was like locating a needle in a haystack. A fucking big haystack. The streets of Tithe were full of colour. Every person I passed was dressed in their best clothes; jackets of deep azures and red dresses so lush that it looked as though they soaked the material in their blood, and I wouldn't have put it past them. Desperation could lead one down a strange path, and the occupants of Tithe were certainly desperate to get the attention of the fey-kind.

In comparison, I looked dull. From my knee-worn trousers, pale cream tunic and the brown leather jacket which had more missing buttons than remaining ones, I stood out in the crowd far more than those around me did. Everything about the way I had dressed screamed my obvious lack of care or interest.

Tithe sang with excitement. It was filled with voices of the town's occupants and had been from the moment I was kicked out of Tom's house until I returned home to find Auriol had already left.

Find her. Mother's voice filled my mind. It wasn't her, of course. The dead stayed dead unless changed by a vampire, and Mother was never given enough time for that to happen. Nor had father when he died weeks later.

I had to shake the thought of them both. If I was to find Auriol among the swollen streets, I would need to focus, not be distracted by the conjured whispers of ghosts.

Living close to the centre of Tithe, there was one window in our home that gave the perfect view to the cobbled-stoned square and lonely ash tree that stabbed through the ground at its heart, and I knew that was where I would find her. No matter the season, the tree never lost a leaf or its colour; a deep emerald green blended seamlessly with the dusting of gold that spread over the thick foliage of the tree.

Leaving home, I ran for the tree and stood beneath its shadow that the endless spread of its foliage cast across the heart of the town. The human that was named Tithe's first Watcher had said he witnessed the tree burst suddenly from the ground, and the elves followed shortly after. It was such an outlandish story that I wished it was nothing but.

I was surrounded by youth. Faces I recognised well were adorned in face paints and hair twisted into ridiculous nests of curls. The boys stood taller, faces unreadable and mysterious, as though they believed their allure would be what the elves would find most asserting.

My eyes flickered across the crowds in search of her.

I had to remind myself to breathe as my chest stabbed with anxious pain. One hand was pressed over my heart, the other gripping onto the vial hidden within the pouch at my waist; its closeness had always comforted me.

"Welcome," boomed a voice so great it made me jump. "I cannot express how warm my heart is to see you all so poised and primed. Tithe has always been overflowing with beauty, and every year I only imagine how hard it must be for our guardians to pick one to take with them. This year may be the hardest choice yet!"

Dameon Slater, head Watcher of Tithe, had ambled his way onto a podium erected to the side of the tree. He was a towering man, white hair always kept from his face which revealed how unkind the years had been to him; lines creased his brow, and deep crow's feet bracketed his eyes. Even when he smiled, like now, the emotion never seemed to reach his eyes.

It was not his appearance that could silence conversations and demand respect, but the knowledge that his family had been one of the first to flee Darkmourn. They'd stumbled across this very place, which years later had come to be what it was today. It was what gave him his title as Watcher. Just as his father had been, or his father's father before that... Dameon Slater was believed to be in direct communication with the elves within their realm.

And as the people of Tithe desired nothing more than to worship those creatures in hopes their lives would change, they treated Dameon as though he was one of them.

Respect was earned, and in my eyes, he didn't deserve a scrap of it.

"Another year has passed, and we are all still here. Safe from the poisoned world beyond without the need for fear or worry. A gift our guardians provide us..."

I forced his baritone waffle to the back of my mind and continued pushing my way through the crowd. It was harder now. Instead of slipping through a moving stream, everyone had stopped and gathered within the courtyard to listen and soon witness the elves' arrival. It was like navigating around immovable rocks.

"Excuse me," I muttered. "Sorry."

"No fucking chance," a woman growled, grey hair pulled across her shoulder in a messy, knotted braid. "If you wanted a better view, you should have got your place earlier. Shift it."

I raised my hands in defeat, forcing a smile before disappearing off into the midst of sticky, sweat-damp bodies.

It was a warm day, not surprising for the turn of summer to autumn. With close to every occupant in Tithe filling the streets, it was as though a furnace of warmth had been lit around me.

"This year is special, for it is the first time in which our visitors are each from the same family. On a good year two, maybe three of you, would have a chance to have your lives changed and your families made for life. This year there will be five. Five luckily souls who will be swept from our dear Tithe and taken on an adventure alongside your mate."

My skin crawled. Just hearing him speak the words aloud had my stomach twisted into knots.

"Let us hear your willingness for the Choosing. Share your excitement with your town and hope our guardians can hear you through our realm into theirs."

The world exploded with cheering. I ducked as dried petals were thrown from balconies of those who watched from the safety of their homes. Arms were thrown skyward, feet stomping on the cobbled streets as the skies filled with cheers and shouts.

That was when I saw Tom. A line had formed, almost in a semi-circle around the base of the tree. Not a single person faced away from it. He, like the surrounding people, was garbed in finery. Clothes I could never have imagined a man like him would ever own.

And my initial thought sent lightning through my veins: He will be chosen today.

His jacket was crafted from a dark velvet, threaded with gold and silver. Naturally, he was tall, but the pads that filled his shoulders and the low cut of his tunic made him look as regal as the creatures he was wishing to impress.

Prick. It had taken until today to realise that he truly saw nothing in the future for us. Even after the evenings of his whispers and repeated promises, this was what he wanted.

He never wanted me. Why would he, compared to a

life of riches and wealth? A life no one truly knew, for when the elves picked their humans, they left and never returned.

I should not harbour a possessive desire for Tom, but I did. Deep down, seeing him scream among those who stood with him conjured an envy I didn't know I possessed over him. For his sake, I hoped he was chosen. It would save the wrath that would follow if he was not.

"Where is she?" I spat, reaching for his arm and pinching it with a steel grip. Tom was so focused on his ridiculous thrill he had not noticed as I had stepped up behind him.

The surprise on his face was genuine. If I was a painter, it would have been an image I would have desired to immortalise forever.

"You actually came."

"Auriol, I need to find her."

He rolled his eyes, a reaction I was all too familiar with. "Even now you cannot just give it a rest. Leave Auriol and let her enjoy the day."

Tom shrugged free from my hand and turned his back on me with dismissal. I could see the disapproving looks from the two girls who flanked his sides before they too dismissed me.

"Tom," I said through gritted teeth. "If you don't answer me, I swear I'll tell the elf that is stupid enough to choose you that your cock is limp and has the inability to create an orgasm that isn't forced."

I was certain even Dameon heard, for his speech dwindled. Everything had become terribly quiet as the crimson spread of embarrassment crept across Tom's face.

Before he spat out his words, I heard her. My name was called out, soft like the flutter of a bird's wing, except it was not a welcoming sound, more broken and breathless.

Auriol. She had stepped out from the line and faced me. My breath stuck in my throat as I caught sight of her. Even the thunderous swear from Tom faded into nothingness as I stared at her. It was as though Mother had called for me. Auriol looked beautiful, not tacky and forced like those around her, but truly remarkable. Natural. As though her very presence among the crowd was justified.

"Your interruption is not smiled upon, Master and Mistress Grey. Return to your stations and wait as those around you are," Dameon called out, narrow gaze fixed on both of us.

I could see that Auriol was mortified by the outburst. Her shoulders had raised, chin forced down to her chest as though she wished to disappear. But she could never disappear, not looking the way she did. The dress she wore was lace and the purest of white. I had only even seen design work so intricate on the spiderwebs in Tom's bedroom ceiling. Her brunette hair was not backcombed and obnoxious but sleek and tumbling, like waves of rich chestnut rolling down her back. She did not need to paint on her beauty, for she was blessed with it in abundance.

I watched, helpless and pathetic, as she dusted off her embarrassment, faced Dameon and delivered a smile so beautiful that even the lines upon his face seemed to soften. "Apologies, Watcher Dameon. It would seem my brother is as excited as I am for the chance to change his fate. Let us hope our guardians pick one of us."

"Yes," Dameon replied, lips twitching. "Your family could do with some good fortune." His comment felt like a slap.

There was no time to dwell as Auriol's pink-blushed lips pulled into a tight line and she gestured to the space beside her. I could see the words form upon her lips. "Here. Now."

Every eye within Tithe watched as I rushed to my place beside my sister. Dameon did not speak as I did so, allowing the muted whispers of those who watched as they burned at my soul.

"I can't believe you are doing this," Auriol said, body pinned straight at my side. She didn't look at me as she spoke but faced towards the tree as Dameon started up once again. "There will never be enough words to express how upset you have made me."

I was frantic, not caring for the scene I had caused, but only for the burning desire to get my sister as far away from the Choosing as possible. "I can't let you go. Not with them."

"Can't or won't? Do you wish for me to be miserable until the end of my days? Cooped up in a hideous home that's haunted by the memories of everything we have lost?"

"You don't understand..."

"No, Arlo, you are right. I don't."

A few of those near us pressed fingers to lips and sneered to silence us.

"If you go, then I will lose you." Just speaking it aloud made my heart crack inside my chest. *If you go, then everything I promised our parents, everything I do to stop the same sickness from taking me, will be for nothing.*

My body was frozen as I screamed in my mind at her.

If you go, then there is no reason for me to stop fighting it. Leaving seals my fate, and I am not ready to face death yet.

I had wished to tell Auriol that I had the same sickness that stole our parents from us. For years, I had fought the urge to speak it aloud for fear of what it would do to her. To us. I had kept it buried, swallowing my words even when my will was weak.

But now, standing before the tree, which would soon ripple like water as the elves passed through from their realm, I desired to tell her more than ever.

Maybe she would understand.

Maybe she would stay.

Or perhaps it would only solidify her desire to run from me.

Auriol surprised me by taking my hand. Her fingers slipped within mine, skin warm and fingers trembling slightly. She gripped onto me like she did years ago, holding on as though she wouldn't dare let go.

"Today is promised, but tomorrow is not. We both know far too well what can happen and I cannot just wait around in a life I am not happy in. Not anymore. Let me have this moment. Arlo, please listen to me."

I bit down on the insides of my cheeks and glanced at her, fighting hard to keep the stinging tears at bay. "I am listening, always."

"There is no saying I will be chosen by them, but I just want this moment to dream. If they leave and I am still here, then I promise you I will try to make better with the life we have been given. But please, just today, let me pretend."

Pretend. That was what I had been doing this entire time. Pretending I was fine. Filling my body with the sickening gore of the undead to just pretend.

How could I deny her that?

"Okay," I forced out, knowing it was still very much far from okay. "But I refuse to leave your side. I can't and won't leave you."

As always, I could hear the smile in her voice without having to look at her. Auriol squeezed my hand, and I returned it with a squeeze of my own. "That is all I could have wanted. Oh, and about Tom... I told you he was an idiot."

I almost spluttered a laugh. "That you did."

There was a shift in the air. It thickened, like when a summer storm settled over the world, and the warm air crackled with lightning as the icy winds clashed against it. It laced a strange taste across my tongue, stifling any further words from spilling out from my mouth.

Auriol's grip on my hand tightened, the crowd inhaling a breath at the same time. Expressions melted with wonder as she and every person looked towards the tree.

I had only ever watched the Choosing a handful of times from the perch of the sole window in our apartment, only a brief glance before I shut the heavy curtains and blissfully blocked out the events from my reality.

Being here was different— thrilling, yes, but that

coiling of fear I had felt this entire time turned from a spark into an inferno.

Then Dameon spoke, his voice crystal clear over the completely silent town of Tithe. "People of Tithe, here they come."

5

The elves swept out through the tree's surface as though the bark were no more than water. It rippled around their frames, not shifting a single hair upon their heads. Not even the light breeze that coursed through Tithe dared touch these creatures; it left them alone. From fear or respect, I was unsure.

I held my breath the entire time, fearful that I would say something obscene from shock or disbelief at what I witnessed. I counted them to keep myself occupied, one by one, as they strode into Tithe from whatever realm lay beyond the strange, unnatural tree.

Like a row of ducklings, the elves stayed in a perfect line, each one moving with a grace that was not possible for humans. It was as if they floated. Everything about them was effortless and perfect. Four, I counted. Not five, as Dameon had suggested. I repeated my tally as though I had missed something.

The air still crackled with impending tension even after they all had left the confines of the tree. It was the movement of the four elves, each glancing over their shoulders with a shared expression of annoyance, that warned that someone was left to come through. The broad, red-haired man tapped a polished boot upon the cobbles with impatience.

Then he showed himself, much to the excitement of the crowd compared to the clear displeasure of his peers. The Elven man stumbled across the threshold; feet awkward as though they were heavy with ale. His sloppy entrance conjured giggles from the surrounding girls, which did not go unnoticed. I expected that he would have enjoyed their reaction, yet his frown remained.

I couldn't focus on a single elf long enough to truly drink in their appearance. Even to blink would have been a crime for missing out on any details of the otherworldly creatures. At that moment, I forgot why I hated them; their aura of beauty blinded me from my preconceived emotions.

"I can't believe it," Auriol said, echoing my thoughts. Even if I wanted to, I couldn't look at her. "I can't..." Her voice tapered off as she finally succumbed to the same spell I was frozen beneath.

The elves had entrapped us, rooted me to the spot as they lined themselves up before the crowd.

S omewhere behind them I was aware of Dameon who hovered upon the podium, out of place and almost displeased that the fey-kind had not paid him any mind.

"Welcome, all—"

"That is more than enough, Dameon. Please cease your tedious chatter so we can get this started." It was the final elf who spoke. Hearing his deep voice rattle with the thickness of some powerful spirits confirmed that he certainly was drunk—that and the subtle sway of his tall frame and the deep-set shadows beneath his piercing gold eyes.

Beside him stood a woman, a lithe figure draped in a dress of emerald and jade. Her skin was a dark brown which glistened as though painted with the dusting of silver stars. She kept an expression of glee across her face. However, I noticed the subtle shift of her gaze, as though wincing in reaction to the elf that had belittled Dameon.

"Now, brother, that is no way to greet our dear host," she said. Her voice was soft, like the tinkering of bells swaying in a gentle breeze. It sent a welcoming chill down my spine, the feeling not as unpleasant as I would have wished it to be. It pleased Dameon also, whose crimson cheeks dulled in tone. He bowed his head as the woman looked at him with an honest smile.

"It is no bother, my lady," Dameon forced out, his smile the greatest of lies.

"Grand. Then, as Faenir so eloquently put it, shall we proceed?" she asked, removing her touch from the drunk elf and clasping her hands before her.

Faenir. His name settled over me like fresh snow. It melted upon my skin, sinking through, chilling my bones, making my body ache. Somewhere deep in my consciousness, I recognised the reaction as ridiculous, pathetic, as though I was pining for a person I had never met before. But that was soon smothered as my attention returned to the drunk.

"Would you not care for a walk around Tithe?" Dameon asked nervously, gesturing with a swollen hand at the surrounding crowd. "This being your family's first year here, we thought you may wish to..."

"That would not be necessary," the woman replied. "We are afraid that our visit to your realm must be kept short. Me and my siblings will pick our mate and leave with haste."

I recognised an urgency buried beneath her words, emphasised by the flickering of the elf's eyes and the slight quiver of her taut lips.

Before, I would have been thankful for the idea of them coming and going without their presence leaving much of a mark upon Tithe. Now, seeing them in the flesh only a few broad steps before me, I never wanted them to go.

Faenir ran a ringed hand through the length of his thick, obsidian hair. It was so long it fell in wisps to his waist. He pushed it back from his face, revealing the two elongated points of his ears and the sharp lines of his jaw and cheekbones. Until now it had fallen mostly over his face, concealing his otherworldly beauty, but the taut lines of his mouth and the endless wonder in his eyes had me fearing him more than those he stood alongside.

Regardless, I wanted his attention. I wished for him to look at me, to trail those golden eyes over me just to see if I was deemed worthy enough for his consideration. It was a haunting feeling, one I recognised to be nothing more than deliria conjured by his appearance. Was this how Auriol felt?

It seemed he settled his narrowed stare upon everyone but me. I hated it. When his eyes found that of Auriol's, I almost jumped before her. It lasted only a moment before sweeping over me and continuing down the line.

I followed his trail of interest where it stopped on Tom. From my position, I caught his handsome profile, one I had enjoyed many times. But compared to the creature before me, Tom paled in comparison. But the elf's attention lingered upon Tom longer than I cared to admit. And that coiling of jealousy made itself known within me once again. Then I remembered Auriol. If Tom was chosen, that would be one less chance for her to be taken from me.

I'd rather it be him.

Or me.

"If that is what you wish," Dameon eventually replied.

Returning my attention to the Watcher, I watched as he paraded towards the edge of the podium, then cleared his throat. Taking a gulping, noticeably shaking breath, he called out again, "As thanks for your continued protection against the evils that lurk beyond the wall, please, the people of Tithe would be honoured to be chosen."

It was the red-haired elf who spoke next. "Ensuring the legacy of your kind prolongs the test of time. We gladly offer our powers up to secure your futures."

He cast his hungry gaze across our line, not stopping on a single person long enough to give a hint who it was that caught his interest. There was something calculating about this one. His eyes were a burning red, as though fires twisted around his pupils in an eternal dance.

"May I, Myrinn?" he said to the elven woman, not once removing his eyes from the crowd.

She replied, gesturing elegantly towards the crowd with a sweep of her hand, "Choose wisely, Haldor."

. . .

A nd choose he did.

His choice lasted only a moment.

Auriol groaned as my hand squeezed hers. I had to relax it, not knowing that I had hurt her without realising. I thought he was walking towards us for a moment, which sent a sharp stab of panic through me. Then someone caught his eye.

Haldor stepped towards the line with sure footing and a chin held high with pride that came from growing up around power. His jacket was fitted across his powerful frame, crafted from a golden velvet that gleamed with the dull light of day. It rippled as he walked, much like the tree that the elves had entered through. As he grew closer, I saw how similar his jacket was to that of a flame, shifting between shades of gold to darker, more warming reds and ambers.

"You," he said, standing before a short, blonde-haired girl that I somewhat recognised. "Tell me your name."

"Her..." Auriol scorned quietly, only enough for me to hear. However, I was certain the elf, Haldor, turned his head slightly as though he had picked her murmur out. "He surely can't choose her."

"Samantha," the human girl replied, looking up at the significantly taller elf through pale lashes.

He stood there, contemplating her name as though it were the oddest thing he had heard. Then he turned towards Myrinn and nodded before returning his attention to the girl and raising a hand.

I was the only one to gasp. Unfamiliar, cold eyes fell upon me, but I couldn't care to see who they belonged to.

Never having witnessed a Choosing, I was confident that the elf was preparing to strike the girl, but he didn't. He placed a hand on the girl's head and the crowd erupted in cheers.

"It is done," Dameon hollered. "The first tithe has been made."

An older woman and man pushed their way through the crowd in a fit of tears and laughter. Haldor stepped back, allowing the girl to be swept into the arms of the couple. It must have been her parents, mother and father coming to say farewell to their child.

Samantha cried alongside her parents, not from sadness or fear, but from happiness. Anyone close enough to her shared congratulations in the forms of hugs and words of praise. Haldor simply stood and waited, his face stoic and expressionless; only the tapping of his boot upon the ground signified his desire for this display to hurry and end.

"That is enough," he finally said, shattering the excitement as though he took it in his hands and crumpled it. "Come, Sam-an-tha. Join me." He reached out a hand for her to take, not because he wished to, but because he had to. Haldor practically pried the girl from her family, and she happily obliged.

One down.

The thought doused the flames of my anxiety for only a moment before I counted the elves that were left. Four to go.

Next to choose was a shorter elf by the name of Frila. She, like Haldor, had pale skin with a bridge of freckles across her pointed nose. Her hair was a tumbling of white that gathered at her waist in braids. As she walked the line

49

of humans, lips pursed in concentration, the bottom of her azure-toned gown slipped over the cobbles like the billowing of water. She chose a male of Auriol's age. I recognised him well and from the exhale of frustration from Auriol at my side; she was not happy to see him picked.

Like Haldor to Samantha, Frila raised a hand and placed it upon the young man's head. She had to raise up on tiptoes to do it. Even I found the action sweet, perhaps sickly sweet, in fact.

His name was James, and he promptly placed his arm into the crook of Frila's elbow before they swept off to stand beside Haldor and his chosen mate.

"Another down," I recounted aloud to Auriol's displeasure. That relief I felt was growing ever so slightly, but enough to notice, as though a weight was being lifted from my shoulders.

Auriol straightened next to me, brightening her smile as she gazed towards the remaining elves. "I only need one chance and I see three. Odds are in my favour."

Gildir was next to retrieve his claim. His skin was golden, his brown hair trimmed close to his scalp. As he drew closer, I could see that each strand of hair was a tight curl upon his head. A feathering of a beard spread across the lower side of his face, which he brushed a thumb and forefinger over as he surveyed the crowd.

"I promise to leave you the best pick, brother," Gildir called back towards Myrinn and Faenir. Faenir's upper lip curled over his teeth, urged by the giggling of Frila, who held delicate fingers over her red-painted lips. It was an odd encounter.

"Gildir," Myrinn scolded through a tight-lipped smile. "Not now."

He spun around on the spot, hands raised to his sides and shoulders, shrugging in a signal of defeat.

I watched Faenir intently, seeing how he whispered to Myrinn, whose expression waned. The crowd was so focused on Gildir as he pointed his finger over them, they did not notice the interaction with the remaining fey.

Faenir boiled with anger. His forehead was furrowed with countless lines, I was certain each one told a story. Even Myrinn looked flustered as she replied. Then the strangest thing occurred. Faenir raised his hand in gesture, and she flinched, stepping back from it in a hurry.

A chill sliced down my spine. I couldn't fathom what I had witnessed between them, nor could I have time to work it out as the crowd exploded around me. This time, it was not all from cheering. Three of the elves had chosen and those waiting somewhat patiently for their chance were growing impatient. Much like Auriol.

By the time I looked back to Faenir and Myrinn, there was not an ounce of tension between them. Well, not from Myrinn at least. Faenir seethed silently at her side now with a noticeable distance between them.

Gildir had claimed a stunning girl with curls of ginger hair that circled her face in a halo. She reacted calmly to his touch upon her head, however, her eyes brimmed with undeniable thrill. No matter how hard she tried to keep her composure, I could see the truth through the cracks of it.

"Whose up next?" Gildir asked as he passed the remaining two. Frila laughed again, silenced only by

Haldor, whose burning stare shot upon her. "May I suggest it be you, sister? Leave the best for last, I think…"

Myrinn shared a look of sympathy with Faenir before sweeping off towards the crowd with a glowing smile. As she did, I caught Gildir whisper into his Chosen's ear. The girl spluttered a cry and practically threw herself away from Faenir, who tried to pretend as though he had not noticed.

But he had. The pain in his golden eyes told as much.

I knew Auriol was safe from being chosen by Myrinn. Never, in Tithe's history, had an elf picked a claim of the same sex. It was a strange concept, to only limit yourself to those opposite to you. Tithe was a place where sexuality wasn't restricted, and it was always a concept of the Choosing I never understood.

When Myrinn passed Auriol, she gifted her a brilliant smile. Auriol, who had only even come home with a boy's name on the tip of her lips, shuddered at the Elven woman's presence as though she would happily have thrown herself before her.

But alas, Myrinn moved on and ended up claiming a strapping young man who towered beside an extremely disappointed Tom. For a moment, I had believed it was him and felt almost disappointed that it wasn't. For my sake, more so than his.

"It will not happen to me, will it?"

I tried to hide my grin as I looked at my sister. Her mismatched eyes scanned my face as though looking for a reason to hate me for my happiness that she was right. I couldn't do it to her. Even though I prayed to anything or anyone that would listen for her not to be taken, I still wished she would have another moment of wishing.

Because when this was over, as she promised me, her want for this chance would be left behind.

"One chance you said. There is one more left to claim," I murmured in support.

Faenir.

"Your turn, brother," Gildir called out again before Myrinn even had the chance to join her siblings. "Don't keep us waiting."

Faenir did not move. His hands balled into fists at his sides, his chest heaving, as though he shared the same anxiety as I. Then he said a word I did not expect. "No."

Gildir laughed to the horror of his Chosen. "Go on, Faenir. Place your hand upon the one you find most alluring and see if she still stands long enough to return home."

"I will not indulge in this fantasy."

"Faenir." It was Myrinn who spoke up. "Please, just try."

"You know what will happen."

"Grandmother will not be pleased if you do not follow custom."

We all watched in complete silence at the interaction. Dameon leaned down from the podium, speaking out of the corner of his mouth. "There seems to be a problem. Accept our apologies if we have disrespected you in any—"

"Silence yourself," Faenir snapped, whipping his temper towards the Watcher, who practically fell back on his arse. The shadows of the tree which the sun cast upon the street seemed to shiver. I blinked, and they were still once again.

"Perhaps it should be left," Myrinn added quickly,

unable to keep up her façade that everything was fine by smiling.

"This is your chance," Gildir said, as if reminding Faenir of something. "To prove her wrong."

Faenir stepped forward, looking from the elf to the line of confused, silent humans.

Myrinn considered her thoughts. "If you do not want to do this, then I will petition Grandmother for..."

Faenir raised a hand into the air, his fingers twitching as he did so. "As always, cousin, my hand is forced. This is what she wants, then I will do as she wishes."

"We should leave," I said without realising. Auriol pulled her hand out of reach as I tried to take it. "Something is not right with that one."

She ignored me, instead muttering the same words under her breath, "Me, please choose me. Please. Please."

Faenir's eyes fell upon my sister and stayed there. He did not smile. His face did not warm at the sight of her. Instead, he looked sorrowful. It was an expression we both knew well. After the death of our parents, anyone we passed, anyone who visited us, looked at us the very same way. I didn't have a chance to understand why as the shift of his cloak hushed across the ground as he walked towards us.

Toward me.

Toward her.

Auriol's breath hitched. My heart stopped. Three words lingered across Faenir's lips as he closed in on us. "I am sorry."

Somewhere behind him, the elves buzzed with a dangerous excitement, Gildir and Frila's voices reaching over the rest of them.

Faenir stood before us, inches from Auriol, as he faced her down.

I tried to move, but I couldn't. My mind screamed for me to say something, do something, to stop him as he raised his hand.

Faenir closed his eyes, handsome face wincing as he lowered his palm towards my sister's willing and waiting head. The world seemed to stop for a moment. All the sound drained from existence until it was only the haunting whisper of my parents which remained.

Do not lose sight of her. Do not leave her as we have. Stay together, promise us.

I broke free from my prison of horror and reached out my hand. Snapping my fingers across the man's wrist, I clamped down with a vice-like grip. His skin was soft like downy feathers, yet it was cold, as if I'd buried my fingers in snow. My hand was not big enough to wrap entirely around the width of his wrist, but my strength was unwavering, fuelled by my desperation to keep him from the only person I had left.

"You. Cannot. Have. Her," I spat, wrist aching beneath the weight of his arm.

"Arlo, stop it!" Auriol pleaded.

Faenir looked at me with widening eyes. I saw my reflection in his stare, stern face twisting among the gold flecks.

No longer did his siblings laugh and coax him on. Instead, they were as silent as the crowd who watched on as I had interrupted the Choosing.

Then he spoke to me, eyes furrowed, and mouth parted in a mixture of disbelief and something else. Something I should have recognised sooner. Terror. "This should not be possible."

Heart thundering like the cantering of a hundred wild mares, I tossed his wrist away and stepped between my sister and him. Like many men, Faenir was taller than me, but I did not let that deter my territorial stance. "Pick someone else. She is not for you."

Faenir cocked his head, looking at me as though he was a hound, and I was something new to him. As he spoke again, I discerned his words were for me and me alone. "What are you, *Arlo?*"

The way he said my name felt as rancid as it clawed up my spine. Not only that, but it was a strange question, one I never imagined being asked by anyone, let alone an otherworldly creature such as him. I replied the only way I felt like I could, "Not of any interest to you, elf."

He smirked, surveying me with those burning, honey eyes. "You could not understand how very wrong you are."

6

The chill which slithered up my spine was not caused by the gale of cold winds that brushed through Tithe. It was the silence, sickening and endless. That was what conjured the reaction. Even with the streets of Tithe full to bursting, I could have heard a pin drop. Every set of eyes were focused on me.

Whereas my attention was frozen upon the elven man.

Faenir stumbled back as though moved by an unseen force. His hands were raised before him, fingers splayed. Without so much as a blink, he studied them as if it was the first moment he had realised he even had hands, turning them over, inspecting every inch of skin with such intensity it seemed he searched for the true meaning of life upon them.

Myrinn was behind him in moments, her movements rushed but still dripping with grace. "Faenir, we should leave."

"Did you see?" he murmured in response, still not taking his eyes from his hands.

Myrinn looked at me, only for a short moment, eyes tracing me from head to toe. "I saw enough. We all have."

Faenir finally broke his concentration and focused on me with the same wide-eyed expression. And he was not the only one who did. Myrinn, Haldor, and the other two fey whose smug expressions had been scraped clean from their pleasant faces. Not a single one tore their gaze from me, not even as Gildir and Frila shared whispers behind their hands.

The human occupants of Tithe also observed in horror at what I had done; some gazes were gentler than others.

Above the lot of them, it was Faenir's I cared for.

His shock was so palpable that it encouraged the hairs upon my arms to stand on end.

"Impossible," he muttered, eyes flicking back and forth from his hands then back to me.

My breathing was heavy, my heart thundering painfully in my chest. The ability to form words failed me as I felt buried beneath the weight of the elves attention. Names were powerful, not something I wished to give out so easily. Father had taught me that.

A tingling spread across my palm. No matter how many times I flexed it at my side the feeling would not stop. Faenir had left his impression upon me, and I was unable to decide how I felt about it.

"Faenir," Myrinn said, turning her back on me as though I was not worthy to listen to. "Now."

Faenir waited for me to answer him. I held my breath, urging him to leave as he was being asked to do.

When he finally turned away, I could have fallen to my knees.

"Wait," Auriol called out, breaking the line as she begged for the elf's attention. "Please, he didn't mean to do that. Take me with you. Let me be your Chosen!"

My skin crawled as I listened to her pleading. Watching her race forward, the skirt of her dress held in two tense fists, I saw the reality of what I had done. The severity of it.

The elves sauntered towards the tree, five with their Chosen mates and Faenir without. *She should be with him. She will hate you for this.*

Dameon didn't have the chance to speak as they brushed past him and disappeared into the rippling body of the tree.

It happened so quickly.

Only when the last slip of Myrinn's straight back passed from view did Auriol turn to me. Her eyes burned, wide and red. A single tear escaped, slicing down her cheek where it traced the curves of her jaw and stained her dress once it fell. It seemed that the ground trembled where she stood rooted to it, but it was her body. She shook violently, physically trying to stop poisonous hate from bursting beyond her pale lips.

The peace lasted a second.

"You ruined everything," she growled. When her mouth moved again nothing more than a slip of exhausted air came out.

"Auriol, I'm..." *Sorry?* No. I wasn't sorry. I did what I had been tasked by our parents to do. I kept her safe. She could hate me for the rest of her life and it would be the *tithe* I would pay for knowing she was safe. Safe from the unknown. Safe from them.

Safe... from Faenir.

Dameon pounced upon the scene, face flushed, scarlet staining his neck and cheeks. He took my upper arm in his hand, pinching my skin between careless fingers. "One of you needs to explain what has just happened. Right. Now. Do you understand the severity? The disrespect would be the downfall of Tithe!"

"Get off me!" The pain Dameon inflicted on me was the anchor I needed to focus. I tore my arm free just as the wave of the crowd flooded over us. Auriol was lost to it, but I had nowhere to go, not with the furious form of the Watcher in my way and the occupants of Tithe at my back.

I was trapped in the net of furious chaos.

"You are not going anywhere, Arlo Grey." Dameon attempted to reach out for me but missed as I began slipping away. "Something needs to be done in hopes to plead forgiveness for your disregard to our customs."

I didn't care for what he said next. Dancing around the crush of bodies, I ran, head down and mind focused as I tried everything to find Auriol.

People tried to stop me, but their effort was in vain. Nothing would prevent me from finding my sister. I had stopped her from being taken from me, I would not lose her now without a fight.

I could hear the song of destruction before I even reached the front door to our home. The shattering of glass. The splintering of wood. My legs burned as I bounded up the stairs, two at a time. I was greeted by our door left ajar. Shards of broken plates and cups littered the floor beyond like blades of deadly grass. My boots betrayed me, announcing my arrival with loud crunching, as did the screeching door hinges that screamed as I pushed it wide.

Auriol waited for me with a chair held above her head. She grimaced, a cat-like shriek spitting out of her as she hoisted the chair forward and threw it towards me. It shattered across the wall at my side. Splinters exploded across the side of my face, cutting and scratching.

"I hate you!"

I lowered my arm, recognising the wet warmth of a cut across my cheek. "I know."

She stood there, breathing laboured and eyes wild with fury. Her hair was unkempt, her dress ruined by the smudging of dirt along its seam. "Do you? Do you know how selfish you are? How completely consumed by your own wants and needs that you cannot see that your actions will be the ruin of us!"

I shouldn't have let her words hurt me, but they did. Because she was right.

"Everything I do is to keep you safe—"

"From what?" She laughed, barking as she interrupted me. "Answer me that, Arlo. Nothing you do is for me. Nothing. It is all for you. Years I have ignored the comments from friends, even from people who I care little for. But I can't pretend they are wrong anymore. They see what you are, and so do I."

I felt heat rise from the ground, through my boots and into every vein and bone within my body. It was a discomforting feeling, knowing that other people spoke about us. I had known the people of Tithe looked at us with sorrow after our parents passed. Was I truly blind to how they saw me?

"Listening to what others say is pointless. Auriol, please consider why I do this. We don't know what happens to those who are Chosen. The risk of the unknown is too great."

She paced forward, arm raised and finger pointed towards me until her nail found my chest and pressed into it. "I know that whatever waits within their realm would be a far better future than what I would have here. Stuck, poor little orphan Auriol whose parents couldn't even stay alive to care for her and whose brother keeps her imprisoned for his own need for control. I want a life without the constraints that have been shackled upon me. And my one chance, the chance I was given and deserved, has been taken by the person I should trust the most."

I lowered my stare to my boots, unworthy of my sister. "I did it because it was what our parents wanted."

Auriol spun from me, moving so fast I was sure she would raise her hand back and slap it across my face. "So you commune with the dead now?"

"Don't be ridiculous," I snapped, stalking after her as she frantically searched for the next item to throw and break. We passed holes in the walls, dents made by the broken objects that lay forgotten at the floor beneath them. "You could never understand the pressure I have been under since they died. Everything I have done is because they asked it of me. It is their wish..."

"They are dead! *Fucking dead*, Arlo. It doesn't matter what they wish or want; if they are not here to say it then it is pointless. When are you going to realise that you act on your own behalf and not that of the dead?"

"That isn't fair."

"Fair? What isn't fair is our dear mother and father gave up on us."

"Auriol!" I couldn't believe the words that came out of her mouth. It was a lie, but as she said it I knew she believed it was truth. "They could not help the sickness that infected them. Do you really think they gave up without a fight?"

I knew the fight, the struggle as my lungs filled up with my own blood, drowning me from the inside out. "You... we cannot even begin to imagine what they went through. You are saying that because you are angry."

"Don't you dare speak on my behalf. You know nothing about me."

I had to keep my anger buried. I wished, nothing more, than to lash out and hurt her with the truth. Auriol didn't understand the very lengths I had gone to ensure our parents final wishes were kept. How I filled my body with the sick gore of the vampires I killed just to ensure she was not left in this world alone.

"What now?" I asked, pacing behind her as she burned marks into our floor which each rushed step. "Are you going to take your anger out on me, on everything we have left? Smash our home into pieces only for us to patch it up together again? You might not understand why I have done what I have, but you will one day. When you are older and realise that you can have a life within Tithe, one you can carve for yourself."

"One where you can continue being my shadow and keep my happiness from reach, is that what you mean?"

This was getting nowhere and if I continued arguing with her I would soon spread my own destruction alongside hers. "I am going to go. Take the time you need to think this over. Perhaps when this entire place is overturned, we can sit down among the mess and chat like adults."

"That's right, Arlo," she sneered, teeth bared. "Run away from the truth. Do what you do best and disappear. You think you do everything to keep this family together when you cannot even stay in this fucking house for long enough to be a part of it. Run to Tom. At least one of us is granted the freedom to live other lives. And do not worry about me. I will be here when you get back like I always am, waiting like the doting sister who is willing to disregard her wants in life to please you."

I stopped myself from telling her then and there. My hand reached for the pouch at my belt and the glass vials within. The urge to tear them free from their leather confines and smash them upon the ground at her feet was almost too strong to ignore. I wished to see the dead, cold blood of the vampire drip through the floorboards and wash away.

It took a will power I did not know I possessed to turn my back on her and walk towards our open door. Each step was forced. My heart thundered in my chest, almost leaping into my throat and stopping me from swallowing or gulping a big enough breath to calm down. I felt a bulging vein in my forehead, throbbing as though it was a worm beneath my skin. And with each step towards the boundary of our broken, split home, I still longed to hear Auriol call my name.

She didn't. And deep down, beneath the anger and embarrassment, I could understand why.

I threw the hood of my jacket up, concealing myself beneath its welcoming shadows, before I reached the last stair beyond the building's outer door. The streets were still crammed with people, no longer alive with excitement for the festivities but horror for what had happened. What I had done.

The worst part of it was that I still felt Faenir's presence across my palm. I needed something to scrub away his touch and the memory of it.

Auriol was right. Only Tom had the power to do that for me.

FAENIR

I was all too familiar with the golden hue of life force. How it glowed around a person's body as though they stood before the mighty sun which burned brilliantly behind them.

All until I touched them and stole it away.

My affliction made me a moth to a flame, always drawn to those who brimmed with life. They teased me, urging me to reach out and touch their warmth, all for me to take it from them and leave them dull and cold.

That was what would have happened to the girl. All before *he* had reached a hand, wrapped his slender fingers around my wrist, and stopped me.

I had never felt anything like it. A decade with only feeling the cold and yet I could feel the boy's warmth as though he still held me.

"He touched you," Myrinn repeated for the umpteenth time since returning to our realm. I sensed her own want to try. My sister, kind and glowing like a star, always hoping for the best for everyone.

"Don't." I pulled back before her fingers could move another inch towards me.

The rest of my relatives whispered with caution as guards came and swept their humans from them. I could see the confusion creased across the humans' faces as they overheard the commotion that lasted a moment as they were removed from the room.

"Queen Claria must hear of this immediately," Frila said. Was that panic I heard beneath her tone?

"Hold your tongue," Myrinn snapped, turning her attention upon our youngest sister. "Until we understand what has occurred there will be nothing to report. As much as you do enjoy the chaos, little sister, I demand that you keep silent about this."

I should have told Myrinn that I did not require her help to fight my battles. It had been years since I had even seen her last and I had done fine coping without her.

"For now," Gildir added, seemingly the most unbothered by the display.

"The Choosing is over," I reminded them all. "What has happened can be forgotten. It makes no difference for I have still returned empty-handed."

As I spoke, I could not stop the wheels turning in my mind. The entrance to Tithe waited behind me. I would have until nightfall to visit and return before the veil between our worlds sealed, if only to see him again and inspect his halo of life, to find the answers as to why he could resist the death my touch granted.

How? Why? Only two of the many questions that swam within my pulsing mind.

My relatives, as powerful as they each were, would not

notice if I melted into the shadows. They had no domain over the darkness, not like I.

I retreated to the quiet chamber within my soul and waited for the conversation to end. With great effort, I forced a smile at Myrinn, who looked back at me with motherly concern that was almost similar to pity. She then turned with the rest and left me alone.

Perhaps I had decided upon my actions before I truly realised.

Impatient and starved for that warmth once again, I slipped into the shadows, pressed through the base of the Great Tree of Nyssa and entered Tithe with my sights and desires focused on finding the boy again.

Arlo.

🦋 7 🦋

I was being followed as I weaved through the bustling streets of Tithe like a mouse. No matter if I stopped and looked blatantly around, or briefly glanced over my shoulder, there was no one there to see.

I narrowed my stare, searching through the shadows of shops, homes and alleyways, just to find the owner of the eyes that caused prickles across the back of my neck.

Still, there wasn't anyone noticeable.

Continuing through the narrowed side streets of Tithe was my best option. Tired, old buildings leaned on either side of the crooked passageways. The shadow they cast across the cobbled path was dense. With my hood up and quick feet, I kept pace.

Dameon likely had a price for my head after what I had done. It was best to stay clear from him until things died down. *If they ever did*. Yes, not all of the fey-kind had left with a Chosen, but four of them did. That was better than nothing. Surely, they would see sense and not punish Tithe for what I had done.

The tickling sensation didn't cease. It continued to flirt with me, spreading goosebumps across any exposed skin it could find. At one point, seemingly alone in the back alleys of Tithe's outer reaches, I almost stopped and shouted for the person to reveal themselves. Seeing sense that I was likely crazed, I kept my head down and my feet quick.

I reached Tom's house to find it empty. The dusty windows were dark and there was not a sound of life from within. I sagged, back pressed against the paint-worn door with the perfect balance of relief and disappointment. He would have likely still been thrown into the throngs of what little festivities were left.

It was not the best choice for me to wait for him to return. So I went to the only place I knew I was welcome.

The Wall.

I needed a distraction, and the ancient oaks couldn't provide that, but it was my only option. I couldn't return home to Auriol, not yet. Perhaps things would have cooled down by the rise of tomorrow's dawn. Until then I would have to wait and play out our argument over and over in my head.

Since I had left Tom's house, I had not felt the presence following me. It was easy to push it to the back of my mind when I had far too much to worry about.

I sat beneath the trees at the edges of Tithe's boundary, hidden beneath the foliage from the towering wall and the Watchers who paraded across it. When evening arrived, I would return to Tom and allow him to divert my mind from my reality.

I only hoped he would.

❦

Night had fallen upon Tithe and with it a chill that sank into my bones. I woke beneath the trees freezing and stiff. At some point I had fallen asleep, giving into the peace of that rather than the punishment my waking brain put me under.

Stretching out my aching limbs, I made my way towards Tom's house, sprinting through shadows. By the time I got there, I was relieved to see the glow of orange and red flames dancing within the windows.

He was home.

"Hello?" I called out, pushing the already ajar door to Tom's home open. It screeched painfully; if they had not heard my call then the noise it made would surely alert them to my presence.

After several moments passed with no response, I called out again, stepping carefully through the threshold. "I would have knocked but the door was..."

My mouth clamped shut, silencing the horror from spilling out as I saw what waited before me.

Tom's mother, Kate, was splayed out across the floor. In her hand she gripped the iron prongs that would be used to push wood about in the hearth. Beside her was a perfectly stacked pile of logs still waiting to be placed into the flames.

It looked as though she had fallen asleep before finishing her task. But Kate was not sleeping. No...

She was dead.

I knew that from the grey sheen of her skin, as though it had turned to stone, cracking in places and allowing blood to spread like a lake of scarlet beneath her. Her hair, once full of warmth and colour, was drained to tones of silver; strands like cobwebs, lying within her blood and staining it in wet clumps.

My stomach jolted. I rocked forward, hands on knees, as vomit erupted out of me; the wet splatter only made me sick again, over and over until my stomach cramped and a cold sweat broke out over my forehead.

I called Tom's name, recognising the deafening silence more than I had before I found Kate's dead body. It was close to impossible to wait for his response or hear it over the thundering of my heart. It echoed through my ears, synchronising with the thumping pain that filled my head.

Perhaps I should have left then, run back out the door and screamed Tithe down until someone came to help us. But my feet moved forward. I sidestepped around the outstretched legs of Kate as though I navigated a narrow path on the side of a sheer-face cliff.

My hand went to my belt and to the short knife that offered its comfort. I gripped the hilt, not pulling it free from the sheath just yet, but I was ready if I needed it.

I found Tom's dad in the darkened kitchen. I almost passed him as I moved for the stairs but stopped when I saw the dark outline of his figure sitting upon a chair by the dining table.

"Are you okay, sir?" I asked, rushing in to help him. In the dark it looked as though he was simply sitting at the table waiting patiently for his supper to be put before him. I was wrong.

The stench of decay greeted me as I got closer to him. With the little light that spilled from the living room I finally saw the truth of what waited for me. Like his wife, he too was dead. His wide eyes were black, bulging from his skull as though the skin around them had retreated. His face was sunken and hollow; it was as though he had died weeks before. What was left of the grey skin still clinging to the bones of his face were melting off before my eyes. It dripped alongside his darkened blood, across the table before him where his hands rested. His mouth was open in a silent scream, the little amount of teeth he still had were yellow and brown; most laid among the dripping puddle of gore beneath him.

My mind raced for what had done this. Vampires? No. It couldn't have been. The Watchers would have been alerted if a vampire had broken through the boundary. Or maybe they had. My disrespect at the Choosing had done what the Watchers had threatened for as long as I could remember. The magic that kept us hidden from sight of the undead creatures had been taken back by the elves and we were left, holed together in a pen like sheep, waiting for the wolves to come and pick us apart.

I unsheathed my pathetic knife, the bone handle worn from years of handling and the blade dull. It was better used to cut steak than an enemy, but it served me well against the vampires that I hunted when I needed their blood.

If there was one here, I would kill it. Take its blood for my own use and call upon the Watchers.

I would be a hero. They would see past my actions and acclaim me for...

No, Arlo. Focus.

Swallowing the urge to vomit again, I lifted the blade to Tom's father's neck. Even in the sagging, melting skin I could not discern teeth marks. I then looked at his arms—

There was movement above me, the familiar creak of

floorboards beneath heavy feet. I could have died on the spot from the fear which crawled up from my feet and spread across my skull; the feeling was painful.

"Tom," I forced out, trying to put as much confidence into my voice as I could muster. I had chased vampires into the darkest pits, far more frightening than this place. But it was different. I was normally the one hunting, but now it felt like I was being hunted. "Please, Tom... let it be you."

I left the dead body in the kitchen and padded quietly towards the bottom of the stairs. My knuckles were white with tension as I gripped the knife and held it out before me.

If it was a vampire, I had to kill it, not because I was desperate to collect its blood this time, but because if it got out of this house and spread its disease around Tithe until it reached Auriol... The thought alone had me taking the steps up to next floor of the house.

I had to keep Auriol safe.

The creak sounded again. I recognised its location from being in Tom's room. I prepared myself to find him dead, like his mother and father. The stairs replied to the noise that waited for me, squeaking its betrayal of my presence.

There was no point in sneaking. Whoever, or whatever, waited upstairs knew I was coming.

I burst into Tom's room, the cry of battle wetting my lips and filling my chest with a false sense of confidence.

"Arlo..." Tom stood still in the centre of his room; darkness danced around him. Only the light of the silvered moon cutting paths through his window illuminated us.

"You are alive."

"It is your fault."

I lowered my knife. The shock at finding him alive sent a violent tremble through my legs. I hardly registered what he said as a new urgency spread through me.

"We need to get out of here, Tom. Whatever has killed your parents will be back." Getting my words out was hard. I rushed, urgent and frantic, as I raised my hand towards him.

Tom stayed still, chin raised high as though an unseen hand had lifted it. "You brought this. You killed them. You..." Tom began to cry now, spitting with each shaking breath. Snot leaked down his nose, spreading with the dribble and tears until it coated his pale skin.

That was when I felt it, a shift of the shadows as a hand reached out behind Tom and hovered in the air above his shoulder. Tom flinched as though sensing the presence but did not turn to see it. It was not the clawed hand of a vampire. The light of the moon dusted across it, catching the almost diamond glint of its skin, perfect nails, and a deep ruby ring set in a gold band that stood proud upon its middle finger.

"Get back!" I shouted, throat dry and tongue feeling too big for my mouth.

"You never answered my question," a voice spoke from the shadows, deep and rich. It caused the air to vibrate as though it danced in command to it. The hand that belonged to the shrouded figure twitched, fingers rising and falling one by one as if he was playing the ivory keys of an instrument.

Tom snivelled like a pig being led to slaughter, eyes rimmed red with the knowledge of what was to come for him.

I pointed my knife, narrowing my gaze as I tried to navigate the shadows for the speaker. It was as though they had thickened into a cloak, and *he* wore it. However, he did not need to step free from his hiding place for me to know who spoke. I recognised his voice as if it was as familiar as my sister's.

"Faenir..." I said his name aloud, hoping speaking it would shatter this illusion. Perhaps I still slept beneath the trees in the outskirts of Tithe. Surely this had to be a dream. This death. This horror. How else could it be explained that an elf stood within Tom's room? When it went against everything I knew about their visits.

As if hearing my thoughts and wishing to prove me a fool, Faenir freed himself of the shadows. He did not move. They did, shifting away from him as if someone else had pulled his cloak free.

My breath hitched. Tom spluttered a light scream that belonged more to a young girl than him.

"I see I have made an impression on you just as you have on me."

I cringed. My skin felt as though it would melt from my bones just as it had for Tom's parents.

"Do not hurt him," I pleaded. "I disrespected you. I refused your Choosing, not him. Why come and hurt these people when they had nothing to do with it?"

It felt natural to close the space between us. I wanted him to know that I did not fear him. But should I? If Faenir had caused the death within this house, then I should be frightened.

"I thought you were *all* free from my curse. Now I see that was wrong." Faenir did not smile as he spoke, although his voice was full of excitement. He did not take his golden eyes off me, not as he lowered his lips towards Tom's neck where they waited a hairsbreadth above it. "You interest me, Arlo. I wished to see you again and make sure that it was not I who was crazed and mad. I almost left without trying again."

"Please," I said through gritted teeth. "Let him go."

"Why?" Faenir pouted, lips growing closer to Tom's neck.

"If you hurt him, I swear I will kill you."

Faenir smiled, welcoming my threat. "I am not scared of death. Why should I fear something that belongs to me?"

He kissed Tom before I could do anything to stop it, pressing his lips into Tom's neck gently and for only a brief moment. Tom relaxed, shoulders lowering, and all creases of fear and panic vanished from his face until he was the handsome man I remembered him to be.

The peace lasted only a moment.

Tom's eyes were thrown open as the first warning. He went to scream but a gargle came out instead. Then, like his mother and father, a shadow of grey passed over his skin. Tom died where he stood; life drained from his body with each prolonged second. I had never seen a body decay so quickly apart from the vampires I had staked myself.

I couldn't mutter a word. The knife shook in my hand, my body rooted to the spot, as Faenir released Tom and he tumbled to the floor like a sack of rotten shit.

"You see what happens to those I touch?" Faenir asked, voice peaked with the question. "Then tell me why you still stand. Why did you not die as you should have when your fingers took my wrist and stopped me? What, *Arlo*, makes you so different?"

I did not take my eyes from Tom's rotting corpse as Faenir stepped towards me. It was as though the shadows in the room closed in around us, blocking out the light from the moon and covering every wall until we stood within a hellscape of darkness in another realm.

"Until you can answer me," Faenir said, voice urging the darkness to creep closer as if his presence commanded it. "You will be mine."

8

I was lost to a sea of darkness. Its current was resilient, dragging me from my feet and throwing my world into chaos.

I had a sense I was moving but not because I was walking. It came in the unsettling jolt that filled my stomach as though I was looking down at the world from a great height, except there was nothing for me to see, only the endless darkness as though hands were held over my eyes.

There was no use in crying out, to scream from fear or wail like a broken-hearted creature from the memory of Tom dying before my eyes. No one would hear me. My throat would fill with the shadows the moment my lips opened, blocking my airway and silencing me with its greedy hands.

Was I dying? It was the clearest thought that I could latch onto. Faenir had reached for me, fingers grazing my cheek in what should have been an affectionate touch. But then the darkness took over.

Perhaps his touch, the one that had killed Tom, his father and mother, had taken me too.

An image of Auriol's face flashed through my mind suddenly. It was an explosion of brilliant light fighting away the shadows so I could see her clearly. Life. That was what the halo that surrounded her frame was.

The edges of the vision were blurry, but the life that encompassed her was bright and frightening. I was beside her. My body glowed with the same aura of light as hers. I could see the horrific embarrassment on her face and the determined hatred in mine. How my mismatching eyes glared at the person's viewpoint I was getting a glimpse of. Faenir. I was seeing from his eyes during the Choosing.

It lasted only a moment.

Then everything stopped. The world stilled. The darkness quietened its siren call.

Only four words seemed to whisper in the silence, so faint, it was the only thing for me to cling to.

You will be mine.

* * *

It was the cold breeze that dusted across my sodden skin that woke me.

Then I heard the gentle brush of... water, lapping up against a shore of smoothed stone which joined in with a chorus of bird calls. I laid there with my eyes pinched closed, enjoying the calming feeling my senses kept me entrapped in.

But then I remembered that in Tithe there was no

body of water large enough to cause such a sound and certainly not one close to home.

I bolted upright, eyes snapping wide, to find that I was laid out across a bed I did not recognise in a room I had never seen before. It was a vast bedroom constructed from walls of white stone with veins of dark grey that spread through them like rivers. Directly before the bed, which was big enough for at least five grown men to fill, was an arched doorway generously giving view to the world beyond.

Sheer curtains moved in the breeze, twisting like ghosts dancing to the chorus of nature.

I focused on the open, cloudless skies and the faint outline of what looked like the peaks of a mountainous range far in the distance. This world was certainly not the one I knew.

I was no longer in Tithe.

Heart pounding, I threw myself from the bed. The sheets that had been draped across me almost caused me to fall flat upon my face as they tangled with my feet. Steadying myself, head thundering in harmony with my heart, my hands went to my belt. One hand clasped the pouch hiding the vials which calmed me somewhat. The other went to the empty sheath that should have held my knife, the one I had last brandished towards Faenir whilst standing above the dead body of Tom.

"I thought it best to keep this from you. It would be foolish to allow a weapon to be kept in your hands when I do not know what you do with it."

I turned on my heel, fists gathered into balls before me, and faced the speaker.

Faenir leaned against a doorframe at the other end of

the room. His legs were crossed at his ankles, rivulets of dark hair falling over his chest like waves of shadow. A shiver spread down from my skull as I watched him, stupefied, as he twisted my knife in one hand with the tip of the metal spinning upon his finger. He pulled it away to reveal a droplet of ruby blood before swiftly sticking his finger in his mouth, raising his golden stare to me, and cleaning the blood with his tongue.

"Where have you taken me?" I hissed, nails cutting crescent moons into my palms.

"To my home."

I wished to take my eyes from the elven prince and glance across the room once again. But I knew that would have been foolish.

Never take your eyes off your enemy, for it is what they do when you cannot see which makes them your greatest threat.

"We are not in Tithe." It was not a question, but more a statement to confirm what my mind had already come to terms with.

"Far from it," Faenir confirmed, flashing pink stained teeth. As he pulled his finger from his mouth, I noticed the cut was no longer visible.

You can take him. The thought was sudden. That possibility faltered into nothingness as I registered the fact that Faenir, as well as being over a foot taller than me, had the power to kill at his touch. If I was to get out of this place, I needed to be alive.

"You killed them..." I snarled, lip curling over my teeth as though I was no different to the vampires I hunted. "Tom. His family."

"That bothers you, does it?"

My skin crawled as his gaze traced over me. Faenir

studied every inch of me, drinking my details like a dehy-drated sailor. I didn't answer his question, aware of my lack of control if I did. Perhaps I would have given into the haunting image of their deaths which lurked at the back of my mind, or even raced across the room and tackled Faenir in a furious hurricane of fists and teeth.

Instead, I inhaled deeply, hoping it would help me stay calm, and presented my demand. "Take me back."

Faenir pushed himself from the doorframe, amusement alight across his devilish face. "I am afraid I am unable to do that."

My eyes frantically searched for signs that he was lying; the twitching of a lip, or the narrowing of an eye that was the usual response when someone was being deceitful.

"Take. Me. Home."

"Are you not going to ask where it is you are before demanding to return to a place which holds no future for you compared to what I can give you?" Faenir was serious as he spoke. Two, perfectly manicured dark brows furrowed above his squinting stare. His angular face was hauntingly handsome. The way he looked at me screamed with confusion as though he could not understand how stupid I could be not to see sense in why I was here.

I stepped closer to him, knuckles white as I still bared my fists. He stared at me and sniggered softly which burned the furnace of anger inside of me to a new level of heat.

"I am not the one to be laughing at, *elf*," I said, muscles trembling with anticipation. "Careful how you regard me."

An urgency was building. I wanted to get home to Auriol and would do anything to make that happen.

"Your threats are meaningless to me, *human*."

"Tell me what you want from me and get this over with."

"You are my Chosen, Arlo." He drew my name out as though enjoying the way the sounds rolled over his tongue. My skin crawled to see his misplaced enjoyment. "What I want is you. Now, are you ready to answer the pressing mystery? I am dying to know."

Nothing else mattered about what he said besides his first four words. "I am nothing to you. Not your Chosen. Not your mystery. Nothing. Now, if you do not take me home, I swear to tear this entire... this... fucking, where the fuck have you taken me!?"

My blustering, wordy anger entertained Faenir who could not hide the twitching corners of his lips. "Haxton."

"What?" I gaped, breathing heavily as though I had run up a steep hill and back down again without stopping.

"You are currently residing in the guest suite of my home, Haxton Manor."

"Well fuck your home," I spat, scowling at the elf who hardly flinched from the droplets of spit that shot towards him. "Smile again and I promise to wipe it clean from your face."

"As you have said," Faenir replied, calmly. Even with me inches from him the elven prince showed no signs of concern. That irked me. "And as I will tell you again, returning home is not possible. I have chosen you, Arlo. Just like my cousins have picked their mates before you, when you so interestingly interrupted. I suppose you simply delayed the inevitable and I admit I am thankful for that. If you had not stopped me from choosing your sister then we would not be here now, together."

Faenir's gilded eyes drifted away from me, lost in

thought. "Perhaps she is the same as you... She can resist my—"

"Do not *dare* think of her." I threw my fist forward, which the elf sidestepped effortlessly. Angered, I tried to punch him again, only to miss for a second time.

"I would not concern yourself, Arlo. My interests are entirely upon you."

I stepped back from him, wishing nothing more than distance as my mind stormed with anxiety. Quickly, I put together the pieces of this scene. Faenir had taken me, unwillingly, from Tithe. Wherever this Haxton Manor was, it was far from the doorstep of mine and Auriol's home.

Auriol. My heart panged in my chest, and I did everything I could not to show him the pain.

Faenir seemed to notice anyway for his face lost all remnants of humour. It was hard to focus on him when my panic made breathing hard. It seemed each breath in was weak and the air too light to have real benefit. My heart was pounding harder, my head feeling as though I had drunk an entire bottle of aged wine or at least had been smacked across the skull with the bottle instead.

"What is the matter?" His voice was quiet as he spoke. Faenir was so close to me now that I caught the scent that clung to his silver-toned shirt, rosewood entwined with something sweeter. I found myself pondering what it was and forgetting about my concerns as he drew closer.

"You..." I muttered, having to look up at Faenir as he stood before me. He was far taller than I first believed. My position accentuated the sharp structure of his face. The tips of his cupid's bow were curved perfectly. His nose was straight and proud. Faenir's skin was kissed by sun, golden like his eyes which only stood out as the tumbling of raven-black hair fell over his shoulders. Up close I could see plaits woven into his hair; red string twisted amongst them.

His closeness only entrapped me for a moment. As Faenir slowly lifted a hand towards the strand of stubborn, blond hair that had fallen over my eye, I snapped out of my stupor and attacked.

"Take me fucking home," I cried over the crunch of my fist as it finally slammed into his face. That perfect nose was not perfect anymore; it was bent. Streams of red blood poured freely; some splattered across my knuckles while the rest spread across the lower half of his face.

"I... cannot." Faenir rocked back, bright eyes wide but not from fear, from intrigue. He raised a hand to his broken nose and traced his finger down it.

I struck out again, slamming my fists into his rock-solid chest. Faenir didn't move an inch. He stood tall, hardly moved by the thundering of my fists. Nor did he stop me. Blood ruined his shirt. *His blood*, pouring freely from the damage I had caused.

"I fear I have made a mistake," Faenir said only when I stopped.

I cried furiously, tears of frustration and desperation rolling down my face. My blood covered hands hurt, the bones in my knuckles each screaming with the demand to rest.

"This is not how I imagined this day to be."

"Please..." I dropped to my knees, not caring for the pain as they met the marble floor. Fat, red droplets of his blood splattered like spring rain around his feet. It was both beautiful and frightening. "I just want to go home."

"Arlo."

I winced as he said my name but dared look up.

"If it makes you feel any better, know that your sister will be well rewarded. Just as the families of the other Chosen are."

I bowed my head, chin to chest, from exhaustion. Deep down I did not want him to see me cry. Holding back such emotion was impossible when one felt lost and terrified.

"Why...?" I said, eyes stinging as I looked back up at him. "You left without a Chosen and came back. Why me?"

Faenir knelt before me, still keeping his hands to himself. I hardly blinked as I watched him with intent, not wishing to miss a single movement. I had seen what his touch could do if he wished, and I was not prepared to die. Even if he had kept himself from me this entire time.

Not yet. My mind raced to the vial of vampire blood in my pouch. One. It would only last near a month at most... that was all.

"If what you desired most in the world was suddenly presented to you on a gilded platter, would you not do what you could to take it?"

Faenir's question was given in answer to mine, however I could not make sense as to what it meant.

"Would you?" he asked again, breath coming out softly. Even with his face covered in his own blood and his deathly power a horrific reminder he was dangerous, I was not scared of him.

"I have faced monsters far more frightening than you, elf."

Faenir paused, regarded my comment and then stood.

"Then you will be well suited to your new home. Monsters." Faenir laughed dryly, turned his back on me and walked towards the open door. "There are plenty of those lurking this side of *my* realm."

"Wait..." I shouted, pushing myself up with urgency.

Faenir stopped briefly. He did not turn back to face me, but instead rolled his shoulders and straightened his posture as though preparing to walk out of this room and into another filled with a crowd of adoring followers. "I suggest you rest. We will speak further on the matter over dinner."

I watched, helplessly, as my captor left the room, his swishing dark ruby cloak the last thing I saw. Even as the door shut behind him, I expected to hear the turn of a lock.

The door was not secured.

Standing deathly still I waited for as long as I could handle, using the thumping crashes of my heart to make sense of the time between when he had left me. I managed until the twenty-fourth count before I gathered myself and followed him.

If Faenir was not going to take me home, I would find my way back myself.

For Auriol's sake.

And mine.

FAENIR

The grace of his touch was the most wondrous feeling in the world, no matter if it conjured shattered bone and blood. I prevented myself from healing, holding back the magic from knitting together my skin and mending the bones that had fractured in my nose. All because I did not desire to forget what *his* touch had felt like for fear I would believe it had never happened.

For years I had felt agony like no other, but not in this way, not as real as this; as physical and undeniable, caused by another's hand. It was always my hands that hurt. Maimed. Killed.

Arlo was the harsh reminder that others, like me, could do just as much damage.

Blood had dried across my bare chest. Some clung within the braids of my hair, making them as stiff as straw. The person who looked back at me in the reflection of the steam-coated mirror was not the same I had grown used to seeing. This one had hope in his eyes, eyes surrounded by purple bruising and swelling from Arlo's attack. I could have looked at myself for hours, spent days even, trying to discern the undeniable truth that Arlo had done this...

With his fists upon my skin, and still lived to do it again.

I reached a cupped hand into the basin of warmed water then splashed it over my face. I did what I could to clean my face and the gore that covered the bottom of it like a mask. Droplets of pink and red splashed across the white stone basin and turned the water a ruddy colour.

Finally, my nose healed, the dark bruising retreated to the glowing hue of my skin. I felt the rush of fresh air as I inhaled deeply, testing the limits of the way my body mended itself.

If I could have put it off anymore, I would have.

Just as I feared, looking back at the pinkish droplets of water that fell from my almost clean face, it was as if it had never happened.

My fingers reached tentatively to the smooth bridge of my nose, expecting to feel some memory of discomfort. But there was nothing. No pain. No bump of bone or cut of skin.

And just like that I forgot. My mind was willing to cling to the feeling of Arlo's touch for long enough to memorise it, just as it had when he had gripped my wrist back in Tithe. It was no more than a dream and I was still the monster whose touch could kill.

9

I required a weapon. *Preferably something fucking sharp and pointy.*

The thought was one of many as I tore through Haxton Manor. It was certainly one of the louder thoughts, alongside my urgency to return to Tithe and get as far away from here as possible.

Faenir had not shown himself again, nor did I feel as though I was being stalked as I trailed through endless high ceiling rooms and chambers adorned in furniture I would never have dreamed of seeing. Grand, stone and wood creations that seemed only suitable for a god, not an elf like Faenir.

He didn't deserve this luxury.

It became apparent quickly that Haxton was a hollow and empty place. Although beautiful, with its marble floors and white stone pillars that helped hold aloft the towering ceiling, it was... dead. It was deafeningly quiet, so much so that what should have been the tapping of my light feet sounded like the thundering of countless hooves as I ran, trying to find my escape. Everything about this place was cold; it seemed to seep from the floor and walls, covering me with its icy embrace.

The endless open windows did not help with the winter-like freeze, but without them I would have felt trapped in a perfectly pristine box with no hope for escape. It was encouraging to see the stretch of azure lake that seemed to wrap around Haxton Manor entirely every time I looked beyond them.

At one point I had stopped to catch my breath, peering out the stone-arched window and looking down to see how far the drop was. Could I have jumped and made my escape easier? A trellis of red flowers that looked as breath-taking as roses but as full as carnations covered most of the wall beyond. The roots and stems were thick and woven amongst one another like the braids in Faenir's hair. They could likely hold my weight but the intense drop that still lingered beneath the window was not worth the risk of trying.

The fall would kill me.

You are dying anyway, I reminded myself harshly. It was what I needed to push from the ledge and carry on running blindly through the wide and empty corridors.

By the time I reached the ground floor of the manor I had broken out into a barrage of hot flushes. My tunic felt sticky on my skin, material clinging unwantedly to every press of bone and curve of what little muscle I had.

Like the windows, the large doors that signalled the main entrance of the manor were wide open. It was much like when Auriol and I would spring clean our apartment in hopes to frighten away the dust and moths who took up residency with us. We would open every window we had just to allow the aid of fresh, spring air to speed up our clean.

Just the thought of her and the memory caused me discomfort. Gritting my teeth and pushing it to the back of my mind, I continued for the door.

Faenir was a terrible captor. It was as though his lack of presence and unlocked doors was his way of encouraging me to take leave. Not wasting the opportunity, I burst out into the open, squinting slightly as the bright glare of sun danced off the swell of water before me. Freedom.

Keep going.

My boots slapped down sloping steps towards a dark stone gravel path that led to the lake.

It is not over until you are home.

I had no idea where I was running to, but something told me Tithe rested beyond the lake. It was as though a compass within me had spun wildly, waking from years of slumber. The arrow twisted and twisted in circles until settling in the direction of the mountains across the lake. To Auriol. I knew it.

The closer I got to the water the more I could see beyond the haze of clouds in the distance. The mountainous outline grew clearer, allowing me to make out the white tipped peaks and harsh giant bodies of each one.

But then I saw what that compass was trying to tell me. The top of a tree, a tree far taller and monstrous than any dared to be. It towered over the tallest of the four mountains peaks but was fainter to look at. Set back at a distance I could see the luscious outline of its full branches and shadowed trunk.

It was much like the tree within Tithe, except bigger by a thousandfold.

Tithe. Home. That was my way back to Auriol. I could not explain it, this feeling, but that tugging of the compass within me was too demanding to ignore.

The lake was miles long. Only a fool would swim it. And I was many things, but a fool was not a title I cared to accept.

My boots left prints in the golden sand as I raced alongside the shore. When I turned back to look behind me, the gentle lapping of water would devour the mark I left as though I never had been here.

Perfect. If Faenir came looking, he wouldn't know the way I took.

Maybe he chased after me now? I half expected to hear my name called out in fury but then the elf did not seem the type to voice his feelings so vocally, not that I knew anything about him, nor wished to.

Eventually I found what looked like a dock of some kind. Wooden and rotten, the panels had holes and the stilts that disappeared into the water looked gnawed and weak. A brown rope slithered within the lake as if toyed with by unseen fish... or other creatures.

This was a good sign at least. Evidence of a boat that would glide across the water far quicker than I could swim it. But if swimming the length of the azure depths was my only option, it would have to do.

The sky was darkening quickly, and with it my hopes of finding a way out. From within Haxton it had certainly felt like the lake stretched around it completely; running along its shoreline only confirmed it.

Haxton was nestled on a piece of land completely

surrounded by water. There was no boat in sight, nothing I could use to get free from this place. And with night fast approaching, the lake went from a soft blue to a darkened grey that no longer looked inviting.

Now, I felt the need to turn away from it and head back to the manor. I couldn't place my finger on why I felt a creeping chill of fear up the back of my neck. But whatever it was did a fantastic job at putting me off giving into my desperation and swimming.

It was when I was close to giving up, I saw something that had my heart leaping into my throat. A light hovered far out in the distance. The familiar curls of fire, orange and red, danced like a bud captured within a glass lantern which hardly reflected over the water it glided across. It was held upon a pole, gripped by a hand of a figure who stood tall on the prow of a small vessel.

A boat.

It was a *fucking* boat.

I waded into the water, waving my hands like a mad fool above my head. "Here!" I shouted, voice skipping over the still water like a stone I had thrown. With each bounce the echo grew quieter and quieter. "Please, I have been taken from my home. He stole me. Please. Quick!"

I walked out further into the frigid water, cringing at the noise my desperate cries made. I was knee-deep when I turned back towards Haxton Manor and the soft, bluish glow that emanated from the many windows. They were like dull eyes, watching my escape as though it was the greatest entertainment it had ever witnessed.

Perhaps Faenir watched in glee, smiling with his shattered nose and blood covered face as I tried to leave. Or maybe he wanted me to; after what I had done to him, he would see that I was the wrong choice and wish for me to return home.

"Hurry up!" I shouted, shivering as the cold water soaked into my trousers. I was waist-deep now.

The boat did not seem to pick up its speed, but it was hard to tell when the darkening sky made every small detail impossible to notice. The view of the mountains had retired to sleep, the tree no more than a darkened smudge across the landscape before me.

I was freezing to the bone, I knew that. My teeth chattered violently, catching the skin of my inner cheeks without prejudice. The water was now up to my chest as I fought my way out as if it would get me to the boat, and the person within it, quicker.

"Please!"

My feet fell from the muddied ground until I was forced to swim.

"Pl-please."

Water splashed into my mouth. Salty but fresh, it made the insides of my cheeks clench and my tongue sting with the distaste of it.

I was not making progress. Turning back towards the shore, it looked so far away that I could not believe I had swum such a length so quickly, yet still the boat and that mocking light did not grow closer.

Something brushed up against me. It halted my breathing, my legs and arms turning to stone. I tried to look down into the dark pits of black that surrounded me and saw nothing.

It happened again, this time beneath me. Something pushed up against my feet and I kicked out, slipping beneath the water in a moment of panic. I scrunched my eyes closed, treading the water with my arms as I attempted to keep myself from drowning.

I managed a single breath before the unseen danger wrapped a grip around my ankle and pulled.

"Arlo!"

The cry of my name was the last thing I heard before I was dragged into the cold depths of the lake.

I threw my eyes wide to see bubbles stream before them, disorientating me. My lungs burned as I held onto the pathetic, final breath I had managed before I was taken under.

I kicked out in vain. It did not dissuade what had me. I had often thought of the creatures that lurked in deep waters but never thought I'd ever set foot in such a place.

Oh how life changed so quickly.

I clawed at the lake as though it would save me, eyes stinging as the harsh, bitter water infiltrated them. Then I saw them. *People.* Figures of silver and white so stark against the dark waters that I gasped at the sight of them. I realised suddenly that my gasp had expelled the little air I had left. My weakening hands reached for the bubbles as though I could take them in my fingers and draw them back to my lips.

A fool you are.

The opaque bodies drifted around me. I followed one, the figure of a small child, a girl whose body was not full but wispy and see-through like morning fog. She drifted beneath me until I saw what had a hold of me.

It was another figure of white shadows. Its hand gripped my ankle, anchoring me through the water with terrifying strength. It glowered, judging eyes cutting straight through me with unmeasurable intent.

Suddenly it was not a lake I drowned within, but a swell of ghostly figures. Each of them reached for me with hard, strong grips and helped guide me down into the pits of my death.

My eyes grew heavy as the swelling pain in my chest faded. Suddenly I did not care for air to fill my lungs with breath and life. It was peaceful, surrounded by the dead as they held me and greeted me, taking me home as if I was one of them.

FAENIR

I refused to look down at Arlo, to study the way his limp body was curled up in my arms, or how his cheek was squashed against the sodden material of my shirt. I didn't need to look to know he was there because I *felt* him.

Arlo's hard press against me was so entirely intoxicating that I could not focus on anything but keeping one foot before the other.

Myrinn waited at the entrance to Haxton, fingernails chewed between teeth as she waited to hear the verdict of Arlo's stupidity. She likely expected him to be dead, drowned by the ruthless shades who dwelled within Styx.

I had not yet dealt with the fact that Myrinn had arrived at Haxton without invitation as though she was above it. Charon would face my wrath for bringing her upon his boat once Arlo was awake; I would take out this feeling on them both.

Arlo would have been dead if I had got to him any later. The glow of life that haloed around his body was the beacon I needed to find him within the waters. Even now it still shone as bright as any star.

I felt rage as though it was a new emotion, furious at myself for being so distracted and letting him get into this predicament. I had convinced myself that Arlo was indestructible because he could withstand my touch. But he was not, tonight proved that.

"He is breathing," I confirmed as I swept past Myrinn.

Myrinn instantly relaxed, pulling her hands from her pale lips and loosing a breath. "Have you not warned him of the dangers that lurk here?"

I paused before replying, trying to focus on her rather than the fluttering of Arlo's heartbeat as it echoed across my chest. I had felt my own before, strong and proud; others would dwindle beneath my touch.

Not Arlo. *But why?*

"He has not been susceptible to conversation."

Myrinn stepped aside to allow me to pass into the manor without slowing a step. "Can you blame the boy? Stealing a mate is certainly the opposite of what the custom is. If we are to keep our relationship with the humans strong, we should not make ourselves seem anything remotely like a threat."

"I care little for what they think of me. Nor did Claria when she sent me to Tithe with the sole purpose of me killing a human for her own enjoyment."

"And yet you proved her wrong," Myrinn replied, pacing behind me on quick feet. "I understand your years of seclusion has affected your ability to think of anyone but yourself; however, your actions have shattered your perfectly crafted cage and left you open to the same rules as the rest of us. Think, Faenir. Keeping your Chosen alive is the first step of claiming your fate."

"His name," the growl slipped out of me without control, "is Arlo. And you truly believe I care for what others wish to see me do with this life?"

The patter of her feet ceased. I almost stopped and turned around, an apology dusted across my taut lips. Instead, I kept my focus on the hallway before me. "If you have come all this way to Haxton to remind me of the repercussions then perhaps it can wait until I deal with this."

Myrinn replied sharply, "Then I will prepare supper."

"That will not be required. You will not be staying long enough to break bread, cousin."

She ignored my disregard. "When he wakes and you both are ready, I expect to see you in the dining hall."

The conversation was closed before I could refuse her anymore. Myrinn's presence retreated into the belly of Haxton whilst I was left to carry the body of Arlo back towards his room.

He had begun to shiver so I held him closer. Only when I was certain I was out of Myrinn's earshot did I dare speak.

"I am sorry," I said softly, knowing it would be the only time I would say the words aloud to him, or anyone. "You are safe with me."

Arlo stirred against me. I slowed my pace just steps away from the entrance to the room he had run from. For the first time since I had reached for his hand in the depths of the Styx, I looked at him. He winced as though dreaming something horrific. I wished to draw my thumb across the lines of worry that scrunched across his forehead until his skin was smooth once again.

I resisted.

10

I bolted upright, a scream clawing up my throat. My hands reached up for my neck as though I expected to choke on water. My legs kicked out to rid them of the phantoms' fingers that pulled me down into dark depths.

But there were no dead here...

Only the tangling of sheets around my frantic legs and the darkened sky which gave a view beyond the opened balcony of the bedroom.

It took a moment to calm my laboured breathing and thunderous heart. Every time I blinked, I believed I would see them again, faint whispers of silver bodies who longed for me to join them in death. They did not come for me, yet I still recognised their presence in the haunting glint of the lake that taunted me beyond the balcony.

"Are you so desperate to leave my home you would throw yourself into shades and think you would simply swim free?"

Faenir stepped into the room with hands full of folded

clothing. He paced straight towards the bed with a pinched expression and fury filled eyes. The pile of clothing thudded upon the bed as he discarded them, then he stood back and folded his arms across his chest.

"If I had known..." I began but swallowed the rest of my excuse and swapped it with something harder. "They were going to kill me."

"Indeed, shades are bitter spirits who dwell within the Styx and harbour the hate and anger that prevents them from moving to another realm of peace. Even I do not dare bother them... often."

Shades. "You expect me to believe that the lake is filled with ghosts?"

"Ghosts, spirits, phantoms. All different words for the same truth. And I do not care if you wish to believe me or not. Thanks for saving your life would have sufficed."

"My captor and saviour," I sneered. "Anything else you wish to add to your ever-growing list of titles?"

Faenir's frown deepened as I pushed myself from the bed. My body ached with every slight move. It felt as though I had been pulled and tugged from all angles and my limbs hated me for it.

Where I had laid within the bed, the sheets were no longer white and pristine but muddied and all shades of brown. The evening breeze drifted across the room and revealed the stench of stale, dirty water that clung to me and the mess I had left behind.

Then I noticed a similar patch across Faenir's chest. He caught me looking but said nothing to confirm what had caused it.

"Your face looks better than it had been when I last saw you," I said through a sly grin.

Faenir ignored my jibe. "I suggest you wash and change before you come down for dinner. Those clothes will have to do until more supplies reach us in the coming days. A bath has been drawn in the chamber beyond those doors, filled with water that is not infested with shades might I add. Clean yourself up and we will be waiting for you downstairs."

"We?" He had said so much but I had only cared for that comment.

"Myrinn is persistent; she wants us both to join and I truly would not ignore that request. She can be rather persuasive if required."

Myrinn, the beautiful elf who had seemed so innately protective over Faenir during the Claiming. Her name and splendour were so unique I would have remembered them until my final day.

"She is here?"

"Arrived with the ferryman, the same one you threw yourself into Styx in hopes to board." Faenir peered at me down the length of his sharp nose. I felt the silent judging in his golden eyes and could not gleam why, someone who so clearly detested me, stole me from my home.

If he hated you, you would be dead.

"You cannot keep me here," I said, fists clenching at my sides once again. "I will not stop looking for a way home."

"I can *and* I will."

It was harder for me not to throw a punch and break his nose for a second time.

"Clean yourself up," Faenir added before turning on his heel to leave. "I trust that this time you will not go searching within Haxton's grounds. If you fear the shades, they will seem like kittens in comparison to what else lurks within my home."

I listened beyond the doors which had been left ajar before me. Pressing my back to their cold, wooden presence I devoured the one-sided conversation that happened in the room on the other side.

It had not been hard to find my way here. All it took was to listen to the voices, for sound was such a foreign concept within Haxton Manor. Sound suggested life, and this place was void of it.

"... must you be so infuriating, cousin? There will be no good to come from trying to entice Arlo to stay when Haxton remains a home for ghosts and regret."

I did not need to peer through the gap to know it was Myrinn who spoke. Her light, powerful tones conjured a vivid image of her in Tithe.

"What is done is done," Faenir replied. He spoke as though every word was an effort. Even from my vantage point I could hear his very want to be left alone. Speaking seemed such an effort for the brooding elf.

There was a familiar scratch of metal against plate, a clink of glass then followed by the glugging rush of liquid. "You are lucky he still lives. Faenir, will you look at me and at least show some interest into what I am saying?"

"This conversation, and your presence may I add, is unsolicited. I did not invite you to visit, nor embark in an inquiry as to what I have done and why I took the human from his realm unwillingly."

"Someone must be the harsh reminder that you have

made a grave mistake stealing him from his home," Myrinn replied, her voice deepening with an unseen power.

Faenir barked, followed by a screech of chair against the floor. The sound made my skin crawl. I held my breath to stop myself from gasping in response.

"You keep suggesting I have stolen him, *taken* him, that my doing is different to what you have partaken in, Myrinn. Did you not willingly enter their realm and pick a mate without asking if they even wished to return to Evelina with you? No. Do not come to my home and look at me as though I am less than. I am simply following the very tradition Claria and the rest of you believed I would fail in. Keeping him here puts all your hopes of succession at risk... that is why you are so invested, I imagine."

Myrinn stood now, evident by the loud clatter of her chair as it was thrown across the floor. "How dare you even for a moment believe I care more for the crown than your well-being."

"Do you not?" His question was quiet, words dangerous as though opening a wound that he knew would cause pain.

I chose that moment to enter. With a gentle push the door swung wide and revealed me standing, red cheeked, and my narrowed gaze locked on my captor. "It would seem your *kind* are not above the mundane limits of arguing with family. Shall I take this terrible atmosphere as the excuse I require to return to my room?"

"Arlo." Myrinn stood straight, face softening before my eyes from one of unleashed anger to controlled temper. "I apologise that you had to hear that."

Faenir said nothing, but his wide, golden stare screamed many silent thoughts.

He didn't think I would come. The rising of his pristine brows told me that he was happy I did.

"Please," Myrinn said, stepping back from the table and gesturing to the vacant chair that waited patiently, tucked beneath the long table before her. "More than anyone, you have been through a lot today. I would feel better knowing you get some food in you. It will help... I hope."

The table had been dressed beautifully; I could not deny that. It was long and made from thick cuttings of dark wood. Across its length, a black runner of material had been laid. Upon it waited silver plates of food, far more than enough for three people to devour. Goblets of wine, deep red and pale grape-white, had been nestled among the delights of food, all mostly untouched beside the goblet closest to where Faenir had been sitting. That one was already half empty.

As I walked into the room, I tried to keep my chin up and my expression unbothered. However, I could not shake the feeling of eyes following me, golden, intense eyes that belonged to my captor. They were the chains that bound me to this place. Heavy and anchoring, Faenir studied me as though he had never seen me before.

"Do all your captive humans get offered such luxuries?" I asked, reaching for the back of my chair and gripping it in hopes they both did not see how my hands trembled. "Because it will take far more than warmed meats and sweet fruits for me to forget that I am a prisoner within this place."

Myrinn winced at that, forcing a smile and a laugh as

she reached down for her chair, righted it and sat back upon it. She was dressed in a gown of silver that complimented her brown skin. Around the narrow bodice was a web of straps and belts that gave structure to her dress before it fell around her waist like clouds of tumbling mist. Myrinn's hair hung across both exposed shoulders, thick braids woven perfectly together with the addition of jewels and golden clasps that completed her regal aura. At the crown of her head, hair had been twisted to give the impression of wearing a tiara.

If I had ever believed in Kings and Queens, I would not have doubted that she was the greatest of them all.

Faenir was the last to move. There was still tension between them both, but it seemed to dissipate with every passing moment.

"If you keep persisting that you are my captive then I will insist on tying chains around your wrists to keep you bound to me. Perhaps that would stop you from being such a... fool."

"Faenir, please."

I ignored Myrinn's pleading as my knuckles turned white upon the top of the chair. "You're insufferable."

"*You* bathed."

I tried to ignore Faenir's strange comment but couldn't. It came out of nowhere and completely derailed the fury that had thickened across my tongue ready to be spat at him.

"It is what you asked of me, was it not? I would not want to displease my captor." I bowed dramatically. When I raised my eyes back to his I held that wide, golden stare in contest.

It took him a moment to reply. Faenir did an incredible

job at keeping most emotion from his bored, frowning expression as though he was not able to show anything else. "Just sit yourself down."

"You arrogant—"

"Perhaps we should begin," Myrinn said hurriedly, reaching for a bowl of what could only be described as a cloudy, thin soup. "Would not want the food to get cold before it is even enjoyed."

Faenir reached for his glass of wine instead of the food. Still holding my stare, he lifted it to his lips and exhaled, fogging the inside of his glass before taking a long sip. He won. I tore my attention from him and sat, hating that I did exactly as he commanded.

In truth I was starving, but the idea of eating food was beyond me. All it took was the reminder of where I was and what had happened, and my hunger ran away from me.

Instead, I focused my attention on Myrinn. "I wish to return to Tithe."

She almost choked on her soup. Carefully she placed the spoon down beside the bowl and raised a napkin to her lips. It was all an act to give her time to decide on her answer.

"That," she said before patting her painted lips, "I am afraid is not possible. As much as I understand... and agree, that your being here is wrong, there is nothing I can do to return you home."

I believed her. How could I not when her gaze was so trusting? I studied her expression and did not see a glimmer of a lie across it.

"I have already told him this. He chooses not to listen."

My hand gripped the knife beside my empty plate. Its polished, bone handle in my hand was familiar. All it would take was a sure aim and a strong arm and it would have been thrown across the table and buried between Faenir's eyes. In that moment I decided it would be leaving this room with me.

Just in case.

"What of your human?" I asked, trying to still the frantic thunder of my heart in my chest.

"Yes," Faenir added, leaning forward with the hint of amusement across his stern face. "Where is your mate, cousin? Is it not custom to spend your first night together?"

Myrinn shot Faenir with a glare that made him snigger into his glass. "Haxton Manor does not scream in welcome. After my brief visit, I shall return to him, do not concern yourself. However, for tonight, I feel that there are more pressing matters to deal with."

"Has he attempted to kill himself already? Escape his fate perhaps?"

My palm dampened as I tightened my grip on the knife.

"You are drunk," Myrinn snapped.

"I need to be to get through this meal."

It was comforting to know that Myrinn also shared disdain towards Faenir. Even though I was still captive, I felt as though she would protect me with more than just her words if required.

Myrinn struck out with a hand as though reaching for something unseen across the table. It was a strange action filled with intent and focus. I followed it and watched, in disbelief, as the wine in Faenir's glass leapt out and splashed across his face before he had so much as a chance to hold in a breath.

Magic. Such an open display scared me more than anything else I had seen.

The glass shattered in Faenir's hand. A growl built within his chest before spilling beyond his lips in a string of anger. "Leave!"

Myrinn stood again, chest heaving and hands open, waiting at her sides. "The years of your chosen solitude has ruined you, cousin."

I watched as power radiated from Myrinn's skin. The air grew heavy with moisture. The goblets of wine trembled upon the table as the liquid within sloshed and twisted like a hurricane controlled them.

"Get. Out. Now." The shadows that hung naturally in the corners of the room seemed to shiver, slithering outwards like snakes that coiled and twisted over one another.

"There is no helping you. Years I have fought your corner with our family. Trying to make them see that your bitterness is simply a making of the way you have been treated. Silly Myrinn, always hoping to see the good in everyone."

"I do not need you or your help. Not now. Not before."

I could do nothing but watch as both elves gathered power. The air crackled with it.

Stories of magic had been left in the history of Darkmourn. Humans capable of magic, witches, had been the downfall of humanity and not a single soul left within the vampire-riddled world beyond cared to speak of it.

Except now I stood between two storms of power that were ready to clash into one another at any given moment.

I could do nothing but watch, knife resting upon my thigh beneath the table, ready in case I had to use it against them.

"This was your chance to prove yourself," Myrinn shouted across the tables, glass cracking beneath the weight of the liquids she controlled. "To Claria, to them all. To yourself."

There was much unsaid between them, a story that I longed to dig my claws into and uncover but all I cared about was getting free of this place and returning to Auriol.

As if sensing my fear, Myrinn glanced towards me, and her power embedded away like water over rocks. The tension in the room retreated as her expression changed from anger to regret.

I waited for her to say something but instead she stood from her chair, leaving her soup forgotten, most of it now splashed across the table and soaking into the dark wood and sodden material; then she dropped her gaze and walked away.

"Wait." I stood, not caring for the shadows that still gathered around us. It was Faenir's power, the same I had seen in Tom's room as he lay dead between us.

Faenir did not stop me as I followed after Myrinn. Nor did he notice as I slipped the knife into my belt that kept the oversized, leather breeches Faenir had supplied, from falling from my thin waist.

"Please, don't leave me with him," I called out, breathlessly chasing after her.

"I am sorry, Arlo," Myrinn murmured, long legs keeping her a pace ahead of me as she moved through Haxton.

"No. If you are then take me with you," I begged. My urgency filled my throat and threatened to make me gag with desperation.

"There is nowhere for you if I do."

I reached out and gripped her forearm. "You have said that my being here is wrong. There must be a way for me to return home. I have to get back to her."

"Your sister," Myrinn said, lips pulled tight. "It is the girl you had stopped Faenir from touching?"

"Yes," I spluttered, almost melting beneath the sorrow in Myrinn's bright eyes. "I am the only person she has left. She is the only person *I* have left. I need to return to her."

"Even if I wish I could, there is nothing I can do for you, Arlo. The veil between Evelina and Darkmourn is weak. Unpredictable. There is a lot to be said about the powers that Queen Claria has sacrificed keeping your kind safe within the boundary wall. Because of this she only has enough reserves to open the door between our realms at the turning of a season. Only she has the power to grant your return home. Even if she does, it would not be until the next turn of the seasons."

I gripped the pouch at my belt and clung to the vial of blood that waited within. As my mind raced, I tried to calculate how long the blood would keep me alive before winter became spring.

"Then you must take me to her! To your Queen."

Myrinn's gaze fell to her feet. "I cannot."

My legs gave out. I fell to the floor, the crack of my knees against the slabbed floor did not dampen the pain that filled my soul and threatened to rip me apart.

To Myrinn it looked as though her confirmation of my fate in this realm had caused this reaction. The truth of what brought me to my knees was far beyond my ability to admit. *Would I die before I could ever return home?*

She knelt before me, skirt billowing out around her. I did not flinch as her fingers reached for my chin and lifted it up so I could do nothing but look at the screaming sympathy that spilled from her.

"I will do what I can to send word to the Watchers of your home and pass a message on to your sister. It is frowned upon, but I will do it as my apology for my cousin's actions. You are a victim of his selfish choice, and I cannot do anything but express my regret for what has occurred."

Tears filled my eyes. I feared to blink for them to spill and reveal my weakness. "I... I need to speak to her."

Myrinn dropped her hand and stood. She towered above me, her frame casting a shadow over my kneeling frame. "You belong to Faenir. You are his property. There are rules we must uphold and interfering with another's Chosen is forbidden. But..." I looked up at her as her whisper settled over me. "There will be a ball within the coming days. Encourage Faenir to take you and I will be there waiting to share news of your sister. Queen Claria will be hosting, if you wish to speak with her then you can do so... but it must seem like it is on Faenir's terms."

"I don't understand what you want from me... what *he* wants from me," I said.

Myrinn turned her back on me in more ways than one. She moved for the main doors of Haxton Manor as she replied, "Faenir is troubled, but he is not dangerous. Not to you at least."

"He kills. I have seen it," I shouted, my words echoing across the empty, cold manor.

"You are different, even I cannot make sense of it. Faenir is many things, but I leave knowing you are safe in his care."

"Care?" I laughed, finally allowing the tears to fall down my cheeks.

"Make him come to the ball, Arlo, and I will give you the news of your sister. Take it as a peace offering between you and our kind."

Myrinn left swiftly, not allowing room for my pleading to continue.

I could have chased after her. But I didn't. Not because I did not want to, but because I knew, deep down, that Faenir watched from the darkness and waited to spring forth and stop me from leaving.

He would not let me go.

Myrinn's own words had confirmed that. *You are his property.* Perhaps my parent's death when I was so young had made the concept of belonging to anyone incomprehensible to me. *You belong to Faenir.* The thought alone made my skin crawl as though spiders danced upon me.

Faenir had me trapped in his web.

Then cut us free.

11

I waited for Faenir to come for me, knife in hand and poised ready to kill.

It had begun with me watching the door with intent, keeping my breathing as featherlight as I could muster to ensure I did not miss a sound. I burned holes into the closed door as my body ached with anticipation for his arrival.

Years of chasing the undead among the forgotten streets and barren landscape of Darkmourn had me in fighting, fit shape. Even with Faenir's unknown powers over darkness and death, if given the chance I would attack before he could do so little as blink in wonder.

After Myrinn had left early that evening and I had returned to the chamber where Faenir had last been, there was only the table of food left untouched. It had been the goblets of wine and water that had seen me though until now. The water dulled the physical pain of my body, the wine calming the wild torment of my mind.

Minutes of waiting for Faenir turned to hours, hours to

days. He never came for me. I had done well to keep the sleep away at first but then I would find myself vulnerable, giving into my heavy eyelids and falling into the comforting embrace of darkness.

When I woke, startling as though a pail of water had cascaded over my head, the knife was still gripped in my hand.

Perhaps reading minds was another one of his sickly powers. Could he sense what I wished to do to him? How my next action would create pain and damage far greater than his healing abilities could battle?

My thoughts of destruction wavered with the time that slipped away. My grip loosened on my knife. Myrinn's promise of providing me with news of my sister burrowed its way into my consciousness and infected my mind.

The more Faenir stayed away, the want to cause him pain turned into desperation for his return. I needed him if I was ever going to get free of this place. I needed him if I was to meet Myrinn at the ball and hear if Auriol was well. Not that I could have done anything about it if she was not okay. We had been torn from one another and kept separated by the steel bars between our worlds.

It was on Faenir's third day of vacancy when my inner thoughts betrayed me. I gave in to walking the many halls of Haxton Manor in hopes to distract myself from what my mind tried to convince me of. *She will be happier without you.* Would she have smiled when I had never returned home? Had she released a sigh of relief to know that the chains I had kept upon her had shattered with my own demise?

Our last encounter had not been positive in the slightest. My disappearance would give her the life she desired, one away from me. Auriol had made her feelings for me clear. Her words replayed vividly in my head, over and over, as punishment.

I grew used to being alone. I counted the slabbed flooring I walked across in my attempts to distract myself. It worked for a short while before the festering poison of my thoughts grew louder.

There was no dulling my anxiety, no counting or distracting that would stop me from hearing Auriol's hate-filled voice. It was so clear, I could have convinced myself that she followed in the shadows as I ambled aimlessly through Haxton.

I forgot my purpose in those three days. Even the knife I had so dearly clung to was left discarded on the bed in the prison I now saw as my room.

For a time, I had to stop myself from leaving the front doors and throwing myself back into the pits of the Styx; at least there would have been peace waiting for me in the darkest parts of that lake.

It was growing dark beyond the manor on that third day when the silence cracked. I had reached the outer doors of the dining chamber and smelt rot and mould. The stench was so pungent it tore me from my thoughts, and I was left standing beyond the room as though I had slept walked the entire way here. Not that I felt hunger anymore, but the smell was enough to ensure I would never wish to eat again.

Haxton was empty, a shell of dark thoughts and vacant rooms. The lack of presence had caused the food that Myrinn had made to spoil and turn. It made sense at least; this was a place of death after all.

There was only a single goblet of paled-grape wine left

within my own room. I had finished the water the day prior. If my own mind didn't kill me before the sickness claimed my body, the lack of sustenance would.

Careless and lost, I wandered back into my chamber to find Faenir sitting upon the bed as though he belonged there and had never left. I stopped, dead in my tracks, unable to fathom what I was seeing. Blinking did not remove the scene, nor did rubbing my closed eyes.

"I made a mistake," Faenir's monotone voice grumbled across the room. My skin crawled in response.

"You left me," my voice was hoarse from days of neglect. I repeated myself, unsure if he could have made sense of the scratchy words. "You left me... alone."

"Did you miss me?" Faenir did not lower his stare although it seemed that he winced ever so slightly.

"Not in the sense you would hope for." I longed for the soft curve of the knife in my hand.

"My leaving you was a lapse in my judgement."

"Why?" The single worded question snapped out of me.

"I believed you would prefer my absence after everything that has happened."

Day's worth of aggression came flooding out of me at once. My weak, tired legs paced the room until I was inches before him. Faenir did little but move his knees apart, allowing me to get closer. I didn't notice this at first, for my gaze was solely on his, not on the way his body moved gently, or how his hands gripped the sheets for support... or comfort.

"If you wish to leave me then I beg you to take me home. Take me anywhere from here, just do not leave me again." I spoke so quickly that I was not truly in control of the words that came out of my mouth, nor the way I said it.

"Do not be concerned," Faenir muttered quietly, so much in fact that the beating of my heart did well to drown out his words. If I was not watching his lips, I would have missed what he said.

"I have no desire to leave your side again... Arlo."

Faenir shifted forward, moving his placement until he sat upon the very edge of the bed. I looked down at him, breathing laboured and face flushed red, as he regarded me from his seat.

"Where..." I felt stupid for asking but I wished to know. "Where did you *hide?*"

"I have found that the shadows provide the greatest solitude when wishing to escape."

"That doesn't answer my question," I said, catching the glint of the knife I had taken from the dining chamber all those days ago. Faenir had moved it from the place I had left it upon my bed, to the oaken side table beside it. He caught me looking but did not make a move to reach for it.

"I was far enough away for you to have time from me, but close enough that I could stop you from doing anything untoward. I admit... time fell away from me. I would not have wished to stay away for so long, but I had believed you made your thoughts clear on our proximity when you shattered my nose."

Was that a smile I caught? A smirk in jest or teasing? Either way I wished to wipe it clean from his face and demand he never raised his lips to me again. "And if you wish to keep your face unmarred then you best tell me what it is you want from me."

"The same as my family wants from their mates."

I caught the retort from leaving me by gritting my teeth into my tongue. *I am not your mate!* The scream echoed in my mind. "Then what do *your kind* want from the humans?"

Perhaps if I knew why they took us, it would lead to the answer of how we could get home.

Faenir sighed, turning his face away from me, his raven black hair ruffled as though moved by a hidden breeze. "There is so much to say, I fear I do not know where to begin."

"Start with me. You left Tithe without a Chosen, but you came back."

His demeanour changed within a breath, turning back to look at me with eyes brimming full of desire. "All my life I have killed just by touching another. I had grown used to taking the glow of life from another as though it was as natural as taking a breath. Not a single person has ever survived my touch."

His deep voice vibrated through me.

"Until me."

Faenir stood then, forcing me back a step to allow him room. It was so sudden that I almost tripped over my footing. "You are smarter than I gave *your kind* credit for."

He mimicked the insult I had not long shared. His slight grin brightened until teeth shone through parted lips. Faenir's smile lasted only a moment as I reached out for him.

My hand wavered in the air beside his face. I let every part of Faenir stiffen. He looked beyond me as though I did not stand before him at all. However, his entire focus was on me, even if he did not truly look.

"You took me from my home because I am the first person who will not die when you touch them," I repeated, fingers inching closer to the carved structure of his cheekbone. "You came back for me. Ripped me from my life... and for what?"

Faenir exhaled a quivering breath, eyes flicking towards the tips of my fingers as they edged closer to his skin.

"The stench of desperation is ripe on you, *Faenir*."

I was not scared of death. The years of prolonging my own demise caused the thought of dying to mutate. It became as familiar as a friend. I had chased the dead to keep my own death at bay, devouring the blood of vampires without much thought. And before me stood the very embodiment of what I had fled. *Faenir*. I had seen what his touch had done to Tom and his parents... and still I reached for him.

"Do not do this..." He exhaled as the tips of my cold, shaking fingers brushed against his sharp cheekbone.

"Why not?" I carried on, ignoring his desperate plea. My fingers melted onto his warm skin until my palm caressed the side of his face. "Is this not the reason why you took me? Because you desired to feel something you have been deprived of for your entire pathetic existence?"

Faenir's eyes flickered closed, too lost in the feel of my hand to recognise my insult. The lines across his brow softened and the frown that seemed permanently etched into his face thawed away before my very eyes.

I studied him, feeling the heavy beating of his pulse beneath my palm. *Or was it my own?*

"Arlo..." he groaned my name, reaching up to place a hand upon mine to stop it from ever moving.

I took that as my moment. Jolting out with my spare

hand, I reached up and wrapped my fingers around his exposed throat. Faenir's golden eyes flew open as I tightened my hold.

"I do not pity you," I sneered. Faenir did not squirm beneath my grip, or wince as my nails dug into his soft skin. "If you think I care for what you have been through, then you could not be further from the truth. I will spend the time you have trapped me here making you wish you never set eyes on me. And if I ever find out that my sister is harmed by your actions then I swear to make you feel pain that you never believed possible."

I was breathless, my knuckles white as I gripped tighter. All the while Faenir just stared at me with a doe-eyed expression that I could not place between fear, surprise or judging.

When Faenir finally broke his silence, all manner of his serenity had vanished. "Have you quite finished?"

I made sure to squeeze into his throat before releasing him, not that it mattered for clearly it did not affect him as I had hoped. I pulled back from him and caught the crescent moon marks my nails had left upon his neck. I grinned, knowing my warning had at least left a mark.

"For now," I replied, turning my back on him and facing the open balcony. I did so, not because I couldn't care to look upon his face another moment, but because my body began to tremble as the adrenaline slowed. I would not let him see the weakness in me. "I think it is best you leave."

"As do I, but first I must know something."

I gritted my teeth. "There is nothing else for me to say."

"I am required to provide confirmation of our acceptance or refusal to my grandmother's pending ball. From your actions this evening I trust you would rather forgo the event than spend it with me."

"No," I spun around, unable to stop the sudden desperation from poisoning my voice, "Wait. I wish to go."

Faenir nodded, his face showing no sign as to him knowing why I wished to visit. "Then I will send word to Myrinn of our decision. Since her departure from Haxton she has been persistent with sending messages. I fear if I ignore her anymore then she will return."

There was nothing for me to say, no words to provide him that would deter my mind from the promise of the ball. I had convinced myself that it had already passed during Faenir's absence. The rush of relief to know I was wrong made my knees tremble.

"Goodnight, Arlo."

"When is it?" I said, failing myself as I tried not to display any more of my desperate nature to him. "The ball... when is it?"

Faenir paused as he reached the door. "Tomorrow evening."

I swallowed my next words. My silence confirmed to Faenir that it was his time to take leave. I could not pretend to care for the ball and what the event entailed; all I could think of was finding out if Myrinn had had word from my sister.

Regardless of the answer, this was my chance to get away from Haxton Manor, from Faenir, and to carve my own way back home.

❦ 12 ❧

Faenir stood and watched me with such interest I almost believed I was on fire. Why else would he keep his stare trapped upon me? Golden eyes trailed me up and down, so slowly, like a dragon guarding treasure, just as the old stories told. I wished to demand that he averted his attention. Instead, I swallowed that urge as I paraded down the steps beyond Haxton Manor to where he waited for me.

It could not have been what I wore that interested him, that was for certain. Before I had left my room, I had surveyed how unimpressive I looked, dwarfed by the oversized, moss-toned tunic and boring trousers that were sizes too large. If it were not for my belt, it would have looked as though I was a child playing dress up in my father's spare clothes.

That, of course, was impossible on two accounts. One: my father was dead, and two: the tunic belonged to Faenir.

The black laces that should have tied up at my collar

were left loose, exposing the skin of my chest. The trousers I wore were crafted from a brown, sun-stained leather that the long boots mostly hid up until below my knees.

I had never been to a ball, for such luxuries did not exist in my world, but I had heard enough tales as a child to know I should have been dressed in finery, like Faenir was now.

It was dark beyond the manor. Night had claimed the skies and brushed its jewelled tones of dark navy so that it appeared black. However, it seemed the moon, proud and glowing white, idolised Faenir for it bathed him in its glow and outlined every possible inch of him.

Faenir's raven hair fell behind him, tousled in the nightly winds. Only the twisted twin braids tumbled across his chest. He was a vision of ruby, white and gold. The tunic he wore was far grander than mine. It was lined with a strand of gold at his neckline which dipped dramatically to expose the shadowed curves of muscle hidden beneath. Across his shoulders were plates of gleaming brass metal which draped into a cloak of similar toning at his back. What kept his outfit in place were the vivid, large stones of ruby pinned at his chest. He dripped in wealth, and I realised quickly that I gawped at him as he did me.

"I was hoping you would have changed your mind and this evening's festivities would be forgotten and thus missed," Faenir said as I reached the gravelled path he stood upon. That was his greeting, not that I expected a polite hello or cared for it.

"You would have liked that, wouldn't you...?" I brushed past him, uncaring, as though I knew where I was walking to. In fact, I did not. What was left before me was the Styx, yet I could not imagine how else we would leave Haxton.

"It would have saved a rather large amount of discomfort, that I cannot deny."

I smiled at the idea of Faenir being uneasy. "What a shame."

The sound of his footfalls, crunching over the pebble-stoned gravel informed me that Faenir followed. Within a few strides he had passed me, strolling towards the stretch of water that spread out around the manor. "Come, it is best the ferryman is not kept waiting."

I didn't get a chance to question him as I was forced to quicken my pace to keep up.

The same wooden dock I had seen days before was now glowing beneath the light of a hovering flame. A boat had moored against it, rocking gently by the lapping of dark waters it rested upon. In it stood a figure draped in heavy folds of material that even the lantern he held could not penetrate to reveal his face.

Although I could not see his features, I felt his hidden gaze follow me, judging and cold. My hand moved for the handle of the knife I had brought with me, buried in the belt of my trousers, one that Faenir did not know about. Or perhaps he did, and he enjoyed the idea of me being armed.

I faltered a step as we reached the haunting figure. Faenir did not share my sudden discomfort as he took to the dock in silence. I allowed myself only a moment of hesitation before I chased after him.

"May I?" Faenir offered a hand as he stood beyond the boat. Not once had he regarded the figure who stood within it or cared to notice that a third person was even among our presence.

I glanced to his outstretched hand and frowned naturally. "That will not be necessary."

I wondered if Faenir could hear the lie in my voice. Standing upon the rickety dock I was more than aware of the shades that waited within the darkness of Styx's water. I could not see them, but their presence was as real as the silent figure within the boat and Faenir's outstretched hand. He did not lower it, not until I forced myself to take a cautious step into the boat which swayed awfully beneath me. It stilled only when Faenir climbed in; his presence was the heavy pressure that kept it from rocking.

"With haste, Charon." It was the first time Faenir spoke to the figure, and I found myself loosing a breath in relief that my mind was not making his appearance up as some cruel vision. "And may I take this moment to remind you that strays are not permitted entry to Haxton without my consent."

The figure turned, hoisting the pole the lantern was draped across. Water sloshed and I soon noticed that the pole extended far beneath the dark waters of the Styx. With a great heave, the boat began to move.

"Myrinn Evelina wished to speak with you, Master," a whispered voice replied from beneath the folds of his cloak. The sound was both awful and pleasant, like the scratching of nails against glass. It rattled the evening winds as though echoing among the dark in which it spoke from. "I cannot deny the bloodline of *life*."

"Bloodline or not," Faenir responded, voice tight as though he held back his true wrath, "You are mine, Charon. Not theirs. If you are so careless to make such mistakes again then you shall find yourself returned to the pits of the Styx where I dragged you up from all those years ago. Do you understand?"

"Indeed," Charon replied softly.

Faenir did not respond, clearly satisfied the hooded figure would listen to the reprimand as a result of escorting Myrinn to Haxton.

Neither spoke again. Instead, their silence gave way to the rushing of water that sang beneath the small vessel as it cut across the lake. We glided across the Styx with ease, aided by the motion of the staff-like pole that Charon pushed in and out of the water.

Faenir simply watched me as Haxton Manor became a dot in the distance. I was glad for the quiet, for I had nothing to say to him. Although the tracing marks his eyes left across my body made me want to itch the feeling from my skin. All I wanted was for this journey to end so I could speak with Myrinn. I cared little for anything else.

"You are cold," Faenir broke the silence suddenly. It was not a question, more a statement, and he was not wrong.

I had not noticed the chill until he spoke. Then I realised the ache in my jaw was from the chattering of teeth and my limbs quivered violently as our boat ripped through the winds.

"Do not concern yourself with—" Before I could finish Faenir had shifted the cloak from his back and threw it over my shoulders. It settled upon me like the falling of a feather, slow and gentle. But I could not deny the warmth his body had left imprinted upon the material. I chose not to refuse him as I hugged it closer to me, giving into a moment of weakness for the reward of comfort.

There was no thanks to share, nor did Faenir expect it.

We fell back into our silence as the boat moved towards the far-off shore and the outline of mountains that crowned it.

Home. Auriol. Run.

My attention fixated on the silhouette of that monstrous tree. The closer we moved towards it, the sharper the edges of its blurred outline became.

Noticing my attention, Faenir spoke up. "The Great Tree signifies the very heart of our realm. Nyssa, it is called by the same name of the Goddess that planted its seed at the beginning of time."

It felt as though I held a coveted book in my hands, ready to open the page and uncover wisdom that no other had the luxury of knowing. No matter how my interest burned I had to show a lack of care to Faenir.

"It looks like the tree back home..." I muttered, breath fogging beyond my lips, fingers tugging the cloak closer around my shoulders to fend off the chill.

"That is because they are linked, intrinsically connected as though they are doors joined by a string that bounds each to one another. Without one, the other cannot survive." Faenir confirmed what that persistent spinning compass within my chest had suggested. It was home, at least my way back to Auriol.

"What makes Tithe so special?" I asked, turning my gaze from the view to Faenir who still looked at me with far more interest.

"Tithe is simply one door among many others. Nyssa is a gateway to all of the world beyond."

"That does not answer my question."

Faenir sighed, blinking for what seemed like the first

time since this entire journey. "Your home is one of the few left standing, unmarred and protected from the deathly curse that has spread across your world."

"What happens if it falls to *them*? The vampires," I asked, mind wandering to the glass vial hidden within the pouch at my waist.

Faenir looked at the hooded figure of Charon who, as I expected, did not utter a word nor the hush of a breath. Knowing that the haunting figure was not prepared to come to Faenir's aid, the elven prince looked back at me with a face of forced steel.

"The end. For us all."

☙❧

A carriage waited for us as we climbed out of the ferryman's boat. At least Faenir climbed, my disembark was more of a clambering on wobbling knees.

The world had not stopped rocking before the ferryman changed course and pushed the boat away from us. I watched as he disappeared, the folds of his obsidian cloak melting with the dark sky in which he moved towards. Within moments Charon, and the ruby flame that burned proudly from the lantern at the crown of his stick, vanished into nothingness.

I had long confirmed, aided by Faenir's prior comment, that Charon was not part of the living world. He was dead, a shade covered in clothing to hide the truth. And the unsaid truth did not concern me.

Faenir hesitated as he waited upon the sandy bank for me. His hand twitched at his side, fingers flexing, as he asked me with forced politeness to follow him into the wooden box on wheels which waited upon a distant path.

There was no hesitation from me to enter. I was the first one inside the darkened carriage, Faenir following shortly behind me. The exchange from the boat into the carriage happened so quickly that I hardly noticed the two bodies who sat upon an elevated seat at the head. They held onto the reins of four, brilliantly white horses. Unlike Charon, these people were very much alive.

As the whip of reins sounded and the carriage jolted gently forward, I decided to break the tension for fear it would devour me completely.

"Is there anything you wish to warn me about?" I asked.

Faenir's attention snapped from fussing over his nails, to me in a heartbeat. "Only that, no matter what impression you receive, we will not be welcome." His reply shocked me.

"Care to elaborate?"

"My *family* has a strained relationship. Not everyone is as pleased to see me as Myrinn has been." There was so much unsaid, evident from Faenir's comment.

"Then I get the impression that I will thoroughly enjoy this evening no matter what it brings."

Faenir grimaced, returning his attention to his nails. "You will not be the only one..."

Within the carriage, we were no longer exposed to the elements of night. Yet still I clung to the cloak Faenir had given to me with no desire to give it back.

Conversation with Faenir was as deathly as his touch. It was clear he did not wish to speak, not that his blatant refusal should have annoyed me.

It did.

He had seemed entirely focused on me within the boat. Now, I could not discern the distance he was putting between us, his lack of care for my presence made clear by his focus on anything but me.

I reached for the velvet blue curtain that blocked the world beyond the carriage and moved it back an inch so I could see. Everything moved past the window in a blur. It was so sudden my stomach jolted, and I fell back into my seat. It took a long moment of frantic blinking to settle my eyes. It was as though the carriage moved at such a speed that it turned the world beyond into smudges of dark shapes.

Faenir did not elaborate. *Of course he didn't.*

There was nothing else to occupy my thoughts but Faenir and his cryptic words. The rest of the journey to our destination went by seemingly quicker than Charon's boat ride. I had busied myself with thoughts of Tom as I felt he was a safer person to fill my mind than Auriol. His memory was less of a punishment until I recalled the dead bodies of him and his parents.

Had they been discarded yet? Stiffened bodies were usually thrown over the wall by the Watchers in order to prevent the dead from rising again as they did in Darkmourn.

Every time I blinked, I could see their bodies falling from great heights, splattering across the grassland and staining it red.

Of course, Tom and his parents would never have risen as vampires. They had not been bitten; anyone with sense knew that the disease spread from teeth devouring skin. I almost vomited at the thought.

"Arlo," Faenir muttered moments before the carriage slowed to a stop. "We have arrived." He sounded less than pleased, but I didn't care.

Urgency and desperation at finding Myrinn blinded me as I reached for the door. Faenir stopped me. He threw out his hand and pressed it upon mine. The sudden touch anchored me back into the moment. "I need you to understand something very important before we do this."

I swallowed a lump in my throat, unable to deny the urgency that lit his golden eyes from within. "Are you worried what your parents will think when they see who you have chosen?" My question hung between us.

Faenir's expression of concern deepened into one that frightened me. It was the first time since seeing him in Tom's room that I truly felt the need to put distance between us.

"Unfortunately, my mother and father will not be joining us this evening."

"Why is that?" I pressed, my bravado faltering with each drawn-out moment.

Whatever he was going to tell me was replaced with something darker. In hindsight I should have kept my smart mouth shut, for I would never have been prepared for what he was going to say.

"Because I killed them." He removed his fingers, leaving the cold press of his touch across the back of my hand. "That is why."

We arrived beneath the shadow of the Great Tree Faenir had named Nyssa. With its monstrous heights, it was not impossible to imagine how the elves believed it to be planted by a Goddess. In a world of vampires and magic, Goddesses were not an impossible fable to believe.

Faenir's words repeated within my head long after we disembarked from the carriage. It was as though he called out into an empty cavern, his deep voice singing back on a loop.

He had not offered me a hand as I clambered out, nor did I believe I would have taken it after he had revealed what he had done to his parents. Although he had not elaborated on the cause of their death, I imagined it was related to his touch more than poison or a dagger.

"Cousin," a shadow spoke as it peeled away from the darkened landscape we had entered. Both of my feet had yet to touch the ground before the speaker was revealed.

Faenir looked into the darkness, positioning his body before mine with a single step and spoke. "Haldor, has Myrinn already come to regret our invite that she sends you to turn us away?"

Haldor. The red-haired elf that had been the first to choose his mate in Tithe. Samantha, I remembered the human girl he had picked and wondered if she lingered within the shadows he had slipped from. That thought was soon banished by an explosion of light. I winced as flames conjured from nothing erupted across the wall of the strange building we had been brought to. Fire danced to life, encouraged by the twisting star of flame that hovered above Haldor's hand. The display of frightening power was so sudden even Faenir rocked back a step but soon stiffened in retaliation.

Besides the light, I was not prepared for the warmth that kissed my cheeks. His flame reached me even from a distance. Bright and all-revealing as it banished the dark and revealed what the tree's shadow had hidden.

"I have no doubt Myrinn would have preferred to have welcomed you this evening; however, she is currently having her precious ear chewed off by our Queen."

Faenir's shoulders lifted at the mention of Claria. It was so clear that even Haldor seemed to notice and shared a smile at his discomfort. "Claria was unaware of our invitation?"

Haldor pouted. The fire within his hand died with a closed fist; only the fire that had sprung along the line of torches across the towering wall remained. Even as the two men's interaction distracted me, I could not help but notice how the wall had the same texture of a tree, rough ripples of oaken flesh that seemed to shiver beneath the flames.

"If Claria had known of your visit, she would have cancelled the ball entirely. And that would have been a mighty killjoy for us all."

Haldor was tall, but still fell inches beneath Faenir's height, made more obvious as Faenir drew closer to him. Now the unease shifted to Haldor for the first time since he stepped from the shadows.

He was handsome, which I could not deny, but even his beauty could not hide his discomfort at Faenir's closeness. Haldor's jaw was cleanly shaven, his ivory skin dusted with freckles. Red curls fell perfectly across his forehead as though twisted by a finger.

"Such a daring choice of mate," Haldor said, narrowing his ember-red eyes on me. For the first time since being taken from Tithe I felt a familiar warmth spread across my groin, a burning encouraged as Haldor's attention devoured me. "I remember this one from the line-up. How could I forget someone with eyes like tha—"

"You would do well to turn your attention," Faenir replied, voice dripping with warning. "He is mine."

I wished to shout at them both and refuse Faenir's comment, but my confidence had seemed to run away from me.

Haldor flashed a wolfish grin towards me which conjured a growl from the man who stood between us. He held it in contest, and I was certain Faenir was going to lash out.

"*She* wishes to speak with you," Haldor said to Faenir whose growl only deepened.

"That was not included on the invite."

"Even you, Prince of Evelina, are not above refusing the Queen for an audience. My suggestion would be that you go and relieve Myrinn before our dearest grandmother unleashes her wrath upon her."

"Myrinn has made her bed. She can deal with the repercussions of orchestrating my visit... we are leaving."

"No," I snapped as Faenir began to turn back towards the carriage.

I dug my heels into the ground, literally, showing Faenir with my firm glare that I was not going back to Haxton.

"You allow your Chosen to speak to you in such a manner?" Haldor enjoyed every moment of this interaction.

"My name is Arlo." I turned my attention to Haldor. "Call me by anything else again and I will cut your tongue from your head."

Haldor laughed. Faenir didn't.

"Trust me, *Haldor*," Faenir said, amusement flirting with his frown. "The human is not lying. If you believe my touch should be feared... well, it pales in comparison to what Arlo is capable of. Take my word for it."

Faenir's strangely placed compliment made my stomach jolt. I had to fight my expression to hide my reaction.

"How well-matched you both are," Haldor muttered. All at once he turned on his heel and faced the carving of a door etched into the strange wall. "Perhaps there is hope for your succession after all."

Nothing else was said as Haldor walked away. I

expected Faenir to force me back into the carriage. Once again, he surprised me.

"Shall we?" Faenir said, gesturing a hand before him in a sweep. There was no denying the trepidation lost within his wincing stare nor the tension that furrowed lines across his brow.

Something had set the elven man at unease. And whatever waited for us alongside Queen Claria conjured something strange in Faenir. Something I had not believed possible for him.

Fear.

I expected Queens and Kings to live within a castle, similar to Castle Dread that languished within Darkmourn, buildings with towering walls and turrets draped with fluttering banners. Each room within should have been full of luxurious furniture and plush beds stuffed with the softest feathers. Every possible detail should have been coated in wealth.

My imagination could not have been further from the truth.

As we followed Haldor through the dark passages, he would throw out gestures towards the walls which then blossomed with a rose of fire. His light revealed all. The walls at our sides were much like what I had seen outside, the rough bark of a tree we now moved *within*.

I had been within many buildings and establishments, but never a tree believed to have been planted by a

Goddess. However, it was not the most impossible thing to believe since being brought to this realm, not compared to lakes filled with ghosts, or elves with the power of fire and death lingering at their fingertips.

The narrow corridors soon opened up to hallways much like that in Haxton. Stone constructions of white and marble, wood from the tree's inners devoured the rooms we passed through; it was the perfect melody of stone and timber. I could not fathom how a tree could have grown to such mountainous heights, nor how an entire dwelling of rooms had been built within the honey-comb maze of the tree's belly.

My fingers trailed the rough walls as I navigated over knots of roots beneath my feet, and I thought of the tree in Tithe. Somewhere within this maze of rooms would be the answers to getting home, I believed it wholeheartedly.

I was all-consumed with my thoughts that I had not noticed when Faenir stopped walking, not until I crashed into the back of him, tripping over his feet and mine.

He did not react to me, I could *hear* why. Towering before us stood large arched doors; they were closed but that did not stop the raised voice within from spilling beyond.

Haldor leaned up against the wall beside the doors, one leg bent which stretched the midnight black trousers that hugged the strength of muscle beneath; I had to force my eyes away to stop my imagination from running away with me.

"Never did I imagine a day when Claria would raise her voice towards her golden child. The right thing to do would be to enter and save Myrinn from her wrath but I admit it is nice for Claria's rage to be placed on another for once," Haldor said.

Myrinn was on the other side of the door, silently taking the muffled berating from the aged voice. I looked to Faenir, and he showed no urgency to enter and help her. Instead, his eyes were pinched closed, wincing every time the voice raised in pitch as though he was at the other end of the ire.

"Do something," I muttered, naturally reaching for his hand. My fingers slipped within his. Faenir's eyes snapped open, and his frown of discomfort melted into one of tempered determination.

He gritted his jaw, muscles feathering. Then, without dropping my hand, he walked us forward and threw the doors open with a powerful push.

"Good luck, Faenir...." Haldor whispered as we passed.

It was not another room that we entered, but another world. A landscape of forest and glade, vines of branches crowned the skies. Pillars of old stone stood like proud guards throughout the area. Swollen buds of deep, red fruit hung from vines; each one shifted on an unseen breeze.

I inhaled deeply, my nose filled with the sweet nature of fruit and fresh flowers. Across my tongue, I could taste it; the burst of strawberries in summer, and the bite of crisp apples picked happily from an orchard. This place thrummed with life. The air sang with it. The moss-covered ground shivered with it.

My eyes trailed the wondrous place until I came across something misplaced in the heart of it. Before us sat a throne made of wood and in it cowered a hunched, old woman.

Myrinn stood next to the throne, her head bowed, and hands clasped before her. She barely looked up as we entered.

"So, it is true?" the broken, rasped voice broke free from the vessel of sagging, wrinkled skin.

"I cannot imagine what you must have thought when you first heard the word, grandmother."

"Faenir," Myrinn groaned, eyes flashing with caution. "Don't."

I tensed at the unspoken tension between the three elves.

"Leave us, Myrinn," the crooked Queen said. "Let our conversation be a reminder that your foolish actions *will* aid in Evelina's downfall. And to think I had high expectations for you when all you wished to do was sabotage our survival due to your misplaced, idyllic thoughts."

"It was never my intention," Myrinn curtsied, voice barely a mumble over the swishing of her elaborate skirts, "Grandmother."

I tried to catch Myrinn's eyes as she swept between Faenir and me. All the while she kept her head down. I almost reached out and stopped her, to demand if she had an update from my sister. With great restraint, I resisted my urge. Because I now stood in the presence of a Queen, and I could only imagine that if anyone had the power to return me home... it was her.

No matter how ancient and weak she looked within her chair, she practically glowed with power.

Myrinn's clipped footfall faded, finally silenced by the slamming of the doors behind us, before Claria spoke again. "Show me." The demand came out of the Queen in a rush.

"There is nothing to see."

"That is exactly why I have asked, which I will not do again."

Faenir turned to me, lips twitching and face full of fury. He extended a hand to me and I couldn't help but notice the twitching of his fingers. I looked at his hand with confusion which lasted only a moment. I soon realised what she wished to see: Faenir's touch and the lack of affect it had on me.

Disregarding Faenir's outstretched hand I took a step towards the throne and ensured my chin did not lower. "He stole me from my home."

The Queen leaned forward. "As I have heard."

I swallowed a lump in my throat and continued. "I wish to return. He has refused and I do not want this... I just want to get back."

Claria studied me for a moment then erupted in bellows of laughter. She threw her head back, the nest of grey hair falling around her sagging face. "Even your mate does not wish to be with you. How does it make you feel, dear Faenir, to know that the only being known to survive your touch wishes to be far from your side? Does it sting as I hope it does? All these years and the one thing you have desired cannot fathom desiring you in return."

I looked between the frantic Queen and the stoic prince of death. My plea faltered on my lips as a great unease settled in the pit of my stomach like a stone thrown into a body of water.

"Unfortunately for us all, human, you cannot return home. There was once a time when your world was full of life and it fuelled Evelina, allowing such transactions more frequently. Gone are those days. Now, only at the turn of the next season, will the veil open again."

Anger boiled in my stomach, replacing the unease. At the tip of my tongue, I felt the need to demand my return, to reveal that I would die without it. But the wild look of madness in the Queen's hooded eyes told me that my demise would please her.

I swallowed my plea and returned, like a wounded animal, back to Faenir's side.

"Do you truly believe I will let you do this, Faenir?"

He tilted his head, deliberating her question with a click of his bones.

"If I indulge in this union, it will be the end of Evelina. I have prolonged my reign to prevent your destructive touch from shattering this crown. Not before. Not now. Not tomorrow or the days beyond."

"I do not want your crown."

My mind tried to piece together what was happening but was distracted by the twinge in Faenir's jaw. His entire focus was on the old Queen. It left his profile open for memorising and I soon noted that the muscles across his jawline had a way of revealing the emotion he fought to keep at bay.

"Your lack of want will not stop it from falling into your hands," she shouted, voice echoing across the landscape and drawing back that sweet power of life as though she was the source of it. "Faenir, your actions have put me in a position in which I wished never to be in."

Her gaze snapped back to me. The pressure of it made my limbs feel heavy. Even if I wished to step back I couldn't. This time her eyes were void of humour, instead narrowed and sharpened like a blade. "Ensuring your union fails before the turn of the season will solidify the court's decision to let the crown surpass you and fall upon one of your cousins."

"Whatever this is about," I started, sensing the presence of the knife beneath the belt of my trousers. If I needed it, it was only a quick swipe from reach. "I do not want anything to do with it."

"A waste..." she sang with fury. It was as though she had not heard me or cared to. "Life is precious, and we need the humans to flourish if Evelina ever has a chance of seeing through these dark times. But if I am forced to sacrifice the life of this one then it would be for our greater cause..."

I gasped as the view of the Queen disappeared. I blinked, wondering if the world had gone dark. But it was Faenir. His body was a shield between us.

"If you even dare to contemplate harming Arlo, I swear to destroy everything your bitter, long life has spent trying to salvage. Do not make me be the monster you so wish me to be."

My throat dried, my lungs constricting as Faenir's words settled over me. There was no denying he meant every word he spoke. It was the first time he had truly retorted with equal power against the Queen. And it nearly took my breath away.

"You dare threaten me?" She pushed forward, long nails pinching into the arms of her throne.

"A promise," Faenir snapped. "I am far too determined to give threats, Claria."

Shadows crept across the luscious landscape like a

living wave. The warmth seemed to vanish from the air within moments. It was Faenir. It was all him.

"Leave," Queen Claria shouted, her own glow of power pushing against Faenir's with contest. "Enjoy the festivities of the evening. For the sake of your life, and that of your mate, I do hope you fail by your own accord. Otherwise, I too will provide a promise and I am certain to keep it for far more years than you would believe possible. *Demon*."

FAENIR

There is no cooling the boiling of my blood. My fury is all-consuming. It thundered across my mind, swelled in my veins until they screamed with the desire to explode.

I could not think clearly, thoughts of sense fell violently between my fingers as though no more than sand. All my mind could capture was Claria's threat against Arlo. It replayed over and over, fuelling a violent crash of energy that built and grew.

There's a storm within me and it's all-consuming. It stole my anger and fed it to the dark mass of power. For years that storm had been kept at bay, the cord of control pulled tighter with each encounter with Claria or my family.

There would come a time when I was powerless to control it.

When the cord would snap.

And soon the storm would break free.

🙌 14 🙌

D*emon.*
Queen Claria had made her lack of love for Faenir clear. Even now, as we navigated the strange maze of corridors on hastened feet, I could hear the hateful title she bestowed on my captor.

Unbeknownst to me, I had found myself in the middle of a family war. Blood against blood. As Faenir tugged me away from Claria in a cloud of screaming silence, I was able to piece together what I had learned. Faenir had killed his parents; still the *how* was a mystery but one I was determined to uncover. His grandmother, the Queen of Evelina, despised him for it as though the crime had been committed recently, her hate potent and undeniable. She kept the crown from Faenir, expecting he would fail to ever grasp the possibility to succeed from prince to something more.

Until now. Until me.

The thought that this man could ever be a King had my footing fumble and nearly trip as I chased after him.

Somehow my presence in Evelina potentially solidified his right to succession and Claria had threatened my life to ensure that did not happen. It was not Faenir's touch that put my life at risk, but his proximity.

The whisperings of music interrupted our silence. First it was so hushed I could barely recognise it over our footfalls, then it grew, building into a crescendo that filled the barren rooms and echoed from all around us.

"What is that?" I asked, fighting to catch my breath as Faenir continued to stalk ahead. It was evident he wished to put as much distance between Claria and us as possible.

Faenir replied through a tight-lipped grimace. "The ball. You wished to partake in it did you not?"

I swallowed, skin shivering in sync with the dramatic notes of the melody. "I would have thought you wanted to leave after..."

Faenir stopped suddenly, his gilded eyes hardly blinked as he surveyed me. There seemed to be so much he wished to say for his expression spoke volumes of unsaid concerns. "You may hate me for what I have done. It is a feeling I am well accustomed to. But I wish for you to know that I will not let anything happen to you whilst you are in my care."

"This is about Claria's threat?"

He nodded softly. "I vow, as penance and apology for my actions, to see you home safely. I will make your stay within our realm as peaceful as I can. Every day that I have with you will be spent proving that I am not the monster they all see me as." There it was. The harsh truth of his inner mind spilling free as though he lacked the control I had grown used to him claiming.

I was lost for words. Even though I wanted nothing

more than to look away from him, I fought myself to hold his stare, no matter how heavy it became. "What if I don't make it to the turn of the season?" I replied, hiding the truth of what I alluded to beneath the real threat of Claria.

Faenir did not need to know that I had only one vial of vampire blood left or why I had it. It would not change how this story reached its finale. Once the blood was gone and my sickness was freed from the prison it was kept in, I... would die.

"That," Faenir said through a harsh breath, "is not an option."

The grey-stoned floor vibrated beneath us as the melody continued to build with tension and beauty. I could not place the instrument that could have conjured such a sound. There was a magic laced within it, something Tithe, Darkmourn and the world away from this one would never have known possible.

I felt as though we were striking up a deal. One that I had, in truth, no choice but to agree to. Since my own parents' demise, I had spent my days convincing myself to prolong the same fate. Every time I left the walls of Tithe in search for my poison, all I did was hold back the ticking hands of my doom's ticking clock. Soon enough it was going to catch up with me.

Now the hands spun quickly. My fate raced towards me, and nothing would slow it down.

We stood there, each of us silently trying to read the other's expressions and failing to grasp the thoughts we hid from one another.

"If your mind has changed about the ball then I am more than willing to take leave." Faenir's arms lifted, his hands reaching out but falling short before they could touch my arms.

Perhaps he expected I would have flinched. I did not.

"No." That was what Claria would have wanted. Our presence here upset her. By leaving Nyssa we would allow her to win whatever game both Faenir and her had been locked within. A game of crowns. A game of family.

I love games.

Before Faenir could lower his hands, I reached out and took one. His mouth parted in a gentle gasp that spread across his face and melted the lines of tension once more. His touch was deadly, mine seemed to be the opposite for him.

"It is clear I do not know your politics, but I can understand that turning our back on this ball only means that the true *monster* has won. I am not one for being a participant and allowing that to happen. So, as you have so perfectly suggested, I wish to make a deal with you too."

Faenir's fingers gripped ever so harder, and it sent a thrilling bolt up my spine. "It would not be wise to poke the bee's nest, for doing so will sting," Faenir whispered.

I wanted to ask how he had heard that saying. It was one Mother had used on me and Auriol many times, a way of warning us that playing with fire always caused hands to burn.

"Faenir," I said, returning the grip on his hand. I was overly aware of the sodden skin and more so the fact he did not hurt me. He could not hurt me. *Why?* That was another mystery I added to the ever-growing list in my mind. "Do not think for a second, I wish to poke the bee's nest. If I am going to be forced to stay here, then I will destroy it instead."

"Arlo, you have a treacherous tongue."

I laughed at that, smiling naturally towards him for the first time. "Oh, you could not begin to imagine."

We entered the ballroom, hand in hand. Of course, I had not known what waited in this strange place for it was a mystery with each turn of a corridor and push of a door. The closed doors blew open without our need to do anything. Beyond them the air swelled with music. A balcony waited before us with twisting, wooden carvings that formed a barrier between it and the great drop on its other side.

Faenir guided me into the room until I could see the sweeping staircase that fell from each side of the balcony until it reached the black and white patterned floor below. We stopped at the edge of the balcony and looked down at a sea of people, and every single one of them looked at us, not a pair of eyes wasted on anything else. Even the music seemed to quiet. The air thrummed with tense intrigue.

I forced out a shuddering breath and held my head high as I stared down at the crowd. This was a symbol. Faenir displayed me beside him as though I was a jewel, and from the look of everyone beneath us they could not fathom what they saw.

Expressions morphed from shock to horror then to disbelief. Some smiled falsely, flashing teeth as though they were wolves surveying prey. It did not deter me, for I was the wolf in this story. Others gleamed upward with pure happiness. Namely Myrinn whose arm was held in the crook of her human mate.

"Faenir Evelina, and his *mate,* Arlo."

I could not see who it was that announced us, nor did I think it was needed. Everyone knew Faenir because of his reputation and thus they had likely heard of me.

"I have not even asked for your full name," Faenir murmured out the corner of his sharp lips.

"And nor will I tell you."

He paused, swallowing audibly. "May I ask why not?"

"Names have power, Faenir. They are also earned, and you have not yet proven yourself worthy of my last name."

He chuckled softly, the sound vibrated across my skin until the hairs upon my arms stood on end. "Then that is all well and good for those who look upon us now will soon expect you to take my last name. That is all that matters to them."

"How disappointed they will be," I replied, pulling away from his side and shifting towards the steps without his lead.

Faenir moved after me, fingers gripping harder on my hand so I could not pull away. It was Faenir's hand woven with mine that finally broke the crowd. The murmuring of conversation began, and eyes turned away from us, all the while I still felt their interest pinned to our union, even if their eyes suggested otherwise.

By the time we reached the last carpeted step the music picked up in volume and pace once again.

"That was an entrance," I said, finally feeling like I could breathe without the weight of so many eyes upon me.

"Indeed, it was," Faenir replied. "It would seem our message has been received. We should leave before any further damage is done."

"And miss a dance?" My legs felt far from dancing as they trembled with anxiety. "I think not."

Myrinn waited for us at the bottom of the sweeping, red-carpeted stairs. Her human was steps behind her as she navigated the swell of the crowd that seemed to press in around us. I was lost in her embrace as she threw her arms around me. "I am so glad to see you. And I am sorry for anything my grandmother has said..." When she pulled away, I could not remove the scent of sea-salt that danced across the breeze. It was not an unpleasant smell, but I preferred the one that clung to Faenir, not that I would admit it.

"Have you heard from her?" I whispered, forgetting instantly of everything that had occurred around me.

Myrinn's smile dimmed, and my heart seemed to plummet within me. "The Watchers have confirmed your sister is well. As the families of all the Chosen, she has been moved to her new settlement and is being provided with thanks for her *sacrifice*."

I wished to ask her more, but Myrinn tactically shifted the conversation. "Faenir, your presence at court is for the best. I hope you know that."

"We will not stay for long," Faenir cut her off with his reply. I glanced up at him, seeing how his mask of emptiness had returned to his face. He spoke to his cousin but looked over the crowd as if hunting for something. "Arlo wishes to dance. Then we will return to Haxton Manor."

"Dance?" Myrinn practically choked on the word. "You?"

He scowled down at her, but not without a glint of something softer in his eyes. "That is what I said."

Myrinn closed her mouth and drew her finger across

her lips. This made the human boy I could still not name chuckle as though she had just spoken the most humorous tale.

"Then Gale and I will join you." She took the human man back into the crook of her arm and beamed from ear to ear.

"That will not be necessary," Faenir groaned.

"Oh do stop moaning, Faenir, it is unbecoming of the future King..." With that she melted into the crowd, a teasing grin brightening her beautiful face.

We stood looking out at the throng of people, side by side, and silent, both as out of place as the other. There was a noticeable space between the crowd and Faenir. If he took a step, they moved. Their potent fear of his closeness left a sour taste in my mouth, one I could not deny.

"Shall we?" I asked, reaching my hand back out for his.

Our fingers grazed one another. There was a reluctance before he took my hand. His eyes left their warm trail from my hand, up my arm, and to my face.

"You can at least force a smile," he said. "We are about to put on a show, are we not? At least pretend like you are enjoying yourself."

I pulled a face, halfway between a frown and a pout. It felt more natural to stick my tongue out like a child; I chose to keep that imprisoned behind my clamped teeth.

"Don't you dare step on my feet," I warned.

Faenir pulled me in close and inhaled deeply. "It is best that you keep up then, Arlo."

🦋 15 🦋

It was awkward at first, our bodies pressed close together, our feet fighting with one another as we stepped on toes and tripped over the strange pacing. I had danced before, but never with another. Usually, it was before a mirror as I imagined a man pressed behind me as I moved my hips in soft circles.

This, undoubtedly, was a different type of dancing. And Faenir, I imagined, had done neither type before. Yet there was no denying that he was a fast learner. Soon enough Faenir took control and we twisted and spun, his hand pressed into the small of my back, mine reaching up and gripping his broad arm for support. The music melted within our bodies until we were one in the same.

It was easy to get lost in the moment, to forget the crowd of elven gentry that stood from the edge of the room and watched as we seized the floor as our own. Soon enough I was aware of other couples who braved the floor and joined us.

Myrinn glided across the tiles in the powerful arms of

her human, Gale. I then recognised the red curls of Haldor and his human Samantha. Another recognisable face could be seen, the youthful, heart-shaped visage of Frila. Her white hair spilled down across her shoulders like strands of silk which swayed as her human mate danced with her.

Evelina royalty danced around one another as the rest of the court watched. Except, there was one elven prince I could not find. Gildir. Perhaps he watched from the crowd, that was close to impossible to confirm as those watching swelled like a wave.

"Your heart is thundering," Faenir said, demanding my attention once again. His fingers tensed on my back, pressing deeper into the skin beneath my clothing. There was something intense about his hold, it had to be as he controlled our movements and kept us dancing. "It is a beautiful thing."

"And yet you still do not smile," I retorted, finding his powerful gaze almost too hard to keep.

"Is that what you wish of me?" Faenir's lips hardly twitched, but his golden eyes seemed to glow as though smiling from within.

"I wish nothing of you," I replied, finding my tongue thickening in my mouth. "However, if you want us to truly leave an impression in spite of your grandmother then perhaps you can convince those watching us that you are actually enjoying yourself."

"Oh, Arlo," Faenir murmured. "Let it be known that I am *thoroughly* enjoying myself."

We were so close now that I felt his warmth spill from him. My chest was inches from his torso. I gripped onto the material of his jacket as his own fingers tapped across my back as though he stroked the ivory keys of a piano.

The music changed the longer we spun amongst the room. The melody slowed then quickened in pace as the sounds began to tell another story.

"Have you danced with many men before?" His question came out of nowhere and had me faltering over the wrong step. Faenir caught me though. His arms wrapped tighter around my waist and kept me pinned to him.

"Not that it matters." I caught Myrinn smiling out the corner of my eye, whispering something to Gale who, in turn, returned her mischievous grin. "No. At least not dancing in the same sense as this."

Faenir's jaw tightened as strands of raven hair blew across his face to obscure the flash of an expression. It did not hide it well. *Jealousy.* It was the reaction I wanted, to toy with him as I would food on a plate.

"I think it is time to leave." He came to an abrupt stop. The crowd audibly reacted to his suddenness.

"Going so soon?" Haldor swept across to us, detaching from the striking Samantha and breaking us apart from his powerful presence. "Faenir, not that you would know, but it is custom for partners to swap during a dance." He then looked to me, hands held out and asked, "May I?"

"Do not—" Faenir began but I cut him off.

"I would love to."

Haldor smiled from ear to ear. "Samantha, dearest, wait for me. It is best my cousin keeps his hands off you. For your sake..." With that Haldor took me into his arms and pulled me away. The crowd took this as their moment to swell onto the dance floor and I lost Faenir to them.

I felt the burning warmth of his eyes bore into me even when I could not see him.

"He will not like this," I muttered, looking up through

my lashes at Haldor. Whereas Faenir did not take his eyes off me, Haldor seemed more interested in the reactions around us.

"Faenir is not one for liking anything," he replied finally, rough hands holding me close to him. His warmth was not as welcoming as I would have imagined. It boiled and crackled, as though a fire filled his veins instead of blood. "But if you are to help him claim the crown from Claria's clawed grasp, then I feel I should do my best to get to know you."

"I get the impression that you all do not like the Queen... which is strange since you are family."

"Family does not constitute love as I am sure you have been led to believe. You cannot choose your family; love is earned not granted just because of shared blood."

My skin crawled at his comment. Auriol had not earned my love, and yet she owned it.

"I imagine you share the same wish that Faenir does not take the crown. Would this not ruin your opportunity to become King?"

Haldor laughed at that. The space beneath his hand grew hotter and I was certain my clothes could combust. "Myrinn is the eldest and thus the next in line."

"You didn't answer my question."

Haldor closed in, his face lowering to mine, and I was certain I felt the ground tremble beneath a far-off growl. "Faenir is many things, and a King is not one of them. Evelina is a place of life. If he succeeds, then he will ruin this realm and everything it stands for."

I tried to pull away but couldn't. My heart picked up in my chest, the music also reached a painful crescendo that vibrated through my bones and skin.

"Is this the part where you warn me?" I scowled at him. "Because anything you are going to say has likely been covered by your most welcoming grandmother."

"I am not going to threaten you," Haldor replied, voice no more than a whisper beneath the music. "Even I know that would be a mistake."

"Then what do you want from me?"

Haldor's hands relaxed. His expression shifted from his narrowed gaze to a softening smile that smoothed out every inch of his handsome face. "The same thing we all want from your kind. A chance."

I could not ask what he meant by that as I slipped from his weakening embrace, and he melted into the crowd. He left me alone. Bodies of strangers pressed in around me. Turning frantically, I searched for a way out, for a face that I recognised.

For *Faenir*.

There was a wave of them, coming in at once and drowning me in rich clothing and judging faces. Although they did not speak to me, I felt their stares trying to drain answers from me. Hands tugged greedily at my arms and tunic, likely testing that I was, in fact, real. For how else could I still be alive?

How I could be touched by the prince of death? Why did I still live when others didn't?

Through the crowd I caught the blur of a body. Gale, long stemmed glass in hand filled with the bubbling of honey-toned wine; in it bobbed seeds of pink. He was moving from the dance floor as though following someone like a lost puppy, likely bringing a drink to Myrinn who he longed to find among the overwhelming crowd.

I followed him. If he searched for Myrinn she was

likely a safer person to be with then Haldor or the grasping crowd. Not caring for those I hurt or upset, I pushed my way through the bodies, not discriminating to whom received a harsh jab of my elbow on the way out. The thought of reaching Myrinn had me rushing forward.

I wanted to know more about Auriol, to uncover how I could send word to a Watcher like Myrinn could. If that was all I could do to feel close to my sister again I would take it.

Gale left the room through an arched door within the shadows of the staircase Faenir and I had come down from. His body disappeared behind the door as it closed. I reached it seconds after him, pushing it open and calling out, "Wait for me. Gale, Myrinn?"

It took me a moment for my eyes to adjust to the darkness of the corridor beyond. This place must have been a hallway for those who worked within this strange place. From what details I could see, there was no wealth or luxury on display here; it was more like the burrowing of a rabbit's den, dark and cramped with a stale moisture to the air.

Footsteps sounded up ahead.

"Gale?" I asked the darkness which pressed in around me. "Myrinn?"

Onward I pushed, but with each step a strange feeling took hold of me. It told me to turn around and return to the main ballroom. Nothing good came from those who lurked within shadows, even I knew that.

I lifted the hem of my shirt and pulled free the knife I had smuggled here, all without a second thought. All of a sudden, I was back in Darkmourn, moving through the ruins of a once brilliant town in search of a vampire. My ears focused on the darkness. My breathing quietened.

The footsteps up ahead slowed, and I copied, except I did not stop. I kept pressing forward just on lighter feet. The outline of a figure came into view and the hand on my knife relaxed.

"Lost?" I called out as Gale turned around to look at me. I searched the shadows for Myrinn but I knew she was not here. Deep down my soul was screaming at me to turn away but it was only Gale. He was alone. Yet I still gripped the knife for instinct commanded that of me.

"I think so," Gale replied calmly, hardly caring for the knife I held between us. "I was looking for something... but I can't find it."

"There is nothing good to come from searching the dark," I said, sidestepping to allow room for Gale as he paced close to me. "We should get back to the ball. Myrinn will be looking for you."

"Myrinn," he muttered, repeating her name another three times as though he could not place why he knew it. Then he said something that tugged at the tension between us. "Who?"

Gale threw himself at me, taking advantage of my sudden confusion. The floor fell from my feet. Strong hands wrapped around my throat and slammed me down until my head cracked into the ground. In a blink I was blinded by pain. My mouth filled with blood as my teeth clamped over my tongue. The gushing of copper choked me as much as Gale's large, powerful hands squeezing my neck.

It happened so quickly.

The anchoring body of the knife no longer filled my

hand. In the fall I had dropped it, not that it would have helped.

Gale straddled me as he strangled hard. I slammed my fists into his chest, recognising the feeling slipping away. When that did not help, and my vision began to blur, I tried slapping his face. My nails dug into his cheeks as I raked down them. At some point, as my eyes began to close and my pain became muted, I felt the warmth of his blood wetting my hands.

Gale was going to kill me.

I stared deep into his wide, unblinking eyes and felt terrifying dread. My vision grew heavy and each time I blinked it seemed to take longer to pull myself from the darkness. But still I tried to focus, to see my frightened, paling reflection in his eyes as my life finally gave up on me.

Perhaps it was my delusion, brought on to protect my mind from the truth that I was going to die, but I was certain Gale was crying.

My lungs burned for air, but his hands ensured that was kept from me.

I closed my eyes and did not fight it anymore. Auriol was waiting there. So was Mother and Father, standing in a line with arms outstretched for me in greeting. Peace. Wondrous, welcoming peace which lasted only a moment.

My eyes flew open as I inhaled a desperate breath.

Gale's presence was gone, only his phantom touch pinched across the skin of my neck. I swallowed mouthfuls of my own blood which now tried its best to finish the job Gale was unable to complete.

Had he run off? Given up at the last moment?

I blinked. Perhaps I had fallen into sleep for a moment

because when I opened my eyes once again, I looked up to see Faenir. He towered above me, sharp-red blood splattered across his pale face. It dripped down his grimace and fell upon me like droplets of fat rain. Then his mouth split open, and he shouted violently until every shadow rushed over and devoured us both.

16

Dark, mottled bruises circled the skin across my neck, a necklace of purples, greens and yellows that I could not remove. I studied them in the reflection of the floor-length mirror, tracing my fingers over the colourful hand marks Gale had left upon me. It hurt to touch, but that didn't stop me from doing so. Each time my fingers even dusted lightly across the tender skin I inhaled through a hiss.

"Looking at it will not make it go away," Faenir said.

I tore my concentration from the bruising to Faenir who sat in a grand, deep green velvet chair. Even in the reflection I could make out his cold expression and his frown that had been on full display since I had woken moments before.

"And prey tell what it is you suggest I do?"

"Rest." His answer came out short and fast.

We were back in Haxton Manor. The last thing I remembered was being laid across the floor in the dark corridor in Evelina, fighting to keep consciousness. My thoughts were a string of disconnected memories that made little sense and only added to the pounding in my head.

"That is easier said than done." I was restless. My limbs ached with extreme exhaustion, but my mind whirled violently as though entrapped by a storm. "How long have I been out for?"

"Not long enough." He leaned forward, clearing sleep from his gilded eyes with a lazy swipe of his hand.

When I had woken back in *my* bed in Haxton, it was to the gentle purring of Faenir as he slept in the very chair he had not yet vacated. Before I had time to even register where I was or remember what had happened his eyes had burst open as my name slipped from his mouth in a gasp. It was a moment of concerned weakness in Faenir that he hid quickly behind a wall of moody temper.

"Please," he said, gesturing back to the mound of twisted sheets upon the four-poster bed. "Sit. Let me look over your wounds."

I shook his offer off, pacing before the mirror instead. "I am fine. I... I just can't make sense of why he would do it."

"Arlo," Faenir said, a hint of warning in his voice.

I ignored him, allowing the pain across my throat and the throbbing at the back of my head to intensify alongside my anxious confusion. "Before you even think to scorn me for following after him, don't waste your breath. I thought Gale was looking for Myrinn, and why else would he have left the room? I only wished to speak with her."

"Arlo," Faenir tried again, his voice deepening.

"Gale was following someone, I am sure of it. But—"

"Arlo, sit!" Faenir snapped, half in a shout and a plea. "You have been through a lot and this incessant movement is not going to help. Do not make me force you back into that bed."

There was something about his warning tone that had my cheeks warming. For an entire moment I lost a grasp on what I was saying. Faenir was standing now, his off-white tunic untied at the collar to reveal lines of hidden muscle. He had rolled his sleeves up to his elbows and left his cloak draped carelessly across the arm of the chair.

"Fine," I forced out, walking back to the bed like a scorned pup. As I clambered back into the sheets Faenir was beside me, moving the full pillows towards the headboard to create a back support.

For a moment we were so close that his breath tickled across my neck. Our eyes locked. I was certain that moment would have lasted a lifetime if I did not force myself to break his gaze.

"I will do my best to answer your questions, but as you can imagine that even I will be falling short on many. Haldor has yet to send word regarding the inquisition that has been raised."

"Inquisition?" I said, allowing the unknown word to fill my mouth and familiarise itself in my mind.

"We must find out what happened and why, the inquisition raised will investigate what happened at the ball."

My throat was equal parts sore and dry. Before I could reach for the glass of water at my bedside it was in Faenir's hand as he brought it to my lips.

"May I?" he asked softly.

I could have refused and taken the glass from him; it was not that I required help to drink after all. But, as if by instinct, I moved my lips closer to him and it was greeted by the cold kiss of glass.

I drank until it was almost finished, muttering my thanks through glistening, moist lips, lips that Faenir seemed to watch intently until I spoke again.

"How difficult is it to question Gale?" I asked as Faenir put down the glass and returned his focus to me. When he did there was dread in his eyes; it shrunk his dark pupils to mere dots that seemed to disappear among the sea of gold that surrounded them.

"Difficult. Impossible, in fact."

I could not remember much of what happened, only that Gale had been atop me and the next he had not. But there was something else, another memory that wished to reveal itself through the haze.

"It was you, wasn't it? You stopped him."

It was Faenir that reminded me. "Yes, and in doing so I have killed him." He flinched as he said it.

My mouth dried once again, but it was not water that would help quench it. "You found me."

"Of course I found you. If I did not get to you when I did then we would not be having this conversation. He was intent on killing you. By the time I found you the glow of life that haloes you was faltering. Another moment and it would have been extinguished."

The truth of knowing that Faenir had killed Gale did not disturb me as I thought it would.

"And Myrinn, is she okay?" She was the first person I thought of as he said it.

Faenir seemed to rock back a step. "Does it not concern you that I killed him?"

"Like you said, we would not be having this conversation if you didn't do it."

I watched as my words physically settled over Faenir and his body seemed to lose some of the tension that had kept him strung tight. As if realising, I noticed he turned his back on me and paced back for the chair.

"Myrinn is coping well considering," he finally answered my question as he took his seat again. "Claria is furious of course but considering the justification of Gale's actions I am free from her open berating for the time being."

"Furious because you killed someone, or furious that I survived?"

Faenir answered plainly. "Both."

"Charming," I muttered. "She can join the line. Haldor is not exactly thrilled that I am here. Gale wanted me dead."

"Excuse me?" Faenir spoke and the shadows quivered. I felt the pressure of his sudden anger as physically as if the air itself pressed in on me.

"When he danced with me..." With each word Faenir's dark mood was intensifying. "It doesn't matter."

"Everything matters. I have put your life in danger, Arlo. By me giving into my selfish desires I have brought you into a realm that does not wish to see you live."

There was so much to unpack from what he said. Too much. However, I could not help but grasp one certain comment.

"This is all because you can touch me and that means you could become King."

"I do not wish for that."

"As you keep saying."

"And yet my family seems to not hear me."

"I hear you," I said softly.

Faenir dropped his gaze, the lines around his eyes smoothing.

"What is it you wish for?" I asked. "You stole me from my home and for what... why?"

"To *feel*," Faenir snapped. "I wish to finally feel the mundane truth of touch without consequence. Such a simple thing for everyone else to experience. So simple that you may not even realise how being deprived of such a thing can drive you to do things you never imagined you were capable of."

"Like stealing innocent people from their homes. From their families."

Faenir looked down, focusing on his hands which were balled in fists upon his lap. "Perhaps I should leave you to rest."

"If you dare leave me. You promised not to leave me again." I didn't expect my sudden panic at the idea of being left alone. Just the thought of Faenir leaving me had visions of Gale flooding back into my mind.

Faenir looked back up at me. Hope swirled within his eyes. "Nothing will happen to you in Haxton. I promise that. Soon the inquisition will find out why Gale wished to harm you and who put him up to that challenge."

I felt numb, defeated and pathetic. Not from what had happened, but how desperate I had been to keep Faenir with me. My captor. The person who had sealed the promise of my death in more ways than one.

"Myrinn is horrified. She thinks you will hate her. Blame her."

"And should I?"

Faenir shook his head, raven hair falling out from its neatly tucked position behind his pointed ears. "Myrinn is not capable of hurting. That is her curse, just like death is mine. And she would not have risked her Claim's life for such a thing."

"Why? Because it takes her out of the running for the crown?"

Faenir pulled a face, but his lack of questioning made it clear that he knew what Haldor and I had spoken about.

"There are many reasons as to why the elfkin take humans from Darkmourn. It is not always about ensuring succession. In fact, that is the rarest of reasons, one only my family are limited to."

"Then why else? Faenir, help me make sense of the world you have forced me to take a part in."

There was hesitation. He opened his mouth but closed it again. I began to believe he would not speak again until words slipped out of taut lips. "I could risk your life by telling you."

That almost made me laugh out loud. I had to swallow back the bubble of frantic chuckles as though I could not believe he had said such a thing. "I think it is clear my life could not be more at risk because of you."

He paused, contemplated his thoughts silently, then revealed something I never could have thought possible. "Our races are linked. Our survival is reliant on one another. If the humans perish in your world, so will the life of this world. We are nothing without one another."

"If that was the case, where was your kind when the vampires spread their disease across the world?" I had always wondered about it. It was one of the reasons why I had a deep hate for elves long before I had been taken to their world.

Why had the elves chosen the desperate moments before the human's demise to show themselves? Sweeping into our world as our saviours, except all they did was throw up walls and concealed us within them.

"There is much to learn about Evelina and its history. We are a realm which has been around far longer than you could even comprehend. But for the sake of your head and my patience you should understand that we thrive off the humans. Their life force feeds Evelina—it keeps us powerful; it keeps us alive. If you, the humans, perish, we follow afterward."

"It still doesn't explain why you take us. If the elves wish for the humans to live then why not leave us in our homes? The more you take, the less you leave."

"Because the elves believe that the only way of ensuring the humans future is by giving them one."

"How so?" I felt myself teetering over the edge of an abyss, with a great discovery lying just out of reach.

"You called them witches, I believe, strange name."

"Those *creatures* destroyed themselves," I interrupted, mouth filling with disgust at the mention of witches. "Darkmourn history tells us that they even had a second chance with the last witch who fell for the creature he was meant to kill and allowed the disease to spread. On two accounts they ruined my world."

"And Queen Claria believes they will save it anew. It was not the plan the elves had for them. The name the elves had gifted them long ago was one more unique. *Halflings*. If we are to give your kind a fighting chance against the vampires that roam the world beyond the walls my ancestors erected, then we will need to right the tip in balance. Magic must return to your realm."

I couldn't believe what Faenir was suggesting. Pinching my eyes closed, the daylight that spilled into the room suddenly became too much to bear.

"Humans are taken and used to sire halflings, beings with power belonging to the elves, but in vessels of humans. Since the downfall of Darkmourn our kind has been creating you an army."

"...that is why they never return."

"I have not lied to you, Arlo. You and any other Chosen can leave Evelina if you so desire. It just so happens that life in Evelina is better than what it can be for you back in Tithe."

I put my head in my hands, finding it easier to block out the world and the horrifying truth Faenir had revealed. There was no denying the intense relief I felt knowing that Auriol was back in Tithe. *Far away.* If Faenir had picked her, and she had the same unknown resistance to his touch, then her life would have not been as she hoped—not one of luxury without costs. Auriol would have been made to bear children. *Halflings.*

"Do they wish me harm because I ensure your succession, or because you picked a mate who cannot sire your children. Which is it?"

Faenir repeated a single word he had said earlier, this time just as cold and sharp. "Both."

I laid down in the bed, unable to hold myself up anymore; I wished only to close my eyes and block out everything that had happened and had been said.

"They see you as a wasted choice, a way of me scorning

their beliefs by spitting at the feet of their rules and customs."

"And what do you see me as?" I asked, rolling onto my side and putting my back to him.

As I buried my head into the feather-stuffed pillow, not even I could drown out Faenir's reply. "The only choice."

❧ 17 ❧

I woke, cheeks slick with tears, my breathing shallow. Auriol's name whispered across my trembling lips. I sat up and found that Faenir was still in the chair. Relief flooded through me, and I fell back onto the pillows.

Faenir slept soundlessly. Simply reminding myself of his presence helped pull me from the dregs of the night terror. He was the reminder I needed to understand I was no longer in that nightmare, for the real world was one far more frightening.

It was hard to focus on what I had dreamt which made me wake with tears. Auriol had been there as she had most nights, waiting for me in the dark. Sometimes she welcomed me, other times she wept as though she could not see me, as though I was already dead.

This time the dream was different.

Her stomach was swollen, her hands cradling it as if she required some assistance with its heavy presence. She sang to it, a beautiful voice full of hope and promise. Then she stopped. Her pregnant belly was gone. She looked down at her hands, now sodden with blood, and she screamed. Auriol's gentle face split into a drawn-out cry that warped her features. She howled and thrashed, begged for her child to be returned to her.

I woke before I saw any more.

I laid like that for a while, looking up at the towering ceiling above whilst listening to the Faenir's soft breathing. Beyond it was the gentle lap of the Styx, one of Haxton's greatest lies. It sounded so peaceful, yet I knew it was far from that. How could both sounds be so calming yet come from such dangerous things?

A chill blew in through the balcony doors, causing the brush of lace curtains to skim over the stone flooring. It cooled the tears across my face and chilled my skin until I shivered from more than just the low temperature.

Despite all the sounds of night it was Faenir's breathing that captured my attention. Soon enough that was all I could focus on. How both his inhale and exhale was feather soft. It was so terribly quiet that I fixated on each breath just to make sure he didn't break his rhythm.

I drove myself mad listening to him.

So, without much thought, I slipped from the bed and padded over to the chair; the floor was cold against my bare feet. Perhaps it was my delusion that drove me to his side. Maybe my exhaustion or the bang to my head when Gale had thrust me to the floor. Deep down I knew it was neither of those things. It was my own selfish need, a want to fill my mind with other thoughts, more delicious and consuming. Tom would have been that distraction for me... but Faenir killed him. Yet that still did not deter me from reaching down and tracing my fingers across the hollow curve of his cheek.

Faenir's breathing faltered; his golden, tired eyes crept open. "Why are you crying?"

Embarrassed, I cleared the stubborn dampness with the back of my hand. "I had a bad dream."

I didn't expect for Faenir to console me, nor did I know why I had come over to him. But his distraction was a powerful thing and I feared if I closed my eyes again, I would see Auriol and I couldn't handle that again.

"Tell me what it is I can offer to help ease your sorrow."

I played with his words, toying with all manner of thoughts that speared through my mind. My legs wove between his, pushing his knees apart with a soft nudge. Soon enough I stood between them, all the while Faenir had hardly moved a muscle; his attitude burned with anticipation and wonder.

"May I?" My eyes flicked to his strong thighs in silent suggestion.

Faenir's hands reached for the arms of the chair and gripped them tightly. He opened his mouth as if to reply but a string of jumbled stutters followed. The chair creaked as I climbed onto it, straddling Faenir's thighs until I sat perfectly upon them. He watched me with wide, unblinking eyes. "It feels as though I am the one dreaming now."

"Isn't this what you wanted?" I asked, leaning into him until my lips brushed across his neck; Faenir still gripped the chair as though his life depended on it. "To be touched. To feel what others do?"

"Arlo," Faenir groaned as my tongue traced the skin at

his neck in intricate circles. "You have been through a lot. You are confused."

I pulled away enough that I could look up at him through the stubborn strands of ash blond hair that covered my eyes. That frown that Faenir wore so well had vanished. "I know what I am doing. If you wish for me to stop, then say so."

"...I..."

"What?" I said quietly. "Believe me, Faenir, if I did not want you, I would not be doing this." I did want him. But I wanted Faenir like I did with Tom, a way of filling the nights with more than just bad dreams.

Faenir shifted beneath me. I jolted as his hips moved and his legs widened in stance. Before I could fall two strong hands pressed against the tops of my ass and held firm. "Careful," he said, fingers tensing. "I would not want you getting hurt."

"But that is the point. You *can't* hurt me."

I almost cried out when he removed one of his hands from my ass. My breath shuddered as his fingers surprised me, brushing across the side of my face and pushing the hair out of it. Faenir's gilded eyes followed the movement of his own finger as though it was the most fascinating thing in the world.

"I still cannot fathom that you are real. Sometimes, for a moment, I trick myself into believing you are just a figment of my imagination, conjured from years of longing and wasted wishes... Yet here you are."

I reached up and gripped his hand so it pressed against the side of my face and could not move away. "Well, I am real. So tell me what you wish to do with me."

Perhaps I had said the wrong thing. My words caused

Faenir to hesitate. The softness in his face hardened, his frown returning to its rightful place.

"Many things." Faenir tore his hand out from under mine and forced himself from the chair, taking me along with him. He was strong. His grip on me was assured and placed to keep me from falling out of his hold. Instinctively I wrapped my legs around his waist as he stalked over to the bed, all without dropping his gaze from mine. "And all can wait until the morning. What I want from you tonight is for you to sleep. Rest and allow yourself to heal after what has happened to you. If you still feel the same about me, come dawn then I welcome you to pick this up where I regrettably stop it. If not, then we will put this all behind us."

I narrowed my gaze, burning holes through him. "I am not the delicate flower that you believe I am. You could pick from me from the root and still I would bloom. I know what I want..."

Faenir lowered me to the bed, depositing me into the cloud of sheets and then stood back at the bedside. "Not once did I imagine you to be delicate. However, I have waited hundreds of years for the chance to feel. I can wait a few more hours if it means I will not need to add the worry of your regret to my mind."

"I do not regret anything," I replied quickly. Desperately.

Faenir looked back at me, rolling back his shoulders as he exhaled his reply. "You will."

FAENIR

I could have taken Arlo, torn the clothes from his body and explored him in ways my mind had tortured me with. I wanted it with such boiling, undeniable desire that it set my skin aflame.

But that would have been wrong to do so.

Not even hours before Arlo sat upon my lap, slowly rocking himself upon me, had he wished me harm. He had looked at me with such disgust and hate that I had once believed I was accustomed to. His feelings could not have changed so quickly. I would not let him make a decision that he would spend the rest of his days regretting.

My conscience was already broken; with that regret upon it, I feared it would shatter completely.

I waited for him to fall back to sleep. Then I waited a few more moments to know that the nightmare that had thrown Arlo into my arms did not return. Only once his breathing had slowed and his face melted into placidity did I leave.

Each step away from the room pained me. I was

breaking his promise, leaving him alone when he begged for me not to again. Part of me expected him to wake suddenly and call out my name, the idea alone was not enough to keep me though, not when my body and mind needed cleansing.

I could not have sat in that room whilst his touch still teased across my skin. Most indulgent of all was the wetness of his tongue. It took everything in my power not to touch my neck and feel the dampness on my skin. If I allowed myself to truly focus on the closeness of his lips and the way his teeth grazed over my neck, I knew I would not have found the restraint to stop myself from devouring him.

Years without touch had not made me a stranger to it. It made me desperate for it.

I walked through the unkind corridors of Haxton in search for the only place with the power to clear my mind. A place of quietness and death. The Styx.

Keep your distance, Charon, I speared the thought across the great lake towards the loyal spirit that lurked within his boat.

His reply shuddered through the link that tethered us, *As you wish, Master.*

Leaving Haxton behind I kept my focus on the dark expanse before me. At night the Styx looked like glass, cut through with obsidian so dark that it mixed seamlessly with the sky. One began where the other ended.

My clothes littered the ground as I closed in on the water. I tore my tunic free with one hand. My trousers came next, undoing them at the waist before they fell to my ankles. I gripped the hard erection that Arlo had cursed me with, forcing it downward in hopes to banish it;

just holding my cock urged it to throb harder. As I reached the shore my toes curled as the freezing water rushed over them in greeting. I did not stop, walking until the water covered my nudity in a cloak of darkness.

Shades drifted towards me, grey slithers of shadow and mist that formed figures. They cut through the water, encouraging me to join them. But they would not take me as they had with Arlo. Even the dead feared my touch.

I let the water slip over my head until I bathed in freezing, endless darkness. Only when the Styx closed over me entirely did the voices start, the shades screaming and pleading for freedom. Begging. Crying. Demanding that I set them free from this place. It was the distraction I needed. At last, my cock softened in my grasp. The water of the Styx did what I required, ridding Arlo's touch from my skin.

When not a whisper was left did I finally forget.

There was no room for thought in the Styx, not as the dead distracted me with desperate pleas for freedom, not when I allowed them to punish me for what I had done to them.

That was what this place was, a prison for the souls I had stolen. A reminder of the monster that Arlo convinced me to forget.

❧ 18 ❧

I had, unwillingly, entered into a tournament of silence. Days passed in a slow and torturous dance of stubborn quiet and close proximity. Faenir, although never straying far from me, hardly spoke a word since that night when I had clambered onto his lap in hopes for more than just a seat. And I, stubborn as Auriol had always told me I was, refused to be the first one to speak either.

It had been three days, although it felt more like an eternity. I counted by scoring marks into the stone flooring beneath my bed using a knife I had stolen. It was becoming a game to store Faenir's silverware like a magpie, hiding it beneath the bed alongside the single vial of vampire blood. I felt carrying the vial around in a pouch at my belt would only raise questions, ones I was not prepared to provide answers to.

When Faenir would leave me alone I felt as though I could breathe properly. It was not that I despised his company, but the silence drove me mad. I longed for him to ask me other questions that did not relate to the rate of my healing or how he fixated on the fading bruises across my neck.

I replied with short, one-word answers yet he still did not seem to understand, or care, that there was a taut string of tension, and it was mere moments from snapping.

It was on the third morning, with the long oak table between us, that the string finally broke.

"I regret it." I slammed my hands down upon the wood, shaking the glass of water Faenir had tentatively poured for me. "Is that what you wish to hear? I regret getting out of bed and throwing myself at you. I should have forced myself back to sleep. If I could go back and change my choices, I fucking would have."

Faenir looked over the parchment of cream paper that he gripped in both hands. It was likely a report from the inquisition into my attack. They had arrived every morning from Evelina's council, every single one lacking real information.

"Is that truly how you feel?" he asked, eyes swirling with interest. Faenir hid the lower part of his face with the parchment, making it harder for me to read him, although I was certain he was grinning behind it.

"Well," I huffed. "That is why you have been practically ignoring me, is it not? Have you finally realised that taking me was a mistake?"

"You," he replied, voice cut with seriousness, "are not a mistake. And we are talking now, are we not? Humans, your kind are strange. If you were so in need of conversation, why did you not start it?"

That stumped me. I swallowed the excuse I was

preparing to throw back at him and picked another root. "You ignored me."

"I apologise if that made you feel uncomfortable."

It felt ridiculous to accept his apology, but rude not to acknowledge it. "So you admit it."

"Perhaps my silence has suggested that I do not care for your company, but rest assured you have been on my mind this entire time."

"Well…" I stumbled over my words. "Don't!"

He lowered the parchment so it no longer concealed part of his face. "Care to elaborate?" Faenir's frown deepened, his pruned brows furrowing like daggers above his eyes.

"Think about me. I have not given you that right."

"That is a fine shame. But with or without it, you have burrowed far too deeply that I do not believe I could pry you out."

My throat dried. I almost choked on the pure seriousness of his expression. I plucked the glass of water and downed its contents in hopes it would calm the rising scarlet in my cheeks.

Faenir grinned and raised the parchment back across his smug, knowing face.

"Usually, the letter is thrown into the fire by now," I said again, not wishing for the silence to return so soon. "Has the council provided more clarity into what happened with Gale and why he attacked me?"

"No," Faenir replied. "Their investigation has not uncovered anything substantial since yesterday's mention of the knife they had found in the corridor. It is still to be determined why Gale chose to strangle you when he could have stabbed you instead…"

"Don't act coy with me, Faenir," I added.

"Ah, that is right. The knife was yours, wasn't it? Or mine to be precise, you just took it from me."

The way his eyes gleamed hinted that he had already known that. Perhaps he too noticed the dwindling supply of knives as the days passed. If only he looked beneath the bed and he would find them.

"And do you blame me? In a world where I am destined for death, it would be foolish for me not to be protected."

"I protect you."

I looked back to the now empty glass of water and wished for it to be filled. Those three words had the heat in my cheeks flooding back in abundance. I felt its hungry presence spread down my neck and constrict around my chest.

Nothing else needed to be said about the knife. Faenir knew I had taken it and did not scorn me further.

"This parchment is not an update from the council." Faenir pushed back his chair, letting it squeak terribly across the floor. Then he walked to me, footsteps heavy, his deep burgundy cloak sweeping behind him. "It... is an invitation."

"Not another one."

Faenir lowered the parchment over my shoulder and held it before me. It took a moment for me to focus on the swirling words upon it as I was too distracted by his closeness.

"Read it to me," he whispered, cool breath tickling my ear. "Hearing it aloud might help me make sense of it."

I stiffened at his nearness. Each blink reminded me of his hesitant touch when I had straddled him upon the chair he still used as a bed.

"Go on..." he encouraged. "I am waiting."

I snatched the parchment from his hands and began.

*Faenir Evelina & mate are hereby invited to the Joining
Ceremony of Princess Frila Evelina & mate.
Proceedings will occur within the capital, Neveserin, by Queen
Claria the Light.
Blessed be.*

"A Joining?" I questioned, looking back at Faenir after I had read it aloud twice.

"Your kind, from my understanding, used to celebrate such partnerships and name it a wedding. This is Evelina's equivalent."

There was no stopping the barking laugh that exploded from me. "A wedding! They have not known each other more than a number of days."

"It is custom." Faenir took the parchment, crumpled it in his hand and threw it with precise aim into the burning hearth, as he did with all the other letters that arrived each morning. The invite crackled upon impact, singeing as the fire devoured it. "Elves who chose a mate will always sanctify their union and Join with one another. It is the first step towards the... necessary."

"Children," I echoed, remembering back to what Faenir had revealed to me. "You pick your human that fits your taste and desire, then marry them before fucking. Seems an awful lot of hassle to get your dick wet?"

"The production of halflings is far more important

than just... sex." I shivered with delight at the discomfort the single word caused the elven prince. "Frila is the youngest of our family, a spritely girl who has always, if I must admit, irritated me with her presence alone. For that we will not be going."

"Hold on," I snapped, twisting in the chair to get a better look at him. "Why?"

"I could list the reasons... The most important is your safety."

I scowled at Faenir down the point of my finger. "Don't you dare use me as an excuse to continue hiding from your family and the responsibilities that come with them."

"May I ask why you show such interest in forcing me to do things I do not wish to do? First it was the ball, now this. It is not safe beyond Haxton, not for you."

I stood from the chair, squaring myself off against Faenir who crossed strong arms over his chest. Standing so close that our toes almost touched, I looked up at him and made sure his gaze was fixated on mine. I wished for him to see the honesty in my soul alongside what I was about to say.

"If we do not go then you allow *them* to win. Claria. Haldor. Anyone who has shunned you for being something you cannot help yourself from being. You may be complacent with letting the bad ones succeed, but I am not. Swallow your pride, Faenir. We're going."

Faenir's fingers twitched, I caught them out of the corner of my eye. "It is not the right decision to make. Believe me, I have spent far more years than you could imagine keeping my distance from family relations. This invite has only reached Haxton because it is a challenge, one I would gladly lose if it means keeping you out of harm's way."

I spun back to the table, snatched the knife from beside the plate and twisted back around all within a blink. Faenir spluttered a gasp, one mixed with surprise and pleasure, as I pressed the blunt blade to his neck. "Don't fear for me. I can handle myself. And this time... I am far more prepared."

Faenir's exhale fogged against the metal of the blade, his chest rising and falling heavily with each breath. "If we accept Frila's invitation we will be openly disrespecting Claria before all of Evelina. I highly imagine she does not have an inkling that the invite has reached us."

"I am relying on that. Which is exactly why I wish for us to go," I replied, reaching up on tiptoes until our faces were inches apart. "Disrespect."

Neveserin, the capital of Evelina, was the most ethereal place I had ever laid eyes on. I drank it in, face pressed against the glass window of the carriage, as though I was a child and freshly baked cakes waited for me on the other side. The city was carved into the mountains that Faenir had named Cul Nair.

The Goddess Nyssa fell from the skies and left her dent in the world. Where she touched, life blossomed. Neveserin is believed to be the birthplace of our kind.

Domed roof buildings and arched walkways connected one another through a pathway of bridges that seemed to float over cascading waterfalls of azure and opal blues. Trees broke up the countless constructions, each locked in the autumnal shades of amber, gold and brown.

Neveserin seemed to be constructed in levels. The lower levels, which melted from cobbled streets to wide pool-like glens of water and fields, housed small buildings. Above them towered far larger buildings, spiralling towers and monstrous stone temples.

I could not fathom how many elves must have dwelled within this city.

Far in the distance I could see the outline of Evelina's heart, the Great Tree we had visited during the ball, Nyssa. If Neveserin was the birthplace, Nyssa was the place where the Goddess went to die. The Great Tree seemed to guard the city with its shadowing presence.

Once the carriage finally came to a stop after journeying for countless hours, I almost felt disappointed. I could have ridden around the city over and over and never grown bored. Being here amongst such architectural beauty made it hard to believe that Tithe was even real and made it even easier to believe in the Goddess; only someone of such great power could have created such a place.

"Do you remember our deal?" Faenir asked as he stood beyond the carriage and offered me a hand. This time I did not refuse it. Still distracted by the city's physical attraction, I was not prepared for the soft kiss of the air and how it hummed with magic. Using Faenir's hand to steady myself, I inhaled a lungful of lavender and cherry blossom.

"Yes," I replied meekly, unable to look at him for longer than a second for fear of missing out on the wonder of the city. "I don't leave yours or Myrinn's sight."

"I understand Neveserin is overwhelming for the likes of your kind, but do not let its grace distract you from the danger that lurks behind it."

I tore my hand from his. "Stop worrying."

"Never."

"You made it," the light, blissful voice called out.

I turned, feeling the easy slip of Faenir's hand fall protectively upon my lower back.

"I cannot express how glad I am to see you. Both of you."

Myrinn watched us from the arched doorway of the grand building that stood guard before us. The lowering sunlight cast a golden glow across her dark skin. Her bare shoulders seemed to glisten as though shards of stars had dusted across them.

It seemed normal for Myrinn to wear only the finest of dresses. Each time I had seen her, she was wearing something that belonged in the pages of books instead of real life. The dress she currently wore was the shade of burnt amber. The cowl neckline was held up by thin straps and the dress seemed to skim across her frame, highlighting each curve and perfectly drawn line of her body.

Faenir tipped his head into a subtle bow. "Thank you for hosting our stay."

I dipped my knees and bowed a beat behind Faenir. "It is good to see you, Myrinn."

Her smile warmed at my comment. Faenir had told me at the beginning of the journey that Myrinn still housed a lot of guilt for what Gale had done to me. I looked forward to telling her that not once did I blame her. She had been the only one to show me kindness since Faenir had brought me to Evelina and I would not forget that lightly.

"As they have been before, and will be going forward, my doors are always open to you, cousin." Myrinn stood aside, sweeping a hand towards the elegant, curved doorway of light cedar wood. "Perhaps we should catch up over wine... there truly is much to discuss."

Tailors fluttered around me like frantic birds; hands pulled at fabric, fingers pinched my skin carelessly. I gritted my teeth as needles wove in and out, stitching a deep navy material to fit my outstretched limbs. I dared not hiss or show my discomfort for fear that Faenir would explode at the handmaids, for he watched from the shadows of the room, leaning against the wall with a knee angled up for support. Not a movement went unseen by him. Myrinn had already scorned him for snapping at one of her handmaids whose needle grazed the skin of my arm.

Myrinn laid across a grand chair, plucking grapes from the plate beside her and inspecting each one with intense interest. "It is important you look the part, Arlo," she said through a breath.

Faenir had refused Myrinn's request for her to escort me through Neveserin to collect a wardrobe of clothes. I guessed he preferred seeing me in his oversized hand-me-downs which he had provided. Instead, in her passive act of defiance, she had commissioned the tailors to her home hours after breakfast that morning instead.

If I cannot bring you into the city, then I will bring the city to you, she had said as the tailors and handmaids floated into the room with arms full of cases overwhelmed with fabric. Faenir glowered and shrunk into the shadows of the room in defeat, yet still he watched.

"He does not need to be paraded like a prized bull," Faenir grumbled from his shadows.

"*He* can speak for himself," I retorted through a hidden smile as Myrinn rolled her eyes dramatically. "If our presence at the Joining is a test, then it is important we prepare to pass it."

"I was thinking of it more as a message." Myrinn popped a purple grape into her mouth and bit down on it. "It is encouraging to know you hold such interest in Evelina's politics. If that is a result of your change of heart to your circumstance, I cannot express how glad I am."

I caught Faenir's piercing gilded stare as Myrinn spoke. Within the reflection of the standing mirror before me I held it, until another needle poked my side and distracted me from him. "It is not like I have a choice in the matter. If I cannot return home, then I must make the most of my visit. I'm not one for hiding from those who wish me harm."

I was certain I heard Faenir swallow hard at my comment.

"Nothing will happen to you during your visit, I promise that." Myrinn glanced subtly over her shoulder towards Faenir. "You will have us both to protect you. After what... what Gale did." She quietened, as though losing herself to a darkening thought. "I will not let it happen again."

"Do not make promises you cannot keep, Myrinn," Faenir grumbled. "Now the inquisition into Gale's actions have been dropped by the council there is no knowing if it will happen again."

Myrinn had been the one to share that update with us when we had arrived the night prior. Queen Claria had closed the investigation and labelled Gale as volatile. Jealous. There was no pressuring the investigation. In the eyes of the Queen and her council, the matter had been dealt with. Except it hadn't, not in Faenir's eyes.

"Rest assured nothing will happen in my home." Myrinn's fingers pinched the grape, letting juice spread down her wrist and staining her silk dress. "And if your hunch behind Grandmother is correct, no pass will be made for Arlo during the Joining. She would not wish to interfere with such a spectacle and ruin Frila's day."

The tailors shared glances with one another. They did not utter a word, but from the look in their eyes I was cautious not to speak ill of the Queen. *Not yet at least.*

"I'm not frightened," I announced, feeling the need to make them aware that I did not need protecting. It was suffocating. Both Myrinn and Faenir, although speaking from a good place, spoke on my behalf. And I didn't like it. For a moment I felt as though I wore Auriol's shoes. "And perhaps the council were right, and Gale was simply mad? When he spoke to me it was like he did not know who you were, Myrinn. His mind was not in a clear place."

"Arlo could be right, Myrinn. What is to say you simply picked a rotten apple from the orchard?" Faenir enjoyed watching Myrinn squirm under his words.

"What is done is done." Myrinn sat up straight, clapping her hands together in dismissal. As though dispersing from the surprise of the noise, the tailors gathered their belongings and parted from the room with haste and whispered breaths.

"We will make the most of your visit to Neveserin, and when you leave it will be alongside a horde of my staff. Now I no longer have a human to host, my rooms are rather full of wasted bodies. I am certain you could find use for them in Haxton more than I can."

"That will not be required."

"It certainly will be," Myrinn replied quickly, rising from her seat. The conversation was done, for now. "Arlo, let me see you."

She winked at me as though recognising the seething elven prince behind. It made me grin, which seemed to calm him quicker. "It is beautiful, is it not?" Her eyes trailed me from head to toe.

I looked down, admiring the clothes the tailors had pinned, strapped and sewed together whilst I had stood for what felt like a millennium. The jacket was a deep shade of navy. It looked almost wet from the way the velvet material caught the spilling daylight that flooded into the room through the glass-domed ceiling above us. The stitching thread was silver. It matched the formfitting trousers, and the unbuttoned jacket revealed the open necked tunic of cream with buttons made from black shell.

"Don't I look stupid?" I asked, running my hands down the arms of the jacket and feeling the small, seven lined stars that they had stitched upon the material. It was as though I wore the surface of the Styx, dark blue with the reflection of burning stars glinting across it.

"No," Faenir said softly. "Far from it."

Myrinn chuckled into her fingers, one brow raised above pleased eyes. "Faenir seems to like it which is the most important thing." She leaned forward quickly and added in a whisper, "So do I. Do not feel *stupid*, but brilliant. If you are to stir the politics of my family, then you may as well do it in style."

"In doing so it will only anger powerful people."

Myrinn took my hand in hers and squeezed. "We are all powerful people. Some—" her eyes flickered, gesturing towards where Faenir lurked. "—more than others."

"It would be best that you do not fill Arlo's head with such ideas." Faenir paced towards us. His closeness made Myrinn flinch slightly, although I could see the regret in her face the moment she did; the reaction did not go unnoticed by Faenir either. "Arlo has a tendency to steal knives. He doesn't need to concern himself with our family."

"He certainly does." Myrinn spun as fast as a viper. "If you are both to complete your own Joining then Arlo will be thrust deep into the heart of our family and its secrets. Hiding from it will only encourage failure."

"Remind me why you care all of a sudden?" Faenir asked, eyes narrowed. "How many years have you all forgotten to reach out to me? The estranged killer of the family. Poisoned fruit, is that not what Grandmother refers to me as during the many dinners, parties and events I have been left out of?"

Myrinn swallowed hard, eyes widening.

"Please," I said quickly. Last time they had come to

blows the room almost crumpled beneath the presence of their magic.

"I wish to hear your answer..." Faenir pressed on, ignoring my plea.

"Faenir, enough." I put myself between them both. "I wish to have some time alone with Myrinn."

"Absolutely not."

"Faenir." I glowered. "It was not a request."

His face softened in outward concern. "*It* is not safe to leave you."

"You can disrespect many things, but not my promise to look after your mate, cousin." Myrinn was not pleased at his blatant disregard of her ability to keep me from harm.

Before he could reply I stepped before him, reached up and cupped his cheek. He practically melted into my touch. "I will be fine. Please."

Faenir bit down on his lip as I removed my touch and let the real world and its worries return to him. Then he nodded, one quick tilt of his head as though he could not utter the words it took to agree.

"Take him beyond the boundaries of your home and I will destroy it," Faenir snapped, frantic and rushed as he took steps towards the door. "And everyone unlucky enough to dwell in it."

Myrinn pouted, wrapping one hand around my waist and waggling her spare hand in a farewell gesture. "He will be returned in one piece. I promise."

My head felt foggy, my arms and legs were heavy and slow. Yet I still drank the wine as though it was water from a never-ending source. At one point I had gone from sober to drunk in what seemed like a blink, most noticeable when I closed my eyes only to reopen them to a room spinning before me. It was not a pleasant feeling, but that did not stop me from knocking back each glass until my teeth felt rough with fermented grape. No matter how many glasses I consumed, I could not get rid of the strangling discomfort that gripped my heart.

"Faenir can hurt with his words, his actions, but you understand now why I cannot begrudge him?" Myrinn did not clear the jewelled tear that rolled down her cheek. "He has been punished... punished from the moment he was born for something he cannot control."

It had been easy manipulating the conversation to get answers that I had longed to uncover. Myrinn was an open book, willing for me to flick through the pages to find out about Faenir and his past.

"How did it happen?"

It felt wrong to ask Myrinn to spill the perfectly crafted chest of secrets without consulting the person it related to, but I had to know. Selfishly, it would help me make sense of him.

"Claria tells it as though it is her greatest story. Repeating it over meals with dignitaries and high esteemed members of Evelina's realm. Anyone who would listen. The part that sickens me the most is that they laugh, chuckle like wild beasts over someone else's misery."

I swallowed a lump in my throat, laying my fingers on the back of Myrinn's hand. "Help me understand."

She gathered herself, inhaling deeply as she regarded me through the low-lit room. "Then I will tell it as Claria has. Forgive me for the lack of sensitivity."

I gripped the glass and watched Myrinn without blinking for fear of missing the truth of Faenir's beginnings.

"Faenir was born to Queen Claria's eldest daughter, my father's sister. Her name was Lilith. During her pregnancy it was prophesised for a child to be born that would finally relieve my grandmother of her duties. Evelina is a place of life. So, when Faenir was born, the perfect vision of our realm was shattered as though captured in a glass ball and thrown from a great height. Lilith died as Faenir passed out of her. Her partner, Faenir's father, Croin, took Faenir into his arms and the moment he did so he joined his beloved in death, all before he had realised what had happened."

I blinked and my mind filled with scenes so horrific I wished never to close my eyes again. A body slick with the grime of birth, skin cold and as stiff as marble. I saw a child, its wailing scratching across my soul like a knife pulled across stone.

The wine was left cold in my hand, my grip on the glass threatening to shatter it at any given moment.

"Claria tells the tale as though she found them. Mother, father and the unknowing maids that rushed to help and calm the crying child. Faenir was discovered, naked and subdued, surrounded by a mound of the dead."

Myrinn was crying hard now. If there was more to the

story, she couldn't speak through the sobs that wracked her chest.

I sat there in numbed silence.

Faenir was branded a monster for simply being alive. His curse was unfair and had moulded him into the person who had seen me in Tithe and acted upon desperation.

Just as I do with the vampires.

Just as I do with suffocating my sister and her life.

In a twisted, warped way, I did not blame Faenir for stealing me. Maybe that was the wine that dulled my sense between what was wrong or right. But in the back of my mind I felt as though I would have done the same.

"How did he survive?" I asked. If he could not have been touched, then it made little sense to understand how a child was nursed and brought up all without even being able to pick him up from the floor.

"He was never meant to," Myrinn replied. "Claria misses this part out in her stories, but our family knows the next chapters well. It took twenty royal guards to return Faenir to his family dwelling. Once bundled in cloth they were able to touch him... he was gathered in a sack and taken home."

"To Haxton Manor."

"They swaddled him in cloth, the first guards dying upon impact with his skin. Those who were lucky enough to gather him from the trail of death were safe for longer moments; protected by the material. Claria did not care for the material that covered Faenir's mouth. Sometimes I imagine she must have wished him to suffocate after what happened to Lilith."

There was a storm in my stomach. It jolted like wild

seas, threatening to break free and spill the morning's food across my new outfit and the chair I sat upon.

"The orders were simple. Take him to Haxton and discard him into the lake."

"No." The glass slipped from my hand and shattered across the floor in a littering of diamond-like shards. "He was a baby!"

"That did not matter. Faenir was a monster from the moment he was born. Claria had him thrown into the Styx in hopes that he would drown. Condemned as poison. His crime of death punishable by death."

I grieved for that child. My heart twisted into knots in my chest, the feeling reminiscent of when my own parents had succumbed to the sickness that claimed them.

"But he survived."

She nodded as the lit candles cast shadows across her striking beauty. "Faenir's power goes against Claria. Life and death. He, like her, is powerful enough to rule a realm. His magic is unexplainable, and Claria despises that. Whatever happened to Faenir in that water changed it forever. You saw what lurks within the waters... you know that death lingers and so does Faenir. Some stories tell that a servant of the family jumped into the Styx and dragged the child free from the water. Faenir has never been one to reveal what happened. Nor do I think he will ever expose that part of his past to anyone."

I stood suddenly, rocking on my feet. "I need to see him."

Myrinn reached out and gripped my arm. "I am sorry if I upset you."

"Before I said I was not scared," I said, my chest rising and falling wildly. "Now I understand that Faenir is not the monster in this story. He is simply the product of another."

She released me. "Go to him. See him in the same light I have for many years."

I paused at that, turning to face her over the shattering of my glass and the melted candle that spilled a river of wax across the table between us. "Why do you treat him with kindness when the rest of your world shuns him?"

Myrinn took a deep breath, rolled back her shoulders and resolve returned into her strong expression. "Whereas everyone sees Faenir as the end to Evelina, I see him as its revival. I do not wish to perish in a dying world."

"And why do you believe he can save it?"

"Because like calls to like," Myrinn replied quietly. "Faenir was destined for birth for a reason. And he is family. He is my blood. I can never turn my back on the truth of that."

$$\text{❧ 20 ❧}$$

Faenir stopped pacing the chamber the moment I burst through the door. By the time I saw him my heart was in my throat and my eyes were blurred with tears. I could hardly hold a full breath for fear of it breaking free in a sob.

"What has happened?" Faenir spluttered, cutting across the room so quickly that I was sure he floated on a violent breeze.

I threw myself into his unexpecting arms. My face crashed into his chest, my hands gripping one another behind his back as I allowed my tears to stain his tunic.

Faenir hesitated to return my embrace. But he gave in, gentle hands reaching for the sides of my face and forcing me to look up at him. "Speak to me, Arlo."

Faenir's thumb brushed a tear from my cheek as I struggled to find the right words to say. The haze behind his gilded stare changed from concern, to anger and back to worry. I could almost see him trying to silently work out what had happened.

"Myrinn," I managed finally, "she told me what they did to you."

He immediately stiffened. I felt his desire to pull away and hide himself from me, but there was no hiding anymore. Even in the darkness of the large room with the amber glow of candles being our only source of light, I saw Faenir clearly.

"Why didn't you tell me?"

Faenir loosed a tired breath and pinched his pained eyes closed. "I had burdened you with enough by bringing you here. It would not have mattered if your time passed without you knowing the truth."

I reached up and brushed my shaking hand down the line of his jaw. My fingers traced it down to his neck, to his chest where I laid them above his heart. "I'm sorry for what they did to you. What they do. I understand now. All of it. I understand." Forming a sentence was hard through my laboured breathing. I spoke what I could, through broken, rushed words.

Faenir's heart hammered beneath my palm, the pace quickening with every passing moment. "Do not cry for me, Arlo," he whispered, opening his eyes once again as his steel resolve had returned to them.

"You have lost so much," I replied. "Even more has been taken from you."

"In this moment I feel like I have everything."

His comment was so precise it stabbed through my soul and buried itself within my mind. It was as though he repeated it, speaking that sentence over and over in torment. It destroyed me. Unravelled me. Devoured me.

"I could give you so much more," I said.

Faenir's eyes widened in knowing. Before he could say

anything further, I gave into the taut tension of our cord, the unseen one that had grown shorter every day during my time in Evelina. Now it was mere inches long; there was no pulling away anymore.

Rising on my tiptoes, cheeks slick with tears, I brought my face up to Faenir's until our lips waited a hairbreadth apart. I felt his breath as he felt mine, a cool and welcoming breeze.

"What are you doing?" he asked.

"What I should have all those nights ago."

Our lips pressed together. At first it could not have been called a kiss. It was feather soft and slow, lips simply touching. Existing as one. Faenir watched through wide eyes as though he feared I would perish at any given moment. It lasted a few heartbeats before I retreated from him. His lack of response made me self-conscious and embarrassed.

Faenir was a frozen statue of disbelief. He did not stop me from pulling away. Instead, he let go of my cheek and raised fingers to his lips and touched them.

The sudden realisation flooded over me. That was Faenir's first kiss. In his long life, that had been the very first.

I turned away before he could see my sadness turn to boiling embarrassment. Then a hand clasped my wrist, tugged me back again, and a body crashed into me.

Faenir kissed me back. This time it was far from gentle and inexperienced. It was heavy and passionate. Our faces melted together; mine held by Faenir's desperate hands as he guided the kiss. It started as lips crushing together. I gripped his tunic in my fists and held him to me. Then my mouth parted, tongue encouraging its way into his mouth to greet his. They coiled. Wet and hungry.

Faenir's hand moved and cupped the back of my head. There was no pulling away, nor did I want to. I gave into the wave of his desperation and happily drowned within it. A spreading of numb tingles filled every finger and toe, all twenty digits until I could no longer feel them. I could have lost myself in him like a maze with no desire to ever escape again.

When we finally pulled away again, I felt disappointment that it was over. Then I recognised the desire in his fiery gaze and I knew that it was far from being done. It had only just begun.

"You taste..." Faenir said, voice a low growl. "Divine."

I smiled, my stomach jolting with anticipated excitement. "For someone who has not kissed before you certainly did well."

"Arlo," he breathed my name as though trying to control himself. "You could not possibly comprehend what the many years of imagination has given me."

"Show me."

Faenir stared at me without blinking. His entire focus was on me, creating a thrilling jolt that awakened every sense in my body. It was as though he was starved, and I was his meal; he contemplated which part of me he wished to devour first.

"Are you certain you want this?"

"I want *you*." And I did, as desperately as he wanted me; I was confident of that. My head was full of him, with no room for any other thought. In that moment it was only us, and the world and the realms beyond this room no longer mattered.

Faenir grinned slowly, his red-stained and swollen lips tugging at the corners. I spluttered a breath as he moved, gathering his raven locks in his fist and twisting it into a knot. I had not seen him so clearly before. With his hair pulled back from his face I could see every perfect curve and line. He was handsome, more so than I had first believed. Everything about him was sharp, from the length of his nose and the protruding of his jawline. His face had been carved from the dagger of the gods.

No. He was a god. In every sense as power curled from his tall, broad body in undulant waves.

"Do *you* want this?" I asked, unable to bear the tense silence as Faenir gathered himself.

"In every possible capacity you could imagine."

"Then have me," I breathed, shrugging off the new jacket the tailors had made for me until it slipped freely from my shoulders and fell to the floor. "Do with me as you wish. I give myself to you, body and all."

"Oh, darling," Faenir groaned. "You cannot imagine how long I have waited to hear that."

Without taking my eyes off him I lifted a finger to pull the dark cords of my tunic.

"No." Faenir put a hand on mine to stop me. "Allow me."

A shiver spread up my spine. I lowered my hand to my side and gave Faenir the control to undress me. He did so with careful hands. Faenir treated me as though I was made of glass. However, all I wished was for him to shatter me.

Patience, his eyes commanded me. The shattering would come.

"Arms up," Faenir demanded.

I listened, raising my arms as he lifted the tunic over my head. His knuckles grazed my stomach; my slight muscles rippled in reaction. I was surprised when he turned his back and walked towards the chest of dark oak drawers. He folded my tunic, placed it carefully upon the chest's sideboard and then turned back to me.

"I do not wish to rush this," he said from a distance.

I stepped forward desperately. "Do you wish to torture me then?"

"Perhaps."

I swallowed hard.

Faenir leaned back upon the chest of drawers. The shadows around him seemed to twist and snake. "Now let me watch you take your trousers off."

My hands fumbled for the belt in haste. The pouch with the glass vials knocked against my hip as I carefully discarded it atop the rumpled jacket that waited on the floor.

"Slower."

I glowered at him. "Give me one good reason to."

"I have waited many years, I can wait a few more seconds."

My tongue spread out and traced my lower lip before sucking it in and nibbling upon it. It was a test for my hands not to shake as I popped the button of my trousers. My fingers were numb as I worked on unbuttoning the final two golden clasps. My trousers fell at my feet and I stepped free of them.

"Oh my, Arlo," Faenir said, pushing from the chest and walking back towards me. "Look at you."

"I do not want you to look. I want you to touch me."

"Is that so?" He closed in on me and brushed both of

his hands across my abdomen. Faenir marvelled at the shivering bumps that appeared across my skin in the wake of his touch. For a man who held such power, it was as though he had only just discovered it. His gilded eyes lit from within, impressed that he could cause such a reaction.

"Take my clothes off," Faenir commanded. "Would you do that for me?"

He asked as though I had the choice to refuse. That would never happen.

I did not take my time to remove the clothes from Faenir's body. My hands fumbled pathetically as I tore them free. He was amused by my manner, lips practically glistening with desire as he bit down on them. As his tunic ripped, tearing at the seams from my hard desperation, he lowered his face to mine and kissed me. I was blinded by his mouth and taste, running my hands over the stone-like muscles that had hid beneath his clothes. I wished to pull away and admire his build, but in the same breath, I did not want to stop feeling his mouth upon mine.

I could not understand how long we kissed for. By the time we pulled apart we were both breathless, my lips sensitive to the touch. Even Faenir's mouth blossomed with red as though sore, but it did not bother him.

My focus moved from his handsome, serious expression to the trousers that still hung from his hips, before shifting back to his face. Staring at him deep in his eyes I lowered myself to my knees. I allowed my hands to trail down the hills of his broad chest to his stomach until they passed from skin to material. My fingers curled into the waistband and pulled it down enough to see the lines that pointed towards the shadowing of coarse dark hair.

Faenir's breathing became laboured, shuddering with each exhale as he watched me unbutton the trousers and tug them downward. I was already aware of the hard mound that rested beneath it. My hand moved over it and my chest warmed. I could not wait another moment to see him in his full, exposed glory.

Yanking the trousers down, his cock fell free, mere inches from my face. My own throbbed within the under-shorts that Faenir had left on me. He, however, did not wear any.

"What is the matter, my darling?" Faenir spoke as he looked down at me with a knowing smile upon his face. "Is there a problem?"

"No," I said, unable to take my attention from the length of his thick, hard cock. "Far from it."

Faenir had controlled every moment until now. But, as I wrapped my fingers around his cock and felt its warmth pool in my palm, the power was handed over to me. No matter how commanding his aura was, up until this moment he soon melted into my touch in a murmuring of pleased groans.

I leaned in close to the pink curve of his tip, mesmerised by the thickness. Tom had been well endowed. But this... This was beyond anything I had seen, held or taken before. My mouth watered at the fact.

"I am going to make up for all your years of wondering," I said, lips brushing against the wet tip. It glistened with his own excitement, flinching in my hand as though it had a mind of its own. "Let us see just how long you can last."

"My darling..." Faenir's voice dissipated into a long,

pleased sigh as I wrapped my lips over him and sucked the head of his cock as though it was a freshly picked cherry.

His taste laced across my tongue as it worked around and around the curves of his tip. My jaw ached within moments but that did not deter me. I started slow, moving up and down his shaft with a quickening pace. There was no fitting it all in, not with this position; the angle was all wrong. I longed to lie him down upon the bed that waited patiently at the other side of the room. There would be more possibilities there... but that would have to wait.

Faenir's groans intensified as my hand joined in. I pulled free from his cock with a pop of my mouth and looked up at him as I licked my palm. He didn't utter a word as he watched my lips retake him, until my wet fingers gripped his cock; he released a swear that made the shadows of the room tremble.

"I forbid you to stop."

"As you wish," I said, words muffled by the mouthful of flesh I held within it. "My lord."

I sucked Faenir until his strong demeanour crumbled; his knees shook, and hands gripped hungrily at the back of my head. Before now I had always done everything I could not to perform for another in such a way. I had found the lack of my own pleasuring dull. This was different. My own cock throbbed with anticipated excitement as I worked away at the elven prince. I knew this was not the end, even as his tip leaked sticky sweetness that coated my tongue, Faenir still held onto control with confidence.

I hardly registered the ache in my knees when Faenir tugged back at my hair and guided me to stand up. Not caring for the spittle that painted my lips and dampened my chin, he dove in for a kiss that burned with passion.

"I was not finished," I said, words smudged across his mouth.

"We." Faenir bent his knees and wrapped his strong hands at the curve beneath my ass. With an effortless jolt he picked me up from the ground; my legs snapped around his waist to keep myself from falling. "Are far from finished."

He paraded across the chamber room with his fingers gripping into the skin of my ass, his hardened, wet cock slapping into me with each measured step the only sound in the room. "Do you wish to know what I am to do next?"

My chest warmed. Heat rose into my cheeks, making my mouth more sodden than I believed possible. I slipped a finger over his red-stained lips to silence him. "Do not spoil the surprise. Show me instead, Your Highness."

He lowered us to the bed until the gentle embrace of silken sheets tickled across my bare skin. "What is with the sudden use of titles? Do you mean to mock me?"

I grinned, turning my head so Faenir could dive into my neck. His lips and teeth tormented me as I spluttered out a reply. "It is a title you deserve."

"How so?" he encouraged, pulling away from my neck as though he came up from the deepest belly of water for air.

"Only a prince is worthy of my body. Take me, Faenir. Show me what you desire. Use me. Destroy me."

"You, Arlo, my darling, are the only person that I wish to be the making of."

The kiss he gave me was softer than the rest. There was no flickering of tongues or clashing lips. It was like a petal falling through a spring breeze which gently landed upon my skin. The brush of a feather. The song of wind.

The calm before the storm.

"I may need your guidance." Faenir's fingers traced down my thighs, digging into my skin but not going so far to cause me discomfort. "The last thing I wish is for you to be hurt."

"You could never hurt me."

"Do not say that."

I reached up, took his face in both hands and pressed my forehead to his. "Enough of this talk. Fuck me until words become meaningless."

He tore my undershorts off me, hoisted my legs up and jolted me forward. I screeched with thrill. "Then fuck you I shall."

Faenir stood at the edge of the bed. My legs were thrown over his shoulders, my ass pressed up against the length of his spit-covered cock that twitched at my entrance. I could not take my eyes off Faenir as he gathered spit in his mouth and, with undeniable precision, allowed a trail of it to fall from his lips and fall upon his cock.

My breathing was heavy, my heartbeat filling my ears as though to block out everything else.

Faenir spat a total of three times. Once he was done his thumb spread out the lubrication as evenly as he could across the curved tip of his cock. Then his hand ran circles up and down his length which drew long, pleasured groans from him.

He had commanded me to touch myself as he prepared for what was to come. Faenir watched with such interest I felt like he was memorising every part of me, searing every single intimate moment we shared into his mind; I could see his enjoyment as he studied me.

There was a second where I had to remove my own hand in a panic, worried that I was going to explode and end this before it had truly begun; the feeling had come over so quickly as Faenir took some of his spit and traced around the sensitive centre of my ass with two, soft-touched fingers.

"Breathe deep for me," Faenir commanded.

This was his first time having sex yet I felt like the one with no experience. The way he looked at me spoke of an abundance of knowledge. There would come a time when I would find out how he could be so confident in the face of a new challenge. Now was not the moment for a history lesson. This moment was for the *now* and *here*.

Faenir Evelina entered me with ease. A cry of pure, devouring pleasure stole my breath away and filled the room. His shadows responded as though singing and muffling my own cries.

I did not catch a breath until his hips pressed into my ass. He was inside of me. All of him.

"You are so deliciously tight," Faenir called out with a dreamy sigh.

I gripped the pillow behind my head and squeezed. What I truly wished to do was rip it from beneath me and place it over my face so I could release the storm of shouts that twisted within me. Instead, I managed a reply, though breathless and broken, "Fuck. Me. I beg you."

I could see Faenir's mask of control shatter with each thrust of his cock. His lips trembled, his hands gripping harder on my thighs as he moved in and out of me. He would not last as long as he wished, as long as I desired.

But there was always time for another try. And another.

I was faintly aware of the darkening room as Faenir's cloak of shadows covered us and left us in the safe haven of their concealment. I did not understand his powers but assumed that the noises we made would not reach past this boundary.

I let go of my inhibitions, giving into the pleasure that stretched me out as he rode within me, and I expelled each overwhelming orgasm in shouts and groans. Faenir soon joined in, unable to hide his growls behind the biting of his lip for another moment. He could not help himself as his grinding quickened. His hands ran across my body, touching every inch. Beads of sweat rolled down his face like diamonds which fell upon me as he leaned over to kiss me. I could tell he concentrated on prolonging this moment.

It was impossible to know how much time passed as he pounded into me over and over. Seeing his thrill had me creeping closer to the edge of bursting and I feared I would fail to stop it.

"Do not stop," I murmured, lips pulling away from his, my fingers interwoven with his knot of raven hair. "I want to feel you."

"I will break into millions of pieces if you dare speak like that," he replied, licking his lips to taste me and the salt of his own sweat.

"Break, Faenir, shatter within me. I wish for it."

My words were the confirmation he needed.

Faenir threw his head back and roared into the shadows. I joined in, my hand moving vigorously in tune with his pounding. We raced towards the edge of the cliff and threw ourselves off as one.

The final orgasm lasted the longest. As Faenir came within me, slowing his grinding to a gentle lull, I finished upon my stomach, uncaring for the splattering of cum that reached my chest.

Faenir crumpled over me, and I embraced him. I closed my eyes to help the sudden throbbing that filled my skull. We laid like that for a long moment, heavy breathing and strong beats of hearts, a chorus of one.

"Words cannot express..." Faenir began sleepily. "I have never felt anything as divine. In a world I had come to believe was full of terror and hate, for the first time I have seen pleasure."

His heart cantered in his chest, echoing across mine as he laid atop me. I held onto him, fingers tracing stars and circles into the damp skin on his back. "You are more than I could have ever imagined."

"You imagined me before this?" He raised his head, a smile creased across his handsome face.

I squinted at him in earnest. "As a monster."

"Entertain me, Arlo, darling. Am I the monster that everyone titles me as such?"

I nipped at his lip, tugging him in so his lips were pressed dutifully against mine once again. "You are my monster. My destroyer. And I count down the moments until you have the energy to terrorise me again."

Wrapped up in his arms I thought of nothing but his warmth. Not of Auriol, of Tithe, nor of the vial of blood that promised me stolen life. There was no past or future to cloud my mind with worry and anxiety.

There was only now, in his arms, and that felt like peace.

"Forgive me, my darling, if my eyes close." Faenir rolled off me and onto his side. I looked down and exhaled at the sight of his large cock resting across the V-shaped muscles of his hip.

"Rest," I told him, closing my eyes and smiling without effort. "We will need it."

"Indeed," Faenir replied, his hand gripping onto mine and holding it tightly. "We shall."

❧ 21 ❧

The skies of Neveserin were filled with song. From the moment I had woken, encased in Faenir's protective embrace, to now as we followed the parade through the city's main road, my ears rang with it. The sound was similar to tinkling bells, as though they had been strung and draped from building to building. Except there were no bells. Elves sang in harmony, crafting sounds I could not have imagined possible without witnessing it first-hand. It was both beautiful, and *haunting*.

My steps were muffled over the fresh layering of scarlet petals that fell around us. *Magic, it had to be*. For there were no trees to cause such a mess. A light breeze danced among the crowds, whipping hair from shoulders and causing dresses and cloaks to flutter like flags in the wind. The petals drifted among the airstreams as though pulled by a ribbon of unseen power, one clearly conjured by Princess Frila who led the procession, sitting upon a carriage of pure, polished wood.

I knew little of magic and frankly did not care to find out, but I had seen enough to know that Myrinn commanded water, her brother Haldor controlled fire, and Frila claimed the air as though she owned it.

That left the fourth sibling, Gildir. He had not presented himself at the ball days prior. And since knowing of my arrival in the city, he showed a lack of interest. Gildir had ignored me with such ease that he made it seem like I had not stood between Myrinn and Faenir as we prepared for the procession. Now he walked beside his twin's carriage like a silent guard. His element must have been earth from his stubbornness alone.

"It will be over soon," Myrinn said as though reading my mind. She offered me a warm smile and I took it. She held a bouquet of white lilies that dramatically spilled a waterfall of orange-dusted ivory petals. The stems glowed with gold powder that matched what was spread across her eyelids and dusted over the apples of her cheeks. The gold complimented the dress she wore. It was crafted from layers of azure and aqua blues and seemed to float like a body of water with each step she took.

"Even that will not be quick enough," Faenir grumbled from my side. Each time he spoke I could not help but smile. It was pathetic. I was dependent and cursed by what had happened between us the night prior. Even now, dressed in the creased outfit that had been left discarded on the bedroom floor where he'd devoured me, I still felt his touch lingering. On me. *In me.*

Myrinn had not outwardly told me that she knew what had occurred. However, the knowing glance she had given me as she greeted us in the main hall of her home was enough to reveal that she knew. Then the blush of crimson across my cheeks confirmed it.

"What is the rush, cousin? Do you have somewhere else to be with more *pressing* matters to attend?"

Faenir shot Myrinn a terrifying glare. She only giggled in response.

"Be on guard," Faenir said, turning his attention back to the crowd ahead but for no other reason than hiding his embarrassment from view. "The day is far from over."

I stiffened at his comment. No matter how beautiful the day had been thus far, he still believed my life to be at risk while being out in public. In truth he likely wished to lock me away to keep me safe, and the thought of that was not terrible, but hiding away was not an option.

"I will tell you again, and a thousand times after that... I will be fine."

Faenir's jaw clenched, the muscles feathering lightly in his cheeks. "The knife you have hidden in your trousers suggests you are, in fact, as concerned as I am."

I had not realised he had seen me slip it from the silver tray provided at breakfast. My mind went to the vial of vampire blood hidden neatly away in the inner breast pocket of the jacket. Had he seen me move it from the pouch at my belt to the pocket? Having the belt ruining the outfit Myrinn had commissioned for me would have surely drawn unwanted attention.

I resisted the urge to reach for the small lump in the material above my heart. "I am not concerned, simply prepared. If anything happens, I am ready to greet it this time."

"Believe me, darling, no one will get close enough for you to be able to pull it free. You have my word."

Myrinn leaned in and whispered with a voice full of glee. "Perhaps, when you are finished with the knife, you would be so kind as to return it."

I bit down on my lip to stifle a grin. "You have my word, Myrinn."

I walked until my legs ached, winding up through the city as though climbing mountains in zigzagging lines. Faenir nor Myrinn showed any effort or exhaustion, whereas I could have fallen to the floor and given up.

By the time we finally slowed to a stop before the grand construction of timber and stone that overshadowed the parade before us, I finally found out the true meaning of relief.

I glanced over my shoulder and admired the thunderous crowd of elegantly dressed elves who had flooded in behind us as we had passed them; it seemed the entire city was here. As I swept my attention over the crowd, I was suddenly aware of just how many of them looked to me and Faenir. Anticipation for our presence was seemingly the most exciting part of the day instead of the pending Joining Ceremony that would soon begin.

The crowd fell to their knees in a bow. It happened in a wave of movement that took my breath away. I almost believed it was in reaction to me, but that misplaced thought quickly dwindled when I turned back around to see the true reason for the display of respect.

Before the door of the impressive construction stood two figures, standing high above us. My heart skipped a beat at the sight of Haldor whose arm was outstretched, aiding the hunched women at his side. Queen Claria was held up by Haldor as though her own minimal weight was too much for her age to bear. Yet no matter how frail and ancient she looked, her gaze screamed with power and authority as she swept it over the city.

Myrinn cleared her throat, which should have been a subtle sound, except the silence around us made it sound monstrous. I looked to my side to find empty space. She, like the rest of the city, was kneeling. Her eyes were wide in a signal as she watched my own horror bloom.

I realised that Faenir and I were the only ones left standing. It did not go unnoticed.

Claria's wrinkled face pinched into an undeniable scowl before she was blocked by the crowd who stood tall once again and erupted in cheers.

"If today had the chance of going well, then I think we have just spoiled it," I spoke to Faenir softly, whose gaze seemed to be lost to a spot in the distance.

He blinked, snapping out of his trance, then turned his full attention to me; I almost buckled under the weight of it. "Respect should be earned," he replied. "Not granted because of the metal placed upon your head."

There was a storm that passed behind his narrowed eyes. His reaction unsettled me more so than Claria's. "What is wrong?"

"All of this," Faenir answered. "I will be content when we can leave this city and return home." He reached out and plucked a crimson petal which had fallen upon my shoulder. I released a hardened sigh as he touched me even only for a brief moment.

"You always seem to be in a rush," I said, watching him pinch the petal between his fingers. It wilted and died, turning brown and falling to the ground at his feet.

"I wonder why."

"You do not deny it?"

Myrinn cleared her throat again, but it was no more than white noise as I focused on the elven prince. He leaned in, both of us hearing the collective inhale of the crowd who watched us. Faenir hesitated as though remembering how exposed we were. He almost pulled away before I scolded him.

"Don't you dare," I said, eyes narrowing. "Touch me. Let them see... even if the reason is that Claria will hate it. Do it."

His eyes flicked in the direction of the Queen as though concerned what she may do if she saw. Then that emotion dissipated within a breath. Faenir's hand lifted to my chin, took it within his thumb and finger and guided my face to his. The kiss was soft and far different to those he had laid upon me the night prior, yet the symbol was clear enough. The crowd had seen that I, unlike the petal he had taken from my shoulder, was left living and well.

I understood their collective shock. Such a simple, mundane act had made the people of Neveserin see Faenir in a new light, different to the picture Queen Claria had painted him as.

"Is that better?" Faenir asked.

"Much," I replied.

Myrinn's hand found my shoulder and Faenir shot her a look that had my knees quivering. She removed her hand almost immediately, but her voice was still firm and guiding. "Your presence will displease grandmother greatly, let our tardiness not contribute to her mood."

For the entire length of the long and painfully drawn-out ceremony, Haldor watched me like a hawk studying a mouse. I tried not to reveal just how much his stare caused me discomfort, or how it reminded me of the underlying threat he gave me during the ball... and what happened after.

My legs became numb from standing as Claria slowly wrapped golden cords around Frila and her human's arms. It was laborious to watch and more so to hear the calling of pleased sighs and comments from those around us.

All the while he watched me. I wished to either escape from Haldor's line of sight or scream threats at him to stop looking.

Haldor had spent more time staring at me instead of paying attention to his human Claim, Samantha. She noticed, grimacing at his lack of interest. I could tell from each perfectly curled strand of sun-bleached hair to the fitting dress of the deepest ruby that Samantha had tried everything to physically capture her elf's attention.

And, for my sake, I wished it had worked.

I had fought myself not to tell Faenir for fear of what he would do. Myrinn also didn't notice as she watched the Joining with tearful eyes.

Did I recognise disappointment from Haldor as it creased the corner of his lips and kept his frown rooted upon his face? Or was I reaching for a reality that did not exist? Allowing my anxiety to clamp its claws into me and conjure stories. Perhaps it was never Haldor's doing in the first place. The inquisition had not listed him as a suspect before Queen Claria had closed it. Regardless, his stabbing interest unnerved me.

Princess Frila and her human Claim, Kai, had not been pronounced Joined mates for a few moments before Faenir stood up and offered me a hand. "Care to take a walk with me?"

"Sit down," Myrinn hissed. "It is not over."

"Unfortunately for you, it is not. Arlo, may we take leave?"

I reached up, not caring for the grumbling of annoyance from the guests who sat nearest to us. Due to their trepidation of Faenir's proximity, the row to his side and those closest to both the front and back had been left empty. It made slipping out of the bustling chamber easier.

"Go then," Myrinn whispered, shooing us away with a flick of her hands. "It is not my wrath you will face." Her soft gaze flickered to Faenir who waited with silent patience. "Do not dare disappear back to *my* home. We have the rest of the evening to survive first. Together."

I smiled apologetically for leaving but felt a great relief to be finally taken out of Haldor's line of sight.

"Save me a glass of something strong," I muttered to her.

Myrinn nodded, pressing a finger to her lips and replied quietly, "You will regret saying that to me."

Faenir pulled me away before I could say anything more.

"Dare I ask where you are taking me?" I focused on not tripping over my footing as we moved through the crowd with haste. It parted as Faenir closed in, elves practically throwing themselves from his path.

"I have sat through that entire service without so much as a moan," Faenir grunted, keeping his gaze focused on the path ahead. "I believe I deserve a treat for my patience and good behaviour."

My cheeks warmed and I suddenly felt aware of every set of eyes and ears that seemed focused on us. Far in the background I could still hear the grumbling chatter from Queen Claria who'd begun untying cords from around Frila and Kai's arms.

Faenir guided us before the grand door of the chamber. On quick feet and pulled by his persistent strength, we made it out into an empty hallway when he stopped just out of the sight of those within the room.

"I cannot wait another moment," Faenir groaned, taking my jaw in his hand. His fingers gripped in desperation and his presence forced me steps backwards until the cold, solid press of a wall met my spine.

I gasped, writhing beneath his touch as my body reacted to our closeness. "Is this all you wanted from me?"

His lack of patience thrilled me. I could see my reflection in his wide, unblinking eyes and the smirk he had conjured; it was sly and all-knowing.

"I despise everything about today. How dare such a self-absorbed event eat into the time in which I could be touching you. The concentration it has taken not to lay you on the pew and take you right there... for all to see." Faenir had to stop to control his breathing. "I want you."

"Why didn't you?" I asked, heart beating heavily in my chest. "Take me, that is? Do not mistake me... I would not care if it was put on display for the entire world to see."

After last night, it was true.

I suddenly felt suffocated by my clothes. I wished to rip them free from my skin until only Faenir's hands could warm me.

"Myrinn wishes for me to make an impression on the people of Evelina. Tearing your clothes off with my teeth and fucking you before them all, I am confident, was not what she had in mind."

I looked around, pouting as his fingers gripped tighter into my jaw. "We are all alone now. No one to see us."

His brows lifted, full lips wetting beneath his tongue. "Tell me you want me."

I leaned in, pulling against his hold until my lips brushed over his. "Faenir, I do not waste time on wants. Only needs. And I *need* you."

As the crowd within the chamber hall erupted in cheers of glee, I exploded in moans of pure gratification. Faenir had twisted me until my cheek was pressed against the stone wall. With the doors still open wide at our side, he called upon his shadows to provide us shelter, especially as the crowd suddenly flooded out in a wave.

Hidden away in our pocket of darkness, none of the guests noticed us as they left the Joining. Not as Faenir, with frantic hands, pulled my trousers down until they laid around my ankles; or as he retrieved his hard cock from the band of his breeches and wet it with the strings of spit from his mouth.

Faenir fucked me before them and not a single one noticed.

"Scream for me," he commanded. "I promise they will not hear a single sound."

Sex with him last night had been beautiful and connective. This made me feel giddy as he ground within me, each thrust hard and enthusiastic as the one before.

I moaned within the blanket of darkness as he pounded me from behind with long, fulfilling strokes. I reached back for him, gripping awkwardly at his jacket, his hair, anything to keep a grasp on reality and not give into the overwhelming wave of pleasure that wished to steal me away.

Bodies of unaware elves flooded around us, outlines blurred as though looking through a murky window. They laughed and spoke highly of the ceremony. Some had Faenir's name lurking upon their lips; I could not hear what they said over my own moaning and Faenir's hefty panting.

I almost broke away when Myrinn moved into the hall, deep in conversation with Haldor who looked utterly displeased. I would have lingered on their hushed words and ruined the mood if Faenir had not pulled himself free of me, turned me to face him, and lifted me from the ground until my back was pressed to the wall and my legs were wrapped around his waist.

"Focus on me," he demanded. "Not them. *Me*."

"Faen—" His cock found its way into me in this new position and my words turned to an exhaled breath. My head clashed upon the stone wall with a thud as I lost myself to the way his cock stretched and filled me. Gone was my concern for Haldor. Of anything.

There was only us, lost, far away from prying eyes.

"You are so beautiful," Faenir said as his eyes rolled into the back of his head.

I wrapped my arms around him, fingers tangling in waves of dark hair. "I forbid you to stop."

"Oh," he groaned, pounding harder each time he pulled his cock free of me. "Arlo, you feel incredible. Tight and welcoming, I would slay a thousand stars to never forget this."

My skin felt sticky beneath my jacket and tunic. I was aware that my hair was plastered across my forehead as I exerted myself with little effort. I, like Faenir, would have wished for this to continue.

It was when our lips met, and our tongues joined in with the dance we were entrapped in that I felt Faenir rush to his finish. As he slowed, burying his face in my neck in a string of moans as he came, I felt satisfied without the need to pleasure myself. My legs gripped him tighter, my fingers pulling on the strands of his dark hair until he peeled free of my skin.

"Do you feel satisfied now?" I asked, noticing how my voice echoed within the cloaking of his shadows.

Faenir pinched his eyes closed and smiled until every line and crease of his usual mask faded away. Pulling himself free from me, Faenir lowered me back to my feet and placed a feather soft kiss upon my forehead. "For now. But I cannot promise I will not steal you away again from the rest of the Joining. I starve for you in ways I never knew possible."

"You are a demon," I said through narrowed eyes. Faenir surveyed me as I pulled up my trousers and buttoned them back up at the waist. "But I admit that even I wish to stay hidden with you. Give me a good reason not to leave like you wished instead of facing the day again."

As the joy of his sex faded and the sounds of the bustling crowds around us peaked through the shadows, I was reminded of what waited. Claria. Haldor. Everything here and far beyond Neveserin.

Faenir took my face in his hands; they felt damp, but I did not care. His touch alone was soothing from the haunting reality that crept back into the front of my mind.

"Believe me, my darling, I wish nothing more than to take you back to Haxton and keep you all to myself. Do not tempt me for I am a weak man and will do it for you."

Remembering Myrinn's story from last night helped me hold my chin high. "No. We face them all together. Myrinn wishes for the people of this realm to see you through eyes no longer glazed with fear. We do not leave until they see you as I do."

Faenir released my face and stood tall. The shadows around us crept inward like smoke dispersing after a candle had been blown out. Soon enough the crowd beyond audibly gasped at our sudden reappearance. I watched as some stumbled back, while others looked at the way our hands held one another and did not retreat with the fear I would have expected.

I was helping them *see* Faenir compared to what his grandmother had made them believe he was.

"Great ceremony," I said softly, forcing a smile at the huddle of elves closest to us. "We do apologise for our sudden... interruption, don't we, Faenir?" I gripped his arm and held him close.

It took a moment for him to force a response as he worked out what I was doing. "Yes. Splendid Joining indeed." He focused on me, and the world faded away once again. "I believe we should get a drink to celebrate dear Frila's special day. I cannot speak on your behalf, darling, but I have built up a rather desperate thirst..."

He winked and I melted.

Faenir gripped my hand and walked through the crowds with focus and poise. Until now I had seen him as he presented himself, different and unwanted in a crowd. But the way he guided me through the cramped hallways of the grand castle made it seem as though he owned it. He was its King and he practically oozed with confidence that only deserved a crown.

Doors were opened for him without the need to ask. People stepped out of the way, not from fear of his touch, but from respect, respect simply earned from his aura.

"We must find Myrinn before she begins to form stories that we have stolen one another and left the city. I would not want to offend our host and I admit, I am beginning to enjoy Myrinn's company. Just do not tell her."

I smiled at his comment, admiring Faenir from his side as we entered a room overwhelmed with the sweet kiss of roses which bloomed across vines that wrapped around pillars of white, carved stone.

"And by the looks of it she is not pleased. Whatever are we going to tell her?"

I locked eyes with Myrinn as Faenir nodded in her direction. She turned from her conversation and beamed at us both, sweeping her arms in greeting, and Faenir's concern fell away.

Before I could call for her, a figure stepped in our line of sight. Someone familiar shouted her name in a tone filled with condemnation. I locked eyes with the person to see the human, Samantha. At first there was nothing strange about her presence despite Haldor not being by her side. She strangled the stem of a lipstick-stained wine glass which seemed to shake slightly.

"Are you lost?" Faenir asked with amusement lightening his voice.

She did not reply. Samantha looked around with wide

eyes and trembling lips. A frown turned her beautiful face into a grimace that looked odd upon such a beautiful face.

I pulled my hand free from Faenir and stepped towards her. Her blue eyes seemed darker than they had before, the pink coating of her lips smudged from the wine glass. "Something is wrong..."

Samantha thrashed out before I had the chance to do anything. I was frozen in shock as the glass she carried was lifted skyward. She smashed it into her skull. Glass shattered and wine splashed, staining her hair red.

Someone shouted her name again; it was Haldor, pushing through the swelling crowd behind her. But before he could reach her, Samantha lunged, face pulled into a silent scream, with the jagged remains of her glass outstretched for me.

FAENIR

I was detached from reality. *Distracted.* Still, as Arlo and I glided on a cloud of pure divinity, I recognised the tight welcoming embrace across my cock which lay resting within the confines of my trousers. The memory of his touch was haunting. It invaded my mind from the night prior until now as we walked into the swell of people who had no sense of what we had done in the shadows.

Arlo's sex made me drunk. Focusing on anything but keeping that feral part of me under control was almost impossible. It was why I had become slow, why I did not act with haste as the human attacked. My body was here, but my mind elsewhere.

Everything happened quickly.

Arlo fell with the human girl, whose name I could not recall. His hand was torn from my own as her weight stole him from me. The room burned with the terrified screams of elves. Many ran, others stayed and watched as the two bodies tussled upon the floor like bickering children. But fighting children usually didn't lead to smashed glass or blood, deep scarlet that stained my vision.

I snapped, breaking free of my thoughts and throwing myself towards them.

"Faenir," Myrinn cried out. She was somewhere at my side. I cared little to check. "They are watching."

The very air before me thickened with moisture. My nose crashed into the wall that had not been there moments before, encasing me in a cage. I slammed my fists against Myrinn's damp power. It did not shatter, yet that did not deter me; not for a moment did I give up. My heart thundered within my chest, and I felt as though it would rupture through my bones, my flesh.

Beyond my watery prison Myrinn threw her hands out towards the scene. Liquid from the glasses upon tables and in hands lifted and gathered within the air. Like the wall before me, she crafted something new, a spike of glistening, sharpened ice that hung suspended; within a blink it shot towards Samantha.

Light exploded. Heat flared. I did not flinch as the warmth collided with Myrinn's wall of power. Water hissed as fire kissed across it. Haldor had met his sister's attack with a wave of his own magic. The spear melted upon impact, leaving a puddle of boiling liquid upon the floor.

"Enough!" Called a voice. Grandmother.

I continued pounding my fists, recognising the roar within my ears as my own which erupted from my open mouth.

"Free me!" I shouted. "Myrinn, I swear..."

Haldor ran towards Arlo, his face pinched in honest and terrifying disbelief. Myrinn didn't have the chance to attack again as Haldor tore his Claim from atop Arlo and threw her across the room. Her head cracked into a pillar with a resounding clap.

Beneath my fury, the sound pleased me.

My anger quickly turned to desperation as I was trapped, unable to do anything but watch. All the while I begged to hear Arlo, to know that he was okay. I fixated on the glow of life that haloed his outline and waited for it to dull with death. To my relief, his aura burned strong, brighter than I imagined stars would be if they were plucked from the sky and held carefully on one's palm.

Myrinn withdrew her power, and I could have fallen to my knees as the wall around me dissipated. Never had I felt so weak before. This time, no one stopped me from running towards Arlo as he lay immobilised on the ground amongst the smatterings of glass. And blood.

Blood.

"Darling." My voice cracked as I knelt beside him.

Arlo's eyes were wide with horror, his skin as pale as snow. He shook violently, his hands reaching towards his chest. It took little searching to find what had caused the reaction. Above his heart, clothes glittering with glass, was the spreading puddle of red; it seeped through the dark material of his ruined jacket, staining his white tunic beneath to a wet scarlet.

"Arlo." Myrinn threw herself to his side and reached out for him. Before her fingers could come near enough to touch, I broke into more pieces than the glass upon him.

"Do. Not. Touch. Him." Each word came out harsher than the one before. "GET AWAY FROM HIM."

The room darkened.

I could not think straight as the one thing I had held so dear began slipping through my fingers like sand. Arlo was hurt. How much so I did not yet know. And my mind dared to torture me with the idea of losing him. It was all that occupied my thoughts.

"I wish to help," Myrinn pleaded, trying again to reach out.

"Did you not hear me!?" Shadows curled between us. I cared little for the hurt that pinched at Myrinn's face. She had kept me from him. *I could have... I could...*

Cold, trembling hands reached up and traced softly across the skin of my jaw. "Faenir... calm yourself down."

Myrinn broke into a sob as she looked down at the boy beneath us. I did the same, unable to truly believe that his touch was real.

"I am okay," Arlo forced out. I did not believe him, but those three words gathered the broken parts of my soul and did wonders to stitch them together again.

"Oh, my darling." My head fell upon his stomach, and I allowed myself to melt into him. "I thought I had lost you."

Bloodied hands gathered in my hair and held on tight. I feared if I looked up the entire chamber would see tears forming in my eyes. They could not see. It was a weakness that I did not desire having attached to my name.

"Arlo has lost a lot of blood," Myrinn recounted aloud as though her thoughts had no limit. She looked up from Arlo, cheeks flushed as she cried out to the watching crowd, "Someone, call for a healer, now!"

A shadow passed across us; in my muddled thoughts I believed it was one of my own, until *it* spoke. "I have had one sent for."

I ripped my head from Arlo's stomach and looked up to see Haldor. Sudden, devouring anger had me standing.

No matter the death my touch could cause him, Haldor did not step back.

"I did not know," Haldor said quickly, grimacing as his eyes flicked down towards Arlo for a moment. "Faenir, I promise you; this has nothing to do with me."

I did not know what to believe. Thinking of anything but Arlo took strength, and I was void of it. In my eyes every person here was responsible. I should never have agreed to come. It was a mistake. One of my gravest.

"Look at me," said the broken, crackling voice beneath me. Arlo tried to sit himself up. Seeing the steely resolve across his face as he grimaced in pain made my knees week. "I am fine," he lied. "It's just a small scratch."

"A scratch would not cause such a spill of blood," Myrinn replied, her voice soft as she echoed my thoughts.

I could barely stand to look at Arlo, not as my mind began pointing the blame back at myself. Seeing him in such a way felt as though glass had punctured *my* chest over and over. I wished for nothing but to steal him into my arms and return to Haxton.

We would never leave again.

Unable to look at Arlo, I focused my fury upon the human girl instead. Her body was unconscious across the side of the room, the glow of life still prevalent around her. The last one who tried to harm Arlo had died before I could question him. This time would be different.

Arlo's blood covered hand reached for Myrinn and pulled her down towards him. Jealousy flared within me, but their closeness lasted only a moment.

"He wishes for me to take him to the healer." Myrinn was already helping Arlo from the floor. Her expression had altered, hardening into a mask to hide something beneath. It was something I was all too familiar with. *Secrets.*

"Absolutely not," I growled, causing those who watched from the outskirts of the room to step back.

"Faenir, Myrinn." Queen Claria cut through the crowd, the tear-streaked face of Frila racing behind. Gildir followed with a hand upon his sword. *Little too late for weapons now.* "I demand an explanation. *Now.*"

"Samantha." Haldor put himself between us, his body acting as a shield, not that I required it. For the first time I felt no fear looking upon my grandmother; there was no room for such a feeling when only anger dwelled within me. "My human attacked him. I saw it—"

"You've ruined my day!" Frila screamed, stamping her feet like a child. "My Joining has been marked by your presence and now you caused this."

"Swallow your tongue, girl," Myrinn snapped, silencing Frila from making another comment that would encourage me to truly ruin her event.

Claria could not hide her half smile. "*He* still lives I see."

"Dissatisfied?" I asked.

Haldor raised a hand to stop me from saying, or doing, anything else.

"It would seem your presence is a bad omen, cousin." It was Gildir's turn to add in his opinion. All the while their words did not affect me; those weapons dulled years ago.

Claria ignored my comment, instead pinning her attention to Myrinn. "Take the boy to a healer and see that he is fit and well. Haldor, gather your mate and the rest of you will meet us in the council hall. The Joining is over."

With the aid of Gildir's arm for support, Claria turned to face the crowd who still watched. "Thank you," she forced a smile that did little but accentuate the deep wrinkles across her displeasing face, "for coming."

Arlo was draped across Myrinn's shoulder. His gaze was unfocused, pinned to something unimportant on the floor as he was lost and confused.

"He will be fine," Myrinn said softly as though her words were only meant for me.

Arlo looked up at me with those mesmerising eyes, one as blue as the skies, the other richer than the earth itself. His lips trembled as they tugged upward at the corners. He winced but still forced the grin nonetheless; it never met his eyes.

"Deal with this," Arlo commanded me. "Find answers. Then come to me."

I swallowed hard, unable to refuse him. If Arlo had told me to kill every person within Evelina in his honour, I would have done it here and now.

No one uttered a word to me as I watched Myrinn escort Arlo from the room. They were not alone as the silver-garbed guards of the Queen's assembly gathered around them in a cloak of metal and steel.

Only when they had left did I turn back on my family.

"When I find out who is behind these attacks, I will take pleasure in causing you terrible pain. Do not think I will let you die quickly. You will suffer just as you have made me suffer."

I looked to Haldor who tugged his human from the floor. She was waking now, moaning as though waking from a night of heavy drinking. Gildir stood guard, unease of the events keeping his usual, misplaced humour silent.

Frila was encased in her human's arms as he wasted his breath trying to console her.

"Hold your threats," Queen Claria said coldly, looking at me with an expression she had not granted me before. "It is unbecoming of a prince."

"Do not mistake me, Claria," I replied, hissing through my teeth to stop myself from screaming. "My words are bond. It is a promise, not a threat. Remember that."

❧ 22 ❧

I held out the broken shards of blood-coated glass, not the shards that littered my jacket, but the smatterings of it that filled the pocket at my chest. There was no need to care about nicking my fingers on glass as I had fished them out of the pocket to show her. Pain was not a luxury I held.

Myrinn had to steady my hand by holding my wrist. It shook so violently that I could have dropped the pieces and let them scatter across the floor. It wouldn't have mattered if I had.

Nothing mattered anymore.

"Help me understand," she pleaded, eyes wide, as though blinking would cause her to miss what I had to say.

It had taken great persuading for me to convince Myrinn to dismiss the healers. She refused at first. Of course she had, as she regarded the blood covering my chest. The pleading in my eyes convinced her to do as I wished.

It was not my blood that coated me. If the healers

removed my clothes, they would have found my skin bruised, but not marked. It would have created more questions than answers.

I could have laughed at what happened. Although I had known that the vial of vampire blood shattered upon impact with Samantha's stabbing attack, it still did not feel real. A dream, a bad one, but surely this was not my reality.

Even as I had whispered into Myrinn's ear, pleading that she kept Faenir away, I still did not fully grasp that I was finally being forced to tell my truth. To face it head on.

When Queen Claria requested that Myrinn be the one to take me to the healers, I almost believed she could read my mind. For a moment, I liked her, because she kept Faenir from coming here and finding out my deadly secret.

I was not prepared for him to find out. Not this way, at least.

"The blood is not mine." My voice was firm. Tears dribbled down my cheeks.

Myrinn tried to reach for my jacket as though to prove me wrong herself by revealing a wound beneath it. She would have found nothing. "You are in shock, Arlo," Myrinn fussed, trying to push me back upon the bed. "It was silly for me to send the healers away... Faenir would kill me if he knew."

"He can't find out," I said, fisting the glass in my hands; every fragment bit into my palm, but I did not care.

Myrinn gasped in response.

"Listen to me," I cried. "Please."

"Okay," Myrinn said, holding her hands up in surrender. "I am listening."

It took me a moment to catch my breath.

"The blood belongs to a vampire. I kept it in a glass vial for the single need to drink it when the time was required. That caused this. It... broke."

The world spun for a moment, as though someone had yanked it harshly out from beneath me.

I allowed my words to settle over her. Myrinn's face twisted from emotion to emotion. Disbelief to horror. Shock to disgust. The expression she settled on turned her mouth into a small O-shape and colour drained from her cheeks.

One word escaped above the rest. "Why?"

"It kept me alive. Without the blood, I will die."

Myrinn shook her head, huffing out an exhausted breath as though she had heard enough. "You are not dying, Arlo. This is just..."

"I am dying, and I do not care if you wish to believe me or not because it is true." I waved my fist before her, letting the minor cuts that broken vial had made across my palm deepen and sting. "This was all that was keeping me from falling to the same fucking sickness that killed my parents. Years I have hunted vampires. Drained them of the very thing they desire from us, then using it for my gain. All to stay alive. To ensure I did not leave my sister in our world alone..."

I pinched my eyes closed as my throat constricted. The pressure of my truth was too much to bear. All this time I had held it all in and refused to let anyone know I hid from death.

But death found me and snatched me from my world. He kept me locked away from my family and now I would never return home. I would truly die here. Except it was not only Auriol I felt guilty for leaving behind. Faenir would lose me too.

"Arlo." Myrinn wrapped her arms around me, and I crumbled within them; my face pressed to her shoulder as I opened the floodgates. "I am sorry... I am so sorry."

There were no questions. No prodding and poking to find out more. There was simply Myrinn, and she held me up with caring hands as she embraced my secret as her own.

"You can't tell him, Myrinn," I said through heavy sobs.

"It is not my secret to share. Your truth is safe with me."

She held me as a mother would, swaddling me against her. If I closed my eyes, I could imagine that it was my mum. Years had gone by since I had last felt the support of another in such a way.

"Does your sister know?" Myrinn asked finally.

I retreated from her embrace and tried to sit up on my own. Although my eyes still leaked, my breathing calmed at the mention of Auriol. "No."

Myrinn chewed on her lip as she lost herself in thought. "How long have you sustained yourself with vampire blood? Our kind only know of the creatures from what we have learned by watching... I cannot imagine how something derived from the undead can keep you alive."

"Before my father died, he had told me a story that was brought to Tithe by one of its founders. An old woman brought tales about vampire blood and its benefits. No one believed her. They condemned her as a powerless witch. No one wished to listen to someone crazed enough to suggest such a thing. When my father had told me this tale, I had dismissed it just like the old patrons of Tithe had... but I became desperate after he passed when I showed symptoms of the same disease that took them both. I had promised them to never leave Auriol. She was still so young and when the spots of blood smudged across my hand as I coughed, I knew what it meant. I couldn't leave her..."

Myrinn placed a hand on my knee to remind me she was here with me. Her touch grounded me from the overwhelming pull of my story, one I never imagined telling.

"Desperate people are forced to do desperate things. Father's story lingered with me. My options were die trying to fix myself or die anyway. I fought."

"You went hunting for death, hoping to find life."

Hearing it aloud broke me. I nodded, confirming what Myrinn had to say as truth.

"My first kill was the hardest. I was sloppy and unprepared. I spent most of my energy breaking out beneath the wall your Queen created. The vampire was practically waiting for me on the other side. I was badly injured by the time I had hacked the creature to death. I drank my fill that night. Fresh wounds healed, and the sickness retreated like a scorned mutt. I never stopped going after that."

Myrinn listened in stunned silence, not once interrupting me as I told my story. Only when I finished speaking did she take a hulking breath in and spoke. "The wall should be impassable. Queen Claria erected it around Tithe to protect your kind from being picked off by the very creatures you have hunted. If you have been able to break free without the Watchers or Claria noticing a tear in her power, then there is no saying how truly weakened she is becoming." Myrinn took my hands into hers and squeezed. "Do you think the blood that you have been taking is what prevents Faenir's touch from harming you?"

I had not thought of it but hearing her ask it made sense. "We will soon find out, I suppose. When the dregs of the last vial I took wear off, my body will fall back into death's grip. Perhaps Faenir will kill me before the sickness in my body finally has its chance to catch up."

Concern spilled across Myrinn's bright gaze. It was hard to watch the pain deepen the lines at the corners of her eyes and mouth. "You must tell him."

"No," I snapped, urgency clear in my tone and wide eyes. "He can't know."

"Why?"

"Because he will lose the only thing that he has ever wanted. That would break him... I cannot bear the thought of watching him know he is losing me... selfishly I cannot handle that. I have been there before with my parents, trapped in the grasp of impending doom... there is nothing more destructive."

Myrinn winced as she replied, "So you would rather he found out when the inevitable occurs? At least prepare him, Arlo. For the sake of Evelina."

I could not explain further why I did not wish Faenir to know. Perhaps I couldn't answer because I did not know myself.

"I wish to help him whilst I have the time left."

"What if we can find a solution? I understand you have been driven to extreme measures to stay alive, but our healers are far greater than those in Tithe, with access to magic your realm has been severed from."

A spark of hope curled within me. I feared to recognise it for getting my hopes up would be detrimental. "If I let you try to help, you must promise me that Faenir does not find out."

"Only if you promise to tell him if I fail."

I bit down on the insides of my cheeks until all I could taste was the sharp tang of copper. "If we are going to make a deal, then I have something I will require from you if I die. My sister Auriol... I cannot stand to leave her in this world alone. Promise me you will watch out for her."

Myrinn dropped my gaze, and the hope diminished in a single breath. "If you die before the Joining with Faenir, much like Gale, then your sister will find the grace we have given her will be taken from her. There is nothing I can do to stop it."

Adding this knowledge atop of everything else was too much. I buckled under the weight, falling back into the white-sheeted bed the healers had ushered me into.

"I have failed my parents... Auriol. Myself."

"Arlo, you cannot think like that."

I buried my head in my hands, the light of the room suddenly becoming too much to bear.

"We can fix it," Myrinn added, fingers gripping onto me with urgency. "Together, we will find a solution."

Sighing through my anxiety, I recognised the way my breath trembled. "I have tried to fix it... for once, I understand that is no longer an option for me. I'm broken, Myrinn, with missing parts."

Noise sounded beyond the room; heavy footsteps followed by the thundering of a guttural growl. Faenir. He had found the dismissed healers loitering outside. Even from beyond the door, I could hear his fury; it shook the very walls.

Myrinn stood abruptly. She angled herself before the door, stance wide, as though to stop him herself.

We had run out of time.

I reached forward, bed creaking beneath me. Scooping up a shard of glass, I brought it to my now exposed chest and sliced it downward. Skin split, blood gushed out over my hands. A rush passed over my mind like a cloud. Somewhere in the distance, as the pain registered and unleashed its scream within me, Myrinn had called out my name.

I blinked, seeing through eyes now filled with agony. Myrinn had torn the glass from my hand just as the door kicked open. She held it behind her back.

There was no time for questioning why I had done it to myself. Faenir had to believe the blood he had seen was my own. That Samantha had caused it.

In my haste, I placed faith in the promise that Myrinn's healers could save me, at least from bleeding out on the bed. And if they couldn't... well, I would die soon anyway.

FAENIR

I felt the fibres of the wood beneath my hands. They cracked and splintered, breaking under my grip, yet I could not let go of the chair's armrests for fear of what I would do. I could take my anger out on it instead of the human slumped in the chair in the heart of our circle.

"Speak, human. Exercise your own free will or be forced to answer," Queen Claria croaked from her throne.

I admit Claria forced just enough concern into her voice to make me believe she wished to know the motives of the human. If I had not glowered across the space towards her, I would not have seen her disinterest deepening the wrinkles across her face.

The human's silence persisted; lips sealed shut as though forced by other means. And perhaps they were.

"Samantha," Haldor said, sitting on a grand chair to my side. He leaned forward; amber brows furrowed over his tortured eyes. He did not care for the human, but more for the knowledge of what was to happen next. "Tell me. Be truthful and I promise to keep you from harm."

I would punish Samantha for her crime against Arlo. Haldor knew that, and he grieved the reality even now. If Samantha died, it would remove him from succession, which made one fact clear.

Haldor was not behind the attack.

Part of me wished he was. I longed to unleash myself upon him, an excuse was all it took. But even in the storm that raged within my mind, I understood Haldor would not purposefully forfeit the only grasp he had on the throne.

Someone had ripped it from his hands.

Who? The question filled my head like a parliament of owls.

My eyes fell back upon Claria and the wood beneath my left hand completely caved in. The snap was so sudden that it made the human gasp out of shock. It was the first sound she had made since the attack.

Claria rolled her tired eyes, which enraged me further. Every wasted moment that we waited for this human to tell us why she had done it was another that kept me from Arlo.

I had to keep myself from blinking. The darkness usually provided me peace and relief, but now it only gave room for the vision of his body covered in blood and glass. Urgency forced me to my feet. "I am not partaking in this game. If the human wishes to cower behind her silence, then I will be forced to act accordingly."

Haldor stood abruptly, calling out for me as I paced towards his Claim. "Don't hurt her... Faenir, please. Allow her to tell us."

"Sit down, Haldor," Claria snapped. "Let Faenir be the

one to kill her. That is what he wants... it is what he always wants. Death. Destruction. He cannot restrain himself."

Frila chuckled into her fingers, falling silent as I gave her my full attention. "Stop hiding behind your hands and say something, Frila. Does it please you to know that you will be Queen if Haldor's mate is killed?"

"Beast," she hissed through bared teeth. For such a beautiful creature, her eyes were feral. "Grandmother is right. You ruined my Joining. Bringing your mate here... what did you expect was going to happen?"

Unseen winds gathered around Frila and twisted her white locks into a vortex. Her ivory dress fluttered like strong wings, snapping in the stillness.

My vision narrowed as my fury intensified. Every shadow around the room whispered into my consciousness, pleading for me to call upon them and carry out vengeance, echoing the sentiments of the furthest and darkest parts of my mind.

And I would have acted then if the small, strange voice that had buried into my conscience didn't speak up. *Prove them wrong. Calm.* I recognised the lullaby tones as Arlo, a siren, cutting through my anger and calming me from the inside out.

"We would not have visited if you had not insisted on sending an invitation," I replied smoothly, "Except your words have clarified that it was never you who sent it."

"Why would I ever wish for you to celebrate alongside me?" Frila said, withdrawing her conjured winds as Claria placed a motherly hand on her arm to calm her. "If you believed the invitation was genuine, then you confirm yourself a fool. Your presence is wrong, and I hate it. I hate you. We all do."

"Enough," Haldor snapped, turning his fiery stare upon her. "This is not helping."

"The truth can hurt," Gildir said, a wolfish grin plastered across his face.

I did not care for her revelation, nor was it required to hear it aloud to know what they thought of me. Their disdain had been clear in the looks they gave me, in the way they had shunned and ignored me.

Claria had attempted to murder me as a baby; that alone made their hate abundantly clear.

Frila may have expected her words to hurt me, to stab into my chest and twist inside my blackened heart. It did not. I wouldn't let them have that power over me.

I looked around the room, allowing my eyes to settle on each of them. Frila, who wouldn't meet my eyes, done with acknowledging my existence. Claria, who cared more about putting a gentle hand upon Frila's to calm her. Gildir, who, as always, cared more about his fingernails than anything else around him. And Haldor, who nodded subtly as I stared at him.

"Which one of you wished for me to bring him?" I asked. "We are all together now. Do not be shy."

Not a single one of them spoke up.

"After all these years, do you truly believe I care for the crown you so desperately clamber over one another for? I do not want it. I do not care about it."

Claria spoke up, turning her sharp eyes upon me and covering me in slashes and cuts. If her gaze could kill, it would. "You think it is that simple, boy? This crown." She gestured to the twisting of gold metal and the deepest red rubies buried within it that sat atop her nest of grey hairs. "Does not care for wants. The people of this world have followed tradition and rely on it. You are the eldest born. You have chosen your mate. They will expect you to take this crown from me."

"Then I will tell them. Remove myself from the race I never wished to partake in."

Claria exploded in light. I squinted as her old, hunched figure burst into whites and golds. Power radiated from her. She was a star among us. It lasted only a moment before she fell back to her chair, exhausted.

"Grandmother," Gildir cried out, leaving his chair and moving to the throne's side.

Panting with shaking breaths and all without opening her eyes, Claria raised a hand to stifle Gildir's worry. "I am fine, dear boy. Give me a moment."

He did so, reluctantly, not before giving me a look of pure disgust.

"Faenir," Claria finally managed. The display of power was inspiring, but equally showed how weak she had become. Time had finally caught up with her and I couldn't help but admit that it did not hurt me to think that she would one day perish.

I longed for it.

"Tradition shall not be ignored simply because you so wish for it."

My hands clenched into fists at my sides. "So you mean to kill Arlo? To take the one thing I truly want just to make sure that fucking crown is kept from me?"

"I do not care for your mate enough to kill him. Time will catch up with you, and I am confident in my belief that you shall complete that task yourself."

"Then who is it!?" I shouted, feeling Claria's back-handed threat sting across my cheek. "Who—"

The human spluttered a wet gasp behind me. I turned to look at her and saw how she clung to her neck; her face painted red; the whites of her eyes darkened with veins.

"Stop that, Faenir!" Claria commanded.

I stared at my hands as though they were to blame, but it was not my doing.

Haldor was up, racing across the space and reaching out for her. "Samantha, I have got you!"

"It is not me." No one seemed to listen to me as chaos gripped the room.

The ground rumbled beneath my feet; stone slabs cracked as Gildir threw out his power towards me. "Enough, leave her."

An icy chill spread through my body. I raised my hands up to my sides, trying to prove that I was not the cause of the human's sudden pain. "I am not doing this."

Claria was the only one left sitting as Gildir and Frila raced towards Haldor to help him. That was when the convulsions began. Samantha's eyes bulged in her head. Foam began gathering past her pale lips and dribbled down her chin. No matter how hard Haldor had hold of the girl, she did not stop the violent spasms that had her body rocking in the chair.

It was over in moments.

Samantha's mouth split into a scream, which never made it out. Her head lolled backwards, neck at a terrible angle. Her body finally stilled. The glow of life that surrounded her extinguished in a blink, as though it was a candle's flame devoured by the weakest of winds.

Dead.

Haldor pressed his head into her lap and wept like a child. Frila expelled a cry of horror which was muffled by the chest of her twin, who gathered her into his arms and shielded her face. The only noticeable reaction on Gildir's stoic face was the peak of a single, dark brow.

Claria sat quietly, watching me with eyes overwhelmed with hate. It twisted her face into a mask of disdain that I had taught myself to mimic. It was an expression that I was most familiar with when looking at my grandmother.

"Are you happy now?" she asked.

I ignored her, pacing towards the dead body of the human. "Haldor, I promise it was not me."

He replied into her lap, his words muffled; I could not make a single one out.

"You demon," Frila spat, eyes swollen but lacked the tears I had expected.

I ignored her. Looking down upon the face of Samantha, I expected to feel relief. She had attacked Arlo, and she deserved death. But the feeling did not rear its head. Peering down upon her, I registered the greying of her skin. It seemed my proximity sped up her decaying as though my aura demanded it. For a moment, it surprised me. Being with Arlo and his resistance to my power had numbed me to a point of forgetting what I was capable of.

I had not been the one to kill her.

A strange, overwhelming urge to place a hand upon Haldor's shoulder overtook my mind. I wished to console him, that felt natural to do so. Instead, I turned my attention to the girl's tormented face, how her wide-open eyes made it seem that she looked at something horrific before her death. I studied every detail of her, searching for the cause, all the while repeating that it was not me, over and over, as though I willed myself to believe it.

As they fussed over her stiffening body, I noticed

something fall from the foam upon her chin. A seed. Haldor looked up, heat radiating from his body, as I reached towards her chin. He said nothing to stop me as he also noticed what had captured my attention. I plucked it from the foam, noticing how cold the human was; where the tip of my finger brushed over her skin, it flaked away as though turning to ashes beneath me.

"What is it?" Haldor whispered; his voice as steady as steel.

As I held the seed, it rotted in my hand. I fisted it, nails digging into my palm as my mind whirled with possibilities. "It would have been easier for you to become King," I said to Haldor, ignoring his question. "Believe me when I tell you I did not wish for death, as you may all think. I am sorry for your loss and more so what it means."

He blinked, grimacing as my words settled over him.

I did not stay to hear what he had to say in reply. As the seed turned to liquid in my hand, decaying quickly beneath my touch, I left the room. No one stopped me. I focused on my breathing, wishing to hear Arlo's calming voice in the back of my mind. But it never spoke up over my inner thoughts that thundered and crashed as violent as a storm.

All I desired was to take him far away from this place. To lock him within Haxton to keep him safe. But how could I do that when my presence still threatened to kill him? Even if my touch would not, just him being mine put him in danger. And the seed that was now nothing but rotten ash in my hand held the answers, I was certain of that.

Each step further from my family was another closer to

him. I should never have left his side, even with Myrinn's promise to...

Myrinn. The invitation.

It was her.

Suddenly I was running, dropping the ash from my hand as I raced through the castle towards Arlo.

My shadows gathered behind me until I felt every part of the castle they graced.

Then I found them, slithers of glowing life among the dark.

Two figures. One burning far brighter than the other.

The other dwindling in life.

Arlo.

❧ 23 ❧

Neveserin passed in a blur of ivory-domed buildings and white pillars. Faenir sat beside me in the carriage, facing his window, not once uttering a word. Silence hummed between us so taut that no knife would have been able to cut it.

Even as wheels clambered over the cobbled streets and the hooves of the steeds clattered evenly, I still could hear Faenir's thunderous fury as he had entered the healer's chamber. I winced at the memory, trying to focus on the details in the world outside this moving box, anything to clear what he had said to Myrinn. He had burst through the door in a storm of shadow; never had I seen someone so far gone to rage as I had Faenir. His anger did not calm when he found me bleeding on the bed with the fresh wound I had given myself.

In a gaggle of fear, the healers had raced in behind Faenir for aid. Strapped beneath their hands as they held me to the bed, I could do nothing but watch as Faenir unleashed himself upon Myrinn.

The pain in my chest had choked me, even if I'd longed to scream and tell him to leave her alone, I couldn't. The scene haunted me as we rode out of the elven city. Guilt was my fresh wound, and it pained me more than the healed slash across my chest had.

It was you.

Myrinn had not denied him.

The invite, you sent it. Not Frila.

I did. Two words, that was all she'd spoken. As fingers had pinched at my skin and white clothes soaked up blood, I found it hard to truly understand those two words.

He could have died because of you. Or is that what you want? It would seem all this time you wished to protect him, yet it was you who has put Arlo's life at risk time and time again.

The mask of steel Myrinn erected had come crumbling down. I'd seen her longing to grab Faenir and shake sense into him; it'd burned in her eyes as they filled with tears.

Myrinn had persisted in her case, but Faenir had kept the blame heavy upon her. Heated words were shared, some I did not think I would ever forget, and at the end of it, there was no solution.

Regardless of what happened with Faenir before he found us, and what came after... I never would have believed Myrinn was to blame. In time, he would see sense. Faenir had to.

I had not seen Myrinn since she stormed from the healer's chamber room. She left, carrying my most precious secret in her hands as though it were a butterfly waiting to be released. Or crushed.

My mind was filled with the promise of death. No matter where I looked, what I thought, it all came back to it. I had grown used to the glass vial's presence. Even now, as we flew over bumps in the road, I reached up for the breast pocket to find it flat. Empty.

It was a painful reminder. All of it.

"You were too hard on her." I severed the silence before the dark thoughts devoured me completely. "If you truly believe that Myrinn is behind the attacks, then I have mistaken you for something other than a fool."

Faenir turned from his window and focused on me. I hated the way he looked at me, eyes searching for pain. His eyes had dulled to tones of honey, as though a light had perished within, yet the worst part was the heavy fear that clung to them. Faenir looked at me as I imagined a poor man looked at coin, with honest, sickening desperation. Part of me wished to snap at him, demand that he look away. If he saw me in such a way now, what would happen if he knew the truth?

He can't find out.

I dropped my eyes to my hands, which fidgeted in my lap. Faenir sighed knowingly.

"Even if Myrinn did not force the hands of the human that hurt you, by her forging that invitation she signed the warrant of your life. I cannot forgive her for tricking us into coming."

"Stop convincing yourself of her intentions when you know little as to what they are."

Faenir recoiled as I threw my attention back to him. Such hot and sudden anger filled my body. I wished to lash out like a child gripped in a tantrum. The new, puckered scar across my chest pulled awkwardly, sending a sharp spread of discomfort across my torso, restricting my breathing for a moment.

"Please," Faenir said, reaching up but hesitating before he touched me. "I should not have said anything to work you up. You have been through a great deal, I only wish for you to relax now."

I was not giving up the conversation that easily. "Stop placing your guilt upon Myrinn. It is not her presence that threatens my life." I regretted the words the moment they left my mouth. Faenir's handsome face screwed into one of agony. If my words were a knife, it would have cut deep.

"I am sorry..." I began as Faenir turned back away and peered beyond the window.

"But you are right. Nothing you said is incorrect. I am to blame, I know that."

I was, but my deliverance did not need to be so careless. "All Myrinn wants is for the people of your realm to see you as more than what you have been painted out to be. There was no malice behind what she has done."

"And she told you this?" he muttered.

"Myrinn petitions for you to become King. She thinks you are the only one powerful enough to prevent the death of Evelina and I think she is right."

"So, she is setting me up and going against my own wishes?"

I reached out and gripped his hand, which was balled into a fist beside him. As soon as I touched him, Faenir released a breath and his hand relaxed. "Beside the fact that you have been told your entire life that you are not to be King, why are you so adamant about not making your own decision on the matter? Tell me, Faenir, help me understand why you do not want such a thing."

"How can I rule a world in which I cannot touch? A

King or Queen should inspire love in their subjects. I embody the very opposite of what love is."

"You do not need to physically touch a heart to make an impact on it. Love is not physical; I only wish you would recognise that."

"*Love.*" Faenir practically shuddered as he spoke the word. It seemed to hurt him. "I am a killer. My own parents brought me into this world as a product of their love and yet I killed them. Everything I touch is destroyed. If the crown falls upon me, then I will destroy it as I have with everything else."

Something white flew past the window so fast that I hardly registered what it was.

"Yet here we are, my hand upon yours, and you have not destroyed me. In fact, I would say you have had the opposite effect. There is love in you, Faenir. You just need to trust it."

Another blur of white beyond the window. This time it thudded against the glass and distracted us both.

"What...?"

I leaned over Faenir, hands propped against his thigh as I peered outside. The carriage moved with such speed that it was hard to focus on anything. Again, another thud occurred as something unmistakably white fell beneath the wheels of the carriage and out of view.

"Slow down!" Faenir commanded, slamming a palm to the wall that separated us from the coachman. He did not need to ask again. We both jolted as the carriage slowed suddenly.

As the world calmed beyond the window, it was clear what was waiting. Lining the streets were elves of all kinds, children, adults, huddled together so close that they formed a wall between the city and us. In their hands were bundles of beautiful white flowers; long, pointed petals so white I first believed them to be carrying handfuls of snow. They threw them as we passed, letting the flowers rain down upon the carriage. They littered the road, crushed beneath the wheels as we rode over them.

"Why are they doing that?" I asked, breath fogging on the glass.

Faenir replied as gentle a whisper, "Lilies. In Evelina, the flowers represent forgiveness. It is a message."

"They ask for our forgiveness?"

"No," Faenir replied sharply. I turned to look at him, noticing the lines of his profile and the returning spark in his golden eyes as he studied the faces of every elf we passed. "They are asking for your forgiveness. For what has happened to you."

A shiver coursed up my arms as I added, "To us."

"No," Faenir said. "They owe me nothing."

"This is what Myrinn wished," I said, pleading for Faenir to see what I now saw. "For the people of this world to sympathise with you. Can't you see? Look at them, Faenir. Truly look at them and recognise the truth in their faces."

"I do not require their sympathy."

"No, you don't." I couldn't hide my smile as I looked back beyond the window and watched as the sky rained with lilies. "But you require their support if we are ever going to see you take what is rightfully yours."

The crown.

"We?" Faenir's eyes tickled across my face. His lips were so close to my cheek that I felt his warm breath.

There was so much I wished to say at that moment.

Looking at the city of elves, at the symbol of their actions, I made my mind up on a decision that I had not given space to think of yet. I did not wish to die and simply cease to exist. If I was going to go, then I wanted to make a mark on the world. It was what my parents had done with Auriol and I. We were their legacy, but until now I did not have one.

Faenir, he is more than my legacy.

"*We* have much to do, Your Majesty."

Faenir tugged me onto his lap and the crowd beyond the carriage shouted with glee as they watched us. He did not care or notice, but I did. "Careful, Arlo, if you speak in such a way, you will force me to rule you; body and soul."

"Do it." I pressed my face towards his until our noses touched. "Rule me."

And he did, cramped in the back of the carriage upon velvet pillows. As our lips crashed together, Faenir reached for the golden cord that held back the curtain from the window and tore it free. We were bathed in darkness.

"That is much better. It would be untoward for anyone to see what I am about to do with you."

Faenir dove into my neck, spreading his tongue and lips across it. I ran my hands through his length of raven hair and held tight. It was easy to forget the world and its worries when pressed to Faenir in the shadows.

"No more talking..." I said, wishing to give in completely to his touch.

"Mhhmm," Faenir replied, his deep voice vibrating against my skin.

I closed my eyes and was greeted with nothing but desire. No death. No thoughts.

Only him.

Me.

Us.

Opening my eyes and slowly adjusting to the dark, I watched Faenir take the golden cord and tie it blindly until my wrists were bound at my back. He gently forced me with a hand until I was on my knees in the carriage's footwell. His bright eyes sliced through the darkness, glowing proudly once again; it thrilled me to see.

"Suck my cock, Arlo."

There was a click of a belt unbuttoning. The brush of material over skin as Faenir pulled down his slacks.

"Of course, Your Majesty."

Faenir groaned, reaching forward and gripping my chin. His large fingers groped around my skin and pulled me towards his exposed crotch. I giggled in the darkness, silenced by the warm, curved flesh pressed to my lips. My tongue lapped up the pleasant coating of his excitement. Faenir growled, and the shadows danced. All before he could capture a deep breath, I wrapped my mouth around his cock and twisted my tongue in circles across the top.

"Fuck."

With my hands tied behind my back, I could only work my tongue to cause him pleasure. Faenir raised his hands behind his head and leaned back. He enjoyed every long moment. There was no stopping my spit from falling beyond my lips and wetting my cheeks and chin.

My jaw had a dull ache, but that did not hold me back. Guided by the sudden presence of his hand, and my ever-constant enthusiasm, I sucked his hardened cock for an unknown amount of time. At one moment the carriage jolted, moving from the cobbled street to something smoother. Faenir's cock was forced deep into my throat, and I gagged, eyes watering.

He chuckled, pulling my head back to allow me to catch my breath. "You are spectacular, my darling," Faenir whispered, clearing the wet spit from my lips with his thumb.

"Don't," I growled, teeth bared, "stop me again. Understand?"

My heart leapt at my own demand, eased by Faenir's chuckle. "Certainly, my darling. I apologise. I am all yours."

Explosions of sweetness filled my mouth as I worked vigorously at Faenir's cock. I knew Faenir was going climax before he likely knew. I tasted it. A warning. I allowed his sweet juices to fill my cheeks and clog my throat. Powerful, that was how I felt. Even with my hands bound and my head held down by Faenir's hand, I was the most powerful creature in the world.

Faenir finished in a string of explosive groans. The hardening in my own trousers throbbed, spreading a damp patch within as I shared the same climax all without the need to touch myself. It was magic. That was what this was. And, even exhausted, all I could think about was doing it again.

Forever.

At least for the rest of my forever, however short that time may be.

🌿 24 🌿

The ferryman's boat rocked viciously as he moored it across the disturbed surface of the Styx. The weather had noticeably changed in the days since our arrival back at Haxton Manor. Perhaps it echoed the storm that brewed with me? Impenetrable clouds did well to block out the sun. The days were overcast, the nights darker, which made everything seem more sinister.

It was not the best of days to stand outside on the stone balcony connected to my chamber. However, it had become part of my daily routine, watching the ferry of new people to help fill the manor and make it feel... alive. A shiver passed unwantedly across my arms. I tugged the rough blanket tighter around me as I watched the visitors within Charon's boat grip the edges as they traversed the dark blue water towards the manor.

Haxton had quickly filled with serving staff that Myrinn had continued sending. I supposed it was her way of apologising for what had happened in Neveserin, not that I believed she needed to.

Other members of Haxton's staff waited upon the shore for the new arrivals, winds battered them from all angles. Children ran in between their parents' legs, sometimes braving the Styx by sneaking up on it, but never did they get too close. Even those in the boat that moved closer with each moment peered over the edge of the wooden vessel in fear. They must have known what lurked and waited beneath the waters. I gathered the shades waited longingly for someone, one poor soul, to fall overboard.

This visit was the second boat today that had arrived. Still, it surprised me when I saw Charon carting the living across to Faenir's home. The prince had done little to refuse the serving staff, but, from his disappearances when new ones arrived, I only imagined what warnings he gave them. He viewed each and every one as his enemy, a threat. I only hoped he would soften in time.

As of yet, Faenir had not permitted me to visit them alone. I understood why but could not ignore my frustration at being kept in a cage like a bird with broken wings.

A door opened and closed in the chamber room behind me. I heard the familiar gait across the marble floor. It was silly perhaps, but I held my breath in anticipation of Faenir and his touch, which always followed. I longed for it more, which only intensified my anxiety, my guilt for the secret I harboured selfishly.

"You will catch your death standing out in the cold," Faenir said.

How wrong he was.

"I enjoy watching them arrive. It gives me something

to do with my mind instead of staring at the same four walls."

Faenir did not miss the lacing of annoyance hidden beneath my tone. "If you wish to go for a walk, simply ask. This is your home for the time being, not your prison," he said.

Finally, I turned to look at him. Faenir carried a silver platter that took both hands to hold up. Piled upon it in a pyramid of scarlet orbs were what I thought to be apples at first. How wrong I was. Pomegranates glistened like fat jewels upon the platter, each one coated with a sheen of mist. My mouth watered in anticipation for the tarty and sweet flavour that waited within the hard, red shell of their outer layer.

"How did you get these?" I asked, rushing to his side.

I had never seen the fruit in person before but had heard of them. Long before the vampire's curse spread across Darkmourn, pomegranates and other unusual fruits came over from far-off lands where the climate was far different to ours.

"Gildir sends his apologies for what occurred in Neveserin. I can assure you; I am equally surprised."

"They," I pointed to the platter, "are from him?"

"Indeed. The first arrivals to Haxton this morning brought the gift with them. If you would prefer I had them disposed of, I would happily do this for you."

"There will be no need," I said, my mouth salivating. "However, I can't stop trying to imagine what exactly he feels the need to apologise for."

Faenir's brow furrowed. "Darling, I believe the saying suggests that great minds think alike."

He placed the platter on the bedside cabinet. As he

did so, the pomegranate that balanced precariously upon the top of the pile rolled from its perch and fell. He caught it swiftly, snatching the fruit in one hand before it hit the ground, which likely would have been better for the fruit because the moment it met Faenir's touch, the pomegranate rotted; it decayed with haste, colour draining from its shell, leaking inky-black liquid between his fingers.

"Such a waste," he said, letting go of the rotten fruit which became ash beneath his touch and floated to the ground. "Gildir would see that as a sign of great disrespect, I am sure."

"I am surprised you have even let me receive the gift, considering how much of a threat you have treated every person who has been sent here. You would trust your cousin is not out to poison me with his gift?"

"They are not poisoned," Faenir said matter-of-factly.

My brow peaked as another shiver passed across my skin. "What have you done?"

"I ate one. Poison would not kill me, but I certainly would sense the effects."

I could not explain why his action had angered me, but it did. "You shouldn't have done that. I do not require you to be my taster... when are you going to realise that not everyone is out to kill me?"

"Would this be the wrong moment to admit that I have been tasting every morsel of food prepared since we came back home?"

I forced out a sigh. Mother had always taught me to pick my battles, and this was not one I had the energy for. Despite my want to fall into his arms and let his touch lighten the storm in my mind, I turned my back on him. I moved back towards the balcony, leaving the disagreement behind me.

The winds had grown stronger in the moments I had been inside. It whipped at my hair, tugging at the blanket across my shoulders until it forced me to hold on tighter.

Charon had now reached shore. The four elves practically threw themselves from the vessel in fear, or relief, I was unsure.

Faenir stepped in behind me and I immediately relaxed into his warmth. I did not protest for space, because that was not what I longed for. His arms came around me, each hand gripping the smooth-stone wall of the balcony as we both watched the swell of the crowds below.

"I cannot express my discomfort at knowing they all dwell in my home."

"Because you long for your own space, or because you are frightened of what might happen?" I asked.

"All my life I have kept a distance from the living. Each one of them burn with the glow of life and sometimes it makes looking upon them hard. Uncomfortable. I imagine it is what it would feel like to stare at the sun for a time."

It made sense. When I had seen Faenir pass the huddles of serving staff dusting long-forgotten frames and sideboards, he always kept his gaze on the floor.

"Give it time. It will become easier."

Faenir's arms closed in on me. His breath joined the winds and played with the hair across my ear. "I hope it does. However, time will not stop my touch with doing the very same as it had with that pomegranate. What is to say I touch one servant by mistake? All it would take is a glance of a hand, a brush of skin, and I would kill them without that ever being my intention."

I took that moment to reach a hand and place it upon his. Mine was deathly cold in comparison. "Faenir, you are far too conscious to act in such a way. Do you see them running from you? Hiding when you pass? I may not be able to speak on behalf of them all, but I am confident they are not scared of you. Take that as you will. Find comfort in knowing that the elves you have allowed into your home understand the risk and still continue as though it is normal because it is. It is your normal and there is nothing wrong with that."

Faenir rested his chin on the top of my head. I could hear his smile as he expelled a laboured breath. "There is power in the way you speak. I am grateful for it."

For it. I longed for him to repeat himself and change his last word to *you*.

The light burst of laughter reached us from the grounds that stretched out beneath us. Three children ran and danced, playing games with one another without a single care in the world. Faenir grunted at their presence but held back any comments.

"Those children," I said, choosing my words carefully, "Are they the halflings you told me about?"

"No," he said. "Not in the sense you are thinking."

"What do you mean?"

"Look closer at them. Tell me what you see."

As I narrowed my gaze on their heads, I thought it was a trick question. I did not know what, in fact, I searched for. "If you wish to provide a clue, I would be ever so grateful, Your Highness."

Faenir lowered his mouth to my ear and placed a kiss upon it, soft lips brushing the rounded tip and pulling away as he whispered, "Look again."

It took a moment to distract myself from his kiss to truly understand the hint he had provided. Then I saw it. The children, hidden beneath hair that bounced as they ran from one another, were ears—as there should have been, of course—but they weren't elongated and pointed like Faenir's. No. They were rounded and... mundane, like mine.

"They are humans..." I muttered.

"It is common for the less noble members of Evelina's community to be burdened with the human babies that are swapped out when a halfling is taken and left in your realm. Although the halflings look human, their blood is far from it; that is the only noticeable difference—so slight, in fact, that the humans would never notice when their blood child was swapped out."

"That," I said, looking at the children in a new light, "is cruel."

"I agree," Faenir replied. "My ancestors had abolished the practice for thousands of years, all until the vampire spread his curse across the world. My grandmother plans to aid the humans' survival by reinstating magic in your realm. Doing so would take years... but it was an investment she was willing to make."

"At the cost of families who bring up children that do not belong to them?"

Faenir stiffened, his stomach hardened like a wall behind me. "Only time will determine if that sacrifice will become beneficial."

"Would you have sanctioned such a thing if you were King?" I asked.

Faenir took a moment to ponder my question. "Claria wants an army to defeat the vampires with the very same being that created the first. Although I understand her efforts, mine would have been different, not that it matters."

I wanted to tell him it did, in fact, matter. All of it did. "I am still trying to wrap my head around all this. Is it possible that I have come across a halfling? If Claria has been swapping children out for years, then surely there is enough of them in Darkmourn to fight back?"

"Not every halfling can become what you know to be a witch. It is magic that lays dormant within them all, but it takes something great and unknown to make it bloom into pure power. The witches that caused the damage to your realm are products of hundreds and hundreds of years' worth of practice, religion and focus. Intervention from our kind helped them along. The halflings in Darkmourn are still young, an army who are yet to understand what they are required for, but an army nonetheless."

Queen Claria had focused her energy on creating an army, years wasted allowing the vampires to devour our kind and keeping us in pens, just for the potential of restoring balance. She played the long game. Not the right game.

My head throbbed at the knowledge Faenir had bestowed upon me. I began racing through my mind, picking out names of people I had known and trying to remember anything that might've suggested that they may have been halflings themselves.

I second-guessed my heritage. The jarring thought was short-lived as I reminded myself of the mismatched eyes Auriol and I got from our mother. And, more horrifically, the sickness I had been unluckily graced with.

"You are quiet," Faenir said.

"My mind isn't," I replied.

Faenir turned me to face him, and I didn't put up any resistance. "Would you like me to fill your mind with other matters?"

His lips curved upward, and I could not help but smile back. Something about Faenir was so entirely consuming. And he was right. It was early afternoon and already I would have preferred to climb into bed and hide away from the world.

"What is it you have in mind?"

Faenir's fingers laced through mine, and he began stepping backwards. He guided me back into the chamber, which was just as cold inside as it was out. "I may not be able to touch Gildir's kind offering of apology, but you can."

"I sense you are missing some elaboration as to what you mean exactly."

There was a glow of mischief behind his gaze. "Follow my commands, darling, and you will find out just what I am thinking."

FAENIR

"There is something I would like to ask you, but if you wish to refuse me an answer, I will understand."

I knew a question was coming, for Arlo's fingers suddenly stopped tracing circles across my skin. He spoke not a moment after placing his entire palm upon my chest.

"I have nothing to hide from you, Arlo. For you, I am a book to open and rifle through the pages at your leisure," I replied.

My heart leapt as Arlo raised his head from its place upon me and looked up at me. His wide eyes glistened. If he blinked, I was certain he would have cried. I longed to know what thoughts had troubled him, so I added pressure onto his back and pulled him close. "Talk to me, darling. What is it that concerns you?"

He looked away, not quick enough for me to see the single tear betray him as it rolled freely down the peak of his cheekbone.

"Seeing the children running through your grounds cannot help but make me grieve a childhood you never had. It is not fair what they have done to you. There is a part of me who is trying to make sense as to why Claria gave the orders to..." Arlo swallowed his words. They stopped so abruptly it conjured a shiver to race across my skin.

"You can say it. The memory is harsh, but I do not give it power to hurt me."

He looked back up at me at that moment. He pushed himself completely from my chest and shifted his weight on the bed until he was sitting cross-legged, facing me. The dull light of early evening danced across his skin. It revealed every mark, every freckle, which I longed to memorise. To touch. As I did every time I looked at Arlo, I gave into the wonder that sang to me. How my shadows and his life light swirled as one. My shadows never took from him. His light was quiet, not demanding as others were around me. Theirs would sing for me to steal it, whereas Arlo's life light simply existed without a melody.

"How did you survive what she did to you?" he asked.

Without thought, my gaze shifted from Arlo towards the cloud-peppered sky beyond the balcony. A storm brewed as it had for days, growing braver with whistling winds and downpours of rain that lasted hours. It was not the weather my mind drifted to, but the sole figure that I felt, even from a distance: Charon.

"Perhaps your answer will be better suited for another, for the mind of a baby cannot remember the details of such an event... even if the trauma left deep scars. It was Charon who found me."

"But he is..." I watched Arlo silently contemplate what he was to say. "Dead, is he not?"

"Charon was once a man who lived and breathed as we

do. During a time when he was not the ghoul that dwells upon the waters of the Styx, he was a man, a member of my family's court. He worked in the gardens and heard me wailing upon the shores. Luckily, he had picked me up with gloved hands. His wife, however, was not so lucky. Nor was my family's head healer. It took three bodies to pile up for Charon to know that he only survived because of the cover he wore on his hands."

It was easy spilling my story to Arlo. The words fell out of me naturally and Arlo listened without interrupting.

"All this time I imagined you had been alone..."

I cringed at the sadness in Arlo's voice, how it passed like a storm cloud behind his eyes. "Do not be sad for me, enough of such emotion has been spent throughout my life. I was not always alone, and with you here, I won't be again."

Hurt pinched Arlo's face. It lasted only a moment as I witnessed him steel his expression. I was certain he bit down on the insides of his cheeks to stop himself from reacting again.

"Charon must have loved you, to look after you even after the unfortunate end his wife met."

Allowing myself only a moment to the dark, I closed my eyes and reached out my shadows to Charon. He, unlike the other shades within the Styx, had been crafted of physical darkness as my grief as a child broke open when he died of natural causes. I could not explain with words as to what I had done to provide Charon such a form when the other souls I stole lingered within the dark waters. Could I release them too? Free them from the eternal prison my presence had locked them within?

"He loved me, I do not doubt that." I said. "When

Charon passed, I had not even reached a decade of age. All the other members of my family's household had fled. They did not desire to be near an omen of such peril, they left only Charon and me. He did his best, with what was provided. I owe that man a debt that I fear I will never be able to repay."

When I opened my eyes again, I could see the thoughts churning within Arlo's mind, hows and whys dancing among each other, deciding which was more pressing to ask first.

"My heart hurts at the thought of you being alone, but I am thankful that Charon gave you his time and love. Knowing you have experienced such simple honours of life makes me happy."

He did not look happy. Far from it, in fact.

I swallowed the lump that had invaded my throat. There was a swelling in my chest that grew the more I looked at Arlo. From his determined stare to the way his spine curved as he leaned forward over his now crossed legs. Everything about him made me react physically.

"Charon has not been the only one to show me such things." I leaned up on my elbows, stomach flexing, and reached a hand for Arlo's knee. I gripped it as though winds threatened to blow me away from him. "You, Arlo, have given me so much more in such a short time."

With bated breath, I waited for Arlo to say something. Anything. I could see he longed to from the subtle opening of his mouth. Silence crept between us, pulling taut, like a cord with knots that wished nothing more than to unwind.

Instead, it snapped completely when Arlo finally broke the silence. "Are you hungry?"

The insides of my cheeks pricked as Arlo reached across my body, his chest brushing precariously over the hardening length, as he snatched a pomegranate from the platter alongside the ivory-bone handle knife. He held it before me, in offering with a grin lifting the corners of his lips.

"Dare I ask what you are going to do with that?"

Arlo exhaled, "Feed you."

I forced my brows to furrow. Arlo lifted the hard, crimson shell to his lips and pressed it there. It took tremendous effort not to take myself into my hand.

"What of the sheets? Careful, or they will become sticky and then where will we sleep?"

He shrugged, pink tongue escaping the confines of his glistening lips as it traced circles across the fruit. He knew what he was doing, the glint of allure in his mismatched eyes revealed as much.

Without saying a word more, Arlo clambered upon my lap, each leg resting on either side of my hips. It did not look as though he moved, but I felt him rock on my cock, encouraging it to throb against his bare skin with equal excitement. He leaned over me, lifted the silver knife and traced it across the mounds of my chest. A shock of cold metal had me gasping, as did the feeling of the sharp edge scratching across the coarse, curled hairs while Arlo ran it across me.

"I am beginning to believe you have an interest in sharp, culinary utensils," I said, eyes flicking between Arlo's smirk and the knife he drew across me.

"You trust me, don't you?"

Nodding, I lifted my arm from the bed to reach for his face. Lightning fast, Arlo jabbed the tip of the knife at my throat. "Ah, ah, ah. Keep your hands to yourself. Let me please His Majesty and show him exactly how he should be treated."

"There is danger in your eyes, my darling," I purred. "Trust, yes. Thrill, even more so."

"Good." Arlo sat back up, withdrew the blade from my skin and brought it to the pomegranate that had, until now, become more of an afterthought during the past moments. "Open your mouth."

A warmth spread across my stomach, hardening the muscles upon it. Shivering anticipation made my hands twitch; to still them I brought them up behind my head to ensure I followed Arlo's command. Between the mischievous glow behind his gaze, and the fluid flashing of the knife, I did not want to disappoint.

Arlo was not as gentle with the knife as he drew it across the pomegranate's casing. It split, and juices dripped in streams down his hand, his wrist, where it splattered across my torso.

"Oh dear," Arlo cooed, not stopping until the fruit was cut into pieces. "It would seem I've made a terrible mess."

"Indeed." It was the only word I could muster strength to form aloud. Every other possibility I wished to share involved much darker thoughts. Things I wished to do to Arlo. Many, countless ideas I longed to see come to light.

Like a cat bowing over a bowl of cream, Arlo lowered himself to my chest. His tongue slithered free, teeth flashing.

My hands gripped the back of my head. The feeling of his tongue lapping the sticky residue of the fruit from my skin made me groan. I pinched my eyes closed but still recognised the throbbing of my cock and shadows which seemed to beat in tune with my heart.

He did not stop. Somewhere the knife and the pomegranate had been discarded for both his hands were on me. My greedy fingers reached behind his ass as he gripped my length and stroked it. His other hand scratched across stomach as though he longed to memorise each dip and peak with his touch. Seeds and spit shone across my stomach. Arlo marvelled at his feast, lips stained red and swollen. There was something feral about his stare, as though he was lost in thought for a moment.

"Have you had enough?" I asked.

Arlo snapped out of his mind, his smile bright, and replied, "Far from it."

I sighed heavily, shivering, as Arlo dipped back down upon me and continued his meal. With Arlo, there was not much room to think of anything but him and the now. Humans should be powerless, but this one defied such concepts.

There was a small concern, eating away at the back of my mind, that attempted to convince me that Arlo filled his mouth with my skin because he did not wish to speak. The conversation had ended abruptly. If I had not been distracted by the kitchen knife and the juices that dried upon my body, perhaps I would have asked what had caused the sudden end.

Such thoughts were impossible.

I closed my eyes as the dripping of fresh juice spilt upon my length. Arlo had slithered downward in the bed, gripping onto the base of my cock to steady himself as he squeezed the fruit in his other fist.

If I watched him, I feared I would race towards the

end before I could stop myself, for I felt the urgency building in the pit of my stomach as though a flock of birds prepared to take flight.

Arlo wrapped his warmth around the tip he held carefully in his grasp. I could not comprehend the sound that burst from my very soul as he twisted his tongue in soft, yet frantic circles. His hand moved in tandem. He sucked the juices from my flesh with burning desire.

It became impossible to control myself. I raised my hips, forcing myself deeper into Arlo's throat. He pushed me back down. The sound he made as he struggled on my length had my blood burning me from the inside out.

As much as I desired to give into his pleasure and relieve myself, I would not. This was not like the carriage ride where he had taken me into his mouth and swallowed everything I gave him. This would be longer. More controlled. Arlo had ways of seeing me pleased, but I wanted nothing more than to tear him from me, twist him upon the bed, and bury myself in him until my hips slapped against his ass.

I could not wait another moment.

Gripping Arlo's head by his hair, I pulled him from my cock. His wet mouth made a popping sound as it came free. The look of surprise and thrill painted across his face was an image I never wished to forget.

My mouth crashed into his. Sweetness burst across my tongue. My fingers wove deeper into his hair until they brushed across his scalp with urgency.

"I am going to take you," I growled into his lips, coming away for breath. "Completely."

My shadows did not need to gather to hide us from sight this time. There were no crowds to watch or Joining ceremonies to defile. I left the shadows alone, allowing our moans to join the thundering rumble of a storm that sang within the darkening skies beyond the room. It was Arlo and me. We were all that mattered in my mind. Not the crown. Not Claria or my family.

"Faenir." Arlo spoke my name as though it was the most beautiful thing in the world. "I was wondering how long I could make you last before you would have me bent over so you could ruin me."

"Ruin you?" I chuckled. Arlo shivered. My cock throbbed. "When I am finished, you will feel remade. Unless you wish for me to destroy you instead?"

"Make me, destroy me. Whatever you decide, do it now."

Arlo turned himself around, lowered his belly down on the bed and kept his knees raised until all I could see was his ass. He presented himself to me, smooth curves of flesh gave way to the light pink star of his centre.

My fingers lifted to my lips. I spat. Once. Twice. Arlo peered over his shoulder, stare narrowed with taunting lust, as he watched me lower my hand to his centre. Arlo's eyes rolled back into his head as I slowly entered my finger into him. His groan was my guide, telling me if it was hurting or not. From the way he bit down on his lip and the way his hands pulled the sheets into fists, he enjoyed it. I did not stop until it was completely inside.

"More," he begged, voice muffled by the sheets. "Give me all of you."

"Soon." The sharpness of my tone surprised me. I wanted this to last. For hours, days or more.

My arms ached, but that did not deter the way I slipped my finger in and out. Arlo loved it. His moans revealed as much. I was able to include another finger which I spat down upon for more ease.

It did not take long for the desire to replace my finger with my cock to overwhelm me. Arlo called out with glee as I pressed the head of my cock to his centre and forced it within. Arlo threw himself back onto my length with a need for pleasure. I gripped his thighs to keep myself upright as I was lost in the tight embrace of his ass. When he grew tired, I began thrusting, pulling out almost completely before thrusting myself back into him.

If I finally gave into death that I had staved off, I would have done so happily. This feeling was divinity. Complete, intoxicating lust that fuelled me with more energy than I could have deemed possible.

I leaned over Arlo for support, still pounding into him although my body was tired and my hair damp with sweat. I spared a hand for him, reaching beneath his hips and gripping his own length. It was selfish for me not to. For a moment I could not find the rhythm of my fucking and my wrist, but as soon as I did our breathing entwined and we raced towards the cliff's edge of pleasure.

There was no understanding of how long we did this for. In another time I would have wished to pick him up and explore other positions but sensing his building pleasure in tandem with my own, I knew we would not last.

Pleasure should be enjoyed, not prolonged. It was for the here and now.

"Faenir, keep doing it."

A growl erupted from me. "Are you close?"

"Yes," Arlo spluttered through harsh, heavy breaths, "Yes."

I could not answer that I too was almost at the end.

My pace intensified, both my wrist and my hips worked faster. Light flashed through my mind, fire boiled in my chest, and the entire world cracked open at the moment we both broke through the sex as one combined soul.

There was nothing to spoil the moment of peace that followed, not as Arlo fell onto his side, drawing me down onto the bed with him. I curled my damp limbs around his body. Arlo panted in my embrace, trembling hands holding onto mine as I wrapped them around his chest.

"Would you forgive me if I wished to be bedbound for the entirety of tomorrow?" I admitted, stifling a yawn. A deep, unsettling tiredness had overcome me. It made my bones feel as though they were made from iron, my blood from hardened silver. "I don't imagine my knees will work for a long while."

"Sleep," Arlo replied, voice as meek as my own. We had driven each other to the edge of exhaustion; it was near impossible to keep my eyes open as I nuzzled into his shoulder. "You have earned the rest."

I wished to say more, do more, but I gave into the wave of peace and closed my eyes. "Good night then, darling."

Arlo inhaled deeply, worming his way back into me until we were completely connected. "Night, Your Majesty."

❧ 25 ❧

Thad lost count of the days which passed both painfully quick and torturously slow. Hidden beneath the bed I was splayed across, etched upon the slabbed flooring, were the marks I had made, my countdown which I no longer had a need for.

Death crept up on me, a silent assassin waiting in the shadows of time to strike. To take me. And I waited for it. My fists clenched and jaw gritted, preparing myself for a fight. I would not be taken without one.

Every day since we had returned from Neveserin had been the same. I woke hours before Faenir, as though freezing waters had been dumped upon me. Each time I took my first breath, I expected to feel pain in my lungs. Every time I coughed; I would pull my hand back as though preparing myself to see the splattering of blood upon it.

If the sickness did not come to claim me soon as it had my parents, the sense of impending doom would likely take me first. Or I would be murdered instead. The person behind the attacks had still not been found, nor did it seem that Claria cared to locate them. How hard was it to locate the killer when all she had to do was look in the mirror to see them? Faenir believed it too, which was why he refused for me to leave Haxton's boundaries again. Faenir trusted Claria would never come to Haxton, whereas I didn't count on that.

I dared move from my position, head resting upon Faenir's chest, feeling the rise and fall and every strong beat of his heart. Unlike most days, when I would come to realise that I was alive and the sickness kept at bay, I happily laid upon him, waiting for him to wake. This evening was different. Today I needed to move, to do something that would distract my mind.

"You have a habit of sneaking out of bed," Faenir groaned, tugged unwantedly from sleep as I slipped from his chest. I winced, face crumpled, as I woke him. Sitting myself upon the edge of his bed, I buried my face in my hands. The bed creaked as Faenir reached over and placed a hand on my shoulder, urging me to lie back down.

I shrugged him off. "I thought it would be a gracious gesture if I offered to help Ana in the kitchens this evening."

Ana was one of the many serving staff that Myrinn had sent to Haxton when we had left. Faenir couldn't refuse them entry even if he wished to. Aided by my demand, he allowed them to come.

During the short time in Myrinn's home, I had grown used to the subtle noise of life. Haxton was desperate for such a thing. Witnessing people as they floated up and down hallways, their chatter echoed throughout the many rooms, had made this place more... tolerable. But my thanks for their presence went far beyond what they did to Faenir's home. It was what they would do for him in time. Faenir would never be alone again and if that was the mark I left upon his life, then it would be a scar worthy of pride.

"Not that I care to speak on her behalf, but she has already got the help. Come back to bed. I can give you something to assist with if you so need the distraction," Faenir replied. "And if I told you I enjoyed helping? It makes me feel less... useless."

Faenir chuckled deeply at that. The muscles across his stomach rippled mesmerizingly. For a moment, I almost forgot what my mind had been set on.

"I am beginning to believe you and Ana are having a flippant love affair with your disappearances," Faenir said, grinning wildly. "Is there something you wish to share with me?"

In all honesty, having company besides Faenir was refreshing. Cleaning pots or helping prepare food worked wonders at taking my mind off my looming death. It was another tactic of distraction that didn't end with having my clothes torn from my body, not that I minded the latter.

"Far too old for me," I said.

Faenir did not miss my wink; he flashed teeth. "What a relief. Now, stop teasing me and get back under the sheets. I am growing ever so cold without you. We have an entire platter of pomegranates that should not go to waste. Just imagine how offended Gildir would be if he knew they were left to rot."

"I'm going. There is nothing you can say or suggest that will make me stay," I said shortly. Images of the night prior were still vivid in my head. Even now, hours later, and the taste of the fruit's juices made my teeth sticky. "May I be the one to remind you I couldn't care for Gildir's gift, or feelings. Let them rot and send them back to him with a ribbon, if you so desire."

"Oh, that would truly be a waste when you seemed to thoroughly enjoy his... apology last night."

"And what about you?" I asked, cheeks prickling from my smile. "Did you enjoy yourself?"

"Enough to not allow you to leave my side!" Faenir said in jest. Except he was not entirely joking. I could see in the concern that darkened his eyes that he did not trust me in anyone else's care.

I stood from the bed, keeping my back to him. "Believe it or not, not everyone is out to kill me. If Ana wished to see me harmed, she could have spoiled many meals and finished the job long before this very moment."

He had undoubtedly struggled with the change in Haxton's climate and the proximity of others in his home. Although he moved out of the way of anyone he crossed, ensuring he was far enough not to cause them pain, he also spent most of his time hiding within this very room. Here, with me, limbs entangled or not, Faenir did well at becoming a ghost in his own domain.

"If you will not be cautious about your own life, then I must."

I could have told him he was wasting his time, snapped and shouted at him for thinking in such a way. But I gathered myself as I had the hundreds of other times. My anger was not a result of what Faenir said, but the truth I kept from him.

My lies were poison, eating me away from the inside.

There had been so many times I had wished to tell him, but every time the words nearly left my mouth, I would see a vision of him, the contorting of his beautiful face into the very expression I had made when my parents died. I was resilient, but not strong enough for that.

"Well, I am going." I forced a smile over my shoulder. I could only bear to look at him for a moment before my knees felt weak. His long, naked body was outstretched across the crumpled sheets, only his modesty was covered by a pathetic slip of material that one gust of wind could move. Locks of obsidian hair splayed out across the pillow in a halo. His tired, rich eyes narrowed upon me with hungry intention.

Surely, he was satisfied. It had been hours since I had last sat upon him as though I was a King, and he was my throne. My chest warmed as my eyes flicked over the knife that lay forgotten on the bedside cabinet. I had to fight the urge to climb back into his arms and distract myself with his company instead of breakfast.

"Then we will both assist Ana if you are so adamant," Faenir said, kicking his legs over the bed to stand. As he did so, the little covering of the sheets fell away from his cock as though reminding me what I was missing out on.

"Myrinn will be pleased to hear that Faenir laboured in his kitchens. What would she say, knowing you are finally *mingling* with the people?"

I threw on a newly made black tunic and matching leather trousers which Haxton's seamstress had made for me. Faenir changed also, his outfit overwhelming with grandeur, from his billowing ivory cloak to the formfitting shirt and trousers beneath. All the while, he did not stop looking at me.

Faenir always watched me as though he were searching for something. It was one of many quirks that thrilled me about him.

Once changed into something more suitable for being seen, we moved through the bustling manor hand in hand. Faenir grew quiet as we passed the many serving staff, who each bowed at him. He kept his gait proud and chin raised, as if he did not see anyone at all. I imagined he expected fear from the people, but the way they looked upon Faenir was with nothing of the sort. Admiration. Excitement. He did not seem to notice it.

In time, he would. At least I hoped.

I realised something was amiss before we reached the kitchens located in the lower levels of the manor. Usually, as we reached the main atrium in Haxton, the air would sing with the smells of freshly cooked foods, cured meats, fried potatoes and an array of delicious wonders that Ana prepared daily.

Today the air was empty. My stomach grumbled in response to the lack of scents. Ana had not yet missed a meal, and she prepared many.

By the time we navigated through the dining room, down the curved steps and into the kitchen, we came to find it void of the songs of cooking and warmth. Ana was nowhere to be seen.

Her maid danced around the cold stone room until he saw Faenir and I. He gasped. The pots he carried clattered to the floor, then the spewing of his apologies burst out as he bowed deeply to hide the scarlet staining his youthful cheeks.

"Your Highness, I am sorry for the delay. Terrible! I feel truly embarrassed that you have had to come looking for food. I have failed you. Please, do not trouble yourself down here. If you would..." He hardly stopped for breath.

"We did not intend to surprise you." Faenir stopped him from vomiting any more excuses; his voice was crisp yet edged with honest concern.

"We came to offer to help," I said, eyes scanning the room for Ana as though she would burst beyond the pantry with arms full of dried goods.

"No help required," he spluttered, then stumbled over his words quickly, "But I don't wish to tell you what to do, Your Highness. If you want to help, then you are welcome. I mean, this is your home, you can do what you like—"

"What," Faenir said, interrupting the panicked boy, "is your name?"

He swallowed hard and loud, the lump in his throat bobbing. "Harrison."

"Harrison, where is Ana?" I asked.

The poor boy looked as though he was about to cry. Harrison's lower lip quivered, and his full cheeks flushed a deeper scarlet. It was not from fear that caused such a reaction this time. He exhaled, dropping his raised shoulders and practically folding in on himself.

I looked up to Faenir, who tilted his head inquisitively.

"I am so sorry..."

"You have got nothing to be sorry for, but please answer Arlo's question. About Ana, what has happened?"

"It is her little girl," Harrison finally said, fat goblets of tears leaking down the curves of his face. Strands of snot joined, spilling ferociously, before he swept them away with the back of his sleeve.

"Go on," Faenir implored as the boy had to catch his

KING OF IMMORTAL TITHE

breath. "If something is the matter, then it is important we know so we can help."

I pulled free of Faenir's hand and edged towards the boy. Taking his shaking shoulders into my hands, I encouraged him to calm down. "Do not be scared. Take your time."

Ana was one of a handful of elves who had brought children to Haxton. The manor had housing for serving staff that was kept separate from the main building itself in the northern grounds; I had passed it on my first day. Forgotten from years of disuse, it had been covered with overgrown greenery. I imagined that was where Ana was now.

Harrison took a moment to steady himself. "Ana's little May is sick. She has been for a while. It's why she had to bring her here. Ana had no family to leave her with in the city."

"What is the matter with her?" Faenir asked, visibly tense from what Harrison said.

"She is dying. Ana didn't come to work because she dreads to leave May's side."

The floor could have fallen away from me at that moment as the reality of what Harrison had said fell upon me. "Take us to them," I demanded as the fingers of dread spread a shiver down my spine. "Now."

FAENIR

The child looked horrifically small, nestled within the arms of her weeping mother. Her body did not glow with the halo of life. Instead, shadows danced around her skin like vipers longing for blood; beneath was a slither of light that they worked hard to suffocate.

I felt the shadows tugging at me the moment we had entered their room, a cord pulling me with urgency. I wished to greet it as the death demanded, to reach out and claim the shadows for my own. If it was not for Arlo's hand in mine and the way his presence grounded me, there would have been nothing stopping me.

The woman, Ana, hardly looked up from the child as we entered. It was as if she expected our company. She was singing a lullaby, rocking the child back and forth. The haunting sound made me want to flee the room, flee this place entirely. I wanted to demand that she stopped, yet it felt wrong to stop a mother consoling a child. Unjust. Monstrous.

Tears fell upon little May's grey hued skin as Ana

finally choked on the lyrics. I believed the little girl was sleeping until two dulled blue eyes creaked open and looked towards where we stood.

Did she sense the pull between us?

"That is the prince, mummy." May's broken voice scratched at my soul like nails across stone.

Ana nodded, swiping her hand over the small forehead of the little girl to gather the damp, red curls that hung around her hollow face. "A special visit for a special girl."

"I want to see him. He is so far away."

Ana looked up and stared directly into my eyes. Without outstretching a hand for me, she beckoned me towards her. "Your Highness, please... for a moment. Come and meet my princess."

I could not reply, could not move a muscle as that ominous shadow lingered across the little child's skin. The room was silent to everyone else, yet to me... the shadows cried out with wanting.

"Go to her," Arlo whispered, sadness thickening in his throat. His voice tore me out of my thoughts.

"I do not wish to hurt them." My voice did not sound like my own. It was distant and echoed as though I stood at the end of a long, barren corridor and shouted at myself from the other end.

"You may find," Arlo said softly, "that your words may have the opposite effect."

He urged me forward, fingers slipping out of my hand with ease. Without him holding me back, there was nothing stopping me from following that sinister pull.

Ana said something to me, but I could not focus, not as the child watched me with doe-wide eyes. I knelt down at her side, squeezing my hands upon my thighs to keep them from reaching out.

"Hello," she said, her small voice wheezing with great effort.

"Hello," I replied, unsure of what else to say.

"You are not scary." May's small, bloodshot eyes raced across my face. Her attention left featherlight touches, like little fingers tracing across my features to memorise them. "They said you were a monster, but you don't look like one."

"Perhaps you are just braver than the rest of them?"

Ana sobbed, pressing a wet kiss to the child's forehead. "May is the bravest of them all. She has faced far greater pains than many could ever comprehend."

"I do not doubt it," I replied softly.

"Mummy," May gasped, wincing as she tried to sit up, but couldn't. "Don't be sad." The girl, with great effort, lifted her hand to her mother's cheek and held it there, not concerned for the tears that raced over her small fingers.

"My sweet girl, I do not wish for you to be in pain anymore," Ana said.

"I feel it going away now, mummy, like you promised. It is slipping away like the sand through my fingers... do you remember?"

"Nothing could ever make me forget."

"I don't hurt anymore."

Because you are dying.

I felt it. Unlike Ana and Arlo, whose bodies sang with the light of life, May did not. I wondered if Ana knew that the child's time was ending. May seemed to know and took comfort in the fact. Had her suffering been so terrible that death was the better choice for her?

For someone so slight, so fragile, I could not deny her strength. I admired it—admired her.

"Why are you crying, mummy?" May asked.

"Because I am not ready to let you go..."

Somewhere in the shadows behind us, Arlo exhaled a cry, stifled by a hand. I wished to find him and comfort him, but May needed me now.

"Mummy is scared," May said with such clarity, "I am dying, and that makes her sad."

"Are you frightened of what will come to pass?" I asked. Perhaps the question was meant for someone of far greater age. Children were a strange concept to me.

May seemed to understand. She nodded, her hand falling from Ana's face before reaching out towards me. I flinched backwards, not wishing for her time to come to its end so quickly. She noticed, face pinching into a frown. "Are you scared of my death like my mummy, prince?"

I sighed, closing my eyes and blocking out the scene for a moment whilst I gathered my thoughts. "I cannot fear death, nor should you."

May replied meekly, breathing taking up most of her ability to speak, "He is not scary, is he, mummy?"

"No," Ana replied, voice a mess of grief. "He is kind."

"Death is not something to be feared. Death is peace. It is quiet. It is relief. It is more than sadness and pain. Death..." It was my turn to choke on my words. I had to stop and clear my throat before I carried on; something strange pricked in my eyes as I did so, opening them didn't help. "Death can be unfair. It does not follow anyone's rules but its own. Yet, no matter when it comes, it will never let you be alone."

"Is that true?" May blinked, as though fighting sleep. *But it was not sleep that was coming for her.*

"I believe you are required elsewhere more than you are here. Such a brave and strong soul. Destiny has another place in mind for you."

"Ahh..." the small, broken child groaned as her mother covered her with a smothering of kisses. "Will you miss me, mummy?"

"So much that it hurts."

"One day, soon or far, you will see one another again," I said, wishing to provide them comfort.

May fought to keep her eyes open. Ana brought the child to her breast and held her close. May's voice was muffled as she spoke, but her words rang true. "I will see you again, mummy. Just like the prince said."

Ana could not respond through her sobs.

"Farewell brave, little May." I stood, feeling my frozen, hardened heart shatter one piece at a time. "May you find rest without pain and burden."

I turned my back on her. Before I fully tore my gaze from the mother and child, I noticed the faint glow was gone from the little girl's skin. Like a candle blown out, or the stars blinking out of existence, May died in her mother's arms.

The harrowing scream that tore out of Ana shook the very foundations of Haxton Manor. It confirmed what I had thought, the child was gone. I wished to throw myself into Arlo's arms to hide from the grief, but he was not standing in the shadows.

Arlo was nowhere to be seen.

❦ 26 ❦

Tears blinded my vision as I ran through the gardens of Haxton Manor. Far behind me I could hear the terrorising scream of grief as it crashed into the darkness. The very stars shuddered beneath it, blinking out of existence as though they too could not bear witness to the death of a child.

The frigid air stung at my face. It ripped the tears from my cheeks greedily, yet more spilled. My throat burned with each inhale, my chest aching as though hands gripped and squeezed. And all I could think about was the way Faenir had softened before the child, his calm and guiding voice as he eased her departure with words of comfort.

Death is not something to be feared.

His resounding voice echoed throughout my mind.

Death is peace.

Since my parents had died, I had never truly felt peace. Chaos ruled my life. I lived on the edge of a knife, kept there only by drinking the blood of the undead. Peace was a concept I had not experienced, until Faenir.

It is quiet.

My mind was roaring as it had since that fateful day, filled with the promise I had made to my mother, my father. *Look after Auriol. Do not fail her as we have.* I had failed them all.

It is a relief.

Was it? Was that what waited for me when death finally caught up? In a way, I believed it, longed for it. No more worry. No more pressure. No more promises.

It is more than sadness and pain.

For whom? For the one who died, or the family they left behind? Because I had lived with shards of grief in my chest, edging closer to my heart every day that passed.

I cut through the night until Ana's screams grew quieter, only stopping as water splashed beneath my boots and the ground seemed to swallow me up slowly. The calm waters of the Styx stretched out before me. Dark waves reached my boots as though encouraging me to give in to it.

Far in the distance I saw the bobbing glow of a light. The ferryman brave enough to journey through the waters patrolled the far edges of the lake. Faenir had commanded it of him, ensuring unwanted visitors were kept away.

I blinked away the tears and attempted to catch a deep enough breath to steady the thundering in my chest.

The waters of the Styx seemed to sing to me, questioning with each lap of a wave against the dark sands of the bank.

Why are you here? What do you come searching for?

Perhaps it was the peace Faenir had spoken about. The quiet. I could have thrown myself into the waters and found peace sooner than the sickness returned. Standing before the Styx, I contemplated ending it. The thought was fleeting and fast, but there undoubtedly.

At least death would be on my own terms. If there was peace, then I longed to find it. It was what I deserved.

"Arlo..." Faenir spoke behind me.

I had not sensed his presence, but as I glanced over my shoulder, face slick with sadness, I saw him there. Wind whipped his obsidian hair around his shoulders as his piercing gaze watched me.

"She is gone, isn't she?" I shouted above the wind. I did not need to ask to know the answer, nor did Faenir need to reply, because the sombre expression etched into his handsome face answered for him. "Death is not fair. It is cruel and wrong."

Faenir stepped cautiously towards me. "My darling, you are not wrong. Death is like a coin, two opposing sides and truths depending on which way it lands and to whom still lives long enough to flip it."

I steeled myself as I turned my back on the Styx. "I couldn't stay and watch. Perhaps that makes me a coward... so be it."

Faenir was close now, hands out, reaching for me. Part of me longed to throw myself into his embrace, yet the other part had me rooted to the spot. As I looked upon him, I could only imagine his reaction when I finally was taken from him. Would he scream as Ana had? Fill the night with his grief until the stars burst and the sky shattered?

"Do you wish to speak about them?" His question caught me off guard. He noticed my trepidation and continued. "Myrinn told me about your parents. She explained your urgency to return to Tithe because of the promise you kept for them."

What else had she said?

I prepared myself for him to drag forth the truth about the sickness and how it, too, claimed me. I, like my parents, was the *tithe* paid to death himself.

I could not speak from fear I would expose myself, or the weakness that longed to burst through the cracks across my soul.

"I understand you will leave me, Arlo, and I do not resent you for it. When the door opens up between our realms, you will return to your sister, and I will not stop you. No matter how hard, I will *not* stop you. I want you to know that."

My knees buckled, and I dropped to the ground. I gripped fistfuls of sand, hoping to feel something real.

Faenir was there before me, hands reaching for my downturned face. "Speak to me, darling. Tell me what is wrong."

"What if I can't leave?" I managed, voice breaking with each word.

Faenir misinterpreted me; I did not correct him. "I long for you to stay with me. Selfishly, I desire nothing more, but I love you enough to know that I must let you go home. It is my punishment for stealing you from it, one I must endure."

I looked up; my eyes once again blinded by grief. "Say it again?"

Faenir's cool fingers dropped from my face, and he rocked backwards on his knees. "What?" He had not realised he said it aloud.

"You love me?"

His stare was lost to a spot on the ground between us, dark brows furrowed as he frowned, trying to make sense of his own words. "I am not worthy of such a thing, but I cannot help it."

Something cold and wet kissed upon my skin. I looked up at the dark clouds that swelled over the night sky like a blanket. Droplets of silver rain fell down over us.

"Who told you such a thing?" I asked. It was my turn to reach for Faenir, who gathered me willingly into his arms. "Let me be the one to tell you how wrong you are, Faenir. Are you truly blind not to see how surrounded you are by love? Do you not see it in Myrinn's admiration for you? Have I not proven to you enough how deserving you are of love?"

Faenir cradled my head to his chest, his hands working in calming circles across my wet hair as the rain fell harder and faster upon us. "I took you from your life because of my selfish and desperate need to feel your touch. Every day, I feel nothing but the burden of guilt for my actions. I do not deserve your love, Arlo."

"Stop it, Faenir," I said, rain and tears blending into one. "I love you. Do you hear me? I love you."

"Say it again," Faenir repeated my previous statement beneath the thundering of a brewing storm. Lightning sparked across the sky. A deep rumbling echoed throughout the blanket of clouds as though encouraging the weather to worsen. Still, we did not move from beneath it.

"I love you," I screamed in chorus with the thunder.

Faenir gathered my face in his hands and crashed his lips upon mine. The kiss was deep and urgent. It was a wave of wordless emotion that gathered me up and covered me. I drowned willingly to it.

"I am not deserving of you, Arlo," Faenir said as he pulled back. "I know it is just to let you leave me, but my soul screams for me to beg you to stay. Our time is limited, I recognise that, but I do not wish for you to go without knowing you will always have a place with me. I will carve out an eternity just for you to be with me."

The lie was the easiest for me to tell, because it was not entirely false, but simply lacking the details that I should have provided him. "I will never leave you, Faenir."

His golden eyes widened. I reached for the strands of wet, dark hair that had plastered across his face and moved them so I could see every inch of his expression. The sharp edges of his jaw, the heart-shaped bow atop his lips. All of him.

"I do not understand, Arlo... help me make sense."

I swallowed the sadness in hopes he believed every word I had to say. "Bond with me."

"Do not say such a thing."

I took his wet face in my hands to ensure he could not look away. "Bond with me. Do so and I will stay by your side willingly. Show me you want me and do it."

He blinked away rain that fell before his eyes. "If we do this, then it will not bode well."

"Because it will solidify your right to take the throne and become King? Do it. Take what is rightfully yours, take me and the crown and you can have me forever."

This was the mark I was to leave on the world. If Myrinn was right, Claria was growing weak. Faenir was the only one strong enough to protect Tithe and keep the wall surrounding my home, my Auriol, strong and secure from the evil beyond it.

Faenir deserved his destiny and if I was to die, then it would be knowing I could ensure Auriol's protection. Deep in the shadowed parts of my mind, I recognised it was my way of keeping my parents' promise.

"I would destroy this world if it meant you would stay by my side."

"Faenir." I cleared a droplet from his sharpened cheek. I could not tell if it was rain or a tear that cooled across my thumb and ran down my wrist. "Do this and I will always be with you. Do it for me, but more so... do it for you." Again, I spoke aloud my half lie. I would always be with Faenir, perhaps not physically, but like the spirits that dwelled within the Styx behind us, I would never be far from him.

Faenir pressed his head to mine and closed his eyes in contemplation. I allowed him the silence as the rumbling storm crashed above us, sky flashing with forks of blue-white shards of jagged light. When he opened his eyes again, they were void of sadness but brimming with confidence. "Arlo, it would be my honour to Bond with you."

I smiled into his kiss, gripping the back of his neck and holding him to me. His wet hair tangled in my fingers as we lost ourselves to one another. Time could have stopped completely as I gave into the relief of his agreement to my request.

"What next?" I asked, my chest full of warmth, as though it would burst with relief.

"If we are to Bond, it must be agreed by Claria."

The bubble popped as soon as he spoke. "She will never agree."

"I know," Faenir replied, lips brushing over mine. "There is, dare I admit, another way."

I looked up through clumped, wet lashes at the determination that oozed from Faenir. "How?"

"We take the throne from her. With the support of Myrinn and my family, it will be enough for the right of succession to fall to *us*."

I exhaled deeply, feeling the hammering of my heart shudder within the confines of my chest. "You mean to kill her?"

Faenir nodded, wincing in discomfort at his confirmation. "If she forces my hand, then so be it. I told you, Arlo, if it means keeping you, I will end them all. After all, it was Claria who had me thrown into the Styx hoping to have me killed. I am only repaying the debt... if it comes down to it, I will do so without guilt. That lack of emotion will be one we both share."

❧ 27 ❧

I woke abruptly, coughing so terribly that my throat burned as though I had swallowed fire. There was nothing else I could focus on but trying to catch my breath. I was panicking, hands clutching at my throat as though it closed in on itself. Each dry inhale was harsh and felt as though daggers pierced my lungs. It took a moment to finally calm myself, forehead damp with sweat and body covered in icy chills—not from the cold, but dread.

I felt the tickling of warmth across my palm and did not need to look to know that blood covered it. There was already the taste of it across my mouth, covering my inner cheeks, the sharp flavour turning my stomach into knots.

I sat there, hands upturned upon my lap, as the blood dribbled between my fingers and stained the white sheets. All I could do was watch it, a physical confirmation of what was to come. An omen.

The sickness rattled around my lungs with each breath. I waited patiently, trying to calm myself, until my breathing cleared and all that was left to prove that what had happened *had* happened was the red across my palms.

There was a storm brewing in the sky beyond Haxton. Each day it was becoming worse, with no sign of it passing; it mirrored that of the one within me.

I was thankful that Faenir was not in bed beside me, lucky in equal measures. He had taken to waking early since May's death to visit Ana; that, and the preparations for our Joining were well under way and consumed most of his time.

With the sun beyond the balcony devoured by the blanket of ominous clouds, it was hard to know what time of day it was. Usually, he would come bearing a tray of food late morning.

Which could be any moment.

Pushing away the discomfort that lingered in my chest, I threw myself from the bed. Tearing the sheets free, I bundled them into a ball in my hands and ran frantically around the room for a place to hide them.

The serving staff could not see the blood without alerting Faenir. And with my plan so close to fruition, he could not know of it either. *Or what it meant for me.*

I bundled the bloodied sheets beneath the bed. Hiding them in plain sight seemed to be one of my only options. As I clambered onto all fours and thrust the sheets forward, I caught a glance at the carving marks I had left on the stone floor, forgotten and pointless.

How long did I have? Days? When the first spotting of blood showed, I would have been preparing to leave Tithe to secure more of the vampire's blood. I never let it pass long enough to play with the knowledge of how long I had left.

Soon you will find out.

Shut up, I scorned myself, inner voices fighting as one.

I raced towards the basin of water that had been left in the adjoining bathing chamber. The cloudy water that filled the brass tub was tepid. Memories of the night prior passed through my mind; Faenir and I, sitting in the water, our naked bodies in constant contact.

There was no room for fussing as I stripped myself bare and climbed into the tub, wincing as it passed every sensitive inch of my body. Until I was completely submerged, blood melting from my hands in smoke-like ribbons, did I finally relax.

I laid like that for a while. Testing out my lungs, I held my breath and lowered myself until I was fully submerged. The tickling in my chest began before I reached the count of ten. Over and over, I slipped beneath the water and held my breath, hoping that this was all a trick. It was not.

I did not leave the bath when an unfamiliar clipping of feet announced a visitor.

"May I come in?"

My hands moved to clutch my groin as Myrinn's voice echoed throughout the marbled room.

"You came," I spluttered, water splashing beyond the tub and puddling on the floor.

Invitations for our Joining had been sent to all of Faenir's family, strapped to the claws of proud crows. Myrinn, Haldor and Gildir had responded within a day. Frila and Queen Claria had not yet responded as of the night prior.

"How could I not? I only hoped Faenir would have agreed to a Joining with you, Arlo, but what powers do you possess to have swayed his mind so quickly?" Myrinn beamed the most beautiful of smiles. It curved her eyes and painted her rounded cheeks with a pink blush. "The moment the invite arrived, I had practically thrown myself into a... what is the matter?"

I dipped my face lower into the water, annoyed that my expression had given my inner thoughts away.

Myrinn, regardless of my naked state, sauntered over to the tub's side. As though reading my mind, she snatched a softened towel that hung upon a wooden railing and thrust it towards me.

I reached and took it, knowing there was no hiding from the conversation. "It is happening quicker than I thought it would."

Myrinn's eyes glanced behind her as though searching for anyone that might hear. She turned her back on me as I stepped free of the tub. Satisfied we were alone, she replied, "I brought my most trusted healer with me. Arlo, I should have gotten to you sooner, but with how things were left with Faenir, I would have had no passage to Haxton if he did not permit it."

"You can look," I said, gripping onto the towel I had wrapped around my body as I was overcome with chills. When Myrinn turned around the pity in her eyes was too much to bear.

"I will send for her immediately."

"No," I snapped, taking a moment to calm my racing heart. "I need to see Faenir first, before he comes looking for me. Your healer can wait until later... not that their visit will have much effect."

Myrinn's hands were warm compared to my skin. She took me by the shoulders and stared deep into my eyes as though searching for my soul. "Have faith, Arlo, it is not over yet."

"And it will not be over until the Joining is complete." I pulled away from her hands and paced back into the bedroom.

Myrinn's light feet padded after me. "I admire your determination," she replied. "However, I cannot help but feel it is misplaced."

My body vibrated with nervous energy. "Frila, and your grandmother, have they bothered to provide a reply?" I asked, changing the subject somewhat, and pulled free the clothing Myrinn's tailors had recently made for me. These, much like the clothes I had arrived to Evelina in, were simple and durable, leather trousers and a plain, simple tunic with loose brown ties around the neckline.

"I would be lying if I said that Frila took a little more convincing to come than the others. However, I regret to inform you that Queen Claria has not been contactable since the previous Joining, although I am sure you are not surprised to hear this."

I could not say I was shocked at Queen Claria's lack of interest to come to the Joining. In doing so, it would mean she accepted our union, which she'd made clear that she did not.

Faenir's words came to mind. *If it means keeping you, I will kill them all.* The more time went by, the less they bothered me; a fact that should have disturbed me had the opposite effect.

"How did you do it?" Myrinn asked. "Convince him? He was adamant he wanted no part in the crown, yet I cannot help but notice that this sudden Joining was a silent acceptance of his fate."

"Faenir believes I will not leave him to return to Tithe if we go through with the ceremony. I have tricked and deceived him, manipulating Faenir's... love to get what I want."

Myrinn frowned, shaking her head. "Unfortunately, it will take more than those words to convince me you do not want this."

"It does not matter what I want. I will die either way. But I will not give up on my life until I am certain the lives of those *I* care for are secured."

"Auriol is not the only one you care for," Myrinn said quietly. "I see the way you look at Faenir. Even those who now work for Faenir have sent word of your love for one another. I understand you are dealing with turmoil that I, nor anyone else, can relate to... but even I do not need you to tell me you are doing this for any other reason than love for my cousin."

I raised my arms at my sides. "Oh, Myrinn, you caught me. Am I that predictable?" I despised the way I sounded, how angry I felt at the world, but everything that was being said was just another slash to my soul, reminding me I was dying and leaving more than I dreamed of ever having behind.

"Love is as predictable as it is a surprise. A blessing and a curse. It is love because it hurts as much as it heals and I wish it was not so, but it is."

"I am sorry," I said, lowering my stare to the floor. "My head hurts and I am tired. I should not have taken it out on you."

Myrinn stepped towards me and embraced me with open arms. I inhaled her scent, salt of the ocean and the light buds of fresh flowers. If I closed my eyes, I could almost imagine it being Auriol.

Ever since my parents' death, it was rare for me to lose myself completely to grief. Often, I had felt the urge, but never did the tears come so violently, until now. Myrinn held my head and allowed the shoulders of her navy silk gown to soak up the tears that spilled from me.

We did not speak. She simply let me be. It was the grief of my future which clamped down on my chest this time, not the sickness. It made breathing hard. Myrinn's hand rubbed circles into my back which helped somewhat.

I focused on her touch to draw me back out long enough to calm myself down. "When I die..."

"If," Myrinn corrected, tone ablaze with her belief.

"If, or when... please send a message to my sister. I have so much to say to her. So many things to apologise for. I cannot say goodbye on my terms, and I know I have already asked a lot from you..."

"Arlo," she said, breathless. Myrinn placed a finger beneath my chin and raised it until our gazes were levelled. "With your agreement to Bond with Faenir, it will not only save himself, but our world. The least I can do is to ensure your message reaches your sister, so she understands what has happened. I swear to you I will make sure she knows... everything."

"You know, I will miss you too," I blurted.

Myrinn chewed down on her lower lip as her azure eyes glistened, mist passing over them. "Never did I think I would care for a human as I do for you."

"What about your mate?" I asked, clearing my tears with the back of my hand whilst Myrinn dabbed hers away with the edge of a napkin she drew from her chest.

"Faenir was blessed to have... picked." We both grinned nervously at her choice of words, knowing how my being here was far more than being chosen as a Claim. "Chosen someone whom he truly connected with. Perhaps if Gale had not perished so prematurely, I may have come to love him too."

"Still no more news on whom is behind the attempts on my life?" I asked, being reminded of what she said.

"All fingers point towards Claria."

A clap of thunder echoed beyond the balcony. Myrinn jumped, both of us turning towards the noise as patter of rain fell heavily outside.

"If you are right, then she will stop at nothing to make sure the Joining is not seen through," I said finally, a shiver creeping up my arms and leaving them covered in goosebumps.

The feeling of dread had become a constant in my life. It twisted among my bones, squeezed through my veins and took root in my heart. This time it was not dread for me, but for the Queen herself, for what Faenir would do.

She deserved what was coming, but at what cost?

28

The storm broke above Haxton Manor, bathing the world beyond in darkness. The building trembled beneath the howling winds. A blanket of clouds coated the sky, split only with beams of jagged lightning; they overlapped one another, some coal grey and others midnight black, each as impenetrable as the next.

Throughout my stay in Faenir's home, I had grown used to the windows always being open. No matter if it was day or night, Faenir had an unspoken lust for fresh air. It was a rarity for them to ever be closed. Now they had each been secured, locked as rain battered across the glass with demanding cracks. Scratching of rain and sleet warred against the glass windows. The noise was terrible.

This weather was far more than any storm I had encountered. This one had brewed for days, only seeming to grow more tempered with time; it crackled with magic. The air was thick and charged. I could not ignore the hairs on my arms as they stood on end. There was no keeping away the cold that had seeped into my marrow until my bones ached. I couldn't discern if it was the weather that caused my discomfort or the growing sickness within me.

Warm hands brushed over my bare chest, drawing me out of my thoughts. I gasped, causing the healer to flick me an apologetic glance before continuing to study my skin, and more importantly, what lurked beneath.

"Is there anything that can be done to help?" Myrinn asked, hardly removing her knuckles from between her teeth.

We both waited for the healer to respond as the golden glow of magic emitting from between her fingers dimmed. The light had been conjured from nothingness, as though the woman clasped a strand of sun beneath her palm. It was not cold, nor warm, but pleasant, nonetheless. "No." Concentration deepened the lines of age across the older elf's face, which only added years onto her age. Her reply was finite and sharp, like a blade driven into one's heart without missing its mark.

Myrinn held her posture straight. However, even I could recognise how hard she focused to keep her honest reaction hidden from me. I watched her, unmoving and straight-backed.

For no other reason but to stop my hands from trembling, I began buttoning my shirt back up, focusing on the task at hand; at least it would stop me from torturing myself with the look of defeat in Myrinn's opal gaze.

"Thank you," I said; each word was as forced as the one before. "For trying, at least."

The healer backed off, her distance truly signifying that there was nothing else to be done.

"Try again," Myrinn said.

"Your Highness, I cannot heal decay—"

"Try again!" Myrinn snapped this time, interrupting the healer who cowered from the lashing of fury. "I refuse to hear your excuses. You have barely tried. Get back and try..."

"Enough." My knees shook as I snapped my attention to the scarlet-flushed princess. "Myrinn, please. It is done."

"It cannot be," she replied. "This is... I do not dare believe it."

I turned my gaze to the healer, whose eyes boiled with sympathy. It made me sick, more so than the extinguishing of hope that her confirmation had just caused. "You tried, which was all I could have asked of you."

"Your lungs..." The healer said, hesitantly looking between Myrinn and I. "Never have I felt such a thing before. They fill with blood, and they feel... wrong. Rotting slowly until..."

"Tarha, that is very much enough." I was thankful for Myrinn's interruption. "I trust I do not need to remind you of the importance of keeping this between the three of us. It would be truly awful if something unwanted was said."

Tarha, even in her advanced age compared to the princess, bowed as though Myrinn was the elder. "Threats are not required, Myrinn, not in my line of care. I simply wish to help ease the pain which," she looked back at me, burning holes into my head, "will come soon enough."

Myrinn blinked, keeping her steely expression. "If Arlo requires your help, then I give him authority to call for you."

"There will be no need," I said, still struggling with my buttons. My fingers were numb. I was more focused on swallowing back the urge to cough. It seemed a tickle had embedded into my throat like a thorn, refusing to clear.

Tarha bowed, dismissing herself without the requirement of another word. As she swept from the room, a worn cream habit clutched in her hand, a shadow passed before the door.

"I have been wondering where you have been."

I fumbled with the remaining buttons as Faenir looked between the escaping healer, Myrinn, and me.

"She came to check on the scarring," Myrinn said quickly, yet still Faenir's gaze studied me as though searching for the unsaid truth. "Being human means his skin will blemish no matter the healing or tonics provided. There is no denying a healer from checking upon their patient."

"Darling," Faenir said, completely ignoring his cousin. "Are you well?"

I smiled brightly, trying not to jump as a violent rumble of thunder echoed beyond the chamber door. "Couldn't be better," I lied.

Faenir did not believe me, that much was clear. Myrinn noticed it too, for she began fussing like a bird as she edged towards the door. She said something about supper and how she would see us there, then she was gone.

Leaving Faenir and me alone.

"Stop looking at me like that," I said, sounding like a demanding child.

"How can I not? I feel as though I have been deprived of your company," Faenir replied, kneeling suddenly beside the chair I had sat myself down on. If I had not, I was certain I would have fallen.

Noticing I struggled with the shirt, Faenir gently

swept my hands upon my lap. His fingers, fast and assured, began buttoning up my shirt. I groaned as his knuckles grazed my stomach. "I have wanted to come for you hours ago, but the rest of our guests arrived at the most inconvenient of times. There has been much preparation, and I did not want to concern you with it."

"Well," I said, trying to stop myself from demanding that he began undoing his helpful work and rip my clothes from me. "You are here now." I leaned forward and placed a gentle kiss on the end of his nose.

The soft touch conjured a purring groan from Faenir as he finished dressing me. "I missed you. Is that pathetic to admit aloud when you have been mere hallways and rooms away?"

"I..." My chest tickled. Panic surged through my body and mind as I prepared for the fit to come.

Faenir's grin faded once again, and he leaned forward, fingers brushing over my chin. "Something bothers you."

I shook my head, giving myself time to appease my breathing. Part of me believed I would open my mouth to reply, and the coughing would begin. If it did, there would be no hiding the truth when blood spluttered beyond my lips.

"It is the storm," I replied, thankful that my voice was clear and the tickle in my chest subsided. "I've never liked them. When I was younger, I would steal into Auriol's room, take her from the crib, and hide inside the wardrobe. Mother would find us come morning and no matter how many times she did, every storm always ended the same." It was a relief to speak aloud the truth to Faenir, to share a part of my past.

"Your sister has always been important to you."

I nodded, eyes pricking. "Even before my parents died, I had wished to protect her. Perhaps on more occasions than required."

"There is nothing wrong with wishing to protect the ones you love."

"Even if they did not wish to be protected?"

As the sickness grew within me, greedily clawing at my body in desperation, I could not forget how Auriol and I had left off. Just as the blood suffocated me as it filled my lungs, I had done the same to her. It would be a regret I would carry with me to the grave.

"I have no doubt that your sister loves you. How could she not?" Faenir glanced towards the closed balcony doors and narrowed his gaze as they rattled in their frames. "The storm will pass as they always do. However, between me and you, seeing Frila and Gildir nearly thrown from Charon's boat into the Styx has been a moment I will not forget in a hurry."

"I feel cheated for not having seen such a wonder," I replied, recognising the warmth in my chest as hope. Myrinn had arrived at Haxton alongside Haldor. It had only been a matter of time before their siblings arrived. "Only one more to arrive."

Faenir looked downward. His hand dropped from my chin and gripped my thigh. "Claria has declined."

I expected it, but still the news stung. "When did you find out?"

"Gildir informed me upon his arrival. It was the first thing he said as sick still dribbled out the corner of his mouth after he expelled the contents of his stomach upon my shores."

I gritted my teeth, jaw aching with tension as I bit

down on my response. "Do I wish to know what this means?"

"Tomorrow I will leave Haxton to speak with her."

"Kill her," I corrected.

Faenir gripped his hand into my thigh and focused in on my eyes as though I were the only thing of importance to him. "She has decided her fate, as I have decided *ours*."

Ours. I blinked and saw the horror in Tahra's face as she discovered the rot of sickness that was unrepairable. There was no knowing how long I could fight it. Even now, I felt weaker than I cared to admit. My neck ached as I held my head up, my arms tired and numb. Our fate raced towards its end, and Faenir did not know it.

"Tonight, we shall feast together," Faenir announced. "With what is coming, I will still need my family's support. I do not wish to go from living with knives at my back to ruling with newly forged swords at our fronts."

"And what if they do not listen?"

"If they turn their back on what I have to say, then they, much like Claria, will seal their own fates." His response was cold and honest, but it did not scare me.

I cared little for Faenir's family and the lack of kindness they had shown me, apart from Myrinn, who had been nothing but supportive; Haldor, Gildir and Frila had shown no loyalty to Faenir. I hoped that changed... for their sakes.

I pressed my forehead to Faenir's, delighting in his proximity. Inhaling, I took him all in, breathing in his scent of sandalwood and feeling the soft brush of his dark hair which tangled in my fingers.

"I can tell something plays on your mind," he said.

"Only that you will be forced to leave me tomorrow."

Faenir's lip brushed closer. "It will not take me long."

"I do not want you to leave me. Ever."

"Oh, darling." Faenir pressed his lips to mine. The touch was so soft, so gentle that if I did not watch him, I would never have known his lips were upon mine. "I will never leave you."

"What if I die?" I asked, not needing to tell him when or how soon it would happen. "You are an elf. Immortal and powerful. I am still a human, and my demise will come far sooner than yours."

A shadow passed beyond his eyes, darkening the gold until they glowed like embers in a hearth. "I command death. It has been my curse. For as long as I control it, I will never let you leave me."

I smiled. "How lucky I am to have found you."

"I hate to correct you, my darling, but it was I who found you. And I vow to never lose you... not in this eternity or the next."

Grief played with me as though it was a hound, and I was its bone. I drowned in the emotions; each wave was both anger and sadness, denial and clarity, not one moment was the same as before.

I closed my mouth upon Faenir's and felt calm. In contrast, the storm outside of Haxton seemed to grow restless. A bolt of lightning flashed throughout the room, highlighting everything so clearly.

Pulling free from him, against my want or better judgement, I spoke, "Not that I wish tonight's supper away, but the sooner it is over, the sooner I can take you away and feast upon you for dessert."

"With promises like that, I would gladly skip the meal entirely."

I smiled into him, and he into me. "It will be worth the wait."

"Darling," Faenir whispered, fingers gripping tighter into my skin. "I have no doubt. Come, let us not keep our revered guests waiting a moment longer."

29

The food laid across the elegantly dressed table was left untouched. Wasted. I felt guilt for ignoring Ana's hard work, but the thought of eating was displeasing. Not a single person reached for a fork or knife. Instead, the six of us clung to the goblets of sweet wine as though our lives depended on it. I could not decide if the lack of feasting from Faenir's cousins was because of an abundance of mistrust or a display of blatant rudeness. I guessed the latter, as they each had no problem with draining their goblets and refilling them without question. If they would have believed the food to be poisoned or tampered with in any way, then they would have left the wine as well.

"It would seem that even the weather is against your union," Gildir said, smiling into the rim of his glass; he revelled in the tension that sparked through the air in the dining hall, toying with it as though it was his to command.

A clap of thunder sounded beyond the walls as though

the storm had called out with its agreement. And Frila giggled softly at her brother's comment, giving him a side-eyed look, wolfish grin contorting her face from one of beauty to beastly.

I could not draw my attention away from the red scratch marks that flexed down the side of his face. No one had made a comment about the scratches, but I sensed everyone had seen them. Shifting my focus elsewhere, I studied the rest of his appearance. His moss-toned cloak was draped across his chair. The tunic that he wore had been rolled up over his elbows which rested—without manners—upon the table. He made me feel over-dressed in my obsidian jacket with the threading of embroidered silver stars across it.

"I care little what nature has to say," Faenir replied, his deep voice rich in darkness. "It is not her support I require. It is yours."

"Support?" Gildir replied, focusing more on the swirling of red wine that spun in the glass he whirled. "I was wondering why you requested for us to visit. Did you think some old wine and dull company would gain our seal of approval for your union?"

Only minutes into the meal and I already wanted nothing more than to throw the wine at him. I grinned to myself at the thought. Faenir seemed to sense my wishes as his hand laid across mine where it rested upon the table; his touch spoke a thousand words.

"That is not why we are here," Myrinn replied, scowling at her brother. "You understand our laws. Grand-mother is the only one who can bless the Joining. Can family not simply be family?"

Gildir glanced towards the empty chair that sat at the

head of the table. "Disfunction is the groundwork for any family, Myrinn, you should know that. So, do you wish to get to the point in why you persist with this Joining so we can get on with our lives?"

"Faenir needs our support," Haldor spoke up, offering me a sympathetic look. "It would seem you have made your mind up, Gildir. Which if that is the case, then care to explain why you are here?"

"Why are we all here?" Frila countered, voice light and sweet, but expression pinched in contrast. "Haxton is a miserable place. I wish nothing more than to leave it and never look back."

"Has anyone ever told you how insufferable you are?" I spat, unable to hold my tongue.

Frila pouted, white hair shifting around her shoulders as an unseen breeze filtered through the room. "Do not dare speak to me... *human*." She spat the word as though it was the greatest of insults.

This was not going well.

"Enough." Myrinn slapped her hand on the table. I felt the wine within my goblet shiver as though listening to her call. "All these years and we still cannot sit together in peace and discuss matters as families should. How do we expect Evelina to survive if we still treat it with such destructive care?"

"Evelina will thrive once Faenir steps down from succession and allows Queen Claria to pass it on to someone deserving." Gildir's knuckles paled as he gripped his goblet, and muscles feathered in his jaw.

"Unfortunately, to your great disappointment, I cannot let that happen," Faenir replied. He was the calmest of us all, back straight as he sat beside me, a rock of clarity, as though unbothered by the growing tension.

"It should first be clarified that I would have happily abdicated the throne. Not once have I ever desired to take it. Of course, all that changed when Claria forced me into Tithe. You see, my choice has never been my own. Just as she has poisoned you to hate me, she wished for the same with the humans. I am certain you do not need me to repeat just how differently that ended."

Faenir squeezed my hand and continued. "Claria's stubborn hate for me will be what kills this world, not I."

Myrinn's glass clattered against her plate as she placed it down. Haldor did the same, not until after he took a swig that drained his goblet.

"May I add... I believe Faenir is the only one strong enough to save our world," Myrinn said. Her gaze brushed over each of us to ensure she had our full attention. "To some of you, this may seem like a game, but it is far from it. Such a decision is serious, and I will do anything to ensure it happens."

"How disappointing," Gildir said, shaking his head. "Myrinn, the golden child. Turning her back on her family for some idealistic idea that Faenir, who kills whatever he touches, will not do the very same when given the crown to rule over our world. Sadly, you are alone in your views."

"No. She is not." All eyes snapped to Haldor, who sat rigid in his chair.

"You seem to have changed your tune so suddenly," Gildir said, lips tugging into a menacing smirk. "Not long ago, you gloated about being the next King of Evelina. Now you are out of the running with the... terrible... passing of your human, you change your mind?"

"It has nothing to do with her murder," he snapped, blazing eyes wide. The many candles that fought against the ominous gloom of the room spluttered higher, fuelled by his emotion. "If you speak about Samantha's death, then do so correctly. Do you not worry that your mate will be next?"

"My mate is secure with our Queen. Do not waste energy worrying about her, dear brother. Instead help us understand why you suddenly desire to see a monster take the throne." Gildir drew out his plea, only emphasising how unserious he was.

"Safe from you, I gather?" I said, glaring at the marks on his face.

Gildir's oak-brown eyes narrowed as he raised fingers to his cheek. "My mate has been hesitant of late. I am sure some heavy encouragement will soon calm her."

Frila giggled knowingly.

"Death rules the human realm thanks to the vampiric disease the witches spread," I said, ignoring the unease in my gut. "Claria does not have the power to counter the hordes of the undead that ravage our world and push it closer to complete annihilation. Faenir... he is the only one with the power to counter it, and I believe, stop it. Regardless of what you think of my kind, without us, you are nothing. You cease to exist."

Gildir studied me up and down with a look of disgust. "I do not understand how Faenir stomachs one with such unwanted—"

Shadows shook the room. Flooding across the table, they snuffed out each candle flame with ease. Left was the dull silvered light that entered from the few windows across the room. It happened so quickly that Gildir swallowed what he had to say next as fear silenced him. A small gasp escaped Frila's taut lips.

"Watch your tongue, Gildir," Faenir growled, now standing from the table with a cloak of shadows twisting at his back. "Speak to Arlo in such a way again and I will use you as an example of what happens to those who oppose me."

I reached for him, threading my hand into the fist at his side. My touch alone had the effect I needed, and Faenir's power seemed to retreat.

Haldor gestured towards the table, and the candles sprung back to life. I flinched at the sudden light as I willed Faenir to take his gaze from Gildir and look at me.

"I shall take the throne," Faenir confirmed his intentions, speaking through gritted teeth. "I requested your presence in hopes you would see sense. To ask that you stand with me, not against me, as I finish what is required. I see now that my hopes have been misplaced with some of you."

Frila glanced towards Gildir, but he did not notice as he watched Faenir with such burning contempt. I was certain he would have burst into flames if he held Haldor's powers. She then stood from the table, chair kicked out behind her. "I, for one, have heard enough."

Gildir stood too, chest heaving with each breath. "If we are done here..."

"Sit down," Haldor shouted. "Both of you. Stubborn as the woman who has poisoned your minds."

"We are wasting time," I said to Faenir out of the corner of my mouth.

"Gildir, Frila, please," Myrinn pleaded, taking another approach as I watched on at the family drama with a parched mouth and headache that thundered far more powerfully than the storm beyond the manor.

"Let them go," Faenir spoke coldly, waving a hand in dismissal. "I have no patience to entertain the minds of fools. Their decision is not important. What is to be done will be done regardless if they stand for me or against me."

The ground rumbled as Gildir flexed his hand. His power over earth echoed across the room. Glasses clinked against plates. Food toppled from their piles and rolled across the table before disappearing onto the floor. "Careful, Faenir, that sounds an awful lot like a threat."

"A promise," I spat before Faenir could gather his shadows again. "Why did you bother coming if you were never willing to listen to what we had to say in the first place?"

"It was not for the wine," Gildir sneered.

"Then what?" I persisted, noticing how Frila pulled back at Gildir's arm as though to stop him.

Gildir puffed out his chest, smiling down his narrow nose as his eyes trailed me up and down. "What makes you so special? That is what I wish to know."

He did not need to explain further what he meant. Suddenly, I recognised Faenir and his closeness, his touch, how it lingered across my body from the last time he had worshipped me.

"All these years and the bodies Faenir has left in his wake, yet you resist it. Why?" Gildir looked to Myrinn and smiled; it was only for a moment. I followed his gaze to find Myrinn looking defeatedly at her empty plate. There was a glint of amusement that passed across his eyes, one that suggested he asked a question when already knowing the answer; Myrinn seemed to confirm it.

My hand edged towards the knife upon the table. I would slit this man's throat before he said another word.

He knows. He knows.

"Is it fate... Arlo? Or something more tangible?"

A ruckus sounded beyond the closed doors to the dining room. My knees could have given way as the attention was quickly diverted away from me. Raised voices and the thundering of heavy footfalls grew in volume. I looked towards the doors the moment before they burst open. They slammed against the walls, shaking the dust from the rafters.

A huddle of figures raced in. Ana was at the head, tired face hollowed in horror. Something was wrong, that was clear before her rushed voice spoke. "There is a fire!" Ana shouted at the table of royalty, not caring who she disturbed; I loved that about her. "In the apartments for the serving staff. We tried to stop it... they are still in there."

As she explained what was going on, I noticed the smudging of ash across her face. The others behind her, panting and breathless, showed signs that they too had been close to flames, cheeks red and skin marked with soot.

"How did it start?" I asked, unsure if she could hear me over the others shouting.

"Lightning. The storm worsens. A bolt struck the building." Ana looked from me to Faenir, her eyes filling with tears. "Children, there are children stuck inside."

Faenir was moving for the door before Ana had the chance to finish. I raced after him, only to be stopped by his firm hand. "No, Arlo. Leave this to me."

I could not refuse him as Myrinn placed a hand on my

shoulder, nodding to Faenir in agreement. "I will look after him. Go."

"The fire, I can stop it. Allow me to help." Haldor was beside Faenir in a blink.

To my surprise, the short frame of Frila joined them too. Her face was void of humour and as serious as the rest of her family. "I will join you both."

Faenir did not waste a moment in accepting or refusing Frila's offer of aid. He was angry, not stupid. Instead, he looked back at me, planted a kiss on my forehead, and whispered a promise, "Stay safe. I will return for you soon."

Myrinn hugged my shoulders as we watched them rush from the room.

"Well, well," Gildir's voice drawled behind us. "It would seem we have some much-required time to discuss some matters."

I could hardly stand how placid he sounded as my mind was filled with the flashing of fire and storm. In the back of my head, I heard the screams of those trapped; they haunted me as I turned my attention back to Gildir. "Why am I not surprised you have not offered to help?"

Gildir smiled, oddly calm, considering what was happening beyond the room. He took his seat, kicking his feet up and resting them on the table, and snatched his glass of wine back. "Because that, human, was never part of the plan."

FAENIR

Frozen sheets of rain hammered down upon me; it stung at my skin, tore at my cheeks and face as I ran towards the fire. My clothes drenched through within moments of leaving the confines of the manor. I bit down on the cold ache that made a home in my bones. My discomfort was an afterthought.

Dark flames towered into the storm-cursed sky. There was nothing that could have prepared me for the destruction. It was both terrible and beautiful. Fire devoured the serving staff's quarters, wood and stone no match for the power of the wild element.

Not days before had I been kneeling before a child in one of those rooms. I glanced in the direction of Ana and May's apartment and saw nothing but flames dancing proudly beyond charred, glassless window frames. Haldor and Frila kept pace at my sides as we reached the blaze. I was thankful for their company. My power was great, but I had my limits. There was nothing my shadows could have done to stop this.

"*Nyssa*," I cursed the Goddess's name above the rain. "Help them."

Haldor stepped up to my left. His amber curls were plastered to his head, ivory skin illuminated as the fire raged before us. His narrowed gaze did not tear free from the fire as he sized it up.

"Can you hold it from spreading?" I asked, voice muffled by the powerful storm.

Determination fortified his expression. Droplets of rain fell from the tip of his nose as he nodded, shouting his reply, "I shall do what I can."

Frila slipped to my other side. Winds ripped around us, howling so viciously it sounded like a chorus of souls crying in pain. Whereas Haldor watched the fire as though it was his greatest enemy, she watched me.

"The winds are feeding the fire," I said. "Deflect the flow away and starve the fire. It will help Haldor attempt to put it out completely."

I did not wait to see if she listened to my command as I threw myself into the chaos.

Ana was aiding people from the scorched doorway. They came stumbling from it as dark, thick smoke billowed around them. Choking, spluttering. Some hardly kept their eyes open as others helped them run free.

Haldor stood before the burning building; arms held before him in worship. He leashed the flames with his power. Immediately, their frantic movements seemed to calm, dwindling slightly, but not completely.

Glass exploded from one of the higher floors. An outward burst of orange and ruby tongues reached out into the night. Not even the heavy rain could aid in putting the fire out.

I was helpless as I watched.

"This is terrible," Frila's small voice whispered beside me. "So much death. None of them deserved such a fate."

I turned to look down at her. Still, she did not aid Haldor. Frila kept her hands at her sides as she marvelled at the destruction.

"You are wasting precious time, Frila!"

Thunder rumbled in the skies above. Not a moment later, a burst of white-hot lightning forked across the sky. It illuminated the darkness, long enough for me to recognise the humour in Frila's wide, grey eyes.

"How are you to protect our world when you cannot even look after your own home? Death follows you no matter where you step. It always has and it always will."

Haldor roared into the night; my name mixed with his cry of desperate pleading.

I wished to turn and help him, but something stopped me; a whisper of my shadows forewarning that something was wrong.

Seared into Frila's cloud-silver gaze was my reflection. Tired, horrified eyes looked back at me. Frila cackled, and the storm echoed in response.

I reached for my shadows a moment too late. Frila was prepared. She threw her hands skyward, and a fork of lightning reached down as though to touch her. Winds billowed as Frila's power fed the storm.

Her storm.

I gathered my shadows in time, for the burst of bright light crashed towards me. The energy crackled across my arms. Inhaling, I smelt singed hair. I threw the cloak of shadows across me as her power slammed into mine. The ground fell away from me, and I spun wildly through the night. A sudden cry tore out of my throat, silenced only as my body slapped back into the muddied ground.

I clutched at my chest, unable to gather a breath. The pain stabbed through me, slicing up my back as though knives slashed out at me.

"What have you done?" Haldor shouted.

I blinked away the rain and looked up at his tired face. Dark smudging of ash had brushed across his cheek. "It is her..."

Haldor turned back, flames spreading across his hands. They hissed as the storm fell upon them, but still they burned bright. He was haloed by the flames that were still devouring the serving quarters as he faced off the deranged figure whose storm whipped around her.

"Dear Haldor, please do not stand in *our* way," Frila groaned.

I pushed myself from the ground, each small movement boiling agony, but my anger soon dulled the pain as it growled throughout me. Darkness swelled around Haldor and me, preparing to shield us if Frila attacked.

"It did not have to end like this, you know..." Frila called out, long-white hair twisting around her as a vortex of power formed into a cyclone. She stood before us, possessed with her element, eyes glowing with the crackling of lightning that she commanded.

"Never did I expect that you had the capacity to arrange such chaos," I replied, breathless from my fury. "Perhaps I should admit I am impressed, but that will not matter with how this will end."

Bolts of white light crackled across Frila's forehead. Even from a distance, I recognised what it was. A crown.

"Not all of my ideas." Frila laughed and thunder rumbled above. "Actually, it was not my idea at all."

"Then whose?" I asked, taking a cautious step forward. Fearing to blink as if I'd miss her next move, I readied myself to hear the name of our grandmother, to confirm what we had always known.

"Take a wild guess," Frila said, head bowing as her grin sliced across her face.

"Gildir," Haldor said.

The ground swayed beneath my feet, sounds diminishing to a soft whisper as Haldor's accusation settled over me.

"How fabulous, you got it in one!" Frila replied. "And I was hoping to play a little game to draw out this finale. Shame."

I had to get to him.

Fire dripped from Haldor's fingers, melting onto the wet ground at his feet. "It makes sense at least, sending you out to do all the hard work to ensure he benefits from whatever this is all for."

Frila pouted. "Oh, brother, are you finally seeing that you are not grandmother's favourite? Do not be too upset, will you?"

"Fuck you!" Haldor roared.

My head throbbed, skull aching as thoughts slammed within it. I took a step forward but the fizzing of Frila's power popped across my skin in warning.

"Now, now, Faenir. Another step and I will be forced to see if you can survive my lightning. I have always wondered what would become of you in the face of my power."

There was nothing else of importance but Arlo and the girl who stood between us.

"Go to him," Haldor said, his words meant for me only. "I will deal with this one."

Frila's fingers tickled the air, and the winds whipped towards us. "Care for me to kill you the same way I did with your sweet little human? Want to feel what she had when I choked the air from her lungs?"

Haldor faltered.

"I would be careful with such claims," I added, sensing the growing heat that spilled from Haldor's presence.

"Claims?" Frila barked. "You have grown soft, Faenir. Gildir was confident you would kill Haldor's human, but it seems compassion has weakened you. Your lack of action simply forced me to do what you could not."

Haldor attacked without another word. He ran forward before my shadows could stop him. Frila welcomed him, bending her knees like a cat ready to pounce. Whips of pressurised fire grew from his fists. He lashed them out towards the place where she stood. Her laugh resounded through the winds, a warning that this was exactly how she wished for this encounter to go.

Haldor stopped dead in his tracks. His fire diminished as his hands clamped towards his throat. His head was thrown backward, mouth pulled open by unseen hands.

The conjured winds grew stronger. Wilder. I forced my way through them as Frila picked her brother up from the ground and dangled him in a web of her power, as though he were only a child's doll. A burst of lightning cracked across the ground before me. Her shot was meant in warning, to keep me in place so I could do little but watch, all without paying much mind to me.

Frila focused solely on Haldor as she ripped the air from his lungs. The glow of life that encased him flickered. His feet kicked out beneath him, eyes bulging out of his skull as the whites turned blood-red.

I pushed on, trying to reach him. The shadows willed me forward, unable to break through the winds which roared between us. More lightning cracked. The ground burned. Hands raised before me, I pushed at the wall of air, trying to force myself through. My body had become leaden beneath her power. She kept me pinned in place, unable to do anything but watch.

"You. Shall. Not. Stop. Us!" Frila screamed, imprisoned by her deranged mind. "It is ours. OURS!"

Desperation clawed out my throat and fuelled my shadows forward. Dark fingers of my power reached out to Haldor. My attempt was futile. The golden light of Haldor's life force spluttered. Before my eyes, it blinked out of existence and bathed him in the shadows of death.

Haldor's arms dropped to his side, his neck falling at an awkward, sickening angle. Then he tumbled to the ground as Frila's winds threw him carelessly. There was a moment of clarity that followed Haldor's death, his shadows reached out for mine and joined as though we were one.

Frila, breathless, fell to her knees and clutched the ground. Not once did she take her wild eyes from the body laid out before her. Then she did something that sickened me. *She cried.* Eyes red and tears rolling freely down her face, she unleashed a howl that broke the storm apart.

The winds were amicable enough for me to walk freely. Frila did not take her eyes from Haldor's body as I stood above her, my shadow falling across her small, hunched posture.

"Was it worth it?" I asked, kneeling before her. Part of me expected a fight, but the realisation of what she had done caused her to break into pieces upon the ground.

Frila did not look away or answer me. I watched the very understanding pinch her beautiful face into a mask of horror. Slowly, she peered up at me. I could only imagine what she must have seen, as my shadows spread like wings behind me.

"It was inevitable," she hissed, fingers digging into the ground. "The tithe to pay for taking the crown. It always was."

The murder of Haldor had broken Frila. She was not made for the burden of death. Only I was.

"Gildir will see that your human dies just as he has with all the others."

I should have left her at that moment, but the hunger that cramped my soul was too powerful to ignore. There was nothing I had left to say to Frila. Words would not relieve my anger. Only death had that power.

I reached for Frila. Determination filled her eyes as my fingers closed in on the skin of her jaw. My shadows flared against her life-light, serpents thirsting for its energy. Willingly, she reached out her dirt-covered hands and gripped the sodden shirt at my chest. It was as though she longed for the release I could gift her. As soon as my touch graced her face, I devoured her. The rush of her life had me crying out into the night. The feeling was euphoric. I gripped her jaw tighter, leaving bruises across her cold skin as I drained the life from her.

I let go long after Frila died. Her skin rotted, melting

from bones as muscles blackened and turned to ash. She crumbled beneath my hand.

Light broke through the thick clouds as they dissipated. At the back of my mind, I was aware of the many servants who watched on. Ana called out my name for aid as the fire still raged on.

My focus no longer belonged to them.

Shadows gathered around me, blocking out the world entirely. The silence I called for was welcome. It did well to drown out the turmoil that warred through my bones and blood. Yet there was only a single name clear enough to cut through the booming in my mind and the agony that clawed through my soul.

One name.

My mate.

Arlo.

30

Dread speared down my spine. It carved its way across my skin and flayed me in two.

Faenir.

Gildir seemed relaxed considering the chaos of the storm and the fire it caused, disinterest smoothing every line of worry that I expected to pinch his face. Everything about his laid-back demeanour made a shiver of alarm spread across my arms.

Myrinn stood by my side, silent as a guard of stone. I glanced sideways at her to see if she too sensed something amiss. She was looking wide-eyed at me, but not from surprise or horror... from sorrow.

"Dare I ask what plan you are referring to?" I glared towards Gildir.

He smiled in return. As he did so the four scratch marks across his jaw flexed as though he was a peacock, and the marks were his feathers.

"Well," he said, voice light and full of amusement. "The one in which we separate you from your oh-so-deadly-mate for a chance to discuss matters."

"The storm..." My tone practically glowed with accusation that I did not need to finish my sentence.

"I am surprised it took you this long to work it out. Was it not obvious that the weather turned alongside our arrival? Frila always loved a show and this one has been spectacular." He raised his glass as though in cheers, then took a long swig with pride.

"Myrinn," I said, unable to take my eyes off the elf as the truth settled upon me. "You need to help Faenir."

"Faenir is not in danger," her reply was cold.

"That is right," Gildir added. "Frila simply needed to remove you from one another long enough for the necessary to occur."

It no longer mattered what Gildir said as I looked upon my friend with horrified confusion. She could hardly hold my gaze, constantly looking down to the hands that she had clasped before her. There was no ignoring the way those hands shook.

"You knew about this?"

Myrinn swallowed hard. "It was never how I wished for this to end."

"To end?" I choked on my words as my mind raced to piece together this puzzle. Myrinn's betrayal stung. A dull ache echoed throughout my chest, and I gripped at it, unsure if the sickness caused it or the revelation.

"I am sorry." Myrinn's reply was short. I stood frozen to the spot as she turned her back on me and paced to the room's edge.

"Would a glass of wine help wash down what we have to discuss or..."

"Fuck your wine," I spat, body trembling with rage.

"What a mouth you have." Gildir chuckled, placing his fingers before his lips. "I must say I can recognise Faenir's interest in you. You are an interesting boy. I only hope Auriol turns out as thrilling as you."

It took a moment for my mind to catch up with the name the elf had spewed. Gildir, who until now enjoyed hearing the sound of his own voice, paused as well, revelling as he witnessed me work out what he had said.

"What did you just say?" The storm became a distant memory as a new roaring screamed within my ears. I paced towards the table, needing to hold myself up for fear my legs would give out.

"Your sister, Auriol," Gildir continued. "Pretty girl I must say. I can speak little of what her mouth can accomplish but I admit her hands, although wild, have great potential."

I watched as he brought his fingers up to his scratched jaw and rubbed it caringly.

"How do you know her name?"

Gildir raised his glass in toast again, this time gesturing towards where Myrinn stood. "My sister shared such interesting information, like your sister's name, not that I needed it to find her. Those eyes... One as blue as cobalt, the other as brown as ancient oak. Such mesmerising eyes and the moment I found her in Tithe I knew her to be your kin. Yet the most interesting news was to learn that you are dying, that all my attempts before have been nothing but wasted effort because you would always have perished in the end anyway."

My legs gave out. I gripped the table, arms suddenly numb, as I tried to hold myself up.

"Arlo." Myrinn was beside me once more, hands reaching out.

"Get away from me," I spat; tears welled in my eyes.

"Steady now," Gildir's calm and steady voice sliced through me like knife through hot butter. "We do not have long before we are to leave, and I need you in one piece."

As my hand fell, my fingers wrapped quickly around the ivory handle of a knife. Neither one of them noticed as I slipped it into my sleeve, slightly nicking the skin on my arm as I did so.

"I don't believe you..." I said finally, breathless as I looked up at Gildir from the floor.

"I do not require you to believe what I have to say. Your trusting of my words will not have an effect on the outcome."

"But you had a Claim..." I spluttered, although my mind kept telling me I had not seen her with him since the day in Tithe. "The door between our realms is sealed..."

"It was. Sadly, the first human I took was rather boring. Auriol, I am confident, will be completely different," Gildir said proudly. "The barrier was closed until I convinced Claria to tear it apart to allow me to retrieve my *new* Claim. Only she has the power to do so, even if it has made her substantially weaker. Grandmother knows her time is coming to an end and with Frila, likely moments from being slaughtered when Faenir discovers the truth, that will leave only myself left to take the crown."

"Why?"

Myrinn winced at my broken, meek voice. "I wanted nothing more than Faenir to take the crown. For years I have petitioned for such a thing. But you are dying..." It pained her to say it, visible from the grimace across her face, and it pained me to hear it. "If Faenir loses you I do not believe he would be strong enough to endure. Evelina has had one unstable monarch; it will not survive another."

"Myrinn saw the light."

"I was given no choice," she snapped. "Do not mistake my decision for anything more than wishing to see this world continue. Gildir, you are the last resort, not the preferred."

"Faenir trusted you." I glowered, ashamed of the tears that ran down my cheeks. "I trusted you."

Myrinn pinched her lips into a tight line. Her dark brows furrowed. She did everything to hide the hurt that desired to flash across her face. She failed at it. "Auriol will be safe," she replied finally. "That is one promise I have not broken."

Safe? The scratch marks upon Gildir's face suggested she felt anything but safe. I almost laughed at the notion before the jolting sickness in my stomach silenced me. The fear I had felt when Faenir had first taken me from Tithe flooded back. Did she feel that same fear now? Scared and lost in a new world filled with danger and betrayal. Where families sent one another to the slaughter for the one purpose of feeling the weight of gold upon their heads.

"So, what now?" I asked, clammy hands holding onto the knife I had taken. If Gildir thought the scratches my sister gifted him were bad, then the one I would leave would be more... lasting. "What was the purpose of all of this?"

Gildir turned his head to the side, studying me as though he was a dog looking at a bone. "Do you wish to see your sister again?"

The question caught me off guard. The answer fell from my mouth as though it was the easiest thing I had ever had to say. "Yes."

Gildir stood from the chair, casting his shadow across me. "Then we must leave before our opportunity fails us."

He offered me a hand. I stared, stupefied, as though not knowing what to do with such a thing.

"Why not just kill me now?"

"Do not tempt me," Gildir groaned, eyes rolling into the back of his head.

"Gildir, stick to the agreement." Warning laced Myrinn's words.

He sighed, dropped his hand back to his side, then glanced to Myrinn where she loitered behind me.

Do it. This was my chance. *Finish him.*

I gathered myself up onto one knee, slipped the knife free and lunged.

The tip of the dull knife gleamed in the candlelight. It was fast. But Gildir was quicker. One moment I was facing him. The next Gildir stood behind me in a blur, hands gripping my shoulders as he turned my body to face Myrinn...

The momentum of my attack did not stop. Myrinn didn't have a moment to blink. Then the knife stabbed through the bottom of her jaw, jarring through sinew and skin, until the hilt slammed into bone. Blood spilled from her open mouth; the gore-stained blade visible between the gaps of her open lips.

I fell backwards, hand letting go of the knife which stayed buried in her face.

"No," I screamed, gagging for breath as vomit filled my mouth before splattering onto the floor at my feet.

Myrinn gargled in response. Her hands violently shook as she reached up towards her face.

"You have saved me a task," Gildir whispered into my ear. He sounded both close and far away. "Two perhaps, for once Evelina finds out what you have done to one of its beloved princesses, they will never wish for you, or Faenir, to take the throne."

I had no fight left in me as Gildir steered my body from the room. Myrinn gagged and spluttered on the blood that filled her mouth. As we left her, I was certain I recognised the thud of a body falling to the floor.

I had killed her.

As my feet moved through Haxton Manor, the thundering boom of the storm still raging outside, I could not stop looking at my hands, at how red they were. My fingers were sticky and slick with her blood. I smelt it, harsh copper that made my mouth water in warning for more vomit.

Soon enough the blood washed away as Gildir pulled me outside. I cared little for the cold, or the sting of the harsh rain that fell upon me. Even with the blood vanishing from my hands I could not stop seeing red. It was everywhere, cursing my mind with each blink. No matter how I willed for it to go, it did not.

"I didn't mean to."

"Yes, you did," Gildir replied, voice raised above the crashing storm.

From somewhere in the distance, I could see the glow of fire. Even through the heavy winds and devouring rain I could smell the harsh scent of smoke.

"She betrayed your trust. She sold your sister to the enemy and for that you wanted to punish her."

"No..."

"It will be easy to convince them all." He leaned in close, lips brushing my ear. "Thank you for that."

The water of lake Styx thrashed furiously beneath the weight of Frila's conjured storm. Charon waited at the end of the wooden walkway that extended over the lake. His boat knocked against it over and over.

Gildir sat me down within the boat which began to slide away from Haxton Manor. I was helpless to stop it. Charon guided us across choppy waters, his dark cloak billowing behind him.

The further the ferryman took us from Haxton the more I could see. Fire grew from beyond the manor, outlining it with a scarlet halo. Dark clouds of smoke stretched up for as far as I could see, mixing perfectly with the clouds as they willingly joined as one.

Faenir's name was a whisper against my sick-covered lips. I wished to say it but the pain was too much. I couldn't conjure up enough energy to do so. Each breath of mine fogged beyond my lips, my lungs rattled as though my grief encouraged my sickness to take me here and now.

"He will come for you," Gildir confirmed; his words did not bring me relief. "But he will be too late."

The storm broke suddenly. I felt the air still as the winds calmed and the waters beneath the boat settled into its glass-like face once again. Above, the clouds seemed to part to reveal a sky blanketed with stars. All at once the magic that had crackled within the air had vanished.

"Ah," Gildir sighed, his shoulders relaxing as he

slumped forward in his seat. "It would seem you are not the only one with blood on your hands this eve. How poetic, the prince of death and his mate cut from the same cloth."

The ferryman skimmed across the Styx like a pebble thrown with force; the speed ripped the tears from my face.

"King or not, Faenir will kill you if anything happens to me."

"I am counting on it," Gildir said through a grin. "He will come and prove himself to be the monster he is. You may have softened him in the eyes of our people but that was doomed not to last."

"Fuck you."

"Careful, Arlo, I would not wish for you to ruin the chance to see your sister before you die. Myrinn told me your wishes... I know you would do anything for her."

I stilled, swallowing hard as the image of Auriol filled my mind. Within my chest, tied in knots around my heart, was a cord. At one side it pulled towards my sister as it always had. The other yanked back towards Haxton, towards the man I had left behind.

"Monsters are for slaying, Arlo," Gildir muttered at my side, facing towards Haxton as though searching the darkness for Faenir as I did, "Never for ruling."

❧ 31 ❧

For the sake of your sister, play your part convincingly.

Gildir's threat clawed through my mind. *Play your part.* During the carriage journey Gildir had explained how my visit to court would proceed. How I would be presented before Claria and the crowd of gentry as a witness to Faenir's crime. Except that was not all I was here for now. My *part* had altered, from being a witness to a partner in his crime.

Myrinn's death was never meant to happen. Gildir wanted me to know that he enjoyed watching my expression as he drove home just how I had killed her... it was my doing. This deviation from Gildir's perfectly planned story only aided in proving both Faenir's and my crime to the people of Evelina as a way of ensuring they would not wish to see us take the crown.

There was no proof that Faenir had killed Frila, but Gildir was confident nonetheless, only confirming to me that he'd sent his own sister, one who'd stood firmly at his side with equal views, to her death.

What of Haldor? He had left with Faenir. Could he have stopped him from falling into the trap laid out for him?

Hope was a strange concept as Gildir guided me through the ominously lit corridors woven within Nyssa. With each shuddering inhale I smelt the thick scents of damp earth. The further we got into the Great Tree of Life, the more my legs ached. My chest tightened with each breath, rasping in the pits of my throat as though liquid was within it.

I could feel my life bleed away with time. The rotting sickness I had delayed for so long finally caught up with me. It was greedy and rushed, racing to claim me before I could dodge it for another time.

Gildir led the parade ahead, a circle of decorated guards who regarded me with all-consuming hatred behind him. To them I was no longer the man who could withstand the touch of death. I was a killer.

There was nothing I could do but keep my stare ahead, focusing on each step to ensure my legs did not give out. The promise of seeing Auriol once more before it was too late kept me going.

What will she think when she sees me? Tired and weak, would she know the moment her eyes laid upon me? In my mind's eye the cloudy vision of my sister broke through the chaos. I saw her glaring at me with the same look the guards shot my way. Gritting my teeth, I could not dwell on what could be, when I was moments away from finding out.

I recognised the destination from my first visit to Nyssa. Unlike before, the doors leading to the throne room were left open due to the crowd of people that overflowed from them, so large that they could not fit completely within.

A path was made between them. No one needed to move a muscle to allow us to pass through. Once they bowed as Gildir swept before them, chin raised and shoulders rolled back, they glowered at me. The weight of their hateful glares forced more pressure upon me. Although I cared little for what they thought, I knew there was no coming back from this, no changing their minds now. Some elves spat across the floor before my feet. Others cursed my presence. Many wept with Myrinn's name, a whisper across their lips.

"Bring forward the killer." Claria's aged voice was recognisable even at a distance. It rang out across the crowd, silencing them. If I closed my eyes, I would have believed that no one was left around us. "I wish to look into his soul when he tells me why he decided to take the life of my darling Myrinn."

A sharp sword was suddenly at my back; it kept me moving until the twisted throne of wood came into view with the hunched figure of Queen Claria sitting upon it like a child. The Queen's expression was void of any knowledge of this charade, yet I could see the satisfied glimmer in her grey-glazed eyes that she was enjoying every moment of this.

Gildir stopped before his grandmother and bowed. The bend of his back was so dramatic I was surprised he did not extend a hand and wave it before him. The crowd was so focused on me that they did not notice the hungry grin he flashed my way before he took his place at the Claria's side.

That was when I saw her. Stiff and straight-backed, her

face covered with a white, lace veil, Auriol stood waiting for Gildir's return. I knew it was her as though I knew my own self. Through the veil I could feel her gaze piercing through me. I longed to see her face, to know the truth of how she saw me, exhausted and covered in someone else's blood. Blood the storm's rain had done more to smudge then wash away completely.

My knees cracked against the ground, the pain no more than a whisper.

"Do you have anything to say for your crime?" Queen Claria bellowed.

Play your part.

As if to remind me Gildir reached out for my sister, longer fingers curling around Auriol's hand. She tried to pull away, but he held firm. As his knuckles paled, I longed to scream out and beg him to stop.

Play your part.

"I have means to make you talk if required," Claria called out, attempting to draw my attention back to her.

"I did it," I spluttered, urgent and rasped. "I killed Myrinn."

She did not ask why because the reasoning did not matter. All that did was the blood staining my clothes and the effect it had on the crowd. "What do you have to say about Prince Faenir?"

My throat closed as though hands gripped tightly around it. As I opened my mouth to reply a spluttered cough came out. It sounded as though stones filled my lungs. It took over my body, cramping and stabbing with agony.

The crowd reacted in a chorused gasp.

My hands slapped atop the strange forest floor as I

tried to catch my breath. Wide-eyed, I watched droplets of deep scarlet fall from my lips and splatter across the stone. They blended seamlessly among the red petals around me.

By the time I pushed myself back on my knees I could hardly stay still. My body rocked. My mind groggy and slow.

His shuffling of feet caught my attention. I drew my eyes slowly from Claria back to Auriol who was being restrained by Gildir. His smile had faded and in place was a fearsome expression of annoyance. The fading scratch marks that she had gifted him gleamed across his skin; that made me smile.

"Faenir will answer for his crimes when he comes for you," Claria said, unbothered. "For your sake he will behave or find that you will meet the same end as Myrinn, as Frila."

"Fuck," I exhaled, blood and spit spilling down my chin, "you."

Claria's shoulder relaxed. Her lips twitched upward at the corners as she turned her attention to the crowd. "I trust another life does not need to be taken to prove that Faenir and his Claim are not worthy to rule our beloved Evelina? Nyssa looks down upon our fading world with great sadness at what has happened... she has lost faith in us. It is important that we make amends before it is too late."

I felt a chill race across the back of my neck. I looked over my shoulder to see if death waited behind me, ready to take me, but only the sharp tip of a sword winked back at me. There was no reason to fear the blade; my sickness would take me long before it could.

Knelt before the twisted, bitter queen of Evelina, I clung to life more desperately than I ever had. Each blink was slow. Claria spoke and her voice seemed muted and muddied. I picked out a few words, trying to focus on them as blood hummed through my ears.

Crown. Gildir. King.

More coughing grasped my body and had me bent over, mouth filling with blood. A strange, starving feeling lingered in the back of my head. It dulled the copper tang of my blood and changed it into something sweet.

"My reign as Queen has come to an end. To give Evelina the chance to stop Faenir and save this world from the undead that steal those we require for sustenance, it is time another takes up the mantle. Gildir, once Joined with his Claim, will be granted my blessing for succession. I hand over the crown and its power willingly. I forfeit my..." Claria stopped speaking suddenly, or perhaps my ears gave up.

All at once there was a silence that thrummed around the room. The falling of soft, red petals from the trees that crowned the room seemed to slow... then stop all together.

I blinked.

Gildir had Auriol's hair gripped in his fist, sword drawn before him as he faced off something behind me.

Claria stood, skin glowing with light as though stars beamed beneath her wrinkled skin.

I wished to see what had scared them, but the world was askew. *No.* I laid splayed across the ground; cheek pressed to the mossy floor bed. As the cough came again, in a wave far greater than before, I could do little to sit myself up. Blood pooled within my cheeks, threatening to choke me where I lay. Unmoving, I was far too weak to hold my eyes open long enough to see what caused the room to swell with disorder.

My eyes closed again. The darkness was so welcoming I did not wish to force myself to see, all until hands brushed over my body. Seeing through narrowed eyes, I looked up at the flushed face of my sister. Auriol. Her lips were moving quickly, the veil ripped from her face to reveal the knowing horror that ruined her beauty. I could not hear her. I tried to say her name but gargled on blood as though my lungs no longer had room for air.

That look... I had seen it upon her face before, when it was much younger, many years ago.

Auriol's ivory dress was stained red. Her fingers dripped with my blood. Droplets even graced the skin of her jaw as slick, horrid coughs continued to devour me.

I gasped for air but the blood filling my mouth, throat and lungs prevented it. The world was far too bright. Before I pinched my eyes closed again, I saw Auriol throw her head back, mouth split as her silent scream made her face feral.

This time I did not open my eyes again.

I was surrounded in darkness, freefalling through it as obsidian winds clawed at my body, pathetically trying to catch me. I went willingly, my mind's clarity was as clear as crystal.

Somewhere in the distance I was aware of Auriol's presence as death guided me away from her. Beyond her was Faenir, a presence of shadow and silence that this calming void recognised. They both occupied my mind. Their memories, both new and old, had my soul singing with glee.

I stopped falling. It felt as though my body hit the floor which had come up to greet me. My conscience recognised something was wrong. I should have kept falling forever and ever until I was so immersed in death that there was no return.

Yet something had stopped me. I felt the dark void regard me, judging my presence as though to see if I was worthy of it. Its decision was clear. Death chewed me up and spat me out. And as my eyes snapped open all I could feel was *hunger*.

FAENIR

I pulled the knife free from Myrinn's jaw. As the metal slipped free of flesh, she let out a howl. It sliced through me, itching nails of urgency across my soul which anxiety had grabbed hold of. I was careful not to touch her blood-coated skin and discarded the blade across the floor.

"Where is he?" My question was a growl.

Myrinn's lips trembled, teeth dark with blood. The only sound she made in return was the whimpering of an injured animal.

I looked across the room, studying the knocked over chair. The emptiness of Arlo's presence.

Gildir.

Myrinn was trying to say something. Each time she forced a noise, more blood spilled from the wound beneath her chin. It gushed across her body, spilling free, until her gown looked as though it was crafted from the richest of rubies.

I stood, leaving her reaching for my jacket. Never had one come so close to touch me willingly, other than those seeking death. The shock of it had my attention snapping back down to her.

Myrinn continued to splutter words that made little sense. I wished to clasp her shoulders and shake sense into her.

"You promised to protect him," I shouted down at her, spittle flying. "You owe it to him to tell me what Gildir has done!"

Myrinn's weak fingers dropped from my jacket, staining the hem red. She gagged on her own gore. It splattered across the floor, almost black in the ominously lit room, as though red wine had been spilled carelessly upon the floor.

A waste.

My world was in turmoil. Still, the fire grew in the servants' dwelling, the bodies of children and their families stuck within. Ana had called after me as I left the bodies of Haldor and Frila discarded across the ground; I did not turn back to help her. All I could think of was Arlo. His name thrummed through my mind. I felt his lack of presence as physical agony. My bones ached as though they grew brittle in my arms and legs. Even the blood in my veins seemed to thicken and boil. The worst of it was the tremendous crack that formed deep within my chest.

Gildir had been behind the attempts upon Arlo's life. Gildir had wanted power at any cost. Gildir had taken him from me—my Arlo, snatched from my grasp. In that moment, I felt as though the meaning of my life had slipped through my hands, never to return. Darkness swelled within my soul, an overwhelming ache that clouded my vision and shackled me with a slew of terrible thoughts.

I will kill them all. They took everything.

Arlo, my heart.

It all shattered.

I felt the Styx shiver as my cry broke free. The souls who slumbered within the dark waters came alive. Even from a distance, I felt them crawl free from their imprisonment. They harboured my hate and *welcomed* my anger, begging me to share my burden so it did not consume me.

Powerful, disturbed shadows spun around me like obedient hounds returning to my side. The presence of the dead pounded within me for release, and I gave it to them. I lost myself to the power. To grief. I cared little for Haxton, for Evelina, and the innocents that dwelled among those who wished nothing more than to punish me for believing alive. They had finally broken me. After all these years, it took a human boy to drive the fatal weapon into my cracked heart to see it shatter completely.

They wanted the monster. They wished for it. For an age, Claria and my family had forced me onto a path I never wished to journey down. Here I was, at the end, alone and broken. Hollow. Carved from the inside out.

They had taken the one thing that kept my love for humanity and life ablaze.

It was time for them all to feel as I do now.

Myrinn's blood-slick fingers clamped around my ankle. Her touch was steel, fingers gripping my skin as nails dug into it. The touch broke through the darkness within me, like sun peeking between clouds. I looked down as the glow of life drained from her body. Her death came swiftly and instant, my shadows fuelled with hunger for it. Had her pain become too much to bear? She wished for peace she likely did not deserve and found it by pressing her skin to mine.

No. It was not that simple.

Before her, strokes of blood had been painted across the floor. She had wished for me to see, her way of giving a message, one provided only with the sacrifice of her life. Drawn in blood was a single word. Even upside-down I could make sense of it.

Nyssa.

My shadows closed in around me so suddenly, devouring my skin, my body, until we were one and the same.

Myrinn's final message was simple. Gildir had taken Arlo to Nyssa.

❦

I could only imagine what those around me thought as I swept into Nyssa. In their wide, horrified stares, I could see myself, passing through the innards of the Great Tree with shadows billowing from my back like the wings of some dark being come to claim its prey. Hidden within my shadows, the dead withered, twisting and coiling among one another like snakes forced into a basket.

Phantom arms reached out towards the crowd that waited beyond the throne room. Their screams of terror set my soul on fire. Some ran, many stayed standing, frozen to the spot. They all shared the same fear, I could taste it, sweet as honey, making my mouth salivate with yearning.

Did they come to witness Arlo's murder? A crowd of people who had once shown us love now thirsted for revenge, to witness Arlo suffer because of falsities and lies.

No one stopped me from sweeping into the throne room. My dark reflection flickered across the metal breastplates from the soldiers who tried to calm the panic my presence had caused.

I lashed out with my shadows in warning to any who got too close. My touch would not be what killed them. The power they had scorned had now changed. It was poison, leaking into my shadows, as though they hungered for death more viciously than before.

The countless elves parted for me. Bodies moved to each side of the forest.

Then I saw them.

Claria sat forward on her throne, smiling with hysterical glee. Gildir stood before her, sword drawn and raised, towards where I walked. It did not deter me from taking another step. I regarded them both, lips curling above my teeth.

Then I heard a sound that seemed misplaced. Crying. I turned my attention to the sobbing woman to my side. She looked up at me, not with horror, but sadness. One blue and one brown eye blurred red with tears. I recognised her. How could I not with such telling eyes? Arlo's sister. Auriol.

There was no time to make sense of how she was here. Not as I regarded the cause of her grief. Arlo was cradled in her arms. His skin was grey. His arms limp at his sides. And the glow of life that I had memorised so perfectly... was gone. In its place was thick, lingering darkness. The mark of death.

"Careful where you step, cousin." Gildir was before me,

his sword still brandished between us. Now there was little distance between the tip of the blade and my chest.

I glanced down at it with no concern. The sword was pressed through my jacket and into my skin. I could not feel it. Did not care. My shadows curled around the blade like armour.

"Arlo is dead," I confirmed aloud.

"It was not I who killed him," Gildir replied. "Did you not know? Did your dearest Arlo not reveal his lie whilst he had the chance?"

I glared down the sharp edge of the blade towards the hand that held it. Unlike the crowds, thin now, as many had run—*clever choice*—Gildir showed no concern at my proximity.

"Lies," I hissed, my shadows echoing the sound as though starved serpents dwelled within them.

He shrugged. "Faenir, for the murder of Frila, Haldor and Myrinn Evelina, it has been established that you are not worthy of succession."

I did not deny it. Their deaths, one way or another, had been caused by me. But their lives did not compare to the one that lay wasted across the lap of a grieving girl.

"You took him from me," I said, shadows crawling up the blade, inching close to Gildir with each passing moment. "All I wished was to be left alone. Never did I care for the crown. For Evelina. For any of this, yet on and on you forced this idea that I wished to rule down my throat... and at what price?"

I spoke to Gildir. To Claria. To anyone left listening as the grinding, painful reality that Arlo lay dead near me slammed through me, and there was nothing I could do;

no power over death itself could prepare me for seeing his cold, stiffening body in the hands of his loved one.

"It was never as simple," Gildir whispered, for only me to hear.

"What have I done to deserve this?" I felt oddly calm as I asked.

"Well," Gildir laughed sharply, as though my question was ridiculous, "you were born." His words had no effect on me. He intended to cause me pain, but pain was an ally. I longed for it, desired it in more ways than one.

"As Nyssa's chosen heir," Claria called out, voice hardly heard over the shouting and screaming and pounding of running feet. "I decree Gildir will be King. It has been decided."

"I lay no claim to your throne," I spat, stepping forward as the sword pierced further into my chest. Gildir's steeled expression faltered at this. His eyes widened only slightly, enough for me to notice his confidence waning. "Have it if you are so desperate. But you will rule over a world of waste, I promise that."

Gildir stepped back. I strode forward, skewering myself upon his blade in hopes it would finish me. I wished to die, to give into that peace which had been dangled before me for years.

I glanced over his shoulder to Claria, who sat watching. "Rather, a powerless runt takes the crown and seals the fate of Evelina. The death of a few may stain my hands, but the destruction of us all will scar yours."

"I will save it."

"Just as Claria has? Keeping the humans in pens like cattle, instead of dealing with the threat that our own creations caused? I look forward to seeing you fail."

Gildir dropped his hands from the hilt of the sword. He stumbled back. Onward I stepped.

"Stand down," Claria warned, bones clicking menacingly as she stood. "You have caused enough damage to this family."

Hate boiled within my bones. My shadows gathered and grew, draining what little light that still spewed from the haggard Queen of Evelina. There was not one person I despised more.

"It is done, Faenir," Claria's voice cracked as she spoke. "My last decree is to banish you to your dark dwelling and ban you from ever leaving its shores for the sake of our people and their safety. You, devil, are not welcome here."

"I will see that you pay." I glared at Claria, then to Gildir, who still looked with shock at his sword, which had pierced through me. Where blood should have spilled, shadows danced in its stead. The forest bed beneath my feet withered and rotted.

"Take your death and leave," Claria warned.

She spoke of Arlo. My death. My Arlo. I could not bring myself to look at him. If I did not look, then it was not real. Even if my shattered soul twisted into knots at the knowledge that he was lost to me.

"Do you wish to know why you could touch him?" Gildir said with a smile.

I looked back at him, shadows screaming for the chance to reach out and drain the golden glow of life that encased him. "I care little for your lies."

"Did Myrinn never reveal what she so willingly told to us? How your dearest Arlo had been dying all along. His life was already entwined with yours, Faenir, even if you were too blind to see it."

I hesitated. Gildir took this as his chance to spill more lies. Where his words did not hurt me before, these cut deep.

"He drank the blood of vampires, concealing his death but not stopping it."

"Liar."

I studied his face for proof that he had lied, the shifting of an eye, or the twitch of a lip.

"Even the very thing you command wishes to escape from you," Gildir said, leaning forward slightly as though preparing to share the greatest secret of all. "And the worst part of it all was my attempts to see that Arlo died were in vain. When all that was required was waiting... patiently... as I have for this day all my life."

My shadows flared like wings at my back. A roar filled my chest and exploded outward as another fleeting cry joined in chorus with me.

Gildir looked away from me, brows furrowing over narrowed eyes at the girl, Auriol, who held the unconscious body of my beloved. I followed suit.

She was standing, arms now empty, and her brother's name carved into her cry. "Arlo!" She looked at Gildir, as Gildir looked at her; it was a strange encounter.

"Impossible..." Gildir muttered quietly, drawing my attention back to him.

My heart jolted in my chest, as though starting again after slumbering in the darkness.

Behind Gildir, with eyes glowing the purest of scarlet against pale, ivory skin, stood Arlo. Clawed fingers gripped Gildir's shoulder, pinning him in place. Arlo's mouth was parted, revealing two sharpened points of teeth that seemed to extend before my eyes.

Arlo regarded me like a predator. His pink tongue brushed against his pointed canines one by one. His attention then fell to Gildir's exposed neck. Spit ran from the corners of his parted lips as though he was a starving hound looking upon a carving of raw meat.

"Darling?" I whispered.

Arlo did not reply, his focus locked elsewhere.

Gildir did not move. Could not move, no matter how he fidgeted beneath Arlo's grip.

"This," Arlo hissed, his voice different from before; it sounded harsh and forced, like nails pulled across stone, "is for them *all*."

Claria could not so much as gather breath to shout in warning as Arlo threw back his head, opened his pale lips wide and dove his teeth into Gildir's neck.

✤ 32 ✤

It was believed the kiss of the undead led to the spread of their disease, teeth sinking into skin, the drawing of blood from a victim until they were left an empty husk of flesh and bone. We were all wrong. I was proof that we were fools ever to believe such a thing. With the nectar-like liquid filling my cheeks and slithering down my throat, I had been brought back not because of a bite... It was the blood that I had drank willingly.

It had poisoned me.

Changed me.

And most of all, it did what Father had suggested, kept me from the grasp of death—now for an unfathomable amount of time.

Before me, Faenir was a creature to be feared. Wings of shadows spilt from his cloak. His golden stare was wide, his head cocked. It took tremendous effort not to close my eyes and give in to the euphoria that filled my body as I drained Gildir, who I had entrapped beneath my grasp. I was stronger than before. Renewed. Famished. *Starving*. I gave little room for Gildir to move, digging my nails through his shirt and into flesh until more sweet, divine blood spilt across his chest; every drop that did not grace my lips was a waste.

The hunger had its own voice, desperate and pleading, like a child locked in a cage in which the key had been long lost. The moment my eyes opened, and I saw Auriol, I almost wrapped my jaw around her arms. Even in my desperation, I knew not to, enough to press away from her and choose my victim. Gildir was the easiest one to pick. Even with the overwhelming thunder of hearts that chorused through my head, or the scent of blood that tickled within my nose, he was the one who called out to me above the rest.

I moaned into his neck; lips smudged with blood. My tongue lapped against his slick skin as though I was a cat drinking cream from a bowl. It was glorious. The more I consumed of him, the more soothed I became.

"Darling," Faenir spoke finally. It could have been seconds or hours since I had first clamped my jaw around Gildir's soft neck. Time was pointless, a silly concept that meant little to me now. "That will be enough."

A strange, unwanted feeling crept into my consciousness. Was it guilt? Disgust... no. It couldn't be when his blood was so holy. So beautiful.

"Arlo," Faenir said again, this time his voice harsher. More commanding. The shadows that spread around him shrunk with each passing moment.

Reluctantly, I withdrew my teeth from Gildir's neck. He groaned, sounding more pleasured than pained. I could only imagine what Faenir saw. My lips were coated with dripping red gore, my chin and chest covered with my ravenous urgency.

"Abomination!" someone cried.

I cared little for the speaker. Words could not hurt me now. Faenir's lip curled above his straight teeth in reaction.

"Your light." Faenir reached out his fingers, toying with something unseen an inch beyond the skin of my arms. "It has gone."

"Because I am dead," I replied, mouth watering as the copper tang of blood teased my nose. My meal still waited, unmoving and spellbound, in my arms.

"That I can see."

I searched his expression for revulsion. There was none to find. Even I was oddly calm with the deep-rooted understanding of what I had become. I did not fear myself or give room to contemplate just what I was doing to Gildir. It simply felt right. Just.

"Why did you not tell me of your sickness?" Faenir asked.

I dropped my gaze downward, suddenly feeling the creeping of emotion flood back into my chest—my empty, still chest. "I cared for you enough to hide the truth. I did not wish to watch you break if you lost me..."

Faenir pondered that, eyes glazed over in deep thought. He was silent for a long moment; I soon believed he would never speak again. "You are far from lost, my darling."

I did not flinch as Faenir reached those gentle, caring fingers and brushed them across my jaw. His touch was featherlight and... real. Warmth like nothing I could have expected. It shocked me. I gasped, lips parting as the points of my teeth nipped at them.

"Skin as cold as forgotten marble." Faenir's voice trembled. His eyes traced across me as his other hand reached out, marvelling at how he did not kill me with his touch.

I groaned into his touch, hands gripping hard upon my prey so he could not escape me.

"I feel as though I should ask how this is possible?" Faenir's question was no more than a whisper. He did not need to elaborate for me to know what he wished to uncover.

My desire to live *had become my curse.*

"Perhaps," I replied, wishing to melt into his hands and forget the world. "We will discuss this soon."

I sensed the presence of someone familiar join at my side. It was Auriol, I knew it from her scent alone. She smelled like home, dust and old wood with the undertones of freshly picked roses. I closed my eyes and saw a bunch of flowers within a vase on the table of our home in Tithe.

"What have you become?" she asked it aloud as though it would make it seem real. "I watched you die in my arms. Arlo, the one I knew has gone... haven't you?"

Part of me longed to reach out and embrace her, to hold my sister close and never let go again but I feared what I would do. My eyes flickered between hers and then her neck. Her skin fluttered above the plump artery, as though enticing me to greet it with my teeth.

I gripped tighter on Gildir's limp, living body as though to anchor myself.

"Perhaps I am still the same. Maybe not. Either way this is my doing." My words came out in a hiss.

Faenir's attention was drawn elsewhere to the clattering of metal and the shouting of an old woman whose voice was likened to the unimportant buzzing of a fly, one I wished to swat.

"How long have you suffered without me knowing? The way you coughed... that sound has haunted me for years. I would never forget such a noise."

I nodded, tongue tracing my lower lip to savour the sweetness that coated it. Her eyes, those same eyes that had tied us together as siblings, watched my tongue as though it was the most dangerous thing she had ever seen.

"It began not months after Father died. I knew from the first spotting of blood that I could not put you through the suffering that still scarred you. Auriol, the choices I made were to ensure you were never left alone. And now I have become a nightmare of flesh..."

"I don't know what to think," Auriol replied, looking towards the limp elf in my grasp. "But I cannot say I am not relieved either way."

"He hurt you, didn't he?" I asked. I feared if the answer was yes, my hands would twist, and his neck would snap beneath them.

"Given the chance he may have. After he came for me, there has been little time alone enough to know his capabilities, although his intention was clear."

"Auriol, I wanted none of this to happen."

"Me being here, or you becoming..." She could not say it.

"Everything."

Auriol grimaced, reaching out her hands, but not for me. "Give him to me."

The protective growl erupted out of nowhere. Auriol did not step back but pushed her hands forward to show she was not scared of me. "Enough blood has been spilled, Arlo. This is not you."

It was not me before. But it is now.

Faenir's demanding voice distracted me. I turned as Auriol took her chance to pry the elf from my arms. I caught a fresh scent on the wind as I regarded Claria, standing guard beyond the throne as though she protected it. Her attention was on Faenir entirely, who had snaked his way towards her.

"This ends now," Claria croaked.

"Indeed, it does," Faenir retorted, wings of shadow flaring out behind him. "It could have been different, Grandmother, I want you to know that."

"No," she spat, eyes wild. "I saw the destruction of our realm the moment you were born. Evil. Death. Decay. Everything Evelina stands against and yet you stand before me, the very omen of our destruction."

"Your words do not—cannot—hurt me."

Claria tore the crown from her head and cowered. There were no soldiers to protect her. They had run from the room along with the crowd who had been led here. "You will not have it. It is not yours."

"If that's true, then allow Nyssa to be our judge. You are not a Goddess as she is. You are a bitter old crone who led this world down the path it is on. Hand in hand, you have guided us to this moment. You may see me as the demon, as you have declared me, but I am merely a product of your hate."

Claria fell backwards, stumbling over her weak footing. Still, she did not let go of the circlet of gold with the inset of opal and rubies. Her wrinkled fingers held on as though her life depended on it. All this blood and death because of that crown. It had inspired hate, greed and malevolence; it represented nothing of life and the beauties that came with it.

"Give it to me," Faenir commanded, the grass rotting beneath his feet. "Make the end easier for yourself."

She pressed her back against the base of her throne. Her gaze flickered between the crown, to Faenir and then to me where I stood. "As breath fills my lungs, I will never lay my blessing upon you."

"Then you force me into a corner that I did not wish to be kept in. Just as you have done from the moment you had me thrown into the Styx in hopes of my demise." Faenir's voice cracked with sorrow. Whereas I wished to rip into her rumpled, old body and drain blood from her veins, he did not want death.

"You. Shall. Not. Have. It."

"I will. Once I pry it from your cold, dead hands."

I watched understanding glaze across her eyes. Her time was up. Her reign ended. Faenir gathered his shadows and sighed, dispersing them until they melted away and he was left mundane without them.

"Do it," I hissed quietly. Faenir flinched, continuing his stride towards his grandmother.

"They will never accept you," she spat, forcing her face as close to his as he knelt down before her.

"*My* people will not have a choice in the matter. Just as they did not have the choice when you were given the crown. I will be forced to prove myself worthy. Earn it. Whereas you believed respect and admiration was given just because of the chair you sat upon and the gold that weighed down your head."

"I hate YOU!" Claria screamed, clutching the golden circlet to her chest protectively.

Faenir replied, calm and clear, "I, Grandmother, forgive you."

Queen Claria Evelina pinched her eyes closed as the King of Death brushed a careful hand across her cheek and claimed her soul as his own.

Days later and I longed for Claria to be alive just for my chance to take my fury out on her withered body. I did not imagine her taste was pleasing, but still I longed for it, now even more so than before.

"Tithe may not be standing by the time we return," Auriol reiterated, looking between Faenir and I.

"What has our captive revealed?" Faenir asked coldly. He sat on his throne, arms resting on each side whilst he twirled a pomegranate around his hand. He always had something in his hand, testing the limits of his renewed power. Days since he'd laid the crown upon his head with the rotting carcass of Claria beneath him, his power had changed.

Even as my sister spoke to him, his focus was never entirely on her. He watched the pomegranate, waiting for its pink skin to melt to black rot. It never happened.

"Claria paid a price of power for Gildir to take me from Tithe. He had no problem gloating about the exchange of magic in which Claria had paid. Taking it from the protection around Tithe to regain energy to open the door between our realms. If the Watchers have failed, our home will be no more than a feeding ground for the..."

Auriol's words trailed off as she looked at me. I held her unwavering stare in contest.

"You can say it," I told her.

"Vampires."

Faenir reached out and placed a hand upon mine. I was perched on the edge of the throne, one hand occupied, toying with the silk of Faenir's dark hair, the other gripping a vial of blood, Gildir's blood. As soon as I felt the singing of hunger, it was safer for me to pop the cork and drink it. It would stave off the famished cry and keep those close to me safe.

"It has been days now and still nothing has been done," Auriol scorned. Her tight-lipped expression proved that she had far more to say but didn't. She had taken it upon herself to become Gildir's keeper, the carrier of the key to his imprisonment. She had yet to tell me what he had, or had not done, when he took her from Tithe. And I learned to keep my questions to myself. Auriol did not need me to protect her, the scratch marks on Gildir's face had proven that.

My sister was determined and clear-headed. Faenir had not asked for her council, yet she provided it brilliantly when it seemed the rest of the elven realm had turned their backs on the new King.

"Something must be done," I said to Faenir, my breath causing the strands of hair to dance.

Faenir nodded softly, contemplating. I wished to reach out my fingers and turn his face to look at me, to help ease the deep-set lines of pressure that had pinched his handsome face the moment the crown and its responsibilities rested upon him. "Auriol, I vowed to ensure the humans survive."

Auriol grimaced, fists clenching at her sides. "Easy words to say sitting comfortably upon a throne."

I winced. Faenir did not react.

"It is clear your grandmother wished for the same. Keeping us penned in walls like sheep hiding from wolves. You should be more concerned with us humans thriving, not surviving. Stop hiding us away. Deal with the issue that your own magic has ultimately caused."

Auriol did not require a sword and armour to make her look like a warrior before us. Straight-backed, chin raised high and eyes burning with fierce determination, she was prepared to take the cause in her own hands and save the world.

I smiled, pride swelling in my chest. "My sister is right, Faenir," I said, catching her quick glance at me. She regarded my smile and her own lips twitched.

Faenir stood from the throne, fingers gripping tighter across the pomegranate until its juices spilled down his wrist. He regarded Auriol. "If all humans share a soul as strong as yours, I do not doubt they will prosper. There are many wounds across your realm and mine that need healing. I only wish you to consider staying with us to provide your strength to aid them."

Auriol had made her wish to return to Tithe abundantly clear, and I had not tried to change her mind. It was her choice to make, not mine. Those lessons had been hard learned. Much had been said between us since Claria's death, and still there were many things left unsaid. I revealed the promise I made to our parents and what I had done to ensure it was kept. I did not do so to encourage her forgiveness for my actions and control, nor had she given it to me.

It took a while for her to look at me for more than a fleeting moment. When she did, she would usually avoid my eyes, now deep red like swirling pits of blood, instead of the once blue and brown that we shared.

Yet it was Auriol who had collected Gildir's blood during her visits to him in his cage in the deep prisons of Nyssa. It was her unspoken acceptance of what I had become, that was all I had needed.

"Auriol, thank you." Faenir bowed to my sister as red petals fell from the trees above her. They landed upon her crown of brown hair as she stood tall. "It is a wonder to have your guidance. I only hope that I do right by you."

If my heart still beat, it would have skipped in that moment.

"What will you do?" Auriol questioned, shifting her stance to prepare to leave us.

Faenir looked over his shoulder to where I sat, lounged across his throne. I still expected him to look at me with loathing at the creature I had become. Never did such an emotion fill his golden stare. In its place was warmth and admiration.

I was no longer living, but beneath his attention Faenir made me feel alive.

"I believe the opportunity is now to infiltrate the hive, to deal with our problems rather than hide them behind walls."

Haxton Manor was deathly silent around us. Peaceful.

I picked up the scents of scorched wood and charred stone. It clung to everything. Faenir had done little to deal with the damage of Frila's lightning. He had revealed that he did not wish to either.

When we had returned to his home, we had found it empty. Ana and those who had survived the fire that Frila's lightning had started had left. Even the Styx was uninhabited; the spirits and souls that had been trapped among the water had found freedom. No longer did they dwell in the dark depths; now they lived within Faenir's shadows. He did not call for them often, but when he did, I saw the silver glow of the phantoms dancing happily among *his* darkness.

Charon had also found freedom. The ferryman's boat was left moored upon the shores of the Styx when we had returned. Faenir did not say a word as he pushed the boat back into the water and helped me inside. Charon, like the dead that left the lake beyond Haxton mundane, had found peace alongside Faenir. I was glad about that.

๑๐๛

Faenir's hands gripped my thighs, the pinch of his nails into my skin was thrilling. He refused to let go as he rolled his hips, encouraging his hard length to push in and out of me.

My arms straddled either side of him, keeping me leaning over him with our lips inches from one another. I looked down at him as I bounced upon him. My sudden control over the sex had him groaning as he bit down on his lip.

"Fuck," I breathed as Faenir's pacing intensified. I gripped the sheets as my teeth grew in my mouth, the tips pricking my lips and drawing blood.

"You take me so well," he groaned; his pleased words warmed me just as his hands did.

"I don't want this to end."

"Arlo, darling." Faenir slowed, moved his hand to the back of my neck, and brought me close to his mouth. "You are mine forever. I am yours."

"Forever is a long time," I replied. "You may grow bored with me."

"Never," he said, thrusting into my ass until his hips pressed against me.

I howled with pleasure, throwing my head back as my stomach cramped with hunger.

Faenir noticed. He brought his wet lips to my ear and whispered, "Drink from me."

I could not deny him. His invitation was what I longed for. I studied him beneath me. Dark hair fanned out across the pillows in a halo of raven shadow. His cheeks were flushed red. Lips glistened as though coated in honey.

"Are you certain?" I hissed, finding it hard to restrain myself from sinking my teeth into his flesh.

"I am going to need you at full strength, my darling," Faenir said softly, "For what is to come."

My tongue traced my teeth, running across the points of my canines as they sharpened. This hunger differed from the emptiness of my stomach. It was lust; it spread across my chest and warmed my cold body from the inside out.

"Come." Faenir continued fucking me, guiding my head down towards his neck. I pressed my hands to the muscles of his chest, my nails scratching across his skin with excitement. "Feast, my darling. We leave soon."

Night was upon us. I felt it coming more than I could see it. Faenir had thrown walls of thick, impenetrable shadow around the room to stop the sunlight from bothering me. The night's arrival signalled our departure. Auriol readied herself back in Nyssa. She would expect our return soon.

"Promise me when we come home, to steal me back into this room and keep me captive just as you always wished," I said, lips pressed to the skin at his neck. My teeth grazed across him, drawing a breathy sigh from my King.

"We are eternal," Faenir replied, pounding softer into my ass as his hands clawed down my back. His touch was warm against my cold skin. It left trails upon it, marks that would linger. "You are my forever."

"Oh, Faenir." My voice was muffled as my mouth was filled with skin. One bite and his nectar would fill me; the thought alone wetted the tip of my hard cock. "I love you."

The King of Evelina pinned beneath me groaned as I bit into him. My teeth spilled through his warm skin as painless as I could make it. Sweet, powerful blood filled my cheeks, and I drank.

Faenir fucked me harder. I closed my eyes as my body burned with euphoria. Faenir squeezed my ass with one hand and held the back of my head to his neck with the other. Above the roaring of pleasure, I heard his breathless reply. "And I love you. My eternal. My forever. My darling."

✤ 34 ✤

WHEN SHADOWS COLLIDE

Castle Dread loomed before us. The shards of dark brick and aged stone was a stain against the landscape of Darkmourn. Its turrets glowed beneath the silver of the full moon. The light did wonders to outline the many details of this haunting place, brick by brick, at least those that still stood. Much of the castle was left in ruins, torn apart by a witch's power countless years ago, yet the great doors at its entrance were left unmarked and closed.

I had never been this close before. It looked empty to the eye, but my keen ears picked up movement from deep within. A shifting of light feet. A murmur of voices.

"They're inside and know we have arrived," I said.

Faenir stood beside me, shadows crawling beneath his hands in readiness. Auriol was at my other side, hand clutching mine tightly.

Even within the shadows of the castle grounds, we were being watched. Stalked. Creatures with glowing red eyes prowled. The warning yip of a wolf sounded from our side. They watched, but never came close enough to be seen beside a flash of red and the sharp snapping of jaws.

We waited beyond the doors of Castle Dread for our host to welcome us.

An elven King. A vampire. And a human.

What a sight.

A shiver passed across my skin as the doors finally opened. The sound of ancient hinges screamed, scratching at my mind with claws of horror. I felt my elongated canines nip at my lower lip as I tried to keep fear from my face, especially when I saw whom we came to visit.

Two figures were outlined by the warming glow of fire within the castle. One was taller than the other. He stood forward as though to reveal himself. Hair of white moon-light crowned his head. His eyes were the richest scarlet. His face was carved and hollow, with strong bones and dark brows that stood in contrast to his ivory skin. Two points of sharpened teeth overlapped his lip which twitched as he regarded us.

"What *do* we have here?" His voice was as deep and rich as the velvet navy jacket that rippled when he moved. He cocked his head skyward, nose flaring as he snatched our scent from the windless night. "I did not realise an invitation had been sent for visitors. Jak, did you call for our guests without my knowing?" There was humour and teasing in his voice. However, there was no denying the sharpness hidden beneath it.

The second figure stepped free from the shadows of the doorway. He was beautiful. Curls of brown hair perfectly laid across his forehead. He wore a loose tunic of white that billowed at his arms and sat low across his shoulders. His skin was deeper in tone than that of the man he stood besides, but it still gleamed with the grey of death. "No, Marius, it would seem they are lost."

I hissed as they laughed in chorus. Auriol squeezed my hand in warning.

Faenir's shadows twisted like snakes as he stepped forward. "I expected more, I admit."

Marius, the vampire of legends, lowered his head and smiled. His tongue escaped the confines of his tight-lipped mouth. He drew it slowly across his teeth, ensuring we each saw the glistening tipped points as though he were a peacock, and they were his feathers. "What do we have here?" Marius said. "Such an unlikely group of visitors, I must say."

"Invite us into your home and we can discuss our presence, among other things," Faenir commanded.

The petite figure, Jak, stiffened. Then flames spread across his closed fists until each hand glowed with curling tongues of orange.

My breath caught in the back of my throat. The last time I had seen such power was in Haldor. The thought alone soured my mouth, especially because Jak was no elf. He was as formidable as the witch-turned-vampire he stood proudly beside. *Witch.*

"This is all your fault," I spat. I did not need to elaborate for them to know what I meant. Vampires. The death. The undead that ruled Darkmourn more than the living.

"Now, now," Faenir sang. "Darling, let us not offend our hosts just yet."

"Your presence alone offends me. Leave before I call for our hounds to chase you out," Jak warned, fire spreading to his elbows. "Or better yet, I could be the one doing the chasing."

Marius chuckled at that. I felt his burning red stare bore into me, studying me from head to foot. Faenir did not like that his attention had turned. "Dare I enquire as to why one of my own creatures," Marius mused, drinking me in, "hangs stakes from his belt as though they were jewels or something of worth? How amusing."

My fingers twitched. I longed to pull out one of the carved stakes to show it off as he had with his teeth.

"Cut the shit. We all know you are not going to turn us away. So, are you going to let us in or not?" Faenir asked, voice raising above the darkness as though to prove he controlled it. "We have come a rather long way."

"Step closer," Marius said, lifting a finger and curling it inward in beckoning. "I do not think I have seen the likes of you before..."

Faenir sensed the danger behind his words but stepped forward anyway, not without snarling in warning at the bloodthirsty creature. Perhaps it was his curled lip that made Marius react, or the fact he finally sensed the elf's power. The strangest thing occurred. Shadows lingered behind Marius like a cloak, a power similar to that of my King. Faenir noticed, flaring his shadows in response. They regarded one another for a moment.

Jak stared, with narrowed and distrusting eyes, between his lover and mine.

"Ah, perhaps you should come in," Marius said finally, breaking the strange competition of power. "You are welcome to join us for a drink. That is as lenient as my hospitality can stretch. However, as our hosting has been forced upon us, I am afraid the wine I offer has long spoiled, yet I see that you have brought your own drink with you."

I wished to stand before Auriol to protect her from Marius and Jak's sharpened stare. Her grip on my hand kept me in place. She snarled, far more deadly than anything Faenir and I could have done in that moment.

"I long to be the one to kill the first vampire," Auriol warned, glancing to Jak. "Perhaps it will be I that finishes the task that you failed at all those years ago."

Jak bucked forward with a snarl. Marius reached out a hand and stopped him, not caring for the fire that burned his skin. Jak recalled his power instantly. Then they both shared a whispered word, before shifting their attention back to Faenir.

"Long have I wondered when your kind would reveal themselves to me," Marius said, releasing his hold on the witch-boy. They both stood aside in offering. "It would seem we have a long night ahead of us." With that, our hosts turned on their heels and enticed us to follow them inside the belly of Castle Dread.

⁂

Jak studied me over the lip of his glass. Eyes like a viper, tongue just as loose, he left a trail of spit across the rim. There was no question that blood filled his glass, and that it was human. I could smell it, pungent, even from a distance. It reminded me of my sister, who sat stiffly beside me.

"Why should I concern myself with the death of your kind?" Marius questioned, bored as he laid back in his chair.

We were surrounded by shelves of books towering on either side of the room. I could have lost myself to the gilded lettering across the spines and the smell of the pages if I was not in such... unpredictable company. Fire glowed in the many hearths within the study; they had been lit before we had entered.

"Have you wondered what would happen to you when the last human is drained of the precious blood that keeps you... reanimated?" Faenir's question was pointed and precise.

"That is not a matter that should concern you, elf." Unseen wind lifted the brown curls from Jak's forehead.

"Oh, but it does. Greatly, in fact."

"Do go on," Marius said, amused. "What holds your interest in whether or not humans survive the might of my kind?"

Faenir had not touched the wine that Marius had poured for him. The cork spun around within the dark liquid; even the bottle was covered in dust, the label unreadable in its age.

"To put it simply, my world will cease to exist."

"And this concerns me?" Marius replied with a disinterested hum.

Shadows twisted from the corner of the room and gathered in a cloak around us. "It should. If pushed, I will do anything to ensure the human race does not perish."

"Ah," Marius breathed, pointing towards where I sat. "Yet if I read your subtle threat correctly, by destroying me you will not only remove the threat of my kind from this world but also your *friend* here... he would turn to ash alongside us all."

Faenir flinched at the term Marius used. *Friend.*

"If that ensures the human race survives..." I said, one brow raised in jest.

"Will you reduce yourself to drinking the blood of rats when you wipe us from existence?" Auriol glowered towards the Lord of Vampires. "And what will you do when you kill the last of those? When all creatures are drained, and you are left to starve? What then?"

"Finally, we reached the heart of this conversation." Marius laughed.

"I'm not one to laugh at," Auriol growled.

Marius studied her for a moment, a grin etched into his demonic yet handsome face. "You remind me of a human girl I once knew."

"What became of her?" Auriol asked. I felt her fingers linger close to my belt and the stakes that waited upon it.

"She willingly gave herself to the death I could gift her. Perhaps I will introduce you to Katherine before you leave... I imagine she would admire your strength a lot. She has such a weak spot for women with spirit of steel."

Jak slapped a hand down on the table, the many glasses chimed in response. "I've been betrayed before by my own blood. What makes you think we will trust you? *Strangers*."

"What if I could promise you a cure? A way of keeping you satisfied," Faenir murmured, drawing their attention back to him.

"You suggest we are in need of fixing?" Jak spat.

Faenir did not flinch at Marius's shadows that joined our conversation suddenly. "Careful, my love, let us not ruin the evening just yet. I have interest in what this... elf has to say."

"I do not mean to fix your curse," Faenir said, leaning forward on the table. "That power is even beyond me. But what if I could provide you sustenance? Blood. An eternal source to keep you and your kind full and the humans untouched. Auriol is right. I do not imagine such powerful beings as yourselves drinking from the likes of vermin. Even I can see that you are above such desperation as that."

It was a gamble coming to Darkmourn to bargain with demons. To play on a weakness that Auriol had brought to light. To pick out a pending concern of blood for the creatures that required it in order to prevent their own inevitable destruction if humans and animals became extinct.

It would seem Auriol was right. Marius and Jak shared a look that sang with concern. It gleamed through the cracks of their confidence and allure.

"Would you like for me to continue?" Faenir's shoulders relaxed as he recognised the reaction before him.

"You have come all this way, elf. Do not stop on our behalf."

"Good." Faenir lifted a hand to his side and flicked his fingers with dramatic ease. The shadows peeled away, revealing another being we had brought with us. Both vampires reacted as though sunlight had burst through the night. "A gift," Faenir looked towards Gildir, who stood rigid as the shadows melted away from him, "A peace offering between us, if you will."

Jak and Marius hissed, nails scratching into the wood of the table. They had not felt, nor sensed, the extra presence and reacted as such.

"What is this!?" Marius growled.

"A trick!" Jak snapped.

I could not fight the smile as their shock melted into expressions of interest. Noses flared and tongues pressed beyond lips as they glanced at the marks my teeth had left upon Gildir's throat.

"We could offer you beings that live as long lives as you. Whose bodies, if cared for, would continue to thrive and provide you an eternal source of the blood you cherish so dearly," I said, revelling in the reaction of the creatures.

Jak broke free from the trance first. "If you are right, one would not be enough."

"Then I would provide you more," Faenir confirmed.

"What *King* would throw his own people into a pit of snakes?" Jak's question hung between us.

"A desperate one," Auriol confirmed, looking between us all. "It is time our kinds come together instead of tearing one another apart, don't you think?"

"Careful, human. Let us not get away with ourselves." Marius's glowing eyes snapped between Gildir and Auriol as though unsure who deserved his attention more.

"I understand the decision has come upon you quickly, but an answer is required before we depart," I said.

Faenir gripped my thigh beneath the table and squeezed. His touch thrilled me. Even in the presence of such creatures, I could not hide my lust that spilled from my pores in waves.

Marius seemed to notice. Jak too, as they both licked their lips hungrily.

"And if we refuse your offer?"

"You die," Auriol said quickly.

"But we are already dead," Marius replied through a wide grin. "That has brought you all here, has it not?"

"You do not know death as I do, vampire." Faenir stood from the table, his hand leaving a mark of warmth upon my thigh. "I wish for you to have the choice of how this meeting ends. Do not mistake my offer for anything more than a request of allied peace between us."

"Peace," Jak barked. "Humans never wanted peace. If they did, we would not be sitting here discussing such matters."

"Yet here we are, together, with a choice to change the world or destroy it."

Marius pondered Faenir's words in a moment of silence. He looked back to Gildir, whose soul had been broken. He no longer moved or made a sound. *Auriol's doing.*

"Such an interesting offer. I admit you may convince me, but the creatures that dwell within the shadows of Darkmourn do not follow my command. Even if I agree, they still have their own desires."

Faenir nodded to Marius in understanding. "I propose a covenant, one that protects our kinds from one another. There would be rules, ones on which we must each agree upon, rules that we would each be responsible for ensuring that our respective people would follow or be punished."

Marius stood from the table and faced Faenir. Both creatures equalled each other in height. But in power? That was not determined. Faenir did not wear his crown by choice. Our presence in Marius's domain was threatening enough; being recognised as a King would paint a bigger target on his back. Faenir was not the King of vampires, nor humans; he had made that clear to me it was not his desire.

"I am interested," Marius said finally, reaching out for Gildir, who did not flinch as the vampire drew a nail across his skin. A bead of deep blood blossomed beneath his mark. Marius drew a finger to his lips, eyes rolling back into his head, as he savoured the taste of an immortal.

Jak stood, unable to resist the smell of the blood; even I struggled to stay in my seat.

"If your suggestion is to work, it may take time," Marius murmured.

"Then we are blessed to have such a concept in the palms of our hands." Faenir lifted an arm and held out a hand in offering. "Are we not?"

Marius looked again to Jak, searching for agreement. The freckles across Jak's nose wrinkled beneath the scrunch of his nose. I readied myself to hear his refusal, but then he nodded.

"There is much to discuss," Marius said, turning back to Faenir. He glanced towards his extended hand as though it held dangers.

You have no idea, I thought as I watched Marius reach for Faenir.

The King of Death and the Lord of Night clasped hands in agreement.

It was done. It had worked.

Auriol relaxed back in her chair, tension evaporating with a sigh. I looked towards her, feeling a swell in my hollow, still chest. It was such a human feeling I almost forgot my lust for blood.

The covenant had been agreed between two great powers of death to cherish life above all else. Yet, as we raised a glass of blood, or wine, I could not ignore the voice that lingered in the far reaches of my mind.

Just as it was Auriol's suggestion for the evening's meeting, it was Faenir's to refrain from mentioning the halflings in our conversation. They were our failsafe, as he had explained. Only time would tell if this agreement would work. And if it did not, there were means to deal with the traitors even if it meant we would be reduced to ash.

For rules, as each of our presences proved, were destined to be broken.

ALSO BY BEN ALDERSON

The *Dragori* Trilogy

Cloaked in Shadow

Found in Night

Poisoned in Light

A Realm of Fey Series

A Betrayal of Storms - Out now

A Kingdom of Lies - Out now

A Deception of Courts - Out January 2023

Darkmourn Universe

Lord of Eternal Night - Out now

King of Immortal Tithe - Out now

Alpha of Mortal Flesh - 2023

The War of the Woods Series

The Lost Mage

Book Two - coming soon

CPSIA information can be obtained
at www.ICGtesting.com
Printed in the USA
LVHW010835160822
726005LV00001B/1